Abou

Mark Yarwood has worked in animation, edited a small press magazine, written for television and the Plymouth Evening Herald. He was born in Enfield, North London and now lives in Plymouth, England with his wife and daughter.

His website is: www.markyarwood.co.uk

SPIDER MOUTH

MARK YARWOOD

BiscuitBooks

BiscuitBooksPublishers

Printed and bound by Createspace

Paperback ISBN-13: 978-1475235050

ACKNOWLEDGEMENTS

A great deal of thanks should be given to the following people: PC Faye Webb and Robert Grant, who have both advised me on police matters in the past. Alan Butler for helping me edit and proofread this book, and Glynis Miller for reading the first draft and telling what she thought. My family for all their continuing support. And Linsey, for putting up with my madness, all the time spent at my laptop, and for putting up with ilene.

Thank you all very much. Once again, I apologize for any errors I have made.

To Linsey, with all my love

PROLOGUE

Sunday, March 10th 1968

The boy knew the old man was dead. It was the smell, the ripe and hideous stench that swallowed him as he stared into the dark hallway of the flat. He stepped over the piles of unopened letters, snuck past the policeman's legs, then froze when he saw the old man sitting in the worn armchair.

'Come on Freddy,' his mother shouted, grabbed him and pulled back out into the bright sunshine. She dragged him to the next door in the tower block, where his aunt lived.

But he crept away again, finding himself heading to the same door, suffering the same smell as he hid in the darkness, watching, unable to take his eyes away from the dead old man.

A policeman walked into the room, and stood watching as another man gently examined the dead man's head, prodding him, twisting him about. The old man's neck made a cracking sound that made the boy shudder.

The man in white overalls took something from his pocket and poked it at the old man's pursed mouth. The instrument glimmered against a beam of light that pierced the drawn tobacco-stained curtains.

The man was meticulous and delicate as he prized apart the yellowed teeth. The boy opened his mouth as the dead man's teeth were removed, leaving a gapping hole in the grey face. All of them, the policeman, the man in overalls, and the boy, stared in horror at the black mouth.

Something had moved.

A flicker in the dark hole in the sunken face. The boy watched as a black stick flicked itself up and across the lips. Another stick reached up and grasped the crusty mouth and pulled its body up into the light.

The spider flexed its joints, reached further out and began to scuttle the rest of the way onto the dead man's chin. The spider's movements were slow and deliberate until it was sitting on the old man's corrugated neck. The spider fell, leaving the boy to wonder why it had made the suicidal leap, until its descent was slowed by a thin glistening web.

The boy walked backwards, feeling for the door, his eyes transfixed on the spider as it scuttled across the carpet and disappeared under the skirting board.

I knew an old woman who swallowed a fly, the boy was thinking, remembering a rhyme from school as he ran to find his mother just outside the door.

When he told his classmates, they laughed and called him names, but his younger brother told him to ignore them, and kept asking to hear the story over and over again.

ONE

Wednesday, 21st April 2004

Fred looked towards the house where the body had been found, then took two more painkillers from his jacket as the pain seemed to stab right up through his back side and into his spine. He pulled himself out of his car, feeling more like an old man than a forty-five year old Detective Inspector. Detective Chief Superintendent Jameson had made Fred take the rest of his annual leave for the sake of his mental health. Now he was back.

He cleared his thoughts, then tried to focus on the crime scene across the grim North London estate. He looked up at the three colossal concrete tower blocks that stood guard over it all, painted in bright pastel colours. They looked as if they belonged in Miami or Spain.

'Morning, sir,' a constable said and handed him the crime scene log. 'It's number 5. It's a real messy one.'

'Fred's seen it all before,' DCI Harris said, smiling as he appeared from nowhere. 'Isn't that right, Fred?'

Fred signed the log and handed it back. 'I've had my fair share.'

'Good to have you back,' Harris said, brightly, looking ridiculous in his polythene overshoes. 'I'm guessing it was either sunny in Spain or you've got high blood pressure.'

'It was alright.'

'I hope there's no hard feelings, what with us having to send you on holiday? After what you've been through…'

'What's happened?' Fred pointed to number five.

'Someone's dead inside, so the usual really. Looks like a junkie. Put some overshoes and gloves on and join the party.'

Fred did as he was ordered, then watched as Harris pushed the door open with his gloved hand, revealing the hallway and the carpeted stairs. The place didn't look like it had been decorated in a long while. Fred noticed a child's crayon scribbles on the wall.

He followed Harris towards the back of the house where the lounge was.

'Through this door,' Harris said. 'Prepare yourself, Fred.'

It had been a long time for Fred, so he breathed deeply, tried to look perfectly unaffected by it all as Harris opened the door.

Nothing could have prepared him for what greeted him. Remains of something, once human, were scattered about the room. He scanned the blood spattered and smeared room, picked out an arm, severed at the elbow, then a leg. The torso was the last thing Fred looked at. The body hadn't done all the bleeding. There was a lot more than eight pints splashed over the room. It was just for the effect.

No head. Where's the head?

The torso. He tried to concentrate on it because it was the only part he recognised as human. It was sitting, propped against the armchair, as if the killer had put it there in a final gesture to them. Another human ripped to pieces, another soul to be filed away. Fred watched the forensic team crawl like ants over everything, ready to bag it all up.

'Pretty rough,' Harris said.

'Seems a little theatrical.' Fred stepped a little closer, wondering where the head was.

'What do you mean?'

'Doesn't seem right, does it?'

'It's a brutal murder. Course it's not right.' Harris took out a voice-activated tape recorder.

'No, I mean, look at all the blood. It looks like the killer was trying to copy Pollock.'

'What?' Harris stared at Fred.

'Jackson Pollock, he's an American painter.'

'I know who he bleeding is. What's he got to do with this? You're a copper, not an art critic, Fred.'

'I'm just saying it all seems a bit staged. There's hardly any blood around the cuts. I'd say the body was cut up quite a while after the victim died. I'm sure the pathologist will back me up.'

'Well, we'll find out later.'

'Where's the head?' Fred was unable to hold in his curiosity any longer.

Harris opened another door, where the kitchen was.

There was a pile of washing up in the sink, rotting food everywhere, but nothing else seemed out of the ordinary. Harris pointed to the oven that was ajar. He took out a pen and pushed the door open wider, then stepped back and let Fred have a better look.

Never in all his years as a detective had he seen something like this.

The severed head. Sitting on a baking tray. The eyes were shut. The face looked peaceful.

Fred stared at Harris.

Harris raised his shoulders. 'See what I mean? A head in the fucking oven? What sick fuck did this?'

Fred was about to reply, but Harris held up a finger

as he took out his mobile phone. 'DCI Tony Harris. Oh yeah, where are you? Right, OK, we're just coming out.'

Harris put his phone away. 'That's the new boy. He's outside. I hope he plays golf.'

'New boy?'

'Yeah. DI Mark South. He's come to take some of the workload.' Harris headed for the front door.

'Some of the workload? My workload?' Pain surged through Fred's backside, just like it had for a long time now.

'Don't take it personally, Fred, it's not about you. We all need a bit of help. If we don't then how will we make time to play golf? Eh? Oh, I forgot, you don't play, do you?'

'Not my sort of thing.'

Out in the street, where the rain was coming down harder, the uniforms had tucked themselves under the shelter of the building. Harris stormed over and said, 'Come on people, don't just stand there! I want you to start house-to-house inquiries. Get over there and start asking the neighbours what they know. Wake your ideas up.'

Fred watched the officers move across the street with their clipboards, preparing to knock on the neighbours' doors. He looked across the street to the cream door opposite the house of death. Fred put on his glasses. He could make out something scrawled on the door.

'Hello?' A tall and well-built man stood in front of Fred.

'Sorry?'

'Detective Inspector Mark South.' South put his hand out and Fred looked at it for a moment, noticing the creases in his skin, the worn metal watch on his

14

wrist. He shook his hand, then looked up into his hard-looking face. South's light brown hair was cut short, brushed forward. He was forty, maybe younger, Fred thought.

'DI Fred Fairservice.' Fred looked over at the door again.

South followed his eyes. 'Is everything alright?'

'Sorry? I was just looking at that door over there. Have you looked at the crime scene? You might want to have a look.'

South looked towards the door to number five. 'They said it's pretty bad.'

'Yeah, just don't touch anything,' Fred said. 'Best thing to do is kept your hands in your pockets.'

'I know.' South nodded and walked over to the flat, then disappeared past the SOCO. Fred turned his attention back to the cream door, focusing on the number, which had long since fallen off, leaving only the bleached outline. The dirty grey curtains were shut. He took a closer look at the mark on the door, deciding it looked like a cross. Perhaps graffiti.

'Oh my God, what the fuck happened in there? Someone said dead junkie, but I wasn't expecting that.' South stepped away from the crime scene, and stood by Fred. 'Any idea what happened?'

'That's what we are paid to find out. What does this look like to you?' Fred pointed at the cross on the door.

South stepped closer, and bent down a little. 'Looks like a cross, painted with red paint or…wait…is that blood?'

'That's what I was wondering. Do you think it could be blood?'

South looked back to house number 5. 'From there? You think the killer came over here and painted a cross on the door in blood? Why would they do that?'

Fred felt rain hitting his head harder now, and got closer to the door, sheltering himself. South stood still, maybe waiting for his answer.

Fred said, 'To draw our attention to it. Can you check with the neighbours and see who lives here?'

South looked at him blankly, then headed along to the neighbour. Fred watched him stroll off as the rain came down in a sudden burst of power, then turned to the door so he could examine the cross more carefully. With all the rain and the dull morning light, he couldn't make out much. He called for a SOCO and a photographer, who eventually came over and started setting up a shelter over the door. Fred took out some more pills and rolled them in his hand, waiting for the SOCO to finish examining the red cross with a UV light.

'The cross was made with the end of a pencil or something similar,' the SOCO said, putting away his UV light in its case. 'It's blood all right, but we won't know if it's human until later. Very strange all this.'

'Any prints?' Fred said, swallowing down the painkillers.

'Like I said, it was done with a pencil or something like it. As for prints, there'll be all kinds all over the door, so take your pick. I'll be over the road if you need me, clearing up a potential murder scene.'

Fred moved to the window and tried to see through the net curtains. It was dark inside and rainwater crawled down his face, making it doubly difficult to see anything but black shapes. He moved back and felt the dirty water filling his mouth.

'Joseph Watkins.' South got under the shelter. 'The neighbour's a young woman, not bad looking. She said he's an old geezer, nice enough. She hasn't seen him for a while though.'

'Nobody communicates any more.' Fred bent over and pushed the letterbox open. 'Hello? Mr Watkins? We're from the police. Mr Watkins, can you please come to the door?'

'No one's home.'

'Right.' Fred got back and lifted his leg.

'What're you doing? You're going to kick the door in?'

'You going to help me?'

South shrugged and got shoulder to shoulder with Fred. They both gave the door a kick. It gave a little. South gave an unexpected kick before Fred could join him and the door flew open.

Fred looked into the dark hallway and noticed they were looking upon the reverse of house number 5. After South found a light switch and turned it on, Fred noticed the carpet was dark green and worn away in places. A sad, familiar smell greeted him. To Fred, it was the smell of loneliness, of the forgotten. He followed the carpet past the stairs and looked at the door to the lounge, which was open. Fred felt South follow him as he walked towards the door and stood before it. 'Mr Watkins? Hello?'

'This better not be another mutilated body,' South said and raised his eyebrows.

Fred pushed the door open, revealing a dark room. The light from the hallway slowly crawled across the carpet, climbed over an armchair and stopped where a figure was sitting facing the window. Fred took it all in. He looked at the old man sitting motionless, facing the antique-looking television. However, his eyes were shut. There was no picture on the television. Fred bent n closer to see if there was any chest movement. None.

'Looks dead to me,' South said, stood in the doorway.

Fred peered closer at the man's sunken face. He noted the man hadn't shaved in at least three days. He prepared himself, half expecting the eyes to spring open, but nothing happened. He could smell death in the room. Something passed through Fred making him flinch.

It was not pain this time, but recognition. He shivered. 'Can you get me a spoon?'

South creased his brow, then headed for the kitchen.

Fred crouched down, stretched out his hands and held the man's head by the jaw. The skin was cold and rough. He noticed the man's enormous ears and the wiry silver hair protruding from his nostrils. This was all so familiar. Just like all those years ago, he thought. Another old man. Another lonely death.

He stared at the mouth, then moved his hand to the crusty lips, while listening to South opening drawers and slamming cupboards in the kitchen. Fred pushed his fingers into the mouth and folded back the lips, revealing yellowish-brown stained teeth. He clenched his eyes shut and grimaced when a soft, but acrid smell drifted out from between the teeth.

South came back and held the spoon out to Fred. He took it, readjusting himself and contemplating his next move.

'Two bodies in one morning? This normal around here?' South leaned against the wall.

Fred pushed the spoon between the teeth and prized open the gates. He nearly fell back.

There! On the tongue!

The spider crawled towards him. Fred's mouth fell open, his eyes bulging. He let himself fall back onto his palms. 'Shit.'

South jumped. 'What? What is it?'

The spider crawled over the old man's hairy jaw

and down his neck and onto the collar of his shirt.

'You OK?' South placed a hand on Fred's shoulder.

'My arse hurts,' Fred said and pulled himself to his feet.

'Is that it? You look like you were going to have a heart attack.'

'I thought I saw something.'

'What? What did you see?'

Fred stood on the doorstep and pulled his coat tighter around him. He looked back at South, trying to judge what sort of man had joined their team. Could he trust him? Did it really matter?

'There was a spider in his mouth,' Fred said, then walked across the street, feeling the rain digging into his scalp. He could hear South striding behind him, his footsteps echoing around the court.

Harris appeared outside number 5. 'The SOCOs have looked the place over. They've dusted for prints and taken photos. But guess what? The pathologist is in there and he said you're right. The blood came from something else. It's not human.'

People had begun going about their daily business by the time the uniforms had finished with their door-to-door inquiries. Fred watched the forensic tent being placed over the front of number 5 and turned to see South sitting with Harris in his car. The residents went by along the street under umbrellas, stopping and gawping at the flat where they knew something bad had happened. Fred didn't blame them as he saw nothing dark about wanting to know what had happened to another individual. It was curiosity, a normal human reaction. It was the people who carelessly walked by who angered him. He had seen so many people die and no one had noticed for weeks, sometimes months, not until the awful smell drifted under their doors.

Fred turned round as he heard someone coming out.

One of the SOCOs came out, just behind the police doctor who'd been called to certify the old man's death. The tall SOCO took off his hood, revealing a bony face and deep-set grey eyes. 'Well, the doctor said he probably died sometime last night of natural causes. Poor old git. They're on their way to pick him up.'

'Nothing tying it to the bloodbath across the road?' Fred said.

'Hardly likely. Just one of life's weird coincidences.' The SOCO put down his case and opened it up.

'What about the blood on the door?'

'Well, it's definitely blood, but frankly it's got me stumped. If the person who did that did come over here and put a cross on this door, then I don't know why. I mean, was he making sure someone noticed the poor old bastard had died? Not the sort of thing a hardened killer does, is it?'

'I opened the old man's mouth and a spider came out.' Fred looked down.

The SOCO looked up from his bag with a smirk. 'A spider?'

'Yeah, it just crawled out of his mouth. Is that unusual?'

'Unusual? I don't think so, not really. I suppose he's slipping into his long peaceful sleep with his mouth slightly open, the spider crawled in and, as he dies, he shuts his mouth. Rare, but I wouldn't say unusual. You hear all that rubbish about spiders being swallowed by people in their sleep, but it's not that common. Why?'

Fred took out his painkillers. 'Nothing really. Just

came as a shock.'

'Don't tell me you're scared of spiders, Detective Inspector?'

'No, not at all. They fascinate me actually. Anyway, can you email the results of the blood on the door? Let me know if it matches the victim in number 5 will you?'

'Sure.' The SOCO picked up his case. 'And I'll hurry them up to pick the old fella up, OK? Bye.'

Fred turned back to the old man's house, and faced the neighbour's door. He walked over, knocked on the door, and heard the sound of a child complaining inside. The door opened after a couple of minutes and a young woman looked at Fred with a hassled expression on her face. Her greasy fair hair hung limply to her shoulders. She began to pull a pram from behind the door. 'Yes?'

'Sorry to disturb you, but I was wondering if I could ask you a few questions?' Fred showed his ID.

'I was just popping out to the shops.'

'It won't take long. Promise.'

The girl looked over Fred's shoulder for a moment, nodded and opened the door. 'Come in.'

Fred followed her into a lilac painted lounge with the artistic illustrations of a young child in one corner. Toys littered the floor, so Fred stepped over them and sat down on a purple sofa covered in stains and cigarette burns.

The girl disappeared for a moment, and came back carrying a sleeping baby. 'One of your lot came around a little while ago.'

'I know, but there was some other stuff I need to know.' Fred took out his notebook.

'Do you want a cup of tea?' she asked.

'No, thanks. Actually, could I trouble you for a

drink of water?'

'Sure.' The girl went to the kitchen.

In the meantime, a little blonde girl skipped into the room. Fred estimated her age at seven. The girl made little eye contact and shuffled over to the far side of the sofa and grabbed a doll.

'Here you go.' The woman handed him the glass of water.

'Thanks.' Fred swallowed another couple of painkillers.

'Got a headache?'

Fred smiled. 'No, kept getting a pain in my back.'

'You better get it checked out. You can't be too careful.' The woman rocked the baby as she sat down.

'So what's your name?'

'Karen. Karen Mills.'

'Right. So, you know your neighbour opposite has been found dead?'

Yeah, It's awful. What happened?'

'We're looking into it.' Fred smiled. 'Did you know him at all?'

'Not really.'

'Not really? So you did know him?'

'Well, we said hello and stuff.'

Fred noticed her eyes looked to her left, then down. He sat forward a bit. 'I see your little girl likes to draw on walls.'

The woman laughed and raised her eyebrows at the little girl. 'Yeah, she's very artistic that one.'

'I saw some very similar drawings on the walls of the house opposite.' Fred looked into her eyes.

The woman looked a little surprised for a moment. 'Well, we went over a couple of times. He seemed alright to talk to.'

'What was his name?'

'Steve. Didn't tell me his surname. He was getting housing benefit though.'

'Thanks. That'll help us identify him. Did he have any trouble? Was there any disturbances or anything like that?'

'No, nothing. He was pretty quiet. Kept himself to himself. I think he was stoned most of the time.'

'OK. Now, what can you tell me about Mr Watkins?'

'The old geezer next door?'

'That's right. Did he know Steve?'

The woman looked confused for a second, then shrugged her shoulders. 'I don't think so. Hardly ever saw the old man out of his house, so no I don't think they knew each other.'

'No, I didn't think so either. Couldn't imagine them going out for a few lagers together.'

The woman laughed as the baby started to wake up. 'Oh no, this one's awake now.'

'Well, I'll leave you then, Karen. Thanks for your help.' Fred got up and headed for the door.

'That's alright.' The woman opened the door for him.

He stopped and thought about the old man and the relatives who might come knocking for him. He knew it was pretty much pointless, but he didn't like the thought of dealing with a corpse with no history, and filing it away without even a little footnote. He held out his card to the woman. 'Can you give my number to anyone who calls around for Mr Watkins?'

'Alright.' The girl took it, looked at the card for a moment, and smiled. 'Do you box?'

Fred touched his nose and smiled. 'No, not really, just been through some rough times.'

'My uncle used to box, had a nose like yours. Steve had a weird nose, all sort of bent. He said it was from boxing, but looked more like he was born with it, if you ask me.'

Fred smiled. 'Well, thanks again.'

When he was outside, Fred noticed Harris and South getting out of the Rover and crossing the road towards him. He hoped South hadn't said anything about the spider; he didn't want to give them another reason to laugh at him.

'Hey, how's it going, Fred?' Harris said with his hands in his pockets.

'Not bad.'

South stood by, looking around the estate.

'Old Mark here is a golfer.' Harris pointed at South.

South stepped forward quickly. 'Well, a bit. I'm not very good.'

'Fred doesn't do golf, Mark.' Harris winked at South. 'You know, I once played a round with Sean Connery in Marbella. Straight up. Just bumped into him and asked him if he wanted a game. So, when we are about tee off, I ask him a question I've always been dying to ask.'

'What's that?' South asked.

'I said to him, "why did you do that last Bond film?" and he turned to me, perfectly straight faced and said, "For the money". As if he needed the money. I ask you.'

Fred could see South laughing along with the joke, but looking uncomfortable. Harris was always the joker. It wasn't a bad thing. In moments of high stress, it took the pressure off, but he didn't have time for it now. Fred was actually finding himself excited about the case. There was some kind of connection between the two deaths. There had to be. He could not help picturing the spider crawling out of the old man's mouth when he was a kid on the way to his aunt's place.

'I'm going back to the station,' Fred said and headed to his car.

'What do you reckon on all this then?' Harris put a hand on Fred's shoulder. 'Come on, what do reckon happened here?'

'This guy, Steve, he was killed and someone cut him up and placed his body parts all over the place. He did this to shock us. I mean, just look at the head in the oven. He got the blood from somewhere and chucked it all over the walls, just to get our attention.'

'Well, it worked,' Harris said and shrugged.

South came over. 'Who was this guy? Why did someone kill him?'

'The pathologist found needle marks in both arms, in his legs, pretty much everywhere,' Harris said. 'There were a few used needles about the place too, all that kind of druggy shit. So I would suggest that some pissed off drug dealer did it and cut him up as a warning to his other clients.'

'Makes sense.' South adjusted his tie. 'When I was in Manchester, we had loads of drug related murders like this. Maybe he was a rival drug dealer.'

It didn't fit with what Fred was thinking. 'If he was a drug dealer, he was small time. Might have been a go between or something…no, look at the way he was living. None of it makes sense. And why did this angry drug dealer walk over the road and put a cross on the old man's door?'

Harris laughed for a moment. 'You still on that? Let's wait until we get the forensic results and the pathologist's reports back first.'

'Well, I'm going back to start on the paperwork,' Fred said and headed to his car again.

Harris' mobile started ringing. 'Yeah, Harris here,

what is it? You're joking? Alright, we'll pop over. What's the address? Right, OK.'

Harris ended the call. 'What is the world coming to? Apparently, a man's come home to find his wife stabbed to death. It's over in Palmers Green. I better get over there. I've been made Senior Investigating Officer in this and now another case lands in my lap.'

South stepped forward. 'I'll go. If you two want to get back to the station?'

'You're keen,' Harris said. 'Isn't two dead bodies enough for one day? OK, why don't you both go? You'll be sharing an office anyway, so you might as well spend some quality time together. Have fun.'

TWO

Fred drove down Fore Street with a mind to get on to Sterling Way, then the North Circular. South followed behind, so close to his rear end that Fred could see the look of concentration on the new boy's mug. Fred took a sharp left into Palmerston Road, a street made up of small, but modern blocks of flats and a long line of 1930s terrace houses that stretched all the way to Wood Green. Palmerston Road was known for car crime, so Fred was careful to lock his car. He watched South park up the street, but didn't wait for him, just found number 123b where a constable was standing outside.

Fred showed his ID.

'Hello, sir,' the constable said. 'Got a woman inside who's been stabbed to death.'

'I know,' Fred said. 'There's another detective coming. Show him in, would you?'

Fred walked into the recently decorated hallway. A nice new burgundy carpet lined the stairs on the right. He kept walking towards the kitchen area where he could see a pathologist and another SOCO going about their business. He looked at the body. She was lying in the middle of the kitchen floor, her legs slightly under the table. Her stomach was stained with blood from several different wounds. A pool of sticky blood had formed around her and had spread across the laminate tiles. Her right hand was stretched far out to her side

27

with a large kitchen knife resting inside it. Fred looked at her face, which looked peaceful, her eyes closed.

It didn't look like murder, but he was never quick to judge.

'Hello,' the pathologist said and stuck his hand out. 'Dr Charlie Farmer.'

'Hello. DI Fred Fairservice. What happened, apart from the obvious?'

The pathologist, who was a short but slender man with receding grey hair, looked at the body. 'Husband came home this morning from his night job and found her like this. Looks like she stabbed herself several times and then bled out. Would've taken a while.'

'She definitely stabbed herself?'

'I would say so,' the SOCO interrupted, his pink face and black eyes peering out of a white hood. 'The wounds are consistent with that. And the spatters of blood around her arms and hands confirm it. She stood there and plunged the knife into herself a couple of times, but not hard enough it would seem. See the sprays of blood?'

Fred looked at blood spatters stretched out across the floor and under the table. 'Means they sprayed out at an angle,' the SOCO said. 'And the ones on the floor are in small circles, droplets, which means she was standing still for quite sometime. The bloody handprint, which is hers, on the table, which told me she was resting upon it. If there were an attacker, he would be standing where you are, and there would a lack of blood on the floor because it would be on him. However, as you can see, there is plenty of blood spatters. No attacker. The blood spatters are piled on top of each other. There are her footprints in the blood and they're the husband's. No one else was here. We've got fingerprints from everything we could find and have taken all the photographs we need.'

Fred nodded. 'Thank you. Makes everything easier…for us, that is.'

'A post-mortem examination will hopefully confirm she killed herself,' Dr Farmer added. 'This is one pretty desperate way to kill yourself. Most people take pills or jump off something or in front of something, but this lady decided to carve herself up.'

Fred stood as close as he could and looked at her face and the way her dark hair was sprayed across the kitchen floor. She was of African descent. He wondered about the husband for a moment, what he must be feeling right now. 'She must have waited until she knew he wouldn't be home.'

The pathologist said, 'That's right. This woman wasn't crying out for help like some do, she wanted to die.'

'Yes, looked very much like it. It's quite a statement she was making.' Fred turned and saw a solitary book, already in an evidence bag, in the middle of the kitchen table. He picked it up carefully and examined the front cover. 'The Complete Works of William Shakespeare. She must have been depressed. Where's the husband?'

'In with the neighbours.'

South appeared in the kitchen, his eyes scrutinising everything as he moved along. Fred saw him look at the body and noticed his eyes focus on her face.

'Quite pretty,' South said and walked around the SOCO, who was collecting the knife. 'No sign of forced entry?'

'No, and there won't be any,' Fred said and stepped around the body. 'She took her own life.'

'Couldn't she have taken some pills or something?' South crouched down and peered at the girl's empty hand, where the knife had been.

'What's the husband's name?' Fred asked the pathologist.

'Terry Hawks. And this young woman on the floor was Michelle Hawks.'

'OK. South, have a look around here, will you?' Fred said and started to leave the kitchen.

'Yes, boss,' South said, sarcastically.

Fred stopped in the hallway for a moment as he felt the pain rising up from his rear. It ached to walk, but he continued out into the front garden. Fred noticed the rain has ceased and a little sun was trying to push past the grey clouds. What a day to find your wife dead. Somehow, Fred felt, finding your wife murdered, thinking some bastard has taken her life from her, was preferable to knowing she gave it away. Fred knew all about rejection. But this, your wife giving you the ultimate Dear John, he couldn't ever understand. Fred stopped and cursed himself. He went back to the kitchen where the pathologist and South were chatting. 'Was there a suicide note?'

The pathologist turned and faced him. 'I wondered when you'd ask that. No, not so far. Maybe the knife in the stomach was the note.'

'Some bleeding note,' South said and picked up the Shakespeare book.

Fred turned, left the house again, and strolled round to next door and rung the doorbell. When a uniformed officer answered the door, Fred showed his ID and walked in.

'Where's Mr Hawks?' Fred asked.

'In the kitchen, sir. He's just finishing a cup of tea.'

'What's your name, son?' Fred asked and started for the kitchen.

'PC Peter House.'

'Could you make another cup of tea? His wife's dead. I know it isn't much, but sometimes it helps. Lots of sugar.'

'OK, sir.'

Fred found Mr Hawks sitting at the kitchen table with half a cup of cold tea in front of him. He saw a young man with old eyes. Maybe was the late nights, Fred thought or the fact his wife has just died. He estimated Hawks' age as mid-thirties, but the bags under his eyes told of many sleepless nights. The next month, the whole year, and much longer, would come with many more.

'I'm sorry Mr Hawks, but I need to talk to you,' Fred said.

Hawks nodded.

Fred sat down opposite Hawks. 'I'm very sorry about your wife.'

Hawks murmured something.

'Sorry?'

'I said I bet you are,' Hawks said, touched his cup and huffed.

'Look, Mr Hawks, I just need to know a few things.' This was going to be hell.

'Like what?' Hawks looked up, his eyes full of fire.

Fred looked Hawks over and noticed he had a fit and strong body, typical of a manual worker. He also had that unspoken, but simmering violent power under his frame. 'I need to know if your wife was depressed.'

Hawks grimaced. 'Yes…yes she was depressed.'

'Was she having treatment?'

'Yeah. 'Chelle's doctor was always giving her pills, but they didn't really help. She was alright sometimes, but other times…'

Fred took a deep breath. 'If I told you that it looked

like your wife committed suicide, would you believe me?'

Hawks looked up slowly, the pain showing in his eyes. 'It did occur to me. I mean, I saw the knife… and well, it was in her hand. I guess I knew…but why would she? I mean, 'Chelle was always so depressed, but why…why like that? I just can't understand it.'

'No, but suicide, well, it usually didn't have much reasoning behind it, just darkness.'

The young policeman placed two cups of tea in front of Fred and Hawks. Fred tried to think of something else to change the subject. 'She liked to read?'

The husband looked confused. 'What's that got to do with anything?'

'It's just that the works of Shakespeare was on the kitchen table.'

Hawks shook his head. 'She didn't read Shakespeare. We don't even own a Shakespeare book. She found all that stuff boring.'

Fred wondered for a moment. 'Perhaps she got it from the library. It looked a little worn.'

'No, didn't sound like her at all. But…well…I don't know...'

Fred sipped his tea. 'Well, I'm sorry again.'

Hawks nodded his head.

Fred was about to leave when Hawks said something. 'Sorry?'

'I said I don't think she even belonged to the library. Her friends sometimes lent her thrillers or whatever or someone would buy them for her birthday.'

'OK, I'm sorry again.' Fred got up, nodded, and headed out of the house. He walked back to the scene of the suicide. The SOCO was finishing with the body, while South drank a glass of water. Fred spotted what he wanted, and picked up the works of Shakespeare.

'They don't own a Shakespeare book,' Fred said.

South shrugged. 'Perhaps someone lent it to her.'

'Just seems out of place.'

'I think the knife in the stomach was pretty out of place.'

'Even so.' Fred took a pair of gloves from the SOCO, then carefully lifted the book out of the bag. He opened up the first page and noticed it was borrowed from Green Street Library. It had been taken out two days ago. He flipped through the pages and stopped when he spotted a red bookmark placed in between the pages of the King Richard The Third play. He looked down the page and saw a red ink mark around a section of text. He read it to himself:

But I-that am not shap'd for sportive tricks,
Nor made to court an amorous looking-glass-
I-that am rudely stamp'd, and want love's majesty
To strut before a wanton ambling nymph-
I-that am curtail'd of this fair proportion,
Cheated of feature by dissembling nature.

It made little sense to him. He was never one for Shakespeare, but he knew it was King Richard telling the audience of his plans to rule after he'd murdered everyone who stood in his way. His hideous deformity had somehow made him evil. He'd nothing better in his life, so why not be king? That's the way Martin had explained it.

'Know anything about Shakespeare?' Fred asked South.

'Not a great deal,' South said. 'Studied it at school, but switched off most of the time. Why? Was she trying to tell us something?'

Fred shrugged. 'Don't know. Might be that this was her suicide note. I want to know who actually got this book out. It came from Green Street Library. Even if she did get this out, why would she go to Green Street instead of Palmers Green, which is closer? They must all have a copy of this.'

'So what's this got to do with her suicide?'

Fred looked up. 'I don't know, but there's something not quite right here.'

Green Street Library sat on the Hertford Road between Ponders End and Waltham Cross. It's situated on Enfield Highway, a strip of suburban shops made up of newsagents, fast food restaurants, a barbers, and a giant continental supermarket. Like the rest of suburban London, Enfield Highway is a remnant of a former industrial town. Having replaced the factories, the lines of shops stretch far into the horizon.

A large pub called the Black Horse sat opposite the continental supermarket. In front of the pub sat a large car park, where Fred parked and stared out at the High Street. South was sitting next to him, having decided to leave his car back in Palmerston Road. Fred hadn't bothered telling him about the car crime in the area.

'My sister lives not far from here,' South said and took off his seat belt. 'That's where I'm living at the moment, until I sort my own place out.'

'That's nice of her.'

'Well, I didn't have anywhere else to go. And she helps look after my son, which is a big help.'

'You've got a son?' South didn't seem the fatherly type.

'Yeah, he's ten. His mother died three years ago.'

South stared at Fred. 'You married?'

'No, not the settling down type.' Fred took the Shakespeare book from the glove box and climbed out the car. South followed him.

The rain started to fall lightly as Fred stood on the edge of the pavement, watching the traffic.

'You live alone then?' South asked as he caught up.

Fred could see the library, which was on the right side of a small supermarket, enclosed by iron railings. 'No, I live with my brother. He's not well.'

Fred stopped outside the library and looked up the three stone steps that led into the small lobby, trying to decide how to handle this. He knew things would be easier with a warrant, but they didn't have time for all that. He wondered how charming South could be, then looked above the door and read the word 'Carnegie' carved in stone above the entrance.

'We may have trouble getting the information we need,' Fred said and stepped into the building.

'Then we'll have to make a fuss then.' South hurried before Fred and stood at the small counter. A middle-aged woman with dark hair was sitting before a computer, typing. She looked up at both of them with a thin smile on her lips.

'Hello, can I help you?' she said.

South smiled and produces his ID. 'Detective Inspector South and this is Detective Inspector Fairservice.'

She looked at his ID with concern. 'What's happened?'

South said, 'I'm afraid there has been a fatality. A young woman has died and we need to get to the bottom of what happened.'

The woman's eyes opened wider. 'That's terrible. She was murdered?'

South shook his head. 'Sorry, can't really discuss that, but you really can help us.'

The woman said, 'OK, how can I help?'

South took the book from Fred and pushed it across to the woman. She looked at it, then up to South. 'The Complete Works of Shakespeare?'

South nodded. 'We need to know who the last person was who took this out.'

The woman said, 'We're not supposed to give away that sort of information.'

'OK, don't worry,' South said and pushed Fred towards the exit. 'We'll just come back with a warrant. I'm just hoping there won't be another victim.'

'Wait!' she called out. 'As long as I don't get in trouble…' The librarian tapped away at her keyboard. After a couple of minutes, a printer on the far side of the room started to moan into action. The woman took the sheet of paper from the printer and handed it to South. 'I hope this helps.'

'Thank you, this will help a great deal,' South said and winked at Fred.

The house they were looking for was in the Brick Lane estate, a crosshatch of streets filled with identical neat little council houses and a school. Fred felt odd. When they passed over the bridge into the estate, and heard a train passing beneath them, Fred looked over and saw his house only three hundred yards away. Too close for comfort, he thought.

As far as he was concerned, they would find a friend of the dead woman, the person who lent her the book. He must have taken it from the library and gave it to her, as simple as that. Why the outlined words? Perhaps they meant something to them both. An affair? Perhaps.

'What do you think we'll find?' South said as Fred turned the car into Gough Road. 'I don't know. I honestly don't know. Probably nothing.'

'I think she was seeing someone else. Perhaps he broke it off and, because she was suffering from depression anyway, she did herself in. I mean stabbing yourself in the gut is pretty passionate. And Shakespeare? That's pretty passionate stuff. Probably left the words marked out for her lover to find.'

'The sonnets are passionate. Not Richard the Third. That's murderous stuff, a different kind of passion. You might be right though. Someone probably just leant her the book.' Fred parked the car and looked at the house. In Gough Road the houses were thin, with an alleyway on the right hand side of each one that would lead along to the back garden. Fred knew the area. His own grandparents had moved there from the East End during the war, avoiding the blanket of bombs that crippled the docklands of London. The war had pushed a large amount of East Londoners towards the north east of the city.

Fred climbed out of the car and listened to South slamming the passenger door. He stood in the road, looked up at the windows and saw the curtains were drawn. He knew how dark these houses got when the curtains were tightly shut. The curtains upstairs were closed too. He walked up the garden and looked into the glass of the door, but all he could see was the beige stair carpet that floated in the frosted glass. He took out the piece of paper and looked at the name of the man: William Lovegrove.

'What do you reckon?' South asked and rested on the front wall.

'Check with the neighbours and see if they've seen him recently.' Fred bent down and opened the letterbox. 'Mr Lovegrove! This is the police. Can you please come and open the door? Mr Lovegrove?'

Fred looked into the glass again. There was

no movement inside, no sound. He looked at the overgrown front garden and guessed at what they were going to discover inside. If he was right about it, something sinister was occurring. Another feeling came over him and took him by surprise; he felt a seed of excitement growing, pushing away his boredom.

South came back, but over his shoulder Fred saw the concerned face of an elderly woman peering from her front door.

'William Lovegrove is an elderly gentlemen,' South said. 'The old dear next door hasn't seen him for a while. Maybe a couple of days, she thinks.'

'I see.' Fred stepped back, feeling the pain in his arse beginning to rise again.

'What the hell is all this about?'

'Someone wanted us to come and meet this man.' Fred took out his painkillers.

'He's dead. Don't you reckon?'

'Probably. Very likely. I think we should go around the back and see if we can get in.' Fred walked under the archway, stood at the back gate, then twisted his arm through a gap in the back fence and unbolted the gate. The back garden was a jungle of weeds, thistles rising above the straw coloured grass and choking the few flowered trying to grow. Fred elbowed the glass in the back door and reached around for the key in the lock. The door opened and he smelt the dust lying on everything. There was a sofa, probably purchased in the sixties, along with a green leather armchair bleached yellow by the sun. Fred hurried up the stairs, his hand running along the wall. He turned and saw South at the bottom of the stairs, concern stamped deep into his face. Fred kept moving onto the darkened landing.

He passed a small bathroom that smelt of damp,

then found a door to a bedroom. He pushed the door open gently. A sliver of light twisted over a bed and outlined what looked like legs under a blanket. Fred moved closer, saw the shape of a head and two large black nostrils in a prominent nose. It was a few seconds before a sour smell reached his own nostrils and he stopped moving. It was a smell you never get used to. He saw a pale hand lying over the sheets and reached out for it. The first touch was strong, tender, and icy. He tried to make his emotions as chilled as the man's body.

'Another poor dead bastard,' South said as he stood in the doorway.

Fred nodded, moved over to the curtains and pulled them apart. The dust swirled in the stream of light, while Fred moved to the man's blue face. His mouth looked like it was pursed to speak or swallow. He looked closer, bending down to examine the mauve lips.

'What is it?' South stepped into the room.

Fred gripped the dead man's head and turned it towards him. The whole neck moved with difficulty, rigor mortis having gripped his body. He pushed his fingers into the mouth, squeezing them past the crusty lips. No teeth. Something stopped his fingers moving in further, the tip of some hard object obstinate against his fingertips. He felt it, closing his eyes, moving his hand around inside the mouth. He felt a lid, then tried to dig his fingertips under it. A small jar. He could feel all of it now as it scraped against the gums, slowly becoming looser until he ripped it from the dead man's jaw.

Fred looked over at South whose eyes were glaring out to him. Fred looked down at the jar and flinched. He held the jar up to the dusty light and saw the spiders moving about inside, clambering over each other. Two household spiders.

'You're joking?' South said.

'I need an evidence bag.'

South fished one out of his pocket and held it open while Fred dropped the jar in. South held it to his face, frowning. 'I hate these little bastards.'

'I can never understand why people are scared of spiders.' Fred looked over the body again.

'They're horrible little hairy buggers. So what the fuck is going on?'

'I wish I knew.' Fred looked around at the room. He saw clothes lying on the floor and old black and white photographs resting on a nearby chest of drawers. How can people be forgotten like this?

'We better get someone over here,' South said. 'Shall I call them in?'

Fred nodded. 'They won't find anything though. Only the spiders.'

As they walked down the stairs, Fred listened to South calling the station, reporting the death. Fred imagined the slow wheels turning somewhere, uninterested voices commenting on another sad lonely death. Except for the spiders, it means little, just one more buried or burnt corpse.

It was brighter outside and Fred thanked the heavens for it, because he could deal with the pain when the sun was out, he just didn't understand why. He kept thinking about the spiders and wondered about their significance. He turned everything over in his mind, concentrating on the two deaths. One was a suicide, they are sure of that, and the other…well, they don't have a clue. He knew the body was in pieces and obviously pointed to murder, but he kept focusing on the theatrical nature of it all. The head in the oven.

The blood everywhere. The blood that did not belong to the victim. In fact, these were not victims, at least not of some murderous soul somewhere. He shook his head.

They would wait for the forensic results and that would be that, everything swept under the carpet for the moment, perhaps forever. He was not looking forward to giving his report on it all.

They travelled back in silence, but Fred replayed the afternoon over in his head as he steered his car into the car park underneath Edmonton Police Station. He dropped South back at Palmerston Road and watched him walk back to his car. Fred hadn't figured him out yet, but decided he was another ambitious officer ready to take charge of the next big murder investigation and ride up to the top. Perhaps he, unlike Fred, would make detective chief inspector or even detective chief superintendent. He had the right look, the right background. His face didn't look like it had been smashed against a brick wall, like Fred's did, and had. Fred didn't really care, he was happy enough to ride out the few years until he retired. Then he could be by himself and forget about the bodies they had filed away, the society outside his four walls that cannibalised itself.

Fred turned off his engine and took out the evidence bag from his jacket pocket. He looked at the jar inside, the remnants of the man's spit and half-digested food still stuck to the glass. He held the bag up and let it twist in his hand. One spider looked dead, while the other crawled about the jar.

Fred headed up to the incident room, walked the long corridor and imagined what it would look like in there. In his mind, he saw the chairs and the police officers sitting, taping away at keyboards or holding phones to their ears. Most of the time they were filling in statement forms, getting details of the crimes they had been investigating. They didn't so much investigate as listen, note down and make report after report.

They often got results, but that's usually because it was pretty straight forward; Mr Smith threatened Mrs Smith or someone, then that person ended up dead. They knew who did it and where and when, they just had to make it stick, build a solid case to hand over to the CPS. It came down to the argument, the pressure and the clever word play until someone admitted something that could be used in court.

Fred entered the incident room. And there they were, his colleagues, busy communicating with other organisations, digging through the dirt to find a single trace of something or someone.

The room stretched before him and, at the far end, on the big whiteboard, he could see photographs pinned up and statements piled up on a large desk. That high up, in the Edmonton Green fortress, he could see North London spread out before him. He looked back into the room and saw DCI Harris in his glass box of an office, bending over the desk. Harris put down his phone and left the office.

'Hey, Fred, when did you get back?' Harris beckoned Fred into his office.

Fred sat down while Harris leaned against the window, his face slowly forming into a smile. 'So, how was the rest of your morning?'

Fred took out his notebook and flipped it open. 'The stabbed woman. Turned out she took her own life. Took a kitchen knife and stabbed herself in the stomach a few times before she got it right. Then she bled to death.'

'Shit. What happened to taking pills or jumping out of windows? Fucking hell, London's getting so depressing.' Harris turned and opened the window a little.

'We found a book at the scene that we thought she'd been reading, but it turned out it didn't even belong to her…'

Harris looked confused for a moment. 'Wait, a book? What's that got to do with anything?'

'Well, it just seemed strange that the book wasn't even hers. The book was The Complete Works Of Shakespeare. A paragraph had been circled in red ink. This is it.' Fred ripped out the page and handed it to Harris.

Harris looked it over and shrugged. 'What's it supposed to mean?'

'Don't really know. However, when we traced the book back to the library it was taken from, we found that the person who borrowed it lived not far away. We went to the house and found him dead in his bed. In his mouth was a small jar that contained two spiders.' Fred took out the evidence bag and placed it on the desk.

Harris picked up the bag. 'You're having me on?'

'No, but I almost wish I was.' Fred adjusted himself as the pain bit into spine.

'You having trouble there, Fred?'

Fred smiled awkwardly. 'Just my backside playing up.'

'Oh dear. Could be haemorrhoids. Ann had real trouble with them when we had Jack. I'd have them looked at.'

Fred turned his attention back to his notebook. 'Anyway, I haven't figured out what's going on, but it looks like all four deaths are connected in some way.'

'But didn't the wife kill herself or am I missing something?'

'Yes, she did, but there was obviously someone else involved. Someone wanted to us to find that book. They led us right to the old man we found today and it all started with the dead man we found this morning.'

'Well, perhaps forensic will be able to tell us something.' Harris stood up and looked through the glass wall of his office. 'Here's Jameson.'

Fred looked around, saw the familiar bulk of his superior officer, and wondered how Jameson's blue shirt kept his flabby body inside. What annoyed Fred about Jameson was the little square of hair he had remaining on top of his forehead. The rest of his head was shiny, but the little tuft of brown hair refused to fade away.

Jameson talked to one of the officers near the door, then looked up, saw Harris and nodded to him. Detective Chief Superintendent Paul Jameson ambled over and entered the office, while Fred turned his back to him and hoped he'd go away.

'Good afternoon lads,' Jameson said, then walked to the window. 'Least it's stopped raining. Anyway, how's everything going?'

'Been pretty shit this morning,' Harris said and sat at his desk.

Jameson nodded. 'Heard you found four dead bodies this morning, Fred. That must be a record.'

Fred looked up from his notebook. 'Yes, it must be.'

Jameson looked deep in thought for a moment. 'Found a fax in your office from the pathologist examining the cut up dead junkie you were dealing with this morning. Seems he wasn't murdered after all.'

Fred looked up and into the eyes of Jameson,

expecting them to be filled with mirth. 'Suicide?'

Jameson nodded. 'Seems he took an overdose of whatever shit he was pouring into his body. Stupid bastard. They never learn. There was no signs of a struggle, no bruising that would suggest he was held down or anything. Anyway, a couple of hours after death he was chopped up. Apparently there was blood all over the place as well. That right?'

Fred nodded. 'Splashed all over the walls and carpet. Looked staged.'

'Well, the claret came from an animal. Most likely a pig. Someone's having a joke.' Jameson folded his arms and rested them on his enormous stomach.

Harris sat back in his chair. 'So, someone must have waited until he was dead and then cut him up and then stuck his head in the oven. Someone's idea of a sick joke.'

Fred was trying to take it all in, to make some kind of sense of it all. 'What about the old man across the street?'

Jameson frowned. 'What old man?'

'Whoever cut up the junkie, they drew a cross in blood on the door of the old man who lived across the street. We found him dead.' Fred looked at Jameson.

'How did he die?' Jameson said.

'Natural causes,' Fred said and knew where it was heading.

'Then there was nothing to look into. Case closed.' Jameson shrugged.

'There was another suicide this morning,' Fred said. 'A woman stabbed herself and bled to death. She had a book that had been borrowed from a library by another old man. We went to talk to that old man and found him dead. In his mouth was a tiny jar with two spiders in.' Fred lifted up the evidence bag.

Jameson took the bag and looked at it. 'Well, I don't know what to say. But if no one's been murdered, what are we supposed to do? We haven't got the man power or budget to look into this.'

Fred knew there wasn't any argument to be had; he didn't have anything he could say to make it seem like something they should investigate. No murdered people, nothing. He could only wait and see what happened.

Jameson walked out of the office door, waving for Harris and Fred to follow him. Jameson stood waiting for them, his back to the whiteboard and the crime photos pinned to it. Fred saw what was coming and sighed.

Jameson turned and pointed at the photo of a pretty blonde girl. It was a school photograph, taken when the girl was in the sixth form. Fred had examined the board on many mornings, staring at her face, trying to imagine what she'd been like.

'This girl, Heather Beckley, is still missing.' Jameson looked at Fred and Harris. 'We need to find her. We need to know what happened to her.'

Harris leaned against the wall. 'When we find her body, then we can get to the bottom of it.'

Jameson nodded, a little sadly. 'Yes, I'm afraid I have to agree with you there, Harris. It's doubtful we're going to find her alive. The shoe, and the blood we found on it, is definitely hers. Her medical records confirmed it. The shoe was found here, a mile away from her home.' Jameson pointed to a photo taken in an alleyway on the way to her work place. 'Now, what else have we got?'

'The boyfriend,' Harris said and shrugged.

'Go on,' Jameson said.

Harris stood up straight. 'Let's face facts, in cases

like this it's usually a family member or a lover or someone close to the victim who's killed them. We know he was seeing someone else, and that his new girlfriend's probably lying about him being with her at the time of Heather's disappearance. I'd say the boyfriend had a row with Heather, it got violent and he ended up strangling her or something. The new girlfriend's lying to protect him.'

Jameson looked straight at Fred. 'Fred?'

Fred was thinking about the four deaths when he noticed Jameson staring at him. 'I have to agree with Harris. I've talked to the boyfriend, Andrew, and he's hiding something. He sticks to his story too rigidly, like he's rehearsed it.'

Jameson said, 'Well, this, my friends, is what we have to kept looking into. I suggest we have a televised appeal using the family of the missing girl and get the boyfriend there too. Let's see how he acts under the heat of the television lights.'

South walked across the office, followed by a woman in her early thirties, her hair long and light brown, framing her oval face. She looked sharp in her trouser suit as she approached Harris and stood next to him, but she always did.

'Morning,' Detective Sergeant Ally Walker said, smiling.

Fred had always found her attractive, but she looked particularly good today, and brighter than usual. She was a great, hard working detective, but she also funny, quick witted and Fred admired her for it.

'It's afternoon, Allison,' Jameson said and looked at his watch. 'Who's this?'

'I'm Detective Inspector Mark South, sir.'

Jameson smiled a little. 'The new boy. Good. Good.

Take good care of him, people. Fill him in on the missing girl. Right, I have a meeting to go to. Violent crime is up in London and the Mayor wants something done about it, apparently. I ask you!'

After watching Jameson walk out, they all relaxed.

Harris turned to Ally. 'You should know Jameson do get irony.'

Ally smiled. 'You mean he doesn't do ironing, more like. Did you see the state of his shirt?'

Harris shook his head. 'Come on, let's do some work.'

South and Fred were left looking at the photographs. Fred nodded towards the door. 'Let's go and see your desk.'

Fred took him out of the incident room, along the corridor and into a cramped office. Fred's desk was under the three windows that opened on to Edmonton. The view was obscured by two tower blocks, but occasionally you could see a red bus circle the indoor shopping market and head off towards Enfield Highway.

Another desk had been pushed along the opposite wall with a nice new leather chair behind it. A couple of filing cabinets sat in the corner, with piles of stuffed folders sitting on top of them.

South looked around and smiled a little. 'Not bad. Not too bad at all.'

Fred watched South seat himself and look over his desk and his computer. He recalled first sitting down in his own office space, loving everything about it, knowing he was on his way up. It all happened in another dimension; a much nicer, and naive dimension.

Fred broke out of his dream as his phone started ringing. The fax machine joined in, grumbling into action. He watched the paper appear, then tore it off. It was from the pathologist, giving additional information on the deaths that morning. Preliminary examinations had been carried out. He looked the sheet over and stopped when he read one particular line as he remembered the information Jameson gave him from the fax left on his desk. They knew the junkie probably committed suicide. Now he was reading something much stranger. Fred lowered the paper and looked blankly at South.

South looked up at Fred. 'What is it? Bad news?'

'It's from the pathologist. Whoever mutilated the dead junkie this morning, also removed some of the body.'

THREE

There was no need for them to have rushed from the building, heading down to the morgue at such high speed, as the dead weren't about to go anywhere. The four witnesses were not about to refuse to tell what they knew. Fred would retrieve all they knew with the help of Dr Charlie Farmer, the Home Office pathologist, short of them sitting up from the slab and chatting to him.

Dr Charlie Farmer was drying his hands as he came out of one of the examination rooms and nodded to Fred and South.

Fred shook the pathologist's hand. Farmer pointed to an office, which was very modern-looking and sparse. Fred noticed the framed certificates from several medical institutions and a couple of classic film posters.

'You said some of the first victim's body was missing,' Fred said and sat on a plastic chair, while South stood in the doorway.

Farmer moved around his desk, seeming to search for something in his drawers. 'That's an interesting phrase you've used, Detective.'

'What do you mean?' Fred said.

Farmer smiled. 'Victim. This dead guy, Steve, looked as if he injected himself with Heroin two hours before he was cut up. There was nothing pointing to him being murdered. Well, apart from the amputations, but they were performed well after he was dead. Unless, when you say victim, you mean victim of society?'

South stepped in. 'None of it makes sense then. Why would anyone cut up a dead person and leave them there? And what about the head in the oven?'

There was a little bit of laughter forming around Farmer's mouth as he nodded. He sat down behind the desk and folded his arms. 'Well, as for the motives of the man or woman who did this, I can't really say. But they didn't leave all of him, as I faxed you. He took a lump of flesh cut from the back of the right thigh up to the buttocks.'

'Why would anyone do that?' Fred asked.

Farmer shrugged. 'Well, there was only one reason I could think of.'

'They took it so they could eat it?' Fred asked, flinching at the thought.

'Maybe,' Farmer said. 'But then there was the animal blood thrown all over the room.'

Fred nodded. 'As if they wanted us to think someone had been brutally murdered, but I think they were trying to grab our attention.'

'Or just hide the fact that they wanted human flesh,' Farmer said. 'Or maybe they're just insane.'

'Perhaps that's it.' South leaned against the doorway. 'Perhaps this is just some crazy person crying out for help.'

'Did you look at the two old men yet?' Fred asked.

'Not both,' Farmer said. 'Watkins died of pneumonia. That's what will be on the death certificate. Nothing out of place.'

Fred knew what he was about to say would sound insane, the ramblings of an old copper who'd spent too much time on the job, but he had to say it anyway.

'When I found the old man, Mr Watkins, I looked in his mouth and a spider popped out.'

Farmer sat up. 'A spider? Just a normal household spider?'

'Yes, just a little spider.'

Farmer smiled. 'I suppose it crawled in there and got trapped. You'd be amazed how many insects and arachnids humans swallow every year while they're asleep. It's not really that unusual.'

'We found a small jar in the second dead old man's mouth,' South said and wiped his nose. 'In the jar was two spiders.'

Farmer raised his eyebrows. 'So someone put a jar containing spiders in the old man's mouth?'

'And maybe one in Watkins' mouth,' Fred added. 'But like my superior said, there hasn't really been any crime committed.'

'But it has to be the same person who cut up the body. There has to be a connection.' Farmer got up from his chair and stretched his arms. 'I'll examine the dead woman first thing tomorrow morning and finish up with the others later. I'll let you know what's what as soon as I've finished.'

Fred shook Farmer's hand. He walked out and South followed, both of them walking slowly back towards the exit. Fred sensed South was about to say something, so turned and raised his eyebrows. 'Yes?'

'So that's it? We have to go and work on this other case? This missing girl?'

'Murdered girl,' Fred said and pushed through a door.

'That's a bit pessimistic,' South said, catching the door before it smashed into his face.

'We found one of her shoes with her blood on it. Now we have to find the body.'

'Still…' South said as they came out into the cloudy, darkened afternoon.

Fred took out his tablets, then pulled a bottle of water from his jacket pocket. 'Still…we have to get on with the job at hand. The day will soon be over and that might be the last we hear from this nutcase. Perhaps tomorrow we'll find the missing girl's body. We do what we do.'

South adjusted his tie. 'Right then, back to the station.'

Fred stopped the car outside his home in Broadfield Square. His eyes swept down the road towards Gough Road, and, even though he could not see it, he pictured the house and the dead old man they found there. He looked away and let the car moan forward and parked it on the driveway. His brother, Martin, would now be sitting with a book in the living room, quietly reading away, absorbing more knowledge that would be used for very little. Fred got out and stood for a moment looking at his car, then around at the square. He watched a couple of kids walk across the litter strewn green, avoiding the discarded parts of old rusty vehicles dumped there. He looked at the other houses that sat untidily huddled around the edge of the square and wondered what happening behind their four walls. He hoped it was all good.

As Fred was about to put the keys in the lock, he heard his name being called, and looked around to see a familiar and attractive, but mumsy-looking woman coming his way.

Mrs Boswell hurried around from next door, smoothing her jeans and pulling her red hair from her face as she came. Fred had always fancied her, but he figured she was just the friendly type, always got time for her neighbours. She'd been kind enough to look in on Martin while Fred was away in Spain. He'd tried to convince his brother to come, but Martin didn't feel up to it.

Mrs Boswell smiled. 'Glad I caught you, Fred. I was wondering how you both were.'

'Oh, we're OK.' Fred noticed she was wearing a tight pink top that her breasts seem determined to escape from. 'I was just going into see how Martin is.'

'I'm glad you enjoyed your break.' Mrs Boswell smiled. 'Must be an awful job to do. Must get you down, I expect.'

Fred didn't like to talk about it really, but he always found people wanted to know about it, trying to dig up any information that might satisfy their dark curiosity. They didn't want to know the truth though, not the real grim stuff, just the highlights, the images of a good old copper slapping the cuffs on another villain. Once he started telling them about the facts and figures, the desperate times when they couldn't catch the guy, when their hands were tied up by the legal process, he noticed their eyes go all cold. He nodded at Mrs Boswell. 'It can be tough. Thanks for looking after him.'

'I didn't do anything. Just popped in now and again. He's very clever. He must have an enormous brain in that head.'

Fred nodded, knowing perfectly well that his brother, his older brother, was much more intelligent than him. Fred had thought about this more often than he'd like to admit, realising his brother should be the detective, wandering the streets and solving crime. He sometimes treated his brother like a living resource book, gaining information from him about various subjects that might help him solve a case. It was like having his own library. He would swap it all though, take it away in a second to have a brother who wasn't dying. The doctor had given him three years to live after quietly, and seriously, announcing that Martin had multiple sclerosis; the Marburg's variant to be precise. That had happened in the doctor's plain and clinical office a few years ago. Martin had got considerably worse since. Fred had watched him slowly deteriorate, until all Martin did was sit and read. Now their pain seemed entwined.

Fred looked into the kind eyes of Mrs Boswell, or Tracey, as she had told him to call her. 'Well, I better go and make him something to eat. He can't just feed himself on books.'

'Unless they're cook books.' Mrs Boswell laughed, patted Fred's arm, then turned and walked away.

Fred entered the front door and looked up the stairs facing him. He heard the sound of the television coming from the lounge on his right, through the doorway. He walked in and saw Martin lying back in the black leather lazy boy chair that Fred had bought him on his last birthday. Fred looked him over and saw that his body was so much thinner than it was a year ago. Martin used to be similar in stature to himself, but now his round head seemed out of proportion compared to his creased bony neck. He never wore anything more than baggy jogging bottoms and T-shirts these days, which made Martin seem even more fragile.

Fred stood in the doorway and put his keys on the table near the door, while Martin lowered his book and looked over to him.

'This is your house,' Martin said. 'Don't just stand there. Come in, sit down.'

Fred smiled, looked at the book, but only caught two names: Hitler and Churchill. He walked into the kitchen where he could still hear the television and the evening news. Fred hated he news and despised the fact that his brother had a habit of watching every news broadcast over and over again.

'I hope you've come back victorious,' Martin said, turning his head.

Fred walked to his brother's chair. 'Wish I could say I have, but it was just another day of naming and numbering the bodies.'

'But that's your job. That's the life you chose. What was it today?' Martin lowered his book.

'Two suicides and two dead old men. No horrific murders.'

Martin slapped the book down.

'Suicides? Two suicides? That's interesting.'

'Yes. But somebody obviously found the first guy and decided to cut him up and stick his head in an oven. The second was a woman who decided to stab herself in the stomach. What do you want for dinner?'

Fred walked out to the freezer. As always it was chock-full of frozen dinners, oven chips and pizzas. Every time he looked in the freezer, he swore at himself for being so unhealthy.

'What happened to the two old men?' Martin shouted.

Fred sat down on the sofa. 'Natural causes it looks like. But the old men and the suicides are definitely connected and...'

'What? Tell me everything.'

Fred sighed. 'Do you remember when Mum took me over to Aunt Sylvia's and the police were next door with that dead old man?'

'When you saw that spider come out of his mouth?'

Fred reached down and took off his shoes. 'Well, it happened again today, with the first old man we found. But what's even stranger is, when we found the second dead old man, he had a small jar in his mouth with two spiders in. I just don't get it.'

'I wonder what the significance of it is.'

'I don't know yet. Maybe I never will.'

Martin grabbed the arms of the chair and pulled himself upright. 'You'll eventually get to the bottom of it, you have to.'

'Not if Jameson has anything to do with it. But he's right though. There hasn't been a murder and we need to concentrate on finding the missing girl.'

Martin stared at Fred. 'She's dead, isn't she? I mean, you think she's dead, don't you?'

Fred pushed his shoes under the coffee table, then focused on the pile of books sitting on the coffee table. Anything to blot out the images trying to climb into his brain, the flashes of her pale, lifeless body. 'Most likely. There isn't much hope.'

'What if this person does it again? The person who put the spiders in the old men's mouths, I mean?'

Fred saw his brother's eyes were alert, wide and interested. 'They haven't done anything. They somehow got into the first guy's flat after he'd killed himself, then they cut up his body. He took a dab of blood and draws a cross on the door of the house opposite, which belongs to an old man called Watkins, who had just died. I don't even know if he did put the spider in his mouth. Maybe that was just some bizarre coincidence.'

Martin gave a disappointed laugh. 'There aren't any coincidences, you know that. You said you found two spiders in a jar in the second old man's mouth, so how can it be a coincidence?'

'But still, there's no real crime been committed. No breaking and entering. Although two people committed suicide around the same time. That's what's bugging me. He had to know, whoever he was, that they were planning to do it. This is ridiculous. I'll make dinner.'

Fred went into the kitchen and found he had the ingredients for Spaghetti Bolognese, and began to prepare it. He defrosted the mince in the microwave, then took it out and stared at it as a flicker of memory sparked in his brain. 'Whoever did it, they took part of the first victim's body.'

'A souvenir?' Martin asked.

'Maybe.' Fred got out a wok and some oil, and began to fry the mince after adding some garlic. He felt the pain travelling up his spine, so took out his painkillers and popped another two into his mouth and washed them down with a glass of water.

After half an hour, Fred delivered the dinner. He put Martin's on a tray and placed it on his lap. 'What do you do all day?'

'I read.'

'I should read more.'

Martin pointed to the television and the cable box sitting underneath it. 'And I surf the net. It's amazing how far you can spread your mind out through it. You can find anything out. You can reach out to people across the world. One minute I'm just sitting here, the next I'm reaching out to the world.'

Fred looked down at the black box that allowed his brother some kind of life. Then he wondered about South, and what he might be doing.

'You told the kids at school about the spider coming out of the man's mouth, remember?' Martin said.

Fred turned to see Martin staring at him, his fork frozen two inches from his mouth.

Fred nodded. 'Yes. They laughed at me. Little

bastards.'

'They gave you a nickname.'

Fred allowed himself to travel back to his school days. He pictured the nasty faces of his so-called school friends. He heard the name being sung all around him. 'They called me Spider Mouth.'

South walked up his sister's front garden and saw some movement inside the house. It was a little darker now and she hadn't pulled the curtains. He hated that. He detested the fact people could see into their world as they walked past. He'd seen them do it, witnessed them take a quick nose into their front room because they could.

He opened the door, stepped inside and heard the hissing of steam. His sister always seemed to be ironing and he liked the smell of clothes having the creases flattened out of them. He walked in and closed the curtains. The sycophantic presenters, Robert and Jilly were on the television, fawning over some US movie star, who looked genuinely bemused by their affection.

'Had a nice first day?' Emma said and folded up a shirt.

'Interesting. Where's Shane?' South pulled off his tie.

'In his room. I don't think he's had a very good day at his new school.'

'I forgot that I'm not the only new boy today.' South unbuttoned his shirt and stretched.

'So did you solve any crimes on your first day?'

South laughed dryly. 'Oh yeah, I blew them away with my detecting skills. In fact, that's it, there is no crime left in North London worth solving. I'm a bit young to retire though, so…'

'Ha ha. You're so bloody funny, Mark. Why don't you go and see your son? He hasn't had such a great day.'

South climbed the stairs and headed to his son's open bedroom door. He could hear Shane talking to someone, probably a toy, so he stood in the doorway watching his son play with his favourite action figure. 'Shane, come back, Shane,' South called out.

'Dad! I hate that.' His son fiddled with his toy, his face screwed up. 'It's so stupid.'

'I know. Sorry. Your Mum liked that film.' South sat on the bed. 'Looks like we both had pretty crap first days.'

Shane shrugged. 'It was alright.'

'I know it's not very nice being the new boy.' He laid a hand on Shane's shoulder. 'They stole my lunch money today.'

Shane smirked. 'No, they didn't.'

'And they stole my favourite pen.'

'Shut up.'

South did his best to look sad. 'I was hoping you could come with me tomorrow and get it back for me.'

Shane stuck his action figure under his Dad's nose. 'Take him, he'll get it back for you.'

South laughed.

'Did you arrest anyone?' Shane asked.

'Can you believe, not a single person?'

'That's rubbish. I'd have them all in prison by now.'

'See, that's another reason you should come with me tomorrow.' South rubbed his son's hair and got up.

Shane looked up with a question in his eyes. 'Are we going to stay here?'

'In this house you mean?'

'Around here.'

'If things go well. I hope so. I'm sorry, Shane, I

know you miss home.'

Shane screwed up his face. 'It's alright.'

'Do you want burgers or pizza?'

Shane smiled as he looked up, then closed one eye as he tried to decide. 'Er...burgers.'

'Come on then. I'll drive us.' South followed as his son hopped down the stairs. He really hoped they'd stay around too. He had needed to get away from the memories of her, but that's the last thing his son needed and yet, he felt it might do him some good to have a new start. Shane would make new friends and so would he. He wanted promotion and his last position had gone as far as it could. It had been time to move on, time to get away from the house and the streets that reminded him of her. For a time he'd felt as if she was haunting him, as if she was just around every corner, sitting in every bar or restaurant they used to go to. He realised one day, as he sat at his desk filling in reports, that she wasn't haunting him at all. He was doing all the haunting. He had to let her go for the sake of his sanity.

Today had been a strange day. He hadn't expected Fred Fairservice to be as unusual as his name. When he'd first seen him, he thought he looked more like a villain than copper. He did like Fred though, somehow. There was something about him, something trustworthy.

South watched Shane hurry to the car, then stand, waiting for his dad to unlock the doors. As he climbed in the car, he thought about the spiders, hoping they could get to the bottom of it all.

There had been no crime committed, he told himself. Perhaps, he thought, it was leading up to something. Then he thought of the real reason he'd moved back down to London and felt ashamed.

FOUR

Thursday, 22nd April 2004

When Fred woke up, he tried to pick out the distant ringing somewhere in the house. He sat up in bed and rubbed his sticky eyes. It was his mobile. He wondered where he'd left the bloody thing and started picking up the files and clothes strewn around his bedroom. It wasn't there. He stepped onto the landing and listened for it. He heard his brother's two walking canes tapping themselves into life.

'It's OK, I've got it, Martin.' Fred stepped down the stairs, found his phone in the kitchen, then saw the time. He'd overslept. He recalled lying in bed, trying to figure out the case. Then nothing.

He answered his mobile. 'DI Fred Fairservice.'

'Hello, Fred, it's Mark South. Where are you?'

Fred sighed. 'I had some trouble at home…my brother.'

'Oh I see. Well, I'm at the Williams Old People's home on Enfield Highway. I think you need to be here.'

'Alright. I'll be there as soon as I can.'

Fred hurried back upstairs and took a quick shower, all the time thinking about what might have happened at the old people's home, the place his mother had stayed.

Fred caught his reflection in the mirror and saw the angry scars over his back. He closed his eyes, pushed away the bad memories.

After he saw to Martin, Fred grabbed some more painkillers from the bathroom, making a mental note to make an appointment with the doctor.

He drove the ten minute journey to the Williams old people's home, which was situated a few yards along from Durant's School. It was a very clinical building, with a large glass and wood front that opened on to the shiny waxed floor of the lobby.

Behind the counter stood a middle-aged woman with black hair tied up in a bun, a shock of white hair running through it. Skunk, he thought, and produced his ID.

'Oh, right,' the nurse said. 'Your colleague's waiting for you along the corridor in the TV room. I'll show you.'

Fred followed the nurse without saying a word, and found himself in a bright room where a few old people were sitting in the corners, dozing away the morning. Rubbish daytime television spewed out drivel from the screen in the corner, high above their heads. South was sitting in one of the comfortable chairs, his head tilted back and his eyes focused on the TV screen. Fred tapped him on the shoulder.

'Everything OK at home?' South got out of the chair and turned to the old dear sitting on his right. 'Take care of yourself, Mrs Stamp.'

'What's happened then?' Fred asked as South directed him out of the room.

'Didn't I tell you on the phone?'

'No.'

'Oh, sorry. Got a dead old guy in the room up here. George Hammond.' South pushed open a door and let Fred enter.

'Anything suspicious? Why did they call us?' Fred

looked over the narrow bedroom, the single bed, the old photos, the armchair. An old man was in the armchair and looked as if he was resting, although his skin seemed grey. His bald head shone, the sunlight glittering over his scalp. He looked like a waxwork. Fred saw the telephone directory sitting in his lap.

'They didn't call us,' South said.

Fred looked at South. 'What?'

'I mean, someone anonymously called the station this morning and reported this. I got over as quick as I could, obviously because of what we found before. A doctor's already examined him. Looked like natural causes.'

'Anything in his mouth?' Fred stepped around the chair and looked into the grey face. He recalled watching the life slipping from his mother's body, holding her small, bony hand. He looked down at the phone directory. Was he trying to call someone?

'There was nothing in his mouth,' South said.

'What's it got to do with us?'

'Look at this.' South put on a latex glove and took something from the bedside cabinet. He held up a glass in which the old man's teeth were sliding about in. Just inside the dentures, Fred could see something floating. South shook the glass a little as if fake snow might start falling. Instead, Fred saw a spider sinking to the bottom of the glass. Fred stared up at South.

'He's got a sense of humour,' South said.

'He's a laugh a minute. Still, it isn't a crime to put a spider in with a pair of dentures.'

'I know, but it's intriguing.'

Fred turned back to the phone directory. 'I wonder who he was looking up.'

'There's only one way to find out.' South walked around to get a better look at the old man's lap.

Fred gently put a hand onto the man's left wrist as if to move it, but didn't. He leaned in and examined the man's fingers, then looked up at South with his eyebrows raised.

'What have you found?' South asked.

'His left hand is trapped inside the book. It's been positioned between the pages.' Fred opened the book, pulled it from the old man's lap and stood up. Keeping the book open, he turned towards the window and kept smoothing his hand over the page. Fred looked down the page, the long list of phone numbers, keeping his eye on each name. He saw nothing out of the ordinary.

South sighed. 'He could've been looking anywhere on these two pages.'

'Then we'll phone them all.'

'I don't think our boss is going to let us spend the time doing that.' South shook his head. 'Wait. There!'

Fred followed South finger as it moved down the page to a name and number that has been marked with a red cross. Fred read the name aloud: 'A. P. Stuart.'

'Do you think our friend marked that?'

'Yes I do. He wants us to go to this address.' Fred ripped out the page.

'55 Northfield Road,' South said. 'Where's that?'

'Ponders End. Not far. Let's go.'

They were outside another house in suburban North London. Fred didn't like it. He'd been thinking about the time they had spent investigating a prankster, someone who likes to pop insects into dead people's mouths. No, not insects, he corrected himself. Arachnids. That was the proper term.

Fred parked a hundred yards further up the road from South. He looked in his rearview mirror and saw

South climbing out of his car, walking up the street, his eyes trying to pinpoint the right address. Fred kept wondering about what they'd find there. Another dead old man?

Fred climbed out and walked towards his colleague, then nodded for him to approach the door. It won't be anything special, he told himself as South rang the doorbell.

South rang the bell again, but Fred saw slow movement inside, a shadow moving up the hall. The silhouette grew larger until the door slowly opened and a man, probably in his thirties, peered out at them. Fred watched the man's eyes flicker nervously between them, his forehead damp with sweat.

'Mr Stuart?' Fred asked.

'Well…' The man looked them over.

'Is he here?' South asked, stepping forward a little.

'No. I think you have the wrong address.'

'No, we have the right address,' South said.

'I don't know a Mr Stuart,' the man said.

Fred looked over at South. 'He lives here.'

The man shrugged. 'Perhaps he moved.'

'Can we come in and look around?' South asked.

The man kept the door where it was. 'I'm a bit busy right now. Can I take a message?'

Fred stepped forward. 'You said you didn't know who he was? Who are you?'

'Who are you?' the man said.

'We are the police.' Fred showed his ID.

Fred saw the worry blossom on the man's face. 'You better let us in.'

'He's letting me stay here for a couple of days,' the man said. 'Mr Stuart, I mean.'

Fred followed South and the man into a nicely decorated lounge. The man stood in the middle of the room with his arms tightly folded over his chest.

South wandered around the lounge, his eyes scanning everything, while Fred stood facing the man. He could smell food. 'Having lunch?'

The man's nervous eyes jumped towards the kitchen, then came back. 'Yes.'

'So, let's start with what you are doing here.' Fred took out his notebook.

The man nodded. 'I'm just staying here for a couple of days.'

'Who's letting you stay here? You said you don't know Mr Stuart, then you said he was letting you stay here.'

'Do you want a cup of tea?' the man asked and headed to the kitchen.

South nearly stopped the man, but Fred shook his head.

'What do you think?' South asked.

'He's nervous about something.'

'You're right. I hope he isn't thinking of doing a bunk.'

Fred nodded towards the kitchen door, so South pushed it open. The man was stood with his back to the cooker, holding a plate in front of him, forking lumps of food into his mouth as if he was in a desperate hurry.

'Didn't finish your lunch?' South asked.

Fred looked at the diced food. Meat of some kind. 'We really need to know where the owner of the house is and we need to know your name.'

With his mouth full, the man mumbled out the answers. 'John. John Kerry. I was told I could stay here.'

Fred stepped closer, noticed the kettle wasn't boiling, and felt an icy cold finger drawing a line down his back. He looked at the man forking meat into his mouth and something, a picture or thought, flashed into his mind. He was trying to grasp hold of what his whole body seemed to be telling him, but like a dream, it quickly faded.

'Who said you could stay here?' South asked. 'Where's the owner of the house?'

'I don't know,' John Kerry said and looked at his empty plate, still swallowing. He lowered it and looked at the kettle. 'I'll put the kettle on.'

'I'll get the milk,' Fred said.

'No, it's OK.' Kerry made a move for the fridge.

Fred blocked his path as he saw a startled look in the man's eyes and more sweat on his forehead. Fred opened the fridge. It was bare and smelt slightly stale inside. He saw a package and looked back at Kerry. 'Not much in here, Mr Kerry.'

'No, I haven't done much shopping.' The man looked down at the floor.

Fred took out the package and began to unwrap it. He heard a gasp of breath and looked behind him. Kerry was doubled over, his face purple and his head was swelling. South moved forward, his hands grasping Kerry's shoulders, pulling him upright. Fred turned back to the package. He unwrapped it. Fred's eyes flickered for a moment at the lump of crudely cut flesh inside the wrapper. It didn't look like any meat he had ever bought and then the thought, the terrible dark thought, leapt into his mind. He turned back to the gasping body of Kerry, his eyes bulging out.

'He's having some kind of fit!' South dropped to his knees alongside Kerry. Fred watched his colleague loosen the man's shirt, his fingers fumbling at the tiny buttons. Fred looked down at the package of meat and dropped it onto the kitchen table and walked over to the now shaking body of Kerry. His mouth opened, gasping, then stopped. Silence. The fridge freezer hummed loudly.

South put his head to the man's chest, while his hands scrambled at his neck, trying to find a pulse. 'He's not breathing!'

Fred watched as South opened the man's shirt and started CPR.

Fred looked into the man's mouth to make sure there was nothing obstructing his breathing, then his eyes lifted and blazed out to South. 'We need an ambulance. Now!'

South couldn't stand the smell. He hated hospitals like a lot of people do. Then he wondered if there were people who were the complete opposite, people who actually get off on the fact they were in a hospital, surrounded by death. There must be people like that, he surmised. There are all sorts of people in the world who like all kinds of weird stuff, so there must be people who are aroused by hospitals. You think of any weird thing, he guessed, and there was someone who got off on it.

'Hello?' An Indian woman dressed in green scrubs tapped him on the shoulder.

South turned round, digging his hands into his pockets. 'Got good news for me?'

'I'm sorry, but Mr Kerry passed away,' she said without much emotion.

'What happened to him?' South moved past her, towards the curtain that separated the dying from the waiting.

'He seems to have had a massive anaphylactic shock.'

'I'm sorry?'

'I'd say Mr Kerry had contact with something he was allergic to. You said he was eating something before he died. What was it?'

South thought back to the food Kerry was shovelling into his mouth, then recalled what Fred had suggested as the paramedics scooped up his body and rushed him away. It made him feel sick. 'Some kind of meat.'

'Well, if a sample of it can be examined that might tell us what set him off. I'd need to see his medical records too.'

South nodded. 'What did he actually die of?'

'The anaphylactic shock brought on cardiac arrest. We tried our best, but it was too late for an adrenalin shot. I'm sorry, but I have to see to other patients.'

'Thanks.' South nodded and watched her hurry off. He turned back towards the waiting room and the worried faces sitting there. He thought about Fred's theory. It made him want to vomit, knowing that perhaps the meat in the fridge was part of their first victim. Victim. He killed himself. And someone took a slice of his body. But who?

Fred waited for the forensic team to pack away the meat and the plate from which Kerry was feasting. Then he looked about the house. He saw the double bedroom of a married couple, family photographs placed lovingly on the dresser. Then he walked into a smaller single bedroom. He looked at the football posters and the ones of a teen pop star. He nodded to himself. Kerry didn't belong there. He'd already talked to the neighbours and found out the Stuart family had gone away to Spain for two weeks. Kerry had a key. A freshly cut key stuffed in his pocket. He would have to get the Stuarts to look at the body and see if they knew him. Chances are they wouldn't. Fred had looked into his wallet and found his home had been in Manchester. He was single. He phoned Kerry's house and no one answered. The local police would investigate.

Prints would be taken from the body and they would see if any of Kerry's showed up at the scene of the first suicide. He had his doubts. There was something about Kerry and the way he acted. Fred didn't think he was the man who cut up the body and put the head in the oven. He was too nervous for that. If he was right, and the meat in the fridge was human, then he knew Kerry had been nervous about them discovering that and nothing else. There was something else too. Fred had found a sheet of paper with the Stuarts' address on it. He took it out of his pocket and looked at it, noticing it had been printed from a computer. It looked like part of an email, although he couldn't see the email address. Kerry must have been told to come to this house, where it would be safe to eat. A safe house for a cannibal, Fred said to himself. If it had been happening on TV, or if he had been reading it in a magazine, he might have found it ridiculous, but it was too bloody real for that.

A SOCO walked up to Fred with a blank expression on his face.

Fred smiled. 'Can I help you?'

'Yes, by buggering off and letting us get on with our job,' the SOCO said. 'You're messing up the crime scene.'

Fred nodded, folded the piece of paper and put it away, then headed past the rest of the forensic people as they carried their equipment into the house. Across the street, a number of neighbours had gathered and stood pointing at the house and chatting to each other. Crime, he thought, was great for community spirit.

He looked at his watch and decided it was time to

get back to the station.

South was at his desk typing away on his computer when Fred arrived. South turned and faced him and said, 'Doing the paperwork.'

'So I see.' Fred went to his desk and saw nothing from forensic. He thought they would've come up with something by now. How long does it take to determine if a food source was laced with poison?

'I got a message from the forensic team, by the way.' South leaned back. 'You were right, the blood on the old man's door was from our chopped up junky.'

Fred nodded. 'Of course.'

'And I talked to the doctor who saw to Kerry before he snuffed it and she reckons he had a massive allergic reaction.'

'The meat he was eating was laced with something. I think whoever cut up the junky arranged for Kerry to stay at that house. I found part of an email I think Kerry had tried to destroy. Perhaps he received instructions to go to the Stuarts' house where he would find his... well, his lunch.'

South frowned. 'Disgusting. How could anyone eat another human being?'

'Survival. In some cultures it's the norm. They eat their enemies so they can take on their powers, their spirit.'

'And you think that's why Kerry did it? So he could munch on the arse of some junkie? Perhaps he was hoping to get high.'

Fred shook his head. 'He wouldn't have known where the meat came from. I think he was just some poor messed up bastard who was desperate to eat human flesh. I think the desire would've been with him day and night. He just didn't have the stomach to kill someone and eat them. That's where our mysterious suicide assister came in. He took the flesh from Steven Murphy and gives it to Kerry. I'm betting Kerry wanted it to be the last thing he ate, as if he couldn't live after giving into his darkest desire.'

'Sounds about right. Well, if the meat was poisoned, then…'

'It's murder,' Fred said.

'Fred?' Harris stood in the doorway, not looking his usual jovial self.

Fred stood up. 'Yes?'

'Come with me.'

Fred followed Harris into the corridor. 'What is it?'

Harris looked into his eyes. 'It's murder now.'

'Who? What case are you talking about?'

'Heather Beckley. The missing girl. She's turned up. She was found on the edge of Epping Forest wedged under a fallen tree. Her hands and feet were tied with string. Looks like she was strangled.'

'The fucking little bastard.' The anger flowed up through Fred.

'What're you thinking?'

'Andrew Nelson, the boyfriend. We need to put the pressure on him.'

Harris nodded. 'That's why Jameson wants us to talk to him. He's in room 3.'

'Me? But I'm dealing with my case,' Fred said and followed Harris down the corridor.

'I thought there wasn't any case, just a bunch of suicides and some spiders.'

'Looks like we've got our first murder today.'

Harris stopped for a moment and dug his hands in his pockets. 'Well, that's great, Fred, but right now I need you to talk to this little wanker I've got sweating in there. I know everyone thinks I'm the joker around here, that I'd rather have a laugh than catch the villains, but I've got news for you lot, it ain't like that at all. A young girl's dead and you can bet your life that this little fucker did it. Now, no offence, mate, but I need your ugly mug staring across that table. It'll scare the shit out of him, maybe get him talking.'

It wasn't anything Fred hadn't heard before. He'd used his ugly mug to his own advantage on many occasions. This would be just one more.

Harris opened the door.

The room was bright and there was a large window that allowed Fred to look down at the rows of takeaways across the street. Harris sat opposite Andrew Nelson, who was sitting confidently in his chair, smoking and smiling.

'Sit down, Fred,' Harris said and pulled out a chair.

'Yeah, sit down Fred, you're making the place look untidy.' Andrew Nelson laughed.

'I get to call him Fred, you call him Detective Inspector Fairservice or sir,' Harris said, calmly.

Fred seated himself and removed the emotion from his face. He knew he needed to say little, just be there and look as if at any moment he might lash out in rage. Most experienced suspects knew the police weren't about to beat them to death, or torture them for information, but of course there was that little doubt in their mind. They might have heard of deaths in police custody, incidents of mysterious circumstances. What really happened? Did they really hang themselves? Did they really just choke on their own tongue? Did they really just have some rare heart condition? And there the doubt grows, until it becomes fear as they face two very angry, threatening policemen.

'So, Andrew, here we are,' Harris said.

Andrew nodded and looked between the two men. 'Yes, here we are.'

'I'm sorry about your girlfriend.' Harris smiled.

'Ex-girlfriend,' Andrew said,

'Oh yes, ex. But still, you must be pretty gutted. You went out for three years, after all.'

Andrew took another drag of his cigarette. 'Of course I'm gutted. She was a good girl. Me and Heather was tight.'

'But not lately?' Harris asked.

Andrew squinted. 'What's going on?'

'I'm just asking you a question.'

'I came here to help. You asked me to help you with your investigation and here I am. I want the fucker who killed Heather caught. Why aren't you looking for him?'

'We are,' Harris said. 'But we need help. We need to ask questions of the people who knew her the most.'

'Me?' Andrew said.

Harris nodded.

Andrew looked suspiciously at them in turn. 'You think it was me?'

Harris raised his eyebrows. 'Did I say that? Fred, did I say that?'

'No,' Fred said.

Harris sat forward. 'We found Heather in Epping Forest, stuck under a tree. She was a very small girl and it was a big tree, so it was quite hard to see her. A woman out walking her dog discovered her. Can you imagine what that's like? Finding a young girl who's probably been dead for a while? It's not nice, Andrew, I can tell you that.'

'So?'

'So nothing. This is a girl who you once cared about. I just thought I might get some emotional response from you.'

'This has nothing to do with me.'

'It has everything to do with you. It's your responsibility to help us.'

'OK. What do you want to know?'

'When was the last time you saw her?' Harris asked.

'Oh God, I've told you this a million times.'

'Tell me again. Pretend I have Alzheimer's. My wife actually thinks I have Alzheimer's. The other night she was waiting for me to come home. Apparently, I had gone out to the pub. Anyway, in the early hours I came stumbling through the door. I could hardly get the key in the lock, she reckons. Anyway, I bounce off the walls until I'm facing my wife and she's steaming with anger. She said, "Where have you been?" I look towards the front door and say, "Have I been out?"'

Fred watched Andrew laugh a little. He knew Harris' way of getting the suspect to relax a little, to help catch them off guard.

'Very funny.' Andrew stubbed out his cigarette.

'Anyway, Andrew,' Harris said. 'When was the last time you saw her?'

'A couple of days before she went missing. She came around to my place 'cause she found out that I was seeing someone else and started ranting and going on. I told her it was over and that was that.'

'Yeah, your neighbours confirmed that there was a girl screaming at your door. But you never saw her after that?'

'No. Next thing I know she's missing.'

The door to the interview room opened and Mark South put his head around it. 'Sorry, but I need to talk to DI Fairservice.'

'I'm busy,' Fred said.

'It's OK, Fred,' Harris said, not taking his eyes off Nelson.

Fred walked out to find South pacing the corridor.

'What is it?'

'Got a call from Farmer. He wants us down there.'

'Why?'

South raised his eyebrows. 'He says the woman who committed suicide was pregnant.'

FIVE

Spread out on Farmer's desk, were the pieces of a jigsaw puzzle. Fred leaned over the desk and tried to make out what the puzzle was supposed to be. He sat on the desk, picked up a piece and turned it in his hand.

'It's supposed to be Admiral Nelson's death scene at Trafalgar,' Farmer said, then came in and closed the door. He placed a file on a filing cabinet, then took off his glasses. 'You got here fast.'

Fred stood up and placed the jigsaw piece back on the desk. 'Sounded important.'

Dr Farmer stepped closer. 'Did you ever think about getting your nose fixed?'

'Never.' Fred nearly touched his nose.

'It's a simple procedure. I should have started with Admiral Nelson himself and then worked from there.'

'What about the woman?' Fred sat down.

'Like I said, Detective Inspector, she was pregnant.'

'How far along was she?'

'About eight weeks.' Farmer examined a piece of the jigsaw. 'This is as close to being a detective as I get. Putting the pieces together.'

'So, not only did she kill herself, she killed her baby too?'

'You have to ask yourself why the woman stabbed herself where she did. She took the kitchen knife and rammed it straight through her abdomen and into her womb. Not her heart. She didn't slash her wrists either. Either way, she would have killed herself quite proficiently. No, she was aiming for her unborn child. That was the very worst kind of abortion.'

'You think she only meant to kill her child?'

'Oh no, she meant for them both to die. But why?' Farmer picked up another piece.

'She didn't want the baby, but she didn't want to live either.'

'Did you notice her hand?' Farmer asked.

'No, why?'

'Of course you didn't. Everybody was looking at the hand she used to take her own life. Her other hand was tucked under her body. It was deformed. Very twisted. Very ugly. She was probably very ashamed of it. Plus, the condition that caused it is hereditary.'

Fred took out his notebook and wrote it all down. 'It made her depressed. Her whole life marred by her deformity. Then she finds herself pregnant...so you think that's why she killed herself and her unborn child?'

'I'm not here to do your job for you.'

'I don't think they pay you to do jigsaw puzzles either.'

'Well, that's why I went into this line of work. I did the general practitioner thing and found my patients were too demanding. So, I decided that the dead would be less...well, fussy. How wrong can a man be? Seems they have a lot more to say than the living.'

'I have to go.' Fred headed for the door. 'Thanks for the information.'

'My pleasure,' Farmer said and examined the jigsaw puzzle. 'By the way, the dead junkie had a huge, ugly nose, which I'm sure you noticed. There might be a connection, so you should look into it.'

Fred didn't go back to the station. Instead, he jumped into his car and headed towards Highlands Hospital where Doctor Sheila Evans had her surgery. He parked, then stood outside for a moment. He opened a bottle of water he'd purchased at a petrol station, and popped two more painkillers. Then he walked in and reported to the reception desk.

He had promised Dr Evans he'd come back. He didn't like it, but Jameson had insisted he talk to someone after the incident. It had all been quite a while ago, and he thought he'd put it past him. But he hadn't quite. He'd been arresting a young, mouthy thug one day when his temper got the better of him. He found himself landing several punches before being pulled off the thug. It was reported and the counselling sessions started.

'You can go in now,' the receptionist said.

Fred knocked on the door and heard the very feminine call of Dr Evans telling him to enter. He found himself in a newly decorated room. The walls used to be plain white, now they were light pink. The curtains were purple.

Dr Evans pointed to the black leather armchair and smiled, then crossed her legs.

Fred hadn't seen her for a month, but she looked the same. Her skin was a little dark, caramel in colour, with light acne scarring around her cheekbones, her dark brown hair tied back as always.

'How've you been Fred?' She leaned over and typed something on her laptop.

'Not bad. It was a bit of a shock going back to work after sunning myself in Spain, but I'm alright.' Fred tried to relax and find somewhere comfortable to put his hands.

'And how is work? How do you feel being back?'

80

Fred looked over at the purple lava lamp that was spewing molten wax. 'It's OK. I've been back two days and it's fine. Just like it always is.'

'Do you still feel bored?'

'I don't think I ever felt bored.'

'Sorry. You said before you didn't feel satisfied.' She smiled.

'I'm sorry about the last time I saw you.'

She waved her hand and smiled. 'It's forgotten.'

'It's just that I was going away and I didn't have anyone to go with.'

'You were feeling lonely.'

'No, that's not why I asked you. I mean, I wasn't just feeling lonely.' Fred sat up and blushed. 'You seem like a nice person…'

'It's OK. What concerns me is your loneliness.' She wrote something down again.

'Anyway, I just wanted you to know that I asked you to go with me because you're nice, not because I'm a sad lonely idiot.'

'But you are lonely?'

He shrugged his shoulders. 'I have Martin.'

'But that's different. You live with him because you feel you have to look after him.'

'He's my brother. He didn't have anyone else.'

'That's my point. You didn't meet anyone in Spain?' Dr Evans' eyes met his, then she looked down at her notes.

'No, not really. I sat in the sun, drank cocktails and then went home. I got plenty of rest. That's why they made me go, so that's what I did.'

She looked up. 'You were made to see me because of the assault against that young lad. They thought it might be related to the attack on you, when those people did those terrible things…'

'Yes, that as well. But that was nearly two years ago.' Fred patted the armchair.

'Have you had any more dreams about it? Have you remembered any more of the attack?'

'No, just the same old stuff. I heard the girl screaming and started running down the street and found the bastards pushing her around. Thing is, every time I remember it, it's like a scene from a film and some hero is suppose to appear and save her.'

'And you arrive.'

'I arrived and get the shit beaten out of me and the next thing I know I'm in hospital.'

'But you don't have any more nightmares?'

'No, none of that stuff. I've forgotten it all really. Didn't bother me.' Fred rubbed the arm of the chair and smiled.

'And work still isn't sparking your interest?'

'Well, there's a case that's got me interested. I can't talk about it, obviously, but do you remember me telling you about the spider thing when I was young?'

'The spider in the old man's mouth? Yes, I remember.' She sat up.

'Well, it all came back to me the other day. I found this old guy with a spider in his mouth. It means something, it must do. It's got me interested. I want to get to the bottom of it.'

'That's good.'

'But there's a new guy I've got to babysit. But he's OK.'

'That's good. You're keeping busy.' She smiled.

'Yes, I'm very busy. But I'm not sure if that's a good thing.'

'So, what's DI Fairservice's story?' South stood at DS Ally Walker's desk while she typed up a statement.

She looked up. 'You are…DI Mark South, that

right?'

'That's right.' South leaned against the wall.

Walker looked at her computer screen. 'He's a good policeman.'

'He looks like he's come back from world war three where he was employed as a battering ram.'

She laughed. 'Well, the budget didn't stretch to battering rams, so we have to do with Fred's face.'

'No, seriously though, should I be worried?'

'Worried about what?'

'Is he prone to violence?'

She laughed harder. 'No, he's just not a good-looking man. Plus, he got beaten to a pulp two years ago by a bunch of yob bastards. Poor git. They took him somewhere and tortured him.'

'Now I see.' South looked around the office. 'Want to get a drink after work?'

'You don't hang around.'

'Well, I don't have any friends around here, so…'

'So you want to make friends? Well, I have to go to the gym straight after work, but some other time would be great. I'll get a few of the others together.'

South straightened up. 'Great. Well, do you know where Fred is now?'

'At his psychiatrist's, but he'll be back shortly.'

'He's got mental problems?'

'It's nothing like that. They just make you see someone after what he went through.'

South narrowed his eyes. 'Being beaten and tortured?'

'Like I said, he was found beaten up with burns on his back. Said he tried to save a young girl from some thugs and they grabbed him and tortured him. Thing is…'

'What?'

'Well, there were no eyewitnesses, no one to support what he said happened and they never found the thugs. It's as if it never happened, but there you go.'

'But he has the scars to prove it?'

'Yes, he does.'

'And now they make him talk to someone about it?'

Walker shrugged. 'Yes, after he nearly beat a suspect half to death a little while back they do.'

'Interesting. Do you have the address of the psychiatrist?'

When Fred walked out of Dr Evans' office, he didn't expect to see DI Mark South leafing through a motoring magazine. He stopped by South and tapped the back of the magazine.

'Thinking of getting a new car,' South said. 'My son thought his Dad should be driving something sporty.'

'Who told you I was here?' Fred walked towards the exit and South followed.

'Does it matter? Don't you want to know why I'm here?'

'I'm not crazy.' Fred opened his car door.

'I didn't say you were. No one thinks you're crazy. I do understand.'

Fred climbed into the driver seat and faced South after he got in. 'What do you understand?'

'You've been through a lot. It can't be easy looking after your brother and being a copper. Being a policeman and looking after a kid is bad enough. And the attack must've really shook you up.'

'I'm fine.'

'I just wanted you to know that I understand.'

'They want to get rid of me.' Fred stared at South.

'Who?'

'Them, up the top and Jameson. They think I can't do the job any more.'

'That's bollocks.' South shook his head. 'I've seen you, you know what you're doing.'

'They're right. They're pushing me and they're right. I'm fucked. I do the job, I go through the motions, but I'm not really here any more. But I'll go because I want to go, not before.'

'And do you want to go?'

'Yes, but not yet. There are things I need to do.' Fred gripped the steering wheel.

'Like what?'

'Just stuff. I want to figure out what's going on with this case for starters.'

'So do I.' South patted Fred's shoulder. 'You need a shag.'

Fred laughed a little. 'Yeah, right.'

'Fred, I haven't had sex in a year.' South raised his eyebrows. 'That can't be right, can it?'

Fred shrugged. 'You might want to try four years.'

'You're fucking joking?'

'Wish I was.'

'You've just made me feel so much better.'

Fred heard his mobile ring. It's the station. 'Yes, DI Fred Fairservice?'

'Hi Fred, it's Ally. Thought I better give you the results from the forensic report, which just got faxed in. The meat and the cooking oil were laced with peanut oil. And they finally got in touch with John Kerry's family. Apparently he was allergic to peanuts. So you've got yourself a murder. Congratulations.'

'Thanks, Ally.' Fred put away his phone. 'John Kerry was allergic to peanuts. And the meat was laced with peanut oil.'

South seemed to think for a moment. 'So, someone

got him into that house, probably had the food ready for him, but already covered in peanut oil so he would snuff it.'

'But why? Farmer said that the woman who knifed herself was pregnant and she also had a deformed hand. The dead junkie had an extremely protruding, ugly nose.'

'It sounds ridiculous.'

'That's because it is. Someone's taking the piss.' Fred started the engine.

Fred was about to enter his home when someone tapped him on the back. He turned to find Tracey Boswell stood behind him, holding a casserole dish covered with tinfoil.

'Hello,' Fred said. He noticed she was wearing a tight beige vest top, which dipped considerably at the front.

'I just saw you park up, so I thought come and have a chat.' She smiled brightly. Her red lipstick glistened. Fred could see some of it had stained her two front teeth.

'Thank you.'

'Busy day?'

'The usual. Murder and mayhem.'

'You are funny,' she said and pushed the casserole dish towards him.. 'I made you some dinner.'

'You made me dinner?'

'Well, for you and Martin. It's just a beef casserole, but it'll taste good. I promise. I make very good casseroles.' She beamed and there were those red teeth again.

'Thank you. That's very kind.'

'You can microwave it.'

'Thanks.' Fred took the dish and nodded.

'Well, enjoy it.' Tracey Boswell hurried along the street and disappeared into her house.

Fred carried the dish into the lounge and saw his brother deeply involved in a book. He put the dish in the kitchen and returned to the lounge.

'I didn't realise that they delivered casseroles to the door these days,' Martin said, but didn't take his eyes from the book.

Fred looked around the lounge and saw vacuum marks in the carpet. The top of the mahogany television cabinet sparkled. 'The house looks clean.'

'Marie was here.' Martin put down his book. 'I told her she didn't have to clean the place, but you know what she's like. She's a social worker with a dirt phobia.'

'Lucky for us.' Fred sat down and took off his shoes.

'Mrs Boswell likes you.'

Fred stared at Martin. 'She likes everyone.'

'No, she pays particular attention to you. I bet Mr Boswell didn't get that much attention. It's probably because you're a policeman. She probably desires your protection.' Martin gave a thin smile.

'She just felt sorry for us.' Fred tidied away his shoes and removed his tie.

'I don't want anyone to feel sorry for me.'

'Sorry.'

Martin looked across to his brother and smiled brighter. 'Do you think she wants to have sex with you?'

'No! She's married.'

'So?'

'She's another man's wife!'

'People have affairs.'

'Not me.' Fred began unbuttoning his shirt.

'You wouldn't be the one cheating.'

Fred shook his head, exasperated. 'Forget it. After all, Mr Boswell is a tall, well-built, builder type.'

'And you are?' Martin raised his eyebrows.

'A copper with a face like a bulldog's backside that's been kicked a few times.'

Martin nodded a little. 'Beauty is in the eye of the desperate housewife who isn't getting any. Your time may have come, brother.'

Fred laughed and shook his head. He looked at the coffee table where Martin's books were piled high. There were more today, probably because Marie had been by and kindly brought some down the stairs for him. At night, when Fred was on the cusp of falling into a well-earned sleep, he could hear the electronic whine, a selection of robotic like hiccups, and he knew Martin was connecting out to the world, reaching out to pull back information. He wondered sometimes, just as his eyelids would began to weigh heavy, what Martin looked for on the internet.

'Any more spiders found today?' Martin asked.

'An old man died in a home. Inside the glass where he kept his teeth we found another spider. On his lap was a phone directory with an address marked. We went to the address and found a man who liked to eat human flesh.'

Martin opened his eyes wider. 'Flesh taken from the junkie?'

'Yes. However, our cannibal friend got more than he bargained for. The meat was laced with peanut oil and he had a peanut allergy.' Fred stepped into the kitchen and uncovered the casserole. He took in the smell. Delicious. He thought about Tracey Boswell and the sprinkles of sweat between her breasts.

'Couldn't have been a nice way to go. But at least you now have a murder.'

Fred came back. 'Do I? What if it was the cannibal guy that did all the other stuff and cut the junkie up and kept some himself and killed himself by lacing it with peanut oil?'

'Where was he when the other stuff happened?' Martin said and raised his eyebrows.

Fred thought for a moment. He hadn't checked. Why hadn't he? God, what was wrong with him these days? He took out his mobile, looked for Ally Walker's number and called it.

'Hey, Fred,' Walker said.

'Hi, Ally.'

'What can I do for you?'

'When you contacted the family of John Kerry, did you find out where he'd been before we found him in the Stuarts' home?'

He heard her take her face from the mobile and speak to someone, then come back. 'Sorry about that. Yes, I asked when Kerry came down to London. He'd arrived that morning. So he'd been in Manchester before then. Is that any help?'

'Yes, thanks, Allison.' He put down his mobile and looked at his brother. 'He was in Manchester when all the other stuff went on.'

'Then it's murder.'

'Let's eat,' Fred said and walked towards the kitchen.

Mark South watched his son pushing a piece of cabbage around his plate. He thought a normal father would tell him to stop playing with his food, but he couldn't stand cabbage either. Maybe another parent, somewhere in the world, might mention starving children, but he thought of the cannibal. How hungry was he? How hungry do you have to be to eat human flesh? Or how messed up?

'You alright?' Emma asked.

'Why?' South putt is knife and fork neatly on the plate and pushed it away from him.

'You just had a weird look on your face.'

He laughed. 'Just thinking about work.'

Emma faced her nephew. 'And what about you? You haven't eaten much.'

'Not hungry.' Shane sighed.

'How was school?' South asked.

Shane shrugged. 'OK. Played football and that was all right.'

'I didn't like school either,' South said. 'But it got better.'

'Can I go upstairs?' Shane asked.

'OK,' South said, and watched his son leave the table and scramble up the stairs. 'Do you think he's alright?'

'No, why would he be?' Emma began to clear away the plates.

'What do you mean by that?'

'His mother died, then he ended up leaving his friends and going to a new school.' Emma put the plates in the sink.

'You blame me?'

'No, don't be stupid. You haven't done anything wrong. You both needed a new start. He'll settle in and so will you. How's work?'

South grabbed the kettle, nudged his sister out of the way and filled it up. 'Weird, but OK. Like you said, I need time to settle in.'

The phone rang.

Emma stared at it. 'Who's that?'

'Answer it and you might find out. It won't be for me.'

Emma went and answered the phone. After some

mumbling, she turned and held it out to her brother. 'It's for you.'

South took it. 'Hello.'

'South?' the voice asked.

'Yes?'

'DCI Harris. Have you got a moment to talk?'

'Of course, sir.'

There was silence on the other end of the phone for few seconds, only the light sound of breathing coming across the line. Harris coughed. 'I wanted to talk about Fred.'

'What about him?'

'How's he at the moment?'

Oh shit, South thought. 'He's OK, I think.'

'You realise that he's seeing someone? A doctor, I mean?'

Office politics. South's mind rewound at high speed to his conversation with Fred that afternoon. He recalled the paranoid words pouring out of the beaten and worn face of his colleague. Not so paranoid now. South never had the makings of a politician, never been able to be that ruthless and lie so effectively. He guessed that if he wanted to get anywhere, he'd have to start playing the game. 'I know he's got problems...'

'Look, we're just worried about him. He's been through a lot and the stuff that's happened to him can generate a lot of anger.'

'He didn't seem like an angry man.'

'Well, he got pretty angry the day he beat up that lad. Listen, you're here because they're getting ready to give Fred the elbow. Best thing you can do is kept an eye on him, report back anything strange. OK?'

'OK.'

'Have a nice evening.'

'Thanks.' South put the phone down and swore at

it.

Ali Saha opened his car window and leaned out. He'd parked a couple of hundred yards from his house, underneath a tree. He looked up and hoped no birds were going shit on his Ford Mondeo. He'd washed it on Sunday. His wife made him wash it, saying she didn't want him picking people up in a dirty car. He tried to tell her that most of his passengers were blind drunk, and wouldn't notice if his car was painted the colours of the rainbow, but she wasn't listening. She never listened, only talked.

He smiled as he took out a pack of cigarettes from his jacket pocket and stuck one in his mouth. He lit it and leaned his head further out of the car, taking hurried puffs, his eyes trying to stretch along the street to his home. He took a few more panicked puffs and threw the cigarette onto the pavement. He got out and trod it into the cracks.

He reached the house and saw the light on in the lounge. Every time he came home, gone midnight, she was still up, waiting for him. He hated it, for two specific reasons: the first was that he knew she would moan about her day, specifically their three children. Secondly, because he'd never get a chance to clean his teeth, or gargle, to get rid of his cigarette breath. He'd come prepared though, and took out some breath freshening mints and began to suck one.

He was too well prepared to be caught out by her, he told himself, and put the keys in the door. Before he could turn the lock, the door flew open and his wife stood there wide-eyed.

'What's wrong with you, woman?' He moved to go past her, but she stood there, her long black hair cascading down her shoulders.

Her eyes darted past his shoulder as she grabbed

his arm. 'Did you see anyone out there?'

'What're you talking about?' He looked behind him, then back to her face.

'I kept seeing someone moving around the front garden.' She gripped his arm tighter and pulled him around and pointed to the garden.

'I can't see anyone.' He shut the front door.

'I'm telling you there was someone out there.' She followed him as he walked into the lounge and sat down on the sofa. He found the television control and turned it on.

'Don't put that on!'

'Nadia, what is wrong with you? Are the children in bed?'

'Of course they are. Are you going to call the police?' She sat next to him, staring angrily at him, and gripped his arm.

'Why? Because you saw someone walk by the house?'

'He was in the garden.'

'Let's get some sleep and see how we feel in the morning, alright, darling?' He patted her back.

'Have you been smoking?'

SIX

Friday, 23rd April 2004

Fred's alarm clock had become redundant. Most mornings he was woken by the rippling pain in his backside. He tried to sit up in bed, pulling himself up and feeling the pain gnawing at his spine. He'd gone to sleep filled with more pills. Did he rattle when he rolled over in his sleep, he wondered? He was beginning to worry about the side effects of pouring so many tablets down his throat. What would be the effect on his liver? Then he realised that it really didn't matter, just so long as he could get through the days, get to the bottom of it, and do what had to be done.

He went to the bathroom, swallowed some more painkillers, and splashed water in his tired face. He looked deep into his blood shot eyes and thought about the day ahead. He got through each day, counting down the minutes until he could take some more pills. Somehow, it made the days seem shorter, each one sectioned off into four-hour parts, something he wished he'd thought of long ago.

Fred started to think about the dead cannibal, the dead junkie, and the woman with the knife in her stomach, penetrating her womb. He pictured the spiders crawling out of the dead old men's mouths. He looked at himself. He didn't look much younger than them; he could be one of them, stuck in a little crappy flat, dying alone with a spider crawling out of his mouth. He wanted to know what it was all about before they got rid of him. He had work to do, a job to finish before they took away the little power he had.

He would change things. Once the spider business was over, he'd be finished.

He turned on the shower, waited for it to warm up, then took off his pyjama bottoms and stepped in, feeling the water dig into his face.

South was a good guy and not a bad police officer. He wouldn't mind him taking his job, but he couldn't let it happen yet. He had too much to do. He made a mental list and, near the top, rising above all the rest, like the chart on Top Of The Pops, was sex. He needed to have sex again.

It was 9 a.m. and the traffic along the A10 was grumbling along, belching out pollution, farting great plumes of toxic smoke towards Ali Saha's parked motorcar. He began to wonder how it could all go on, when every human was jumping in their cars and racing off somewhere, vomiting more fumes into the air. No wonder more children were getting asthma, he thought, and ate a sandwich his wife had made. He was no better; he drove his taxi around filling the air with the same poisons. No, he was different in a way, because he transported people from one place to another. Each person he delivered to their destination, was one less car poisoning the air. He was saving the planet just a little bit. He said so to his wife one night, and she laughed in his face.

Right, he said and sat up. He'd had his morning sandwich break, which he had at that time every morning, parked pretty much in the same spot. It was time to get back to work.

The back door opened and someone got in.

'Sorry, my friend, but I'm just off to pick someone

up.' He turned to see who'd climbed in.

He felt the sharp object dig into his neck, then a hand grab his shoulder.

'Enfield Town!' the voice growled. 'Take me to Enfield Town or I'll cut your throat!'

Ali Saha froze, trying to think for a moment, weighing up whether or not he could jump out of the car. As if the man read his thoughts, Ali felt the knife digging into him. 'Start the engine and drive!'

'Please, just leave me alone,' Ali said, gripping the steering wheel.

He felt the knife again, more pressure this time and the slow and menacing words that were as sharp as the blade. 'I'll fucking leave you alone when you've done what I want. Now fucking drive, you little shit!'

For a moment, a split second, Ali looked in the rearview mirror and saw the eyes screaming out to him through a mask, a balaclava. He started the engine, trying not to move too much, the blade digging into his neck. He felt sick as the engine roared to life.

He turned left into Carterhatch Lane and drove, keeping the car at the legal limit, waiting for some kind of demand. Ali looked at his radio set and heard another driver letting headquarters know his position. He wondered if he could grab the radio.

'Don't do anything stupid, Ali,' the man said.

For a second, he wondered how he knew his name, but saw his identification card stuck to the dashboard.

'That's it, Ali, don't go over the speed limit. Wouldn't want to get pulled over.' The knife was pressed harder into his neck. Ali lifted his chin as he watched a car overtake them. One car had a mother and child in, probably being dropped off at school. He hoped for a second that he'd be seen and rescued.

In Enfield Town, the knife man told him to follow

the one-way system and drive into the town centre. Ali pulled out a little and braked sharply as a double-decker bus cut him up.

'That was close.' The hijacker laughed, but didn't take the knife away. 'This is not a driving test, Ali. Get going. See that shop halfway up the street with the red and white front?'

Ali looked up the street, saw the shop, and read the sign above the window. 'The Deformity Society?'

'Yes. You're going to drive up there and park your car inside that shop.'

'You're crazy! I'm not going to do that!'

'Then you'll die.' The knife brushed his neck.

'I have a wife and three children.'

'So?'

'They need their father.'

The hijacker huffed. 'I've seen your family, Ali. I've been hanging around outside your home, waiting for the right moment. I picked you out especially. Just drive into the shop and it'll all be over.'

'I can't!'

Ali felt a coldness brush past his leg and looked down as blood soaked through his khaki trousers. 'Shit. Shit. Please don't.'

'Then drive. For your sake and your family's.'

The engine roared as Ali put his foot on the accelerator. He looked for a gap in the traffic, then joined the flow. With a few toots of their horns, the other drivers let him over to the right lane. He saw the Deformity Society getting nearer, the clothes and books in the window. He gripped the wheel.

'Put your fucking foot down. Now! Do it!'

Ali turned the wheel and suddenly everything went into slow motion. It seemed to take an age for the car to mount the pavement. It smashed through the wood and glass of the shop front, hats and dresses hitting and sliding off the windscreen, caught up in glass and wood. A hat stand, then a dress rail, penetrated the windscreen. Ali jerked backwards as a mannequin rolled up the bonnet and rolled down again. Please let it be a mannequin.

The car hit the back wall, and the airbag boomed and hissed into Ali's face.

Then there was silence.

'No, I want to speak to Mr Hawks, not his supervisor,' Fred said calmly, seeing Harris step into his office. 'Yes, please. Thank you.'

The woman on the other end of the phone told Fred that Mr Hawks couldn't be found. 'Can you give him the number I gave you before? Yeah, that's a direct line to me, Detective Inspector Fred Fairservice. Thank you.'

Harris smiled as Fred put down the phone. 'Don't you fucking hate people?'

'I was just trying to arrange for him to come in and talk to us some more.'

Harris looked over the desk at the paperwork and Fred's notebook. 'I thought I'd better tell you that there's a young woman who wants to see you downstairs.'

'What? Who?'

'Sharon West. Said she's the girlfriend of the dead junkie we found.' Harris winked at Fred. 'You better go take care of her.'

Fred got up and fiddled with his tie.

'Very nice, and quite sexy, but not my type,' Harris said. 'Perhaps you should try it on. You know, must be a while since you got any.'

Fred shook his head in disbelief and turned for the door. 'Where is she now?'

'I told a WPC to bring her up and put her in number 2.' Harris walked away, whistling.

Fred put a hand through his hair and stood before the door to interview room number two. He hated meeting the people left after the act, the remnants of someone's life. It had to be done though, so he opened the door and walked in.

He smelt perfume or soap as he entered the room. The young woman sat hunched over in a three quarter length jacket that looked too big for her. Her hair was black, bobbed and silky.

He walked around and smiled, noticing her face was attractive but slightly gaunt. 'Hello, I'm Detective Inspector Fred Fairservice.'

She looked up with a look of expectancy in her eyes and a tinge of sadness. 'Steve's dead, isn't he?'

Fred took a seat and folded his arms. 'Would you like a cup of tea?'

The girl shook her head. 'Just tell me. It's him, isn't it? I found out where he was staying and when I went round there, this woman said the police had found him dead and cut up into pieces.'

Fred coughed. 'We found the body of a male aged about twenty-seven. He was known as Steve…'

'Steven Murphy.' She quivered.

'What did Steve look like?' Fred looked at his hands.

'He had dark hair, a bit wavy. Brown eyes…'

'Did he have any distinguishing features?'

'Well, he had a large nose. He was very self-conscious about it, if you know what I mean?'

Fred nodded. 'I'm sorry, but I think it probably is your boyfriend.'

She shook her head. 'Ex-boyfriend. He was living

with me and my mum and my kid. But I chucked him out a few months ago.'

'I see.'

'So someone killed him and cut him up?'

'That's the problem. The medical examiner said he died from an overdose of heroin, self-administered, as far as he can tell. At least there were no signs of a struggle. There were old needle marks over his body.'

She nodded. 'Yeah, that's why I kicked him out. He was nicking stuff and taking money from my mum. The bast…sorry, I shouldn't say that.'

'Do you know why he moved there?' Fred asked.

'No, I just got an email at work from him giving me his new address. The email said that he wasn't supposed to tell anyone where he was. I only got the message yesterday. I haven't been at work, you see?'

'Where would he have sent the email from? We didn't see a computer.'

The girl examined her nails. 'If he had one, he would've probably sold it for drugs. Probably the library in Edmonton. He used go there and use chatrooms. He was sad like that.'

Fred nodded and did his best to smile.

'He owed me a hundred quid.' She looked at Fred as if she expected him to dig into his pocket and produce the money.

'Well, thanks. I'll get someone to show you a photo of…well, of the forensic photo taken of Steve so you can identify him. But that's all really.'

She nodded and got up.

Fred gave a file of photos to a constable and asked them to show the girl a non-gruesome photo of Steven Murphy for her to identify, then said goodbye again, and walked back into the incident room.

Harris walked over after putting down his phone,

grabbed Fred's shoulder, then turned him back towards the door. 'You look like you could do with getting out. Maybe do some window shopping.'

'What?'

'We need to go to Enfield Town.'

'Where's Mark South?' Fred asked as he drove Harris to Enfield Town.

'He's in Epping Forest, where Heather was found,' Harris said. 'Jameson thought it would be better if he got dirty working with the team on that. You know, get some mud on his nice shiney shoes.'

'What about my case?' Fred followed the one-way system around Enfield Town, tucked behind a 121 bus.

'Not sure, Fred. Things is, it's just a couple of suicides. Maybe if you're lucky, Jameson will let you carry on looking into it.'

'I need to go to Edmonton Green Library to check something out.' Fred followed the bus and slowed down as he saw the back end of a car sticking out of what used to be a shop window. He pulled over quickly, parking in front of a uniformed officer who tried to get them to drive around the scene. Harris jumped out and showed his ID, while Fred focused on the firefighters who kept rushing from their fire engine and into the shop. He got out of the car and followed Harris and the uniform. There were several uniforms holding back the crowd behind the police cordon, which stretched from the lamp post to the shop front, and around the back of the car.

'Some people don't understand the concept of window shopping,' Harris said.

An overweight man in a creased white shirt walked towards them. His thinning straw colour hair was matted with sweat, while his hands untidily tucked his shirt back into his trousers. Harris smiled at the man and held out his hand.

'Hello, Tony,' the man said and wiped some sweat from his forehead. 'What a mess, eh?'

'What exactly happened? Apart from the obvious.' Harris looked around at Fred, then dragged him towards the overweight man. 'Do you know Fred? DI Fairservice? Try not to laugh at his name.'

The man shook Fred's hand. 'Nice to meet you, mate.'

'This is Detective Inspector Peter Baxter, Fred. He's from Enfield nick.'

Baxter nodded at Fred, then said, 'Apparently a cab driver found himself with a knife to his throat this morning and was forced to drive straight into this shop window. I'd say it was a case of smash and grab, but nothing was taken. If it was a smash and grab, it may be that they got the wrong shop, seeing as it's a charity shop, and not a jewellers or electronic goods shop.'

'Where's the knifeman?' Fred asked.

'He done a runner through there.' Baxter pointed to the smashed back window of the car. Shards of glass cover the boot, the pavement, while the sound of the uniformed officers grinding the glass into the ground filled the air.

'So, why are we here?' Harris slapped Baxter's shoulder.

'Right.' Baxter nodded and looked at the Firefighters who were heading back towards their fire engine. 'Apparently the cabby was told to give you lot a message.'

Harris raised his eyebrows at Fred, then looked back at Baxter. 'And that was?'

'He just said, "tell the police that they could not live in an unsympathetic world any more".' Baxter shrugged. 'Weird, isn't it?'

Fred peered in through the damage, focusing on the till that was sat right on the far wall, inches from the front of the car. 'Very. Anyone hurt?'

'An old dear has been taken to Chase Farm. They don't reckon her chances much.' Baxter loosened his collar a bit. 'I'll kept an eye on her. Want to meet Mr Saha, the taxi driver?'

'Where is he?' Harris asked, looking towards an ambulance that was parked in a side street, next to a bright yellow coffee house.

'Paramedics looked him over, then I sent him in a car over to our station.' Baxter pointed a thumb behind him. 'Come on, let's go and get a shit cup of tea, then talk to Mr Saha.'

South looked up, risking taking his eyes off his feet. The sun pricked at his eyes before the trees blotted it out. Under his feet, he felt the dead leaves and damp soil move as he walked behind the meaty frame of Jameson. Jameson took off his jacket. South could then smell the forest, the damp earth, rotting foliage, and the slight musty smell of sweat. Further ahead, a uniform strode through the woods, prodding the ground with the white pole he carried.

Something caught the corner of South's eye and he turned his head sharply to see a squirrel scampering up a tree.

He recalled as a kid how his family might sometimes go camping, setting up their tents on the edge of a forest. He'd poke his head out and look into the darkened trees, imagining something evil was peering back out at him. He wondered if Heather Beckley was alive when she was brought here, perhaps kicking and screaming, her eyes focused on the darkness and the spookiness of it all. There had definitely been

103

something evil in the woods that day.

Jameson stumbled along, his fat hands grasping the bark of the trees. South looked down, saw the mud caking the bottom of his shoes and trousers, then groaned.

The uniform stopped them as they come to a clearing, his hand reaching out and pointing to ten other uniforms standing lined up, all swiping white sticks at the undergrowth.

'Where was she found?' Jameson asked the uniform.

'Just over there.' He pointed to where a small enclosure has been set up. A SOCO entered the area and stood on the metal duckboards that protected the crime scene, while the uniforms kept searching for any evidence.

'The poor cow wasn't killed here,' Jameson said, his eyes jumping to South.

'Then where?' South tried to brush some dirt off his trousers.

'I wouldn't bother doing that, boss,' the uniform said. 'You've got to walk back through that shit to get back to your car.'

'Thanks, Gary,' Jameson said. 'You better join the rest.'

Jameson took out a handkerchief and wiped his forehead. 'What a place to end up. Thing is, she's not the only one and she won't be the last. If you've killed someone in North London and you want to get rid of the body, then you come here. There must be loads of people buried here. People who were never reported missing.'

'But Heather was,' South said and watched a uniform bending down and examining something with his gloved fingers.

'We've got one hell of a job.' Jameson stepped over

to a tree and grasped it, his thick neck twisting as he looked towards his men as they searched the floor of the forest. 'We have her shoe and now we have her. When you've got a shoe with blood on, you can be damn well sure she's not coming back alive. That fucking bastard of a boyfriend.'

South stepped forward as a twig snapped under his shoe. 'How sure are we that it's him?'

'There's no doubt in my mind. You can look into the eyes of a shit like that and know.' Jameson turned around and faced South. 'How many guilty men have you faced across that little table?'

'A few. It's hard to say.'

Jameson nodded. 'You've put them away, but you've had doubts? Yeah, I know. It's hard not to have doubts when the media are constantly going on about wrongful convictions, but you have to say fuck them or you have to quit. You're a copper, so you have to see the guilt in their eyes even if you don't really see it.'

Jameson turned away before South could ask what he meant.

'What about Fred?' Jameson turned back around. 'What do you make of him?'

He knew this would come today, but he hadn't been expecting it so soon. A nice trip to the woods, he said, get the feeling for the crime scene, get motivated to catch the killer. The fat DCS was all friendly, with lots of pats on the back and sweaty, stale breath one minute, and the next he's full of prying questions. 'He's a good officer.'

'You've only been working with him three days.' Jameson laughed and prodded South's chest playfully. 'He won't be around long though.'

'What do you mean?'

The laughter sank from the fat policeman's face.

'He's a liability. He's an accident waiting to happen.'

Wondering how many more clichés Jameson would fit in, South moved closer to the search. 'He's seems OK to me. I know he's got problems.'

'He's got problems alright. His brother's dying. In two years he'll be alone and that's not a good position for any policeman. You need family to ground you, to kept you sane. Fred has a lot of anger and resentment inside him.'

South spun round. 'Really? He seems sort of calm and...'

'He was sent on leave because he was acting strangely. I finally made him go away when one of his fellow officers reported that he hit a suspect. I wasn't having that, but I didn't want to boot him out either. But I might have to anyway. I'm getting pressure from up high. The fuckers.'

They both turned when they heard feet trampling the ground behind them and saw a constable jogging towards them.

'Sir,' the uniform said.

'What's happened?' Jameson said and grasped the uniform's shoulder.

'We found an abandoned car a few hundred yards from here. We ran it and it's registered to Andrew Nelson.'

SEVEN

Harris leaned against the wall and flicked through Saha's statement, then threw it at Fred. Fred missed the catch and watched it drop to the floor. He picked it up, gave it a quick glance, and handed it to Baxter. More police constables came down the corridor and they squeezed out of their way, watching them pass through. Enfield nick was tiny compared to their Edmonton fortress.

'Probably didn't know anything,' Baxter said and opened the door to the interview room and let Harris and Fred enter.

Ali Saha's head sprung up and he looked at the three officers with watery eyes. Baxter let Harris and Fred seat themselves, then stood by the door.

Harris coughed. 'Hello, Mr Saha.'

'Hello.' Saha looked at them all. 'Am I in trouble?'

Harris laughed. 'Well, that depends, Mr Saha. We've read your statement and we need to go over a few things with you.'

'What happened?' Fred asked. 'He just jumped in the car with you?'

Saha nodded. 'Yes. He just jumped in the back and then he stuck a knife to my throat. He told me to drive, so I did.'

'What else did he say?' Harris leaned forward.

'Don't really remember. Just the message he told me to give you before he ran off.

'And when he told you to drive to Enfield town, you just drove? Harris asked.

Fred stared at Harris. 'He said the man had a knife to his throat. What would you do?'

Saha's eyes burned. 'I did say I wouldn't take him and look…'

Saha lifted his leg up to show them. There was a bandage over the wound, a little blood showing through. 'He cut me. I had to drive and he said he knew where I lived.'

Harris said, 'he said he knew where you lived?'

Saha nodded. 'My wife said she saw someone lurking around our house. I didn't take much notice, but now…'

'Did he say why he wanted you to drive into that particular Shop?' Fred tried to sound friendly.

Saha shrugged. 'Because he's mad. He didn't give any reason. I drove into that window because he had a knife to my throat and now that lady's probably going to die. How do you think I feel? I sat there after it happened, after we crashed into the shop and all he said was to say hello to you lot. I don't know why.'

There was a smirk on Harris' face when he turned to Fred. 'Sounds a bit funny to me, what about you?'

'Try and remember if he did or said anything else, Mr Saha, it could be very important.' Fred tried to make the words sound full of meaning, desperate pleas for the sake of some possible future victim.

Saha's eyes flickered for a moment to his chest, then his hand slowly moved up to his top pocket. He reached in slowly, his face showing great uncertainty as he pulled out a slip of paper. 'He put this in my pocket after we crashed into the shop. I nearly forgot.'

'Drop it on the table,' Fred said, then turned to Baxter. 'We need an evidence bag and some gloves.'

Baxter nodded and left the room. Harris sat forward, looking down at the paper. 'There's definite writing, I think.'

'Probably another message,' Fred said.

'Another message?' Harris asked.

'Yes. Remember the marked passage in the Shakespeare book?'

There was confusion growing on Harris' face, his eyes narrowing. 'You don't even know if there was a connection. Anyone could have marked that passage.'

The door opened and Baxter threw an evidence bag at Fred and a pair of surgical gloves. Fred picked up the note and carefully unfolded it.

They all stared at the short paragraph:

'Deform'd, unfinish'd, sent before my time
Into this breathing world scarce half made up,
And that so lamely and unfashionable
That dogs bark at me as I halt by them'

Harris gave a bemused laugh. 'OK, so I was wrong. Big deal. Fuck him.'

'Have you two finished with our witness then?' Baxter asked, picking up the note and slipping it inside the evidence bag.

Fred got up and looked at the minicab driver. 'I'd forget all about it if I was you, Mr Saha.'

Harris left the room, leaving Baxter, Saha and Fred alone.

Saha looked up at Fred. 'You don't think he'll try and find me?'

'I don't think so. You've served your purpose. Just go home and forget about this.' Fred tucked his chair back under the desk.

'What about the lady that was hurt?' Saha asked.

'They'll take care of her at the hospital. She's in good hands.'

When they had left the room, Baxter said to Fred, 'She'll be fine? That old lady's going to die.'

'What else was I going to say?'

'I suppose you're right.' Baxter looked along the corridor to where Harris was standing reading a bulletin board, holding a cup of tea. 'What's this whole thing about anyway?'

'We don't know really. Just another loony. Anyway, I have to go to the library, so thanks for your time.' Fred shook Baxter's hand and walked towards Harris.

'That probably means we've got two murders to deal with now,' Fred told Harris.

Harris nodded, still transfixed by the bulletin board. 'I can't remember if Baxter plays golf or not.'

The red Peugeot was sitting a couple of feet from the road, tucked under the trees, one of the doors still open and its wheels caked in mud. The ground all around the car was muddy. Jameson stepped around the front of the car, while South and Sergeant Knight stood and watched. South was staring at the door, stuck in a daydream. He shook himself out of it and approached Jameson. 'What're you thinking? You think he's done a bunk?'

Jameson did his best to crouch down and look under the car, but he failed and lifted himself back up. 'Probably. I know for a fact that Nelson works in Loughton, so this is his route home. He probably had someone waiting for him here with another car. He got out, got in their car and they were away. The bastard.'

Sergeant Knight walked over, looking at the mud. 'There was signs of a struggle. I think you're right about the other car, there are tyre tracks over there, but looked like someone was dragged from this car to the other car.'

Jameson and South look down at where Knight was pointing. South nodded. 'I think he's right. Better get all this photographed and get the car into the pound so we can check it out, dust it for fingerprints.'

'Right, Sergeant, get on it will you. Call in and get this taken care of. Better get forensic to look it all over.' Jameson put a hand on South's shoulder and directed him away from the scene as Knight talked on his radio.

'So, what case should you really be on?' Jameson asked.

South shrugged. 'That's up to you, sir. I mean, the whole thing with the cannibal and the spiders, that's Fred's thing, I suppose. I can't even make sense of it to tell the truth.'

Jameson took out his handkerchief and wiped his top lip. 'I know what you mean. Didn't make any sense to anyone. Better just to let Fred stumble around it and spend the rest of his time chasing his tail. I know that sounds harsh, but it's for the best really. You could have a good career ahead of you, South. We need more men like you at the lodge.'

'Sorry?'

'The Masonic lodge. Never mind, we'll talk about that another time.' Jameson started to cross the road. 'Let's get back to our cars and head back to the station. There's a lot of paperwork to sort out and we need to go over a few questions with some witnesses. And you and I need to have a chat at some point about the real reason you were sent here.'

Fred hadn't been inside Edmonton Green Shopping City for years. The smells woke his memories of childhood. The stench of the fish market and rotting vegetables greeted his nostrils like an old friend. Before he reached the centre of the market, he stopped, turned right, and looked at a clothes shop that used to be a burger bar about thirty-odd years ago. He walked towards the glass and looked inside, letting the women's clothes and lingerie vanish, and the old tables, booths and greasy counter appear. He pictured the chef standing behind the counter, getting his food orders from a middle-aged Italian woman with oily black hair. He even recalled the hairy mole on the side of her face.

His whole family would sit in a booth in the back corner. On the table would be the cutlery and a ketchup container shaped like a tomato. The smell of the French fries cooking came back to him, filling him full of warmth. They were the times when they were all together, happy with their lives.

Fred turned and strode through the market, hearing the calls of the men and women on the market stall, children screaming, laughing, echoing around the high corners of the concrete interior.

He walked into the library and ignored the shelves of worn books, thumbed by millions of readers, and walked up to the counter where a man in a baseball cap and black shirt stood looking at a computer screen.

Fred took out his ID and stuck it under the man's pointed nose. Fred watched the man read the ID card, noticing that there was something not quite right about his face.

'So, what can I do for you?' the librarian asked. 'Detective Inspector Fred Fairservice?'

'I need some information. You may be able to help me. What's your name?' Fred turned his head and looked into a narrow room just a few feet from the counter, where a few young people faced computer screens.

'Scott Brown.'

Fred turned back to the librarian. 'Sorry?'

'That's my name. Scott Brown.'

'Right, sorry. Look, I need to know if you remember a man who used to come in here. About average height, longish dark brown wavy hair. And a very prominent nose.'

Brown smiled. 'S. Murphy. Real ugly-looking nose.'

'That's right.'

The librarian ducked under the desk, giving Fred the chance to scan behind the counter. He looked over the worn office chair, the scanner for checking out books, and the computer it was attached to. Brown placed a ledger on the desk, opened at a particular page, adjusting his hat as he put the book down. Fred looked at his dark blue hat and the 'NY' embossed on it. 'You must get hot in that hat.'

'Not really.' Brown pointed to the names in the book. 'These are the people who've used the internet. We get them to sign this book. There… S. Murphy.'

'So, he only came into use the internet?' Fred looked at the untidy, scratchy signature.

Brown nodded. 'Yeah, came in quite often, sometimes early in the morning when we've just opened or when we were just about to close. What's he done?'

Fred looked into Brown's eyes, noting that they didn't look quite right. 'Nothing really. He's dead.'

'Shit. That's terrible.' Brown shook his head. 'Seemed an alright bloke. Is this anything to do with the weird website he used to log on to?'

'Why? What was it?' Fred leaned forward.

'Well, I probably shouldn't say this, but I once walked past and saw he was viewing this site called

113

The Solution. I logged on after him and realised it was a site for people obsessed by suicide. It was about famous people who had topped themselves like Curt Cobain, Marilyn Monroe, Michael Hutchins and other people recording their failed attempts in the past. Really sick stuff. There was a chatroom too.'

'That's interesting. Well, is this website still up and running?'

'Think so. I'll write the address down.'

Fred looked around the library, spying the college people taking out textbooks and a mother picking out a book for her kid. He remembered his mother reading romance novels just before their father left.

'Here,' the librarian said and gave Fred a scrap of paper. 'Was it murder or did he…I mean, did he…?'

'Suicide, I'm afraid.' Fred put the piece of paper away, feeling the pain in his backside flare up again.

'No business for you then.' Brown smirked.

'Still got to be cleaned up. Thanks for the information, by the way.' Fred nodded and walked out of the library.

Outside, the clouds had gathered, all grey and threatening. Fred looked up and heard a rumbling somewhere and wasn't sure if it was thunder or some young wide boy blasting out music from his car. Fred took out his painkillers, swallowed a couple, feeling them scratch his throat. He told himself he should make an appointment with Dr Silverman.

He imagined this was how birth felt like, being sucked out of the warmth of sleep, a drift in comfort and hearing the outside, but not really wanting to be part of it. You're ripped out and the light is so strong that you kept your eyes closed for hours, perhaps days. But this wasn't the same, nothing like it at all. Andrew Nelson was brought out of the comfort of sleep and there was no light, just blackness.

He sat still for a moment, letting his eyes adjust to the dark, hoping that he'd see shapes or objects. Nothing came, no outline or anything. He tasted the bitter gag around his mouth. He tried to move his arms, but something like a rope, rough against his skin, kept his hands behind his back. He moved his legs, but his ankles remained locked together. He listened to his feet scraping against a dusty floor.

Then he felt it.

His leg twitched. Did something just touch his leg? Then he felt something on his arm. A shiver climbed his back. He started imagining someone was lurking in the darkness, reaching out a hand and teasing him.

What did he remember? He recalled driving home from work and the car behind flashing him desperately. He'd pulled over and sat in the car, watching through the darkness, trying to see who was sitting in the car behind him. Someone got out of the car and started walking up to his window. He grabbed his torch and got ready in case it was someone crazy. He looked up and saw the mask, but it was too late. There was sudden pain and then nothing.

He looked up as a beam of light appeared, stretched out below what seemed to be a door, like on a garage. The light spread, crept across the dusty floor, letting a little light illuminate what was around him. There was enough light to see what was climbing on him.

No. No. Get it off! He looked at the creatures crawling up his body, tapping at his clothes with their hairy black legs. More of them moved up to his chest and neck, crawling up to his face. He tried to call out, but no sound escaped the gag.

Outside Edmonton Police Station, the rain was coming down hard. Fred lifted the files off his desk and put them down again as he searched for something, anything that made sense. He looked up at window on the other side of the office and watched the rain hammering at the window, then the streaks of grey water cascading down the glass. The only sound in the office was the rhythmic beating, the sound of nature trying to get in through the window. It was somehow nice. Comforting.

Fred looked at Saha's statement that was faxed from Enfield nick a couple of hours ago. Nothing, but a cab driver being hijacked and made to drive through a shop window. He'd called up and asked about the prints on the taxi, but he knew the outcome already. The witnesses said he was wearing gloves and a balaclava. Any hair and fingerprints would be lost among the hundreds of others in Saha's car. The outside was clean, but the inside was just dirt piled upon dirt. There were some fibres on the windows, caught on the shards of glass, so they were filed away, ready for when they had a suspect. A suspect for what? The murder of a cannibal, the hijacking of a vehicle, and the probable manslaughter of an elderly woman? Hardly crimes of the century.

He laughed loudly. He heard his own laugh and the self-disgust contained within it. He rubbed his tired eyes, took out his painkillers, then a bottle of water and swallowed some pills.

The rain kept beating down on the windows.

He knew they'd kept him working on the case until it came to nothing, a dead end – the same place his career would end up too. They wouldn't let him anywhere near the Heather Beckley case. They don't want his face all over the television and papers, not when they can have a young up and coming copper like Detective Inspector Mark South.

It was fine with him. He'd got his job to do and he'd finish it.

Fred picked up a report from the lab that told him no other prints were found on the cooking utensils and ingredients in the Stuarts' home. Just Kerry's.

The door to the office opened and Mark South came in, his shoulders and hair wet from the rain. Fred got up and opened a cupboard behind him and grabbed a towel. He threw it at South, who caught it and dried his hair.

'Thanks,' South said and sat down at his desk. 'Got caught in the downpour walking back to the car.'

'Pain in the arse,' Fred said and opened his notes and read what Mr Hawks had to say. He'd tried to contact him again, but there was no reply.

'Andrew Nelson's done a bunk,' South said, looking for somewhere to chuck the towel.

Fred looked up. 'Really? Stupid idiot. He's just making it worse for himself.'

South looked thoughtful for a moment. 'That's if he did do a bunk.'

Fred heard the doubt in South's voice. Why? What do you think happened?'

'I don't know. We found his car abandoned. Looked like there might've been a struggle, but who knew? Perhaps someone decided to make him pay for killing the girl.'

'He hasn't been proved guilty yet.' Fred looked at the website address. When he got back to his office, he'd phoned the IT department, the special section that collects incriminating data from computers. They were the team that got sent for when someone's suspected of downloading child porn. They had said they would send someone down eventually.

'That didn't matter to an angry parent, does it?' South asked, and put the damp towel on a radiator.

There was a knock on the door, then a pasty-looking face appeared in the office. Fred told him to come in.

'I'm from IT. You wanted someone to come down? You Detective Inspector Fairservice?' The man, aged about thirty, had light brown, shoulder length hair, but shaved around the ears. Fred noticed the silver nose ring and the earrings. The man looked out of place in the trousers and creased shirt he was wearing.

'I'm Fairservice.' Fred got up and shook his hand.

'Rich Vincent.' The young man looked around the office. 'What did you want to know?'

'There's a website I'm interested in and I want to know who set it up.' Fred gave Vincent the piece of paper with the address on.

He looked at it, still nodding, then looked at Fred. 'Isn't there a contact email address or anything?'

'I went to the site on my computer, but I couldn't find anything. I think they want to remain anonymous.' Fred turned his computer screen towards Vincent.

South got up, came over and rested on Fred's desk. 'What is this website? Is this to do with the cannibal, spider thing?'

Vincent sat at Fred's desk and began typing on the keyboard, staring up at the screen. 'Yeah, the site's still going. Oh yeah, this is good stuff. A suicide website. Cool.'

Fred turned to South. 'I think Steven Murphy, the dead junkie, found the place he stayed at through this site. I think the person he contacted set up this site. If my theory is correct, then I think Michelle Hawks might have viewed this site too. He probably needed two people who were on the edge of taking their own lives.'

'Why?' South said.

'For this little crazy game he's playing.' Fred put a hand on top of the computer, as he turned to face Rich Vincent. 'So, can we find the person who ran this site?'

Vincent turned to face Fred as he tied back his hair. 'The answer to your question is yes and no...maybe.'

Fred sighed. 'Can we or not?'

Vincent shrugged. 'Depends how clever the person who put this site together is. I could find out where the site was hosted from and get it removed if you want?'

Fred rested on the desk. 'Forget removing it, I want to find them.'

Vincent chewed the inside of his mouth. 'I might be able to. However, the likelihood is that the site will be on a server at a company who specialise in hosting websites. When you connect to the internet, you use a service provider, an ISP, like Freeserve, for example, and so you get an IP address and these are made up of a set of numbers and every one is unique.'

Vincent turned back to the screen. 'Now, when this mysterious person created his website, he must've uploaded the web pages to the web server using a computer connected to the internet, which means he would've had an IP address and that will lead directly to the computer he used to upload the site.'

Fred nodded. 'So we can trace him?'

'No, because after he logged off that address would've been used by a few thousand other people.'

South dropped his head into his hands. 'Fucking hell. So is there anyway we can find the bastard?'

Vincent frowned. 'If you're really determined, and can get a warrant, then probably, but with some hard work. You see, just about everything on the internet is logged somewhere. You could ask to see the logs. The ISP company would have to look through their logs to find out who logged on and uploaded the web pages. That's if they gave their real details. But you could probably still get the phone number of the line they used. But there are millions of lines of information on the logs to search.'

'But it's possible?' Fred asked.

Vincent nodded, his hands brushing over the keyboard. 'I could run a programme to sift through them, but it'll still take some time.'

'It would great if you could do it,' Fred said.

'They would've probably covered their tracks pretty well, if they are smart,' Vincent added. 'But smart people get caught all the time using the internet to upload a virus or something. People just don't understand how the internet works. They think if they use an alias like throbbing purple bang stick, then no one will know it's them, but they can always be found out.'

South raised his eyebrows. 'Well, that was an education.'

Fred thought of something. 'Actually, Rich, if you're not busy right now, I could use you on a job.'

Vincent shrugged. 'Sure.'

The engine of Fred's Vauxhall Astra fell silent, leaving Rich Vincent's drumming on the dashboard the only sound in the car. The IT expert looked over to Fred, then over to the houses they'd parked in front of. 'Which one?'

'123b. Just over there,' Fred said and climbed out of the car. He looked at his watch to check how long it's been since he took a painkiller. Not that long. He felt OK, he decided and walked up the front garden and rang the bell. He heard Vincent behind him, slapping his hands on the sides of his legs. Fred turned to him. 'You in a band?'

Vincent nodded, a broad grin stretching across his face. 'Yeah, The Holy Sanctions. I'm their drummer.'

'Thought so.' Fred rang the doorbell again.

'You sure he'll be home? It's only three, he's probably still at work.'

Fred shook his head. 'He works nights. He'll be sleeping.'

'Oh great.'

Down the stairs came the sound of angry steps, so Fred stepped back a little. He heard the grumbling of a man's voice, then the lock opening. Terry Hawks peered out, his eyes puffy. 'What do you want?'

Fred took out his ID. 'Remember me, I'm Detective Inspector Fairservice? I came to see you after your wife's death? I'm sorry to disturb you, but I'd like to ask you something.'

Terry looked at Vincent. 'Who's this?'

Fred looked at his colleague. 'This is Rich Vincent. He's one of our IT experts. I was wondering if we could take your computer away to be examined.'

Hawks sighed. 'I don't understand. My wife killed herself. What has my computer got to do with it?'

Fred took a deep breath. 'Can we talk about this inside?'

Hawks sighed and opened the door wider. Fred and Vincent walked through to the hallway. Fred looked towards the kitchen and could see that the floor has been taken up. Now a large piece of carpet covered what was left of the bloodstain. He wondered what, if he were in this position, he would do. Would he sell the house?

'You want a cup of tea or something?' Hawks asked, blinking.

'You go and sit in the lounge, Mr Hawks, Rich here will make the tea.' Fred ushered Hawks into the lounge, then turned to Vincent.

'Thanks,' Vincent said sarcastically, then walked to the kitchen.

Hawks was sitting on a dark blue sofa, facing the blank screen of the television. Fred walked in and sat in an armchair that matched the sofa. 'I'm really sorry about bothering you again, Mr Hawks.'

Hawks nodded. 'It's alright, it's your job.'

'Yes, but it didn't make it any easier. Look, is it OK if we examine your computer?'

'If it helps in some way, but I don't see how. What's going on?'

Fred took out his notebook and his pen. He opened the book, fiddling with his pen, trying to delay the questions, trying to decide how to approach the whole subject. 'A man called Steven Murphy killed himself the same day as your wife, or at least the night before. Evidence at the scene led us to a door opposite his flat where we found a dead old man.' Fred stopped. He couldn't mention the spiders. It would sound crazy and he had to kept some of the details back. 'After your wife took her life, we found the book that was on your kitchen table. Do you remember? The Shakespeare book?'

Hawks' eyes looked tearful as he nodded.

'Well, we traced the book to an old man who borrowed it from the library. We found him dead too. Both old men had died of natural causes. Now, I don't know what all this means, but I do know that Steven Murphy had logged on to a website all about suicide. I think there might be a chance your wife did too. Do you know if she spent a lot of time on the computer?'

Hawks nodded. 'Yes, she did. Michelle was always on it. Even if I came home early, say ten at night, she'd be on that thing. I didn't have the time myself.'

'Well, that's why we need to examine the computer,' Fred said and watched Vincent come in and put two teas on the coffee table.

'Take it,' Hawks said. 'It's upstairs in the spare room. Please, just let me know what this is all about if you ever find out.'

Fred signalled for Vincent to get the computer. 'Again, I'm sorry.'

Hawks cleared his throat. 'I went to the library and found that book and read it. That little bit anyway.'

'I'm sorry?'

'The bit in the book she'd circled,' Hawks said. 'I sat there and read it and read it again. I don't know anything about Shakespeare. When I was at school, if they were teaching that stuff, I'd usually bunk off and end up smoking and drinking round a friend's house. I was a stupid prat back then. Anyway, I was reading that bit and I thought I understood what it meant.'

'Really?' Fred opened his notebook.

'This King Richard bloke is deformed, crippled or something. It's like he's deformed and ugly on the outside, so people think he must be the same on the inside. So, because everyone thought so, he becomes bad. Maybe Michelle thought everyone looked at her like that because of her hand. I don't know really.'

Fred noted it all down quickly, his brain taking it all in, adding it up and comparing his theory to what's happened so far. He nodded to himself. He'd been real stupid. He looked at the tired eyes of Terry Hawks and got up. 'Thanks for your time. I'd better be going.'

Hawks saw Fred to the door. The rain had ceased before they'd arrived at Hawks' house, but now the sky looked heavy again, desperate to flood the streets for a second time that day. Fred turned to see Hawks at the door, watching Vincent putting the hard drive in the back seat of Fred's car. The front door closed.

Fred took out his mobile phone and dialled DCS Jameson's number. Jameson answered, coughing.

'Sir, I think I know more about my case now,' Fred said, 'I think I understand more of what's going on. This person, whoever's doing this, won't stop now. They'll do more damage. They'll kill again.'

'You think so?' Jameson said, eating something. 'OK, you better tell everyone tomorrow morning. I'll arrange for a few bodies to be in the incident room tomorrow, early. Including Mark South. Let's talk then.'

Fred put away his phone. He knew what was going on, he thought, and he knew what he was going to do next. He smiled as he walked to his car.

After Michael Byrne jumped out of his car and beat the shit out of the bastard following him, he'd plead insanity. He looked at the lights of the car that was driving right up his arse. Looked like a Ford something. The car's light came on bright, blinding. Byrne pulled over and took off his seat belt. He opened his door and heard the roar of the engine as the Ford sped past. He stood there for a moment, watching the brake-lights of the mysterious vehicle, seeing it turn off towards the town centre.

He jumped back into his car and parked up closer to the Bare Club. It was wedged between a clothes shop and a dentist. The old shop front had been redesigned, changed from plain glass to black metal shutters that had the food menu and bar price list painted on them. The entrance led down to a staircase, which twisted down into the open-plan expanse of the club.

Michael Byrne straightened his suit as he prepared to cross the road, his eyes looking over the front of the place, the sign and the doorman standing outside. He stepped into the street, seeing a car out of the corner of his eye. He heard the engine roar, then jumped back onto the curb as the car ripped through the evening air, almost clipping him.

The same car.

'You fucking bastard!' he shouted after it.

'You OK, Mr Byrne?' the doorman said, turning his head towards the car.

'Yeah, Dan, I'm fine.' Byrne looked down the road, towards Enfield Town. 'That fucker, he'll get the shit kicked out of him one of these days.'

'I'll kept an eye out for the car,' Dan said, and got his meaty frame back by the door.

'You do that. I need a drink.' Michael Byrne put on a grin, even though he was burning with anger. He walked down the stairs hearing dance music being churned out by the house DJ. It was a little smoky, and crammed full of customers, most of whom he knew. They were sitting in the corner booths and on the tables set out close to walls. He reached the square bar at the centre of the room and waited, knowing that Mario the barman would be over in a second.

'Your usual, Mr Byrne?' Mario asked and grabbed a glass.

'Yes, Mario and make it a fucking double. Busy in here tonight.'

Mario nodded and mixed a Black Russian for his boss. 'Yeah, they really like the new look.'

A hand gripped Byrne's shoulder and he turned around to face a short man with black spiky hair and a big grin.

'Hey, Lee, you little fucker.' Michael shook his friend's hand. 'Get this little shit a drink, Mario.'

Lee poked Michael in the stomach. 'Hear you're

going away tomorrow morning. Already leaving the place?'

Byrne smiled and lit a cigarette. 'I can't do everything. I need my time in the sun, so tomorrow I jump on a plane and meet Kate in Marbella.'

Lee nodded and looked around the bar. 'What about the Inland Revenue? I thought they had their eye on you?'

'They're always after someone. Sod them. I'm off. If they want some pissy amount of money, then they can have it. They can kiss my arse.'

Lee laughed. 'Well, if you need any help with this place?'

'I'll let you know,' Byrne said and looked up towards the stairs. He put his drink down on the bar. 'I'll be back in a minute, Lee.'

He hurried up the stairs and reached Dan. 'Seen that car again, Dan?'

'No, no one been by. I'll call you if I see it. Who are they?'

'No one,' Byrne said and stared up the street.

EIGHT

Saturday, 24th April 2004

It was after midnight when Fred came in, his hair soaked and his shoulders and back damp. He took off his jacket and hung it up in the hallway. In a few hours he'd be giving a lecture to his colleagues about his theory. He didn't feel nervous, even though it had been a while since he'd talked in front of his fellow officers. It didn't matter, he told himself, they could either listen or bugger off.

Martin's eyes met his. Fred stepped into the room, smiled at Martin, and began to take off his tie. 'Thought you'd be asleep.'

Martin seemed to be watching his brother carefully. 'You'd better get dry, or you'll catch a cold.'

Fred nodded, got a towel, then sat down.

'Been working late?'

Fred looked over at his brother. 'I had a lot of paperwork to do, so I thought I'd stay and do it. Everything alright, Martin?'

Martin looked towards the windows. The curtains were open, and Fred saw the amber streetlight and the rain that speared through the night air. There was a rumbling outside and a flash of light illuminated the room. 'Mrs Boswell was here.'

'Really?' Fred got up and pulled the curtains.

Martin nodded and folded his arms. 'She came to see you. She brought us dinner again.'

Fred laughed. 'She's crazy that woman.'

'She likes you.'

'What? What's that look for?'

Martin gives a slow thin smile. 'She'd do anything for you.'

'I've got enough to deal with, without some mad neighbour to worry about.'

'How is the case going?' Martin asked.

Fred took off his shoes. 'I think I know what it's all about. Well, sort of anyway. I'm giving a talk tomorrow, this morning I mean. Going to tell them what I think.'

'Nervous?'

Fred shrugged. 'Not really. Did you know there are sites about suicide on the internet?'

Martin smiled. 'If there was something you want or need, then you'll find it. It didn't matter what it is.'

Fred looked strangely at his brother. 'Are you still talking about the internet?'

Martin nodded. 'Every obsession, every little perverted little secret fantasy, they're all out there floating around. It's like a breeding ground for the weird and whacky. It's like one big menu of perversion.'

Fred can't help asking. 'And what do you look for?'

'The facts.'

'Really?'

Martin smiled again and pulled his blanket up to his chest. 'She'd fuck you.'

'What?'

'Mrs Boswell. If you took her out, I guarantee that she would let you do it to her.'

Fred got up quickly. 'I need to get some sleep.'

'Think about it, brother.'

Fred shook his head.

There was a light rain falling on him when Byrne left the club and said goodbye to Dan. It was gone 3am and all the customers had staggered off home drunk or lurched into kebab shops to give the staff trouble there instead. Michael Byrne pulled his suit jacket around him, and walked towards his Mercedes. He crossed the road, his eyes scanning the empty streets, seeing the rainwater glisten and hearing the wind brushing through the trees along Silver Street. He pointed his key fob at his Mercedes and heard it beep, flash and unlock. He climbed in, feeling the chill of the interior.

He saw something in the corner of his eye. A red Renault Magane crawled along driven by a smiling young woman, her fella grabbing and messing her hair. He sighed. What the hell am I so afraid of? He owned clubs and pubs across North London, not forgetting the massage parlours. He wasn't a man to mess with. People know that. When they come to one of his establishments, they know that they have to behave themselves. He knew it all sounded like he was trying to play the bad boy gangster, but there was little choice when you had risen to his business level. The violence came with it, whether you liked it or not. He had to deal with things his way, because the law wasn't on his side. Not all of them anyway. There were some who didn't mind doing him a favour for an envelope of cash.

He started the engine, pulled into the road, did a three point turn and headed towards Bush Hill Park. He put the radio on for a bit, but it was all dance music, so he turned it off again.

He checked his rearview mirror. Shit.

Where the fuck did that come from? He looked and saw the same car from earlier behind him, feeling his

129

heart pulsating a little. He could only make out the shape of the driver. The car got a little closer, its lights trying to blind him. He looked down at the floor and saw his wheel lock. He shook his head. He opened his glove compartment, reached in and took out a flick knife. He put it on the passenger seat.

The car roared up behind him, flashing its lights. Fuck this, he thought, pulled the car over, and braked sharply. He opened the door and climbed out as the other car swerved around him. He watched as it slowed, turned left and stopped. The car crawled slowly along until he could only see the tail end. He reached in the car and scrambled for the knife.

Right you bastard, he thought, and stormed towards the car, holding the knife down by his leg. The blade flicked out. As he approached the car, he saw the driver's door was open. The fucker's done a runner. He looked into the car and saw no one in the front or back.

The arm came from nowhere, clamped around his neck, pulling him backwards. Byrne lifted his hand up, pointing the knife upwards, ready to strike. The attacker gripped Byrne's knife hand and twisted it. Byrne tried to take the pain, but couldn't, released the knife and heard the blade drop to the pavement. He was pushed forward, his hands automatically jerking out to block his fall. He smashed down onto the car. He tried to turn around, but a bolt of pain pierced the back of his neck. He fell to his knees, then tried to scramble to his feet.

Not like this! He thought of Kate. He imagined her, in that split second, having to identify his body.

He flipped over and looked up at his attacker, who was big and broad, and wearing a mask. The eyes burned out to him as the baseball bat came down at him. He held up his arms, then screamed out in pain, when the blow smashed down on his wrist. He pushed himself back and started kicking out with his legs. The bat was lifted high over the attacker's head again, then down at Byrne's knee. A spear of pain spiked through his leg. He looked up at the crazy eyes staring at him. 'Please...listen...'

The bat came down, hard, smashing his head against the pavement. The bat came down again and again.

They were all in there, every one of the personnel who Jameson had said should know the ins and outs of the Spider Mouth case. Spider Mouth. Fred had been called that as a boy, when they picked on him after he made the mistake of standing up in class and reading his story aloud. Until that moment, he'd just been a ghost in that classroom, more a spirit than a real person. He'd brought the nickname on himself. Perhaps he was about to do it again.

He stood in the doorway with his glasses on, and looked down the incident room. He could see the backs of their heads. The back row was filled with uniforms, specially picked to help with taking statements, talking to neighbours. There would be the chance of overtime.

Fred looked over at South, Ally Walker and Harris, who were all sitting by the whiteboard. Harris was stretched out, nearly asleep.

Jameson stepped out of his office, approached the team, saw Fred and beckoned him.

As Fred walked towards the front, to face his audience, he looked over at the whiteboard and the photos stuck to it. Photos of his suicides. Next to his photos are the shots of a young Heather Beckley, once missing, now accounted for, but still not avenged.

Jameson started by waving his hands above the group, waiting for the chatter to die down. 'Come on, people, let's have a bit of silence. Don't forget we are part of the Serious Crime Squad, not the circus.'

'Now,' said Jameson. 'I know it's Saturday morning and some of you aren't supposed to be here, but that's that. The fact is there are still crimes going on out there. Look at this board behind me. Heather Beckley's killer is still out there somewhere, whoever he might be.'

'Probably done a bunk,' someone shouted from the back.

Jameson shook his head. 'As well as Heather, we've also got the death of John Kerry to deal with, as well as the other strange goings on of late. Now I want you to listen to what Detective Inspector Fairservice has to say about it all. Fred?'

Fred nodded to Jameson and stepped forward. He looked at their faces and tried to blot out their eyes, imagining deep black holes instead. 'Thanks. This won't take long.'

'Good,' Harris said and sat up. 'I've got to get over to Kent this afternoon to play golf with my mate, Rob.'

Fred turned and pointed to the shot of Steven Murphy's decapitated head. 'This was Steven Murphy. We found him in a flat in Edmonton Green, just up the road. He'd been dismembered. Dr Farmer, the pathologist, said that he actually died of an overdose of heroin. Seeing as Murphy was a smack addict, it's too far fetched to think he did it accidentally. There were no signs of the victim being held down or signs of a struggle. But of course we are still treating the death as suspicious because of the way his body was found. So, we have the dead drug addict as our first victim.'

'Good riddance,' someone commented.

Fred coughed. 'Now, there was a lot of blood at the scene that didn't belong to Murphy. I think this was purely theatrical. They also took a lump of his flesh. I'll come back to that in a minute. Whoever cut him up post-mortem did it to get our attention. They also took some blood and, I believe, marked a cross on the door of the flat opposite. In that flat was an old man who died of natural causes.'

He watched his colleagues turn and comment to their neighbours. He took a deep breath. 'In the mouth of the old man was a spider. At the time, I thought perhaps it was a coincidence, but then we found our second suicide. Michelle Hawks had taken a kitchen knife and stabbed herself several times in her abdomen. She not only killed herself, but also her unborn child.'

He turned and looked at the photograph of Michelle Hawks, a holiday shot of her and Mr Hawks in some hot country. Fred guessed at Spain. 'I think you'll agree, this was a pretty extraordinary way of taking her own life. Now it gets stranger. On the kitchen table was a book of Shakespeare plays that did not belong to the Hawks. We traced it to the library it was borrowed from and then to a Mr Lovegrove. Also dead. Also with some spiders in his mouth.'

Fred caught South's eye and got the thumbs up. 'The next morning the death of an elderly man at an old people's home was reported to us. A spider was found in the glass in which he kept his false teeth.'

Laughter spread across the room until DCS Jameson quietened them down.

Fred continued. 'Evidence at the scene led us to an address where John Kerry was staying. Kerry was, when we arrived at the scene, in the middle of eating his lunch. Which consisted of the flesh cut from Mr Steven Murphy, our first victim.'

There were grimaces in the room, mixed in with sounds of awe and confused laughter. Fred nodded in agreement. 'The flesh had been laced with peanut oil and Kerry suffered a massive allergic reaction, making this a murder investigation. There also seems to be evidence linking this case to an incident yesterday when a taxi driver was hijacked and made to crash his vehicle into a charity shop window.'

Harris laughed to himself. 'Not a very charitable act that.'

Fred kept his eyes on the front row. 'An elderly woman is still in hospital in a critical condition. We could be looking at two counts of murder. Now, you might be wondering what this all means. Well, Murphy had a severally deformed nose as you can see. Michelle Hawks had a deformed hand that had damaged her psychologically. I think Kerry's disability was his desire for human flesh. I think it would have consumed him day and night. Pardon the pun. I think all this because a paragraph from Shakespeare was underlined in the book. It's all about how people see your body and your defects. As if the ugliness on the outside, makes you rotten and ugly on the inside. That's what Shakespeare was saying and, well, it's all we've got to go on.'

A hand went up at the back.

Fred nodded. 'Yes, Sergeant Knight?'

'So this person doesn't like people with deformities?'

Fred shook his head. 'No, I think he's trying to point them out to us, show us the error of our ways. When you see someone ugly or deformed you tend to look away. Some people might even tease them. I think he's trying to make us realise that we're at fault.

I don't know why. Perhaps a member of his family were deformed or something.'

'What about the old men?' Ally asked.

'I must admit, that's got me stumped,' Fred said, 'but I hope to look into it and I'll get back to you.'

'The spiders must have some kind of significance,' Ally continued.

Fred shrugged. 'Perhaps because spiders are misunderstood. A lot of people hate or fear them because of the way they look. I don't know yet. But I do know that we need to go around to all the neighbours again and ask them about any strange visitors. He would've researched his victims.'

'I thought all the victims killed themselves,' a voice piped up from the back.

'We can't be a hundred percent on that at the moment,' Fred said, shrugging a little. 'In the case of the Hawks woman, we have a forensic report to back up that theory. There was no sign of breaking and entering.

Harris stood up, then slowly clapped his hands. 'Everybody thank Freddy boy here. Don't forget Andrew Nelson is out there. We need to ask that bastard some more questions.'

Jameson heard the phone ringing in his office and strode in. South walked over and squeezed Fred's shoulder. 'It's starting to make sense now.'

'I hope so,' Fred said.

Jameson came back into the incident room and held up a hand. The room fell silent. 'Right, that was some more hot off the press news. A body of a man has just been fished out of the River Lea. Looks like he's had his brains bashed in. Tony, South, and Fred, get down there now.'

The incident response car turned left past an old

pub on the corner, across from the lock gates. With the river by the side of them, all green with algae, they parked up. The response car stopped a few yards up the river, close to the SOCO van. Fred got out and looked down towards where the body was lying. He could see Farmer on his knees, peering down at the head. Fred looked around him as he walked behind South and Harris, his eyes scanning the view. A middle-aged man and his son were sitting on one of the pub benches, their fishing gear piled up beside them. A uniform seemed to be asking them some questions. He looked back down to the body as they all got closer. The arms were out stretched and the hands were grey. The dead body was clothed in a suit. Maybe a good suit, but now it was soaked with the Lea's polluted water.

'Oh, lovely.' Harris knelt down after pulling his trousers up a little. He dipped his frowning face closer to the blue swollen head, which was also bruised and contorted. 'Beaten senseless and pushed in the water. Been under long, you reckon?'

Farmer crossed his arms. 'No, I'll risk saying, without examining the body too closely, that the cadaver has only been in the water a few hours maybe less. Of course, I'll know more later.'

A SOCO officer strolled over, his body covered in a white protective suit. He stepped towards Harris and held up an evidence bag with a wallet inside, a small amount of dirty water sitting at the bottom of it. 'The dead guy's wallet. Mr Michael Byrne. I've counted the money inside, so don't pinch any.'

Fred looked over the body as it was bagged up, ready to be taken to the mortuary. There it would be laid on a table for Farmer to take apart, discovering the events leading up to the victim's death.

'Well, I won't miss the bastard.' Harris crouched down, gripping his knee, looking into the bulging face, and the grey and pruned hands. 'Probably a revenge killing or something.'

Fred stood with his hands in his pockets looking down at the body as the SOCO was about to zip up the bag. Fred bent his head, stared at the battered head, then pointed at the mouth that seemed puckered for a kiss. 'What's wrong with his mouth?'

Farmer looked at Fred, then down to the body. 'Something probably got wedged in there. Let's take a look.'

They all watched as Farmer knelt down, and prized open the blue lips. Water trickled across each cheek as Farmer's gloved hands pulled at something inside. He grabbed a pair of forceps, grasped the object, then tugged. Fred got closer and saw the bag, wet with dirty water, appearing from Byrne's breathless mouth. From the mouth came a yawn, a last gassy gasp filled with the smell of every rotten thing in the Lea.

Farmer untwisted the bag. They all stepped closer, including the SOCO. Farmer shook his head as he looked at the dead spiders all curled up in the bottom.

'Fuck me,' said Harris and laughed.

'Who's Michael Byrne?' asked South.

'Let's get some breakfast and then I'll tell you,' Harris said as a rumble travelled across the sky.

NINE

There was a flash of lightning. The thunder seemed to travel along the walls of the café, then along the floor to their feet. Fred felt the storm travel along his spine and up to the top of his skull. Outside, the rain ripped hard from the sky, ricocheting off everything, shooting back upwards and soaking the air. Fred looked beyond the curtain of rain, beyond the pub that stood alone on the opposite side of the street. He looked at the sun trying to shine behind what remained of the factory buildings of Brimsdown, the industrial heart of Enfield.

South came in through the door, his hair soaked and his jacket dark with giant spots of rainwater. He put his mobile in his jacket and sat at the table where Fred and Harris faced each other, nursing their teas.

'Well, seems Byrne's bit of stuff reported him missing today,' South said. 'Apparently, she was in Spain, staying at his villa with a couple of her friends. Byrne was supposed to meet her out there at some point. But she never heard, so came home.'

Harris picked up his tea and sipped it. 'So, looks like you two get the nice job of breaking the news to her.'

South reached for his tea, then looked at Harris. 'You not coming?'

'Sorry, but I'm playing golf this afternoon.' Harris grinned.

'It's pissing down,' Fred said as a young Greek-looking man arrived with two plates piled up with bacon, eggs, beans and toast.

Harris looked at his plate, rubbing his hands together. 'It'll be clear by then. The storm's heading away from us. And the sun's going to come out.'

South tucked into his fried breakfast, his eyes jumping between Fred and Harris. 'So, who is Michael Byrne?'

'A statistic now,' Harris said and shovelled bacon into his mouth.

A plate of toast arrived for Fred. 'He was a small time mobster.'

Harris stared at Fred. 'I think mobster is a bit strong. He owned a few clubs and pubs. Oh, and a few massage parlours.'

South raised his eyebrows. 'And? What did he do?'

'The usual,' Fred said. 'Lent money and crippled people who didn't pay it back. Ran a prostitution ring out of his massage parlours. There were rumours of his people selling drugs in his clubs. I heard his staff would make sure outside drug dealers that got inside were harshly dealt with.'

'So he could sell his stuff,' Harris said, picking up his tea. 'Nothing was ever proved though. Never any evidence, just word of mouth that managed to get back to us. This was a few years back. Me and Fred were the ones trying to prove it all. But we had nothing. We once found traces of coke in his house, but not enough to prove he was dealing or anything. Now he's gone. Good riddance.'

Fred stared across at Harris as he ate his breakfast. 'We failed.'

South bit into some toast and nodded. 'So what's he got to do with our case then?'

139

'That's what you two are going to have to find out,' Harris said and finished the last of his bacon. He took a serviette to wipe his mouth, then grinned again. 'Right, I've got to get home, change and then get over to Rob's place. I'll see you lot on Monday.'

Fred ate his toast, his eyes following the figure of Harris as he opened the door, looked up into the rain and sprinted along the street.

'Is that all you're eating?' South asked.

'I'm not very hungry.' Fred took out his painkillers, swallowed a couple and washed them down with the remainder of his tea.

'Your back still playing up?'

'Yeah. You got an address for Byrne's wife?'

'Yep. Wellington Road, Bush Hill Park.'

Fred got up. 'Nice place to live if you can afford it.'

Andrew Nelson's head sprung up as he heard a car engine outside the garage. He tried to work the gag from his mouth with his tongue, but it was tied too tightly. The car engine faded off, getting further away. He wondered what time it was. From the light coming from under the garage door, he knew it was sometime in the day. It was still very dark in the lock up, but now he could make out the objects that surrounded him, like the timber that was piled against the wall. Every time he breathed, he felt cement dust slip down into his lungs. He listened to the nearby heavy traffic that constantly hurtled by to his left, trying to work out where he must be. It was a main road that only became quieter at night. Looking down to the dusty floor, he saw the bottle of water. A French brand, probably bought from a newsagent for an extortionate price. Then there was the sandwich wrapper near it. It was a stale cheese sandwich, but he was still grateful for something to eat. He recalled all this, brought all these thoughts to his mind, to stop him thinking about the fact that he might die.

It was last night that the man appeared through the garage door. He was startled as the figure put down a bag, stepped closer, revealing his masked face. A knife was held to Nelson's throat, while the man's gloved hand removed the gag. The man then held a finger to his lips, shoved the bottle of water to Nelson's mouth and made him drink. He was fed the sandwich, then more water. Before the gag was replaced, Nelson's captor asked him only one question.

'Did you do it?' the deep voice asked. 'Did you kill her?'

Nelson only had time to shake his head before the gag was pulled over his mouth. The man picked up the bag and walked out of the garage.

Andrew Nelson felt a tear emerge from his eye. Please God, forgive me.

Wellington Road is long and dotted with Victorian semi-detached, three story houses. Fred parked outside the one Michael Byrne used to own. Kate Morcom still lived there. He noticed the incident response car sitting outside straight away.

'Have we been beaten to it?' South said, and climbed out.

Fred climbed out and felt a light rain darting at his head. 'I wonder.'

'That house must've cost a fortune.'

'Probably worth about four hundred grand now,' Fred said and walked up to the glass porch, his hand reaching out to open the door. His hand retreated as he saw two young-looking police constables stepping out of the house. He recognised the female PC as Kerry

Philpot, and smiled at her. The male constable nodded and headed back to their car.

Philpot laughed and took off her hat, revealing her brown shiny hair, all tied up in a bun. 'Hello, Fred. Haven't seen you for bloody ages.'

Fred nodded. 'Been busy. What you lot doing here?'

The PC pointed back to the house. 'Been a robbery.'

'Really?'

'Anything valuable taken?' South asked and leaned on the porch.

'Well, a few items, nothing really expensive. But Miss Morcom in there reckons her fella kept a gun in a locked drawer. But the drawer's been busted open and now there's no gun.'

Fred looked up at the house. 'Great. Well, nice seeing you again.'

Philpot squinted suspiciously at Fred. 'So, what are you doing here?'

'We've got the wonderful job of telling the lady of the house that we just fished her bloke out of the River Lea this morning.'

Philpot raised her eyebrows. 'What a lovely day she's having. Well, see you later. Pop by Ponders End sometime.'

'Will do,' Fred said and watched the constable slip inside the response car. He rang the bell and put a blank look on his face when he heard the door opening.

Kate Morcom looked South and Fred over. 'Hello.'

Fred took out his ID, which seemed to confuse her as she watched the police car drive off and said, 'I've just had the police here.'

'I know.' Fred put away his ID as South stepped forward.

'Can we talk inside?' South asked and pointed into the hall.

'What's this about?' Morcom asked.

She was slim, beautiful and young, Fred noted and wondered how she ended up with Byrne. Then he thought about the money, the nice car and the house, and it all made sense. 'It's about Mr Byrne.'

Her face changed. The annoyance turned to quiet panic as she opened the door and let them step into the large hallway. Their steps echoed around the room as Kate Morcom walked before them, dressed in a yellow summery dress that clung to her slender frame. Fred looked down the hall to the enormous square kitchen, which looked as if it hadn't hardly changed since the house was built in the Victorian era. He slipped on his glasses and spied the old servant bells that the Victorians would have pulled to call their staff.

South touched Fred's arm as Kate Morcom disappeared into the lounge. 'How old was Michael Byrne?'

'About Forty-ish.'

South tutted. 'She must be about twenty-five, the lucky bastard.'

'Let's just concentrate on the timeline,' Fred said and followed the young woman into the large, high ceilinged lounge. French windows looked on to a perfectly landscaped garden. He turned to see Morcom taking a couple of handfuls of tissues from a box, but still no tears.

South walked across the carpet towards a large canvas on the wall. It was modern art, with several multicolour stripes blending into an orange horizon. 'Nice.'

'Michael liked his art,' Morcom said. 'Just looks like a mess to me.' She screwed the tissue up in her fist as she sat down in an armchair.

Fred sat on the sofa. 'I'm afraid we have some bad

news.'

She looked at her hand. 'Is he dead?'

South looked down at her. 'Yes. I'm sorry.'

'What happened?' she asked.

'We don't really know at this stage,' Fred said. 'He was pulled out of the River Lea this morning. We're working on it. Looked like he was beaten about the head very severely.'

Fred tried to make his smile comforting. He found it hard, remembering the sort of man Byrne was. 'You reported him missing two days ago?'

She nodded. 'I'd gone to Spain with a couple of friends and was waiting for Michael to join me. I didn't know when he would be coming out to the villa. And I couldn't phone him to find out.'

'Why not?' South asked.

She turned to look up at South. 'He had this thing about people trying to contact him. His catchphrase was "I'll call you, don't call me". He'd get really pissed off if I would phone him. He didn't even have a mobile. Not a social one, anyway. After a few days, I tried to find out where he was, but no one knew.'

'Who did you talk to?' Fred asked.

'People at his clubs.' She sniffed. 'I found out that he'd been last seen in the Bare Club in Enfield town. That's the one he opened a little while ago. The doorman, Dan Goodis, told me he said goodbye to him early Saturday morning.'

Fred took out his notebook and pen. 'Do you know the exact time?'

'About three in the morning, I think.' Morcom stretched out the tissue between her hands.

'You got an address for this Dan Goodis?' South asked.

She nodded and got up. She left the room. In a

couple of minutes, she brought back a piece of paper with Goodis' address on it. 'He's one of those body builder types. Always in the gym. I don't know why women go for men like that.'

'What about the break in?' Fred asked.

Morcom looked into Fred's eyes, a little surprise showing on her face. She shook her head slightly. 'No, it wasn't a break in. They didn't find any sign of anyone breaking in. Anyway, this place is a fortress. They must've had a key. And all they did was go into Michael's office.'

Fred nodded, then scribbled down all the information. 'And what about his gun?'

'It was for protection. The drawer where he kept it was busted open and now it's gone.'

'What sort of gun?' South asked.

She shrugged her shoulders. 'Don't really know. It was small.'

'Revolver or semi–automatic?' South said.

'What's the difference?'

'A revolver has the chamber where you load your six bullets,' South said. 'It spins around.'

'Yeah, one of those.' She nodded. 'And it was silver with a black handle.'

'Was there anything particularly strange going on in Michael's life or business affairs?' Fred asked.

'Nothing that he told me about. His clubs were doing their usual business. Nothing unusual, no. You think someone he'd upset got to him?'

Fred shrugged. 'At this point we have no idea. We'll probably be back to ask you some more questions. Do you want us to send an officer around to help you at this time? Someone to talk to?'

She smiled. 'No, it's OK. I'll probably stay at my friend's. Thanks.'

Fred got up, made eye contact with South, then nodded towards the door. 'We'll go then.'

She saw them to the door and, as she opened it, said, 'So, if they killed Michael, they could have taken his keys and got into the house? So his killer might have his gun?'

'Quite possibly,' Fred said.

They were sitting in Fred's car, watching the red brick building in which Dan Goodis had his flat. They had driven to the address while trying to find out anything they could about the bouncer. There was nothing in the system that gave them any reason to believe he had anything to do with Byrne's death. South was holding a copy of the Enfield Courier in his hands, his eyes scanning over the pages. He turned his head towards Fred as he saw him take out his painkillers. 'So our killer might have a gun now?'

Fred nodded. 'Sounds like it.'

'So what's this got to do with our spider case? Does Byrne have some deformity? Perhaps something he kept hidden, like he had two cocks.' South laughed, then stopped as Fred glared at him. 'You knew Byrne. What was he like?'

Fred glanced at South. 'He looked very business like. He even came across as friendly, and accommodating. When we used to go and ask him questions, you'd think we were old friends. But don't make any mistake, he was a right bastard underneath it all. Evil.'

South lowered the paper. 'Evil? That's a strong word.'

'We could never prove it, but we knew he was getting in young girls from Eastern Europe and using them as prostitutes. These girls would think they were being rescued from a life of hardship, but they were

146

being smuggled in and forced to have sex for money. They were very young girls.'

South closed the paper, imagining the terrified faces of the girls. 'And how do you know this?'

'A grass put me and DCI Harris in contact with a girl who called herself Mel. She'd come from somewhere in the Ukraine, I think. She was scared and wanted to get away. We met her once in a pub. She must've been about seventeen. She said there were girls that were even younger, maybe fourteen.'

South shivered. 'Shit.'

'Exactly. The girl said she was going to stay working with Byrne so she could help the younger girls. I told her not to, but Harris thought she was right. He convinced me that it was for the best. The stupid fucker.'

'What happened?'

'Mel turned up one day. Well, her torso. Wrapped up in a bin liner, inside a suitcase. Thrown in the Thames. But we couldn't prove anything. There was nothing actually connecting her to Byrne. No one talked. We went to the two massage parlours Byrne owned and we didn't find any young eastern European girls. Nothing. Eventually the council closed them down. Me and Harris never really let on how close we came. We kept it between us.'

South stared at Fred's battered face, suddenly understanding why he had so much sadness beyond his eyes. 'So, now Byrne's found with a bag of dead spiders in his mouth. I just don't get it. I can understand a rival or old enemy killing him, but not this.'

Fred nodded. 'There must be some kind of connection. And now maybe we'll find out.'

Fred pointed across the street to the red brick building. A Peugeot parked up and a stocky man with a shaved head climbed out carrying a gym bag.

Fred nodded, so South opened his door and started across the street. He turned and saw Fred behind him, taking out his painkillers, then looked back to the building and saw Goodis was about to go inside. 'Dan Goodis?'

The man stood still, his face full of suspicion. 'What do you lot want?'

'The usual,' South said. 'We want to ask a few questions. We are nosy like that.'

'Don't I know it,' Goodis said and looked Fred over. 'Where are your IDs?'

South showed his ID. 'Who's a little bit paranoid today?'

Goodis smirked. 'Just being sure. When you work doors like I do, you can upset people. I've had blokes jump out of vans with baseball bats coming after me. They usually bottle it though.'

'Nice,' South said. 'Can we come up?'

'Yeah, but don't expect a cup of tea.' Goodis went in and jogged up the two flights of stairs to his tiny flat.

Fred and South followed him in and found a small lounge with a sofa bed in one corner and a wide screen television opposite. South made himself comfortable in an armchair as he listened to Goodis putting something away in his bedroom. Fred stood by the door, his eyes flickering about the room.

Goodis came back in holding a can of lager. 'Want a beer?'

'No thanks,' South said. 'I don't know if you know, but we pulled your boss out of the River Lea this morning.'

The can of beer stopped halfway to Goodis' lips. 'You're fuckin' joking?'

'No, I'm not.' South sat back. 'He was beaten to death.'

Goodis raised the can to his mouth. 'The fuckers.'

'Any idea who might've killed him?' Fred asked.

The bouncer lowered his beer. 'Your guess is as good as mine, mate.'

'Any enemies?' South asked.

Goodis laughed a little. 'Of course. He was Michael Byrne. You either liked the bloke or you fuckin' hated him.'

'And you liked him?' South smiled.

'Well, he was my boss, so I did my best to be friendly to him. We didn't have romantic meals together, but I didn't hate him either.' Goodis laughed again.

Fred stepped forward, shoving his hands in his pockets. 'Far as we can make out, you were probably the last person to see him alive.'

'I didn't fuckin' do it.' Goodis' eyes jumped from Fred to South.

'We didn't say you did.' South grinned. 'Anything weird happen the other night? Byrne left the club about 3 a.m. we believe and you waved him off.'

Goodis grabbed a wooden chair and sat down. 'That's right. It was more like half three. He said goodnight and fucked off. That's about it.'

'Nothing else happened? Fred asked. 'Nothing out of the ordinary?'

Goodis thought for a moment. 'Oh, there was this car that nearly knocked him down when he was crossing the road to the club.'

'Just an accident or what?' South sat up.

The bouncer shrugged as he sipped his can of beer. 'Well, I'd say the bastard in the car put his foot down. I'd say he was definitely trying to scare him.'

'And what was this car like? South asked and took

149

out his notebook. 'You get a registration number?'

'Na, he took off too fuckin' fast. I think it was like a dark Ford Mondeo or something like that. Sorry.'

South nodded. 'How much do you know about Mr Byrne's business dealings?'

Goodis looked strangely at South. 'Nothing. I was just paid to keep the wankers out. I know he had his hands in a few dodgy deals.'

'Drugs?'

Again, Goodis shrugged. 'Don't know about that.'

'But if there were drug deals going on in his clubs, you'd know about it, right?' South stood up.

Goodis shook his head. 'Don't know anythin' about any drugs. Don't touch the stuff.'

'I didn't ask if you touched the stuff. I'm not interested in your personal habits.' South stepped closer to Goodis, looking down at him. 'What about the gun that Byrne had in his house?'

Goodis' eyes narrowed. 'If Byrne had a shooter, it's news to me. But it wouldn't surprise me.'

'Why not?' South asked.

'You never know if someone you've upset is going to come after you.'

'What about young girls shipped all the way from Eastern Europe? What do you know about that?'

Goodis' head sprung up, his face showing total confusion. 'What're you going on about? You lot have always been on his case. Far as I know, he just owns a few clubs. He used to own a couple of massage parlours. Whether or not it was to do with prostitution, I don't know. End of story. I don't know what this has got to do with my boss endin' up in the river.'

South shrugged, then smiled. 'No, nor do I. Thanks for your time, Mr Goodis.'

South walked out of the flat and Fred followed.

They moved fast down the stairs and then stopped outside. South ran a hand through his hair and looked up at the sky and saw the sun trying to shine.

'What was that about?' Fred asked.

'Don't know. Just don't like his type.'

'His type? What type is that?' Fred adjusted his tie.

'Bouncers. I hate bouncers. All the ones I've met have been right yob bastards. They kick the shit out of some young kid and ask questions later.'

Fred started walking to the car. South followed, thinking about what it all means, why Byrne ended up in the river with a bag of spiders in his gob. 'Do you really think our man did Byrne in?'

Fred opened his door. 'He had spiders in his mouth, didn't he?'

After opening the passenger door, South stood there shaking his head. 'What if someone took this opportunity to knock Byrne off? They see that all these weird murders and suicides are going on, so they decide to do Byrne in and make it look like the same thing.'

'But they'd have to know about the spiders. That hasn't been released to the public. This whole case has been low profile so far.' Fred climbed in and started the engine.

'Yeah, I know. But someone could've found out. It's not impossible. And anyway, apart from the spiders, Byrne's murder doesn't fit the pattern.'

Fred put the car in reverse. 'I'm not sure there is a pattern any more. I think the person who's doing all this is just out of control. They'll probably do themselves in and that'll be that.'

Fred's mobile started ringing. He took his phone out. 'DI Fred Fairservice.'

South watched his colleague talking into the

phone. He watched the old man bobbing his head and thought to himself that Fred wasn't that old, not really, he just looked that way. He was a rock that had been hit by a rough sea too many times.

'Who was that?' South asked.

'Farmer. We have to go and look at Byrne's body.'

TEN

South stepped into the room and immediately felt his nostrils burn from the cleaning fluid they used to disinfect the surfaces. He hated the place as much as he hates hospitals. He looked over to the table where Michael Byrne's swollen and grey body was lying. He expected him to sit up at any moment. It was the only time he'd meet the legendary Byrne, but the conversation was going to be very one sided. But then again, he thought, Byrne might still have plenty to say.

Farmer was dressed in his scrubs, with his hands in latex gloves. South's eyes went to the body and the stitches that kept Byrne's chest together. He looked over and saw the scales and knew Farmer would have cut open his chest, split his ribcage, and weighed his vital organs.

'I was right about him being in the water for a few hours,' Farmer said. 'They must have killed him, then dumped him straight in the water. When he was beaten, I'd say he was lying on a surface like a pavement. I found traces of paving dust in his wounds. His skull was cracked right open. Whoever did this was very angry. They must have battered him well after he was dead.'

'Lovely,' South said, stepping a little closer. 'So they killed him, then dumped it in the river? Why? He wasn't weighed down. They must've known he'd be discovered pretty soon.'

Farmer leaned on the table, looking into Byrne's contorted and bloated face. 'Well, perhaps the assailant wanted him to be found. After all they did put a bag of spiders in his mouth. They were sending a message.'

'Strange,' Fred said.

'How long had the bag been in his mouth?' South asked.

'That was placed in his mouth at the time he was placed in the water, I'd say.' Farmer took off his latex gloves and dropped them in a nearby bin.

Fred crossed his arms and walked around to the right side of the corpse's head. He looked closely at the wounds. 'So, you think this our killer?'

Farmer frowned. 'It doesn't really fit the M.O. of your suicides does it?'

Fred looked up at Farmer. 'What if he planned it like this? He does all this suicide, messed up stuff, then kills Byrne, his real target. He put the rest of his plan into action and then let us find Byrne's body now, just so it seems like he's just another victim.'

South shook his head. 'Just doesn't make sense. All the other stuff, Murphy, Hawks, the cannibal and the hit and run, they all have some kind of connection. We can link each of the dead old guys to it as well, even if we don't really know why. But this is just a bludgeoned small-time gangster with a bag of spiders in his mouth. I think someone else took the opportunity to knock off Byrne and stuck that bag in his mouth just to confuse matters. They're copycatting just because it suits them.'

'Well, you two are the detectives,' Farmer said and started pulling a green sheet over Byrne's naked body. 'You'll have my full report soon.'

South followed Fred down a long corridor, watching the back of his leather-like neck. He could make out the sweat marks on his shirt collar and the little bit of dandruff on his suit jacket. He felt like reaching out and dusting off the flakes. 'Still think it's our man?'

'We can't rule it out at this stage,' Fred said. 'But I must admit, it's not looking that likely at the moment. All the others are deformed, angry with the way they look…but this…Byrne…he was just a vicious bastard. No, I don't think they're connected.'

'Where now?' South asked.

'I think we should go and see that old dear in Hospital.' Fred walked towards the car. 'I phoned this morning and she's still hanging on.'

Tracey Boswell opened the door with the key Fred had given her, just so she could look in on Martin. She closed the door behind her and stepped into the lounge. She turned to see the usual sight of Martin reading a book, but stopped dead when she saw him staring at her.

'Come in, Tracey,' Martin said, his chin resting on his bony fingers.

She smiled and looked about the room. 'Want some lunch?'

'I'm not hungry.'

'You should eat.'

He raised his eyebrows. 'Why? Because I might waste away?'

Tracey looked down at the carpet.

'Sit down Tracey.' He pointed towards the armchair opposite. 'I hardly get to talk to anyone these days.'

She looked at the chair, then sat in it.

'Do you like my brother?' he asked, his face showing no signs of emotion.

'Fred?' What a strange question, she thought. 'Of course. He's a nice man.'

Martin nodded and smiled. 'As nice as your husband?'

'He does his best. He's a hard worker.'

'Sometimes I can manage to sit by the window and look down the street.' Martin gestured to the window and the outside world beyond the glass. 'I see him drunkenly stagger from his van up to the door. I've heard your arguments.'

'Well, lots of people argue, Martin.' She didn't know what else to say. She didn't like the way the conversation was going and felt like running for the door.

'I'm sorry,' Martin said and looked down at his legs.

She felt bad. 'It's all right. You must get lonely all by yourself.'

'So does Fred. More lonely than I'll ever get.'

She smiled and smoothed her hand over her jeans. 'That's a shame.'

'He really likes you.'

When she looked up, she saw Martin nodding and confirming his declaration.

She laughed a little. 'Of course he doesn't.'

'He does. He's told me.'

'That's silly.' She blushed.

'Why is it? You're a very attractive woman. Do you like him?'

Tracey hadn't thought about Fred like that before. But she already knew the answer. She didn't find him attractive, but found him interesting, mostly because of his job. No, she could never see herself running off with him. 'He seems like a really nice person.'

Martin smiled. 'You want to leave your husband, don't you?'

'Martin!' She jumped up from the chair.

'I bet if you did, you could both go far away from him. He's just a drunken bastard anyway.'

'I've got to go now.' She turned away from him, heading for the door, her anger and embarrassment rising.

'Wait,' Martin said. 'Let me just say one more thing and then you can go. Please, just one more thing.'

'I hate hospitals,' South said, as he followed Fred up the dirty stairs that used to be white a long time ago. South's eyes flicked to his right. He was sure he saw something move across the floor. He'd heard most hospitals are overrun with cockroaches. They took the next flight, with Fred breathing heavy. South passed him, while watching Fred open the packet of painkillers that he'd taken from his coat.

'No one likes hospitals.' Fred pointed to a large yellow door. The sign on the door read: THE QUEENSLAND WARD.

'Right, let's go see Mrs Earl.' South put out his hand, ready to pull the door open.

'Could you go down to that drinks machine and get me something? I need to swallow my pills.' Fred showed the two pills in his open hand.

South shrugged and looked down the long corridor with the low hung fluorescent lights. He saw a nurse walk out a room and talk to a young couple sitting on a red leather bench against the wall. All their faces looked sickly in the yellow light, he thought, and walked towards the drinks machine. He took out some change and looked back towards Fred as he heard him pull open the ward door and walk in. He grabbed a fruit drink, then went to find Fred in the ward.

Fred was sitting by the first bed, his back hunched over. South looked at the empty bed. There was only a mattress. Fred's hand reached out and slowly patted the bed.

'Are we too late?' South asked and dropped the drink into Fred's lap.

Fred looked at him blankly.

'Fred? What's happened?'

'She died an hour ago.' He opened the bottle and swallowed the pills.

'So, we're not going to find much out?' South looked down the ward at the other beds, the other elderly bodies. A television screamed out the news.

Fred leaned forward and reached into the bedside cabinet. He produced a jar with Mrs Earl's dentures in it. He passed it to South. Holding it up to the light, South nearly laughed as he saw the tiny spiders spinning about in the dirty water. Then he spied a nurse walking by. 'Excuse me?'

The nurse turned to him. 'Yes?'

'Did Mrs Earl have any visitors?' South asked.

'I think her sister came by a few times. Why?'

'Drop it,' Fred said and got up. 'Anyone could have dropped them in that glass. Let's go.'

'Thank you,' South said. He turned to Fred and held the glass out to him. 'What about this?'

'You bring it.' Fred walked out of the ward carrying his bottle of fruit juice, his shoes squeaking against the polished floor.

South raced after him. 'What's wrong with you?'

Fred's eyes seemed empty. 'Nothing. It's time to get back to the station.'

'Don't you give a shit about anything any more? You're just walking around on autopilot. If it's got anything to do with the pain you're in, I suggest you go to the doctors and find out what is wrong with you, because you're starting to get on my tits and I'm sick of seeing you popping pills.'

'Fine. Now let's go back to the station.' Fred pushed past South and headed down the stairs.

Detective Inspector Mark South walked into the incident room and saw the desks lining the walls, the bodies sitting and holding phones and typing information into computers. It was all he'd seen for the last few days. Fred Fairservice walked past him, then stopped dead.

'Have you seen these?' Fred handed South three letters inside evidence bags.

'Letters?' South took one and saw it was addressed to the station.

'They're from the people who committed suicide. Suicide notes to us, signed by each one of them, all expressing their willingness to die. Even our cannibal friend and the old woman. They arrived today.'

'We will have to verify their handwriting…' South began.

Fred took back the letters. 'I know, but looks pretty much like they wanted to die. No murder case. All we can do him for now is helping them kill themselves.'

South nodded, because he didn't know what else to say. Fred shrugged and kept on walking across the room. South watched Jameson beckon Fred into his office.

'You busy?' a voice asked behind South.

South turned to see Detective Sergeant Ally Walker smiling at him. 'No, what's up?'

Ally pointed a thumb towards the corridor. 'I need you to come and look at some information I dug up.'

She turned and walked down the corridor. Her dark brown hair was pulled back and pinned in place. He hadn't had that much time to get to know her, but he recalled Jameson talking about her, remarking how clever she was and how she always seemed one step ahead of everybody else.

Ally went behind the desk in the small office and opened a file. She looked up at South as he stood in the door. 'Sit down, Mark.'

He sat in a chair. 'Didn't realise we were on first name terms.'

She smiled and looked down at the file again. 'I decided to look for similar unsolved crimes like the ones you and Fred have been looking into.'

'You found something?'

She held up a finger. 'Well, I only found two cold cases. One in Scotland and one in Wales. What I was initially looking for were possible suicides that were a little suspicious.'

South nodded. 'Does Fred know you did this?'

She looked up, then sat back in her chair. 'No, not really, but we are supposed to be a team and I will tell him. I actually thought…'

'That I was going to be put in charge?' South raised his eyebrows.

'Anyway, I found this one case in Nairn, Scotland, where this disabled guy, Harry Bruce, was found hanged in his own home. His mother had just popped out for half an hour. When she came back, she found him hanging from a beam. It seemed as if he'd tied a noose to the beam, climbed onto a chair and well… that was that.'

South shrugged. 'So?'

'Henry Bruce was paralysed from his neck downwards.' Ally raised her eyebrows.

'Interesting. What about the other case?'

Walker rotated the pen in her fingers as she bent down and looked at the file. 'Swansea. 1997. Ryan Brint was found alone in his flat, with a single gunshot

160

wound to his temple. His brains were splattered up the wall. The report said that it was as if he'd taken the pistol and placed it against his head and pulled the trigger. The pistol was right next to his body, as if he'd dropped it after firing the shot. The front door was locked and there were no signs of forced entry.'

South grinned. 'I'm waiting for the punchline.'

'Ryan Brint was born without arms.' Ally smiled.

'Any prints on the firearm?'

'None. It was completely clean.'

'And where did the gun come from?'

'Was an old gun, belonged to Brint's grandfather. Was kept in good condition. So, what do you reckon?'

South shrugged. 'So, this person could've come to London? That's what you're thinking? He might've been working his way down?'

'Both victims had talked of taking their own lives. Could it be we have a serial suicide assister?'

'If we get this person in a courtroom, their defence could be that they merely helped these people to die.'

South laughed at how ridiculous it all sounded. Then he recalled the case in Germany where the cannibal killed and ate a willing participant. He wanted to be breakfast, lunch and dinner. His desire was to become a midnight snack. If you could think of the craziest thing, the ugliest, hideous desire, and, even if it made you sick to your stomach, you'd know there was someone out there who wanted to do it. They would find it erotic or healing. South found it plain sickening. 'He's still committing a crime.'

'And what about Michael Byrne?'

'I don't think it fits. I can't see Byrne being the suicidal type, not with all that he had. No, our killer has a purpose and he sticks to that. He has a pattern. He kills those who want to die. And it looked like he removes himself from the scene.'

Ally looked confused. 'What do you mean?'

'Our suicide assister makes it look as if he wasn't even there. Like he's death himself going about his work. Byrne was just plain murdered.'

Fred looked away from Jameson, who was arguing with someone on the other end of the phone, and let his eyes drift over to the whiteboard. He looked at the photographs of the victims – or whatever you call someone who took their own life. Victims of life, he thought, and then looked at the photo of a young Heather Beckley. He tried not to let his eyes move over to the photograph taken when she was found; half her body covered by the tree, her hollow and pale face scattered with dirt and leaves, the bruises around her neck. Her hand were bound with thin rope. The image of her seared his eyes, remained in his vision wherever he looked. Looking back over to his side of the board, where a pyramid of his suicide photographs were pinned, he felt a little empty. Nobody was taking his case seriously, not now the suicide letters had turned up. Even the murder of Michael Byrne was being torn from his grip, marked down as a copycat killing.

'I said, have you seen this, Fred?' Fred turned to see Jameson holding a copy of the Enfield Courier.

Fred grabbed the paper and looked at the photograph of Michael Byrne on the front cover. It looked like a passport photograph, with a blue curtain pulled behind him as a background. Like all passport photos, it made him look suspicious, his mouth serious and hard. Maybe, Fred thought, passport pictures brought out what was below the skin. Fred read the headline to himself: ENFIELD CLUB OWNER BEATEN TO DEATH.

Looking up, Fred saw Jameson's simmering anger. 'It was only a matter of time before the press got to hear about it.'

Jameson pointed at the paper, a little spit appearing at the corner of his mouth. 'The bastards even mention the bag of spiders in his mouth. One of our people has leaked that.'

'Not necessarily. There were witnesses present at the riverbank. Someone could've been watching from the pub, and gone to the papers. You want me to go along to their offices?'

Jameson reached up and loosened his tie, then looked at his watch. 'No, that'd be a waste of time. I've got enough problems with the press on the Heather case. At least we can use the press to help find her killer. Do you know they found blood in his car?'

'Sorry?' Fred looked down at the paper again.

'In Nelson's car. Looks like someone got him to pull over. Probably flashing him from behind. He probably pulled over and they came up to the driver's side and hit him with something. There were blood spatters over the door and steering wheel. So we might have a vigilante on our hands and that's going to fuck up our case.'

Fred was looking deeply into the photograph of Byrne, focusing in on his eyes. 'It's not an ideal situation.'

'Did you go and see the therapist?'

Fred looked up. 'Yes, I did. But you know I did.'

Jameson nodded and smiled a little, his face still red. 'Yes, I do. She said you seem better, like your anger has been eased. Spain must have done you some good.'

Nodding, Fred folded the paper and put it on Jameson's desk. 'But…'

Jameson breathed deeply. 'I think it's more appropriate for Detective Inspector South to take over the Byrne caseload.'

'And what about the suicides?'

'Those too.' Jameson picked up the paper. 'Work with him Fred and help him along. I'm sorry about this, but we need to put people like South at the head of investigations, to give them the experience. He's never led a team before, but we have to give him the chance. Orders from above. I know you'll work well together.'

'I'm sure we will.' Fred got up and turned towards the door.

'Time you got yourself home now, Fred,' Jameson said and pointed to his watch.

Fred smiled and walked out into the incident room. He saw Sergeant Knight looking at him, his hand clenching a piece of paper.

Knight came over and gave him the paper. 'Checked the CCTV camera footage from outside Byrne's club and the ones in the town centre, but nothing. Got some images of the car, but whoever was driving masked their registration plate.'

'You better tell DI South,' Fred said and pushed the piece of paper back at Knight.

Andrew Nelson's head sprung up as he heard the garage door opening. His eyes felt the light spear into his eyes, like acid being dropped into his irises. He blinked and smelt cement dust being kicked up by the feet that walked in. He saw the familiar shape turning towards him. Light beamed out from a torch and Nelson followed it over every object it slid across. He saw the beam broken by a pile of timber and a few sheets of plastic, the kind you might wrap a body in.

The light moved quickly to his face, burning bright, so he closed his eyes. Pink circles swirled in his vision until he felt the light drift to his chest. He opened his eyes again and found the man was closer to him, the masked face staring down at him.

A gloved hand reached out and pulled the gag from Andrew's mouth.

'You're going to kill me, aren't you?' Nelson asked, and prepared himself for the answer.

He saw the eyes change. They have became wrinkled at the corners, denoting a smile. This was not good, Nelson told himself. A smile. Something that should represent happiness was now something so sinister.

'Let me ask the questions, and I might give you an answer,' the deep voice said.

'What?'

'Did you kill her?' The man stepped back.

'No.'

'You raped her, then strangled her, didn't you?'

'Are you going to kill me?'

The torchlight flickered off. Nelson could no longer see the man's eyes or his outline. Then the sound of boots crunching dust seemed to come from near the garage door. 'I might let you go if you tell me the truth.'

'I've already told you the truth,' Nelson pleaded. 'I didn't kill her. The last time I saw her she was fine. I don't know what happened to her.'

'You're lying.'

'I'm not! If you think I did it, just hand me over to the police.'

There was laughter in the darkness. 'The police? What? So you can get six years? Then get out again and strangle more women? Fuck that.'

'Don't kill me. Please.' Nelson heard his own pleading voice, tasted the puke rising in his throat.

'Did she beg for her life?'

'I don't know, because I wasn't there.'

'Did you see the plastic sheet on the floor?'

'Ye...yes...'

'If I don't get the truth the next time I ask, you'll be wrapped up in that. But you won't be alive to experience it.'

Nelson sucked in his breath as he felt the hands pulling the gag up to his mouth, tightening the knot at the back. The boots crunched the dust and dirt until the sunlight stretched out across the floor, creeping along until it nearly reached Nelson's shoes. He was engulfed by the man's shadow as the garage door opened. The door shut and he found himself alone in the dark again.

Nelson saw visions of his own death, his body wrapped in the plastic sheet. Tears began to leak down his cheeks.

Fred looked at his watch after turning off the engine. He was parked on the driveway, looking at the net curtains of his own home. His mother's old home. She had been stuck in that home, not able to get around, withering away. He recalled every crease in her deeply yellowed-skin. Already dead. They just had to find a place for her to die. Now Martin, the only family he has left, faced the same fate; he was sitting in the house, waiting to die, soaking up knowledge, stretching his mind across the world wide web, like he would somehow live forever as a thought, an electric pulse transmitted into space. We all die. Then the electric light in us is switched off.

A face appeared at his car window and Fred jumped.

He pressed the electric window. Tracey Boswell's face was one big smile.

'Sorry, I made you jump,' she said and rested her hands on the door.

Today she was wearing a more provocative perfume. Something more expensive. He realised he didn't know if she had children. What a great policeman I am, Fred thought. He smiled. 'I was just sitting and thinking.'

'You shouldn't do too much of that.' She leaned in more, her cleavage filling his view.

He laughed and tried not to look at her chest. He could no longer deny his desires. It was not right for a man to be that alone for that long, he thought. Every night his bed seemed bigger, colder. But she was married. 'How's your husband?'

'Him? He went to work today and now he'll be in the pub. He'll come home drunk, if he comes home at all.'

Marriage was an alien world to Fred. An alien world he'd seen close up, but never really understood. His parents' marriage appeared fine until the split. He never saw it coming. Then one day, a summer's afternoon, at a funeral, he heard something that made everything in his world crumble. In his grandfather's little house, after his funeral, he watched his old relatives smoking roll ups and consuming sausage rolls, swapping stories he'd heard a million times before. Then he was in the kitchen, making Aunt Doreen a cup of tea when he heard some croaky voice say that his grandfather had had to marry his grandmother. She'd been pregnant. The words 'shotgun wedding' hung in the air as he poured hot tea all over his hand. He was the result of an accident a long time ago.

'What are you doing tonight?'

Fred came out of his dream. 'I'm sorry?'

'Do you fancy going for a drink?' Tracey smiled.

He wondered what a 'drink' would involve and felt himself being drawn into a trap. 'Well, I have to sort dinner out for Martin and see that he's alright.'

'That's taken care of, Fred. I've cooked dinner for him. Come on, come for a drink with me. I need to get out for the evening.' She playfully punched his shoulder.

He sniffed a little and her perfume invaded his nasal cavities. Her scent, like her sexuality, was now consuming him, inside and out. He looked towards her house, a quick glance to make sure an angry, drunken builder wasn't heading towards him. So what if he was? His need was greater. 'That would be nice. What time?'

The fire brigade had alerted the police to the burnt out Mercedes. They had been dealing with a house fire when one of the officers wandered over and examined the charred vehicle. He called it in, wondering if some-one was missing a car that would have once looked expensive. The car sat on a small piece of greenery at the end of a row of houses between Enfield Town and Bush Hill Park, tucked behind an old cricket pavilion.

South parked up and looked over to DS Walker as her eyes followed the uniformed officers already cordoning off the scene. South climbed out and felt the breeze and damp air rush towards him. He looked at the houses and wondered if anyone saw what happened to Byrne's car or Byrne himself.

'One of our boys is waving to us.' Ally pointed to the houses, where a young looking officer talked on his radio and waved his hand.

The uniform let go of his radio. 'One of you Detective Inspector South?'

'That's me, son,' South said. 'This is Detective Sergeant Allison Walker.'

'PC Tom Harding, sir.' Harding turned and pointed towards the semi-detached houses that faced a pub and an off-licence. 'Old girl in number 214 said she saw the Merc being followed right up the backside by another car. Said she saw them stop here. The other car went around the corner and then she couldn't see them any more.'

South looked towards the corner, then back towards the pub. 'It was three odd in the morning, what was she doing up?'

'Said she gets pains all over and it woke her up,' Harding said.

Ally walked towards the corner and stopped. She turned to South, her finger pointing to the pavement. 'Perhaps this is where he was killed. Farmer said the wounds were caused by his head hitting some paving.'

'It's been pissing down since then. No hope of finding any evidence.' South walked past Walker and stood looking down at the paving. He crouched down at where a particular paving slab is cracked. He saw another, then noticed Ally's shoes near him. 'Better get someone to try and find some blood or something. See if there was any CCTV cameras nearby too.'

South pulled himself up and groaned.

'Looks like they might've found something.' Ally pointed over the road.

South looked back over to PC Harding and saw an old woman with him, her leathery skin wobbling as she wrapped her arms around herself and chattered away. He walked across the damp grass, trying to spot where the killer drove the Mercedes onto the grass. He

169

walked with his head down, his eyes scanning each blade of grass, watching them flicker in the wind. Then he crossed to his right and saw the tyre tracks, deep and now very muddy. He followed them right up to the back of the car, standing just behind the police cordon.

The SOCO lifted the charred baseball bat that was wrapped in an evidence bag, showing it to Ally. 'Could there still be DNA on it?'

The SOCO looked at the black bat and shook his head. 'I wouldn't get your hopes up, Detective. Whoever did all this, did a beautiful job. Nothing better than fire for disposing of evidence.'

'Don't suppose you found a gun in there too, by any chance?' South asked and looked at the burnt out car.

'No, no gun.'

Ally turned to South and gently grasped his elbow. 'We still have some wanker out there with a gun. Byrne didn't have a registered weapon, and his killer will know that. Whoever killed Byrne is walking around with a weapon that he knows we have no way of tracing.'

'Who the bloody hell's he going to kill next?' South asked.

'He could be waiting to shoot anybody. All we can do is wait and see what happens.' Ally shrugged.

'Unfortunately, you're right.'

ELEVEN

Fred and Tracey were sitting in a corner of the Moon Under Water Pub in Chase Side, in a booth away from the younger customers who crowded the bar.

Fred wondered what he was doing there as he turned his glass on the beer mat, trying to avoid looking into her eyes. She'd gone to some effort to look good for him, wearing a knee length black skirt. Her legs weren't really slim and perfect, but they looked good to him. He looked up to the beige blouse and saw a couple of the top buttons were undone, tantalising him with a glimpse of her cleavage. He looked up into her eyes and smelt her perfume, mixing with the cigarette smoke that drifted up from the ashtray in front of him.

'I didn't know you smoked,' he said and sipped his drink.

She took a puff of the cigarette and smiled, a little guiltily. 'Only when I'm drinking in pubs. Sorry.'

'It's OK.'

'I always imagine coppers to be a bit more aggressive.'

He laughed. 'I suppose that's what people always think. I think I used to be when I was younger, when I was just out of Hendon. I was raring to go then, but eventually the job wears you down.'

'How long have you been a policeman?'

Fred sighed. 'Too long.'

'Go on. I want to know.'

'Twenty-odd years now. Years of sitting in a room typing up information, getting statements signed and filing stuff away. Sending evidence to the courts, hoping for a conviction and not getting one.'

'Oh…that's the sound of someone who got up on the wrong side of the bed.' She smiled, and touched his hand for a moment. 'Martin worries about you.'

'Does he? He shouldn't.'

'Of course he does, he's your brother.'

'He's the one…' He stopped and grabbed his beer.

'Who's dying? I think he's a very brave and strong man.'

'It's funny, but people always say that.' Fred laughed. 'People who're dying always seem strong to everyone, but what else are they supposed to do, just cry all the time?'

She shrugged. 'I suppose. Didn't he want to travel or anything? See the world, do something?'

'I asked him that after we found out about the MS, but he said he didn't want to go anywhere. Martin's been everywhere he wanted to go long before he found out he was ill. And anyway, he said that wherever he goes, he'll still be dying.'

'Bleeding hell, it must be fun in your house.'

Fred nodded. 'You should see us on lottery night, holding that ticket, our fingers crossed.'

She laughed, but her face became serious again. 'Martin mentioned what happened to you.'

He looked up from his drink and saw she was pointing at his head. 'All in the line of duty.'

'He said you heard a woman in trouble and when you went to help, they jumped you. Must've been awful.'

'It's what you've got to expect.'

Her eyes grew wider. 'Got to expect to be beaten

up? I don't think that's in the job description. What did they do to you?'

He sighed. 'Just gave me a bit of a kicking, that's all.'

'He said he didn't see you for a few days. He seems to think they kept you somewhere.'

Fred gripped his glass, keeping his eyes on it, blocking the memories.

'Well?' Tracey Boswell lowered her head so she could see into his eyes.

'He's got lots of time to sit around and make up little theories.' He put a smile on his face.

'But you were gone a few days though, weren't you?'

He let out a deep breath. 'Yes, I was in hospital.'

'Hospital? That's terrible. It must've been a lot worse than them just beating you up a bit. He said they made you have counselling.'

'He got you to come out with me, didn't he?'

She sat back a little, her eyes fluttering. 'No, of course not.'

'All these questions. They could be coming out of his mouth. Thing is, I know Martin would never ask them. He loves soaking up the knowledge all around him, but never from me. Oh yeah, he'll want to hear about the cases I'm working on and all that stuff, but he stays away from the personal stuff. So, he finally found someone who he thought can manipulate me, twist me around their little finger.'

She blinked, her mouth open. 'I'm sorry. I was just concerned.'

'I'm sorry. It was a bit worse than a beating. I was in hospital for a couple of days. I was unconscious for most of that time.'

'That's awful. Why haven't you left the force?'

He shrugged. 'I didn't want to seem a coward, I suppose. Just didn't want to give anyone the satisfaction of thinking they beat me. But now it looks like I'm getting the shove anyway.'

'And that will be that?' Tracey picked up her drink.

'Well, I've still got some work to do and then I'll fade away.'

She laughed. 'Let's get out of here.'

He lowered his glass, disappointed the evening might be ending. 'If you want.'

'I've got somewhere else in mind.' She winked and smiled.

Amy Glade climbed down the steps of the coach, making sure her small rucksack was still with her. She looked around Victoria Coach Station and took in all the people hugging each other and pulling enormous holdalls and suitcases towards the exit. Another large coach pulled in and she watched the faces of the passengers, their heads pressed up against the window, trying to see if anyone had come to greet them. She looked out into the darkness beyond the station exit and saw the inky sky of London. A light rain was falling, the same kind of rain that had been falling in Birmingham when she left.

She lifted her rucksack onto her back, then pulled her woolly hat around her ears and started walking through the exit, ignoring the men who were standing around asking if anyone needed a taxi.

She turned left and walked, looking at another coach entering the station. She passed a couple of families and was surprised when they smiled at her. Smiles shouldn't be around her now, she thought and moved on, her head down and her right hand in her jean's pocket, gripping a piece of important paper.

The rain fell a little harder as she hurried across the road towards Victoria Train Station. She ran under the shelter and narrowly missed a Chinese woman stepping out with her umbrella already up. She stood back and watched the downpour. This was what she imagined London would be like on that day. Of course, she'd been down on the train with her friends before. The few friends she had. But she knew they only felt sorry for her, only hung out with her to make themselves feel better.

She stepped out into the rain that was now much harder. The rain felt like wet fingers tapping her cheeks. She stepped back and pulled her rucksack off her back and opened it. It was black like everything she owned these days. The inside of it was like a black hole. She put her hand in and hoped she'd be sucked in, never to be seen again. She moved her hand around and felt it, then pulled out the object by the handle. She held the mirror in front of her face, the lights from the station illuminating its surface and her reflection. She closed her eyes for a moment and imagined her face was OK. She opened her eyes and saw the purple birthmark down one side of her face. She held up her hand, covering one side, allowing herself to see how pretty she might have been.

She wiped away the tears and put the mirror back in the bag, then grabbed something else. She was careful, pulling it out by the handle. She looked around and saw that no one was nearby. She pulled out the large kitchen knife and stared at it. Rain fell on the blade, but she kept staring at her distorted reflection in it.

After she put up her red umbrella, Tracey turned to Fred and signalled for him to follow her. He listened to the drops of water hitting the umbrella, the beat slowly speeding up as they stepped away from the entrance of the pub. They stepped back from the curb as a minicab pulled in and nearly spat rainwater over their clothes. They walked around the car and across the street. Tracey stopped on the other side of the street, her bottom lip between her teeth. He looked into her eyes as she lowered the umbrella.

'I want to ask you something,' she said and looked sheepish.

He smiled, feeling a little lost. 'Alright. What is it?'

'How do you feel about sex on the first date?' She raised her eyebrows and looked over at the large yellow building behind them.

He blinked. He waited for her to start laughing, then followed her eyes until he saw the sign above the pale yellow building that read: The Young Buck Hotel.

'I don't know what to say.' He shuffled his feet and shrugged his shoulders.

'You don't want to?' She looked sad.

'No…I mean, you're very attractive, so of course… but…'

'But I'm married?'

He heard the regret in her voice, the way she said marriage like it was a lump on her body which needed removing. He looked at her, the way she'd dressed so provocatively, but not like a tart, not like some of the younger women in the pub. He wanted to grab her and pull her close, but he turned towards the hotel doorway. 'Let's go in and get out of the rain.'

She smiled as they walked into the hotel. He looked around when they got inside, peering into the restaurant that's partitioned off from the small lobby. He saw the diners eating and chatting, sipping wine.

'There's a bar through there.' Tracey pointed to an archway. 'Get us some drinks while I go sort my face and hair out.'

He watched her walk towards the toilet and disappear inside. He sat in the bar and ordered them a drink. He didn't know what would happen with Tracey Boswell, but he felt less lonely, more part of the world than he had done in a long time. It's Saturday night after all, when the world goes out and has a good time. Usually it was his night for putting his feet up and watching his brother slowly die out of the corner of his eye.

Fred felt a hand on his shoulder and turned to see Tracey Boswell reach for her drink.

She seated herself next to him. 'This is a nice place, isn't it?'

Fred made a show of looking around his environment and nodded. 'Yes, very nice.'

'I've got us a room.'

He stared at her. 'You've got us a room?'

'Is that OK? Thought we could dry off and just talk for a bit if you wanted to?' Her eyebrows rose for moment as a thin smile formed on her lips. Life is short, he thought and smiled.

'That's better,' Tracey said and patted his hand. 'You've got a nice smile.'

'If you spend most of your time frowning at suspects, you sometimes forget how to smile.'

'Shall we go up then?' Tracey got up.

He quickly finished his beer. 'Let's go.'

Fred let her walk in front of him, watching her body as she glided through to the stairs. He realised he didn't know how to approach this situation, it had been so long. Tracey, he decided, was a woman who knew what she wanted. Just sit and talk, he told himself. Let her make a move if she wants.

South listened to the engine of Ally's Peugeot quiet down, then turned to her and smiled. They'd parked outside his house and he could see the lights were on, his sister sitting and watching television. She hadn't pulled the curtains again.

'Sorry?' Ally asked.

'Just talking to myself. My sister's left the curtains open. People walking by can see into the front room.'

Ally laughed. 'You take your privacy very seriously, don't you?'

'Of course. My private life is just that, private.'

'Well, you better get in there and pull the curtains then.' She nodded towards the house.

South looked into the lounge and imagined another night chatting about nothing in particular to his sister. Looking at Ally, he got an idea. 'What are you doing now?'

She looked. 'Now? Going home and having a bath probably, why?'

'Just thought you might like to come in and chat for a bit. We could discuss work or anything you like.'

She smiled, then gave him a suspicious look. 'You don't want to sit on your own on a Saturday night, do you?'

'Not really. What do you reckon?'

She gave her phone a quick glance. 'OK, just for a bit.'

'Great. I'll make us some tea or coffee.' South jumped out of the car and got out his door keys. Ally followed after locking the car. Inside the house, the television blared out, and South's sister shouted something out. South walked into the front room and saw Emma sipping a glass of white wine.

Emma was about to open her mouth, when she saw Ally behind him. 'Hello.'

'Hi. I'm Allison.' Ally smiled.

'Is he in bed?' South nodded towards the ceiling.

'Yeah, he went over to a friend's this afternoon.' Emma finished her glass, stood up after grabbing the rest of the bottle.

'A friend from school? A new friend?' South smiled.

Emma smiled too. 'Yeah, good news, isn't it? Looks like he's not the only one.'

South laughed. 'We've got work to discuss.'

Emma winked at South as she left the room. 'Well, goodnight then.'

South went into the kitchen and put the kettle on, while Ally stepped over to the stereo, bent down and looked through the extensive CD collection. 'You like Oasis?'

'Doesn't everybody?' he said.

'I can't stand them.'

'How can you not like Oasis?'

'I just don't like their sound. And I don't like their whole attitude either.'

'OK, I see. Tea or Coffee?'

'Coffee. Black, three sugars.'

Back in the kitchen, South made the coffee, and watched Ally walk in and stand by him. She opened her mouth, then closed it.

'Go on and say what you were going to say.'

She looked awkward. 'I was going to ask what happened to your wife.'

'She got breast cancer.' He took a gentle sip of his coffee. 'She had two lumps on her breasts, but she didn't say anything for a while. By the time it was diagnosed, it had spread. Didn't take long.'

Ally touched his arm. 'I'm sorry.'

'I guess that's why I feel so sorry for Fred, because I know what he's going through.'

'He used to be such a different person. Much more alive. He's never been that social but you could still have a laugh with him. Now, he's just a shell. He used to tell me that he could meet a suspect and he'd know straight away if they did it or not.'

'Well, he seems to be lost with this spider business. I think it's just some crack pot and they'll end up doing themselves in or coming to us.'

'Perhaps. Anyway, let's talk about something else.' Ally smiled.

South heard a phone ringing. 'Is that my phone?'

He fished the phone out of his pocket and answered it. 'DI Mark South. Hello?'

'This is DS Canter. Got a girl in the middle of the all night supermarket in Church Street holding a knife to her throat. Said she's going kill herself.'

South let out a sigh. 'Why can't you lot deal with it? What do you expect me to do?'

'Sorry for living, mate, but she asked for you by name.'

Tracey opened the door to the room and stepped onto the beige carpet. She looked around the room, nodding and turned to Fred and smiled. 'It's lovely.'

Fred stepped in, hardly taking in the room. He saw the digital alarm clock and phone, then looked through the gold curtains at the streets of Enfield. He stood there and couldn't take his eyes off Tracey as she hurried about the room, touching objects and opening drawers. She came out of the bathroom holding some shampoos. 'I'll be taking these with me.'

Fred smiled and looked for somewhere to sit that wasn't the bed. He felt his damp trousers sticking to his legs as he took off his suit jacket and put it on the back of a chair. Tracey came out of the bathroom again and stopped in the doorway. He loosened his tie, then looked at her, and caught her look, a sorrowful stare. Then a bright smile stretched across her skin.

'You look soaked through Fred.' Tracey looked him over, shaking her head. 'You better take off your shirt and I'll put it somewhere to dry.'

Fred looked down at the damp shirt. He couldn't take it off. If he did, she'd probably not want to touch him. 'I'm alright. It'll dry now we're inside.'

'No, no, you're taking that off.' She lunged for his buttons and started to undo them, then sat on the bed. He looked away as she opened his shirt. Her sudden intake of breath told him all he needed to know.

She peeled the right side of the shirt back and looked up at Fred, her eyes a little wet. Then she opened up the left side of the shirt and shook her head. 'Oh my God. Is this what they did to you?'

Fred looked at his body for a moment, but no longer saw what she saw. He didn't see the devastation. He just saw his body, in all its horrendous glory. She moved around him and started to pull his shirt away from his shoulders. She let out another hard breath as she stood transfixed by his back and the scars running parallel and diagonal with each other. He felt her hand reach out and hover over a spot where he knew there were burns. The skin was raised and angry. A couple of the burns on his back were like tiny lips, two small mouths puckering up for a kiss. He felt her fingers gently touch the scars, then her whole palm moving over his back. Fred sat forward and let her do what she wanted. He felt just the way he did when he was medically examined, the cold, unemotional hands prodding his wounds. The wounds. They were part of who he was. It was what drove him to do what he does.

'He was right, wasn't he?' Tracey asked. 'They took you somewhere and beat you and cut you. What did they burn you with?'

Fred looked down at his hands. 'I really don't want to talk about it.'

'I'm sorry.' She grabbed his hand and pulled him out of the chair and onto the bed. He looked up at her as she took off her blouse, stared at her breasts as she slowly slipped her bra off and threw it on the floor. When she moved herself into his arms, Fred wrapped his arms around her, feeling her smooth skin against his scarred body. Her mouth moved to his and he closed his eyes. He forgot everything else that had happened to him before that night and everything that might yet happen. He allowed himself this moment of madness. He felt his trousers being pulled from his legs and he smiled. It happened all so fast. He was quickly under the sheets with her as she pushed her body up against him. He could hardly believe his luck.

Fred sat up in bed, trying not to look at her. She was supporting her head, looking over at him, her hair all messed up. She put a hand on his arm and caressed him. He wanted to jump out of bed and get dressed, but he sat there staring across the room.

'I wouldn't worry about it,' she said.

All he kept asking himself was why? Why? She was beautiful, and there were no strings attached. He never used to have erection problems, so why now? He'd been warned this might happen. With all that had happened to him in the past and lately, he knew sooner or later his body wouldn't be up to much. It was a side effect and a pretty devastating one at that.

'Do you want to talk?' she asked.

Fred could feel part of her was already dressed and

out the door. 'Not really. You better go.'

She sat up. 'I'm not going to leave you.'

He turned to her, letting her see how serious he was. 'Please go. I really think you better go home to your husband.'

Tracey slowly got out of bed and dressed herself. He could feel her eyes on him as she buttoned her blouse and brushed her hair. He sat staring out the window, still tucked up in bed. She stepped across the room and smiled at him. 'I'll come around and see you.'

He nodded, and looked back out into the night.

When he heard the door close, he peeled back the covers and looked down at his limpness. 'You little bastard.'

It seemed the local population of Church Street had gathered outside the twenty-four hour supermarket, while a scattering of uniformed officers kept them from entering the glass doors. The streetlights illuminated the faces of the crowd as South walked along beside them. He pushed himself through the crowd and heard complaints from behind him. A female police constable stopped him until he produced his ID.

'Sorry, sir, but it's been hell tonight,' the PC said.

'DS Canter round here? Is he hiding somewhere?' South looked round the crowd, standing on his toes as Ally appeared at his shoulder.

'He's inside dealing with the situation. The girl's at the back of the store and she won't let anyone near her. She's holding a large carving knife to her throat.'

'Do we know her name?' Ally said and looked in through the glass of the door.

'Amy, and that's all we got,' the PC said as her radio started squawking. 'They've got a doctor in there trying to talk to her.'

183

'Right,' South said. 'Let's get these doors open.'

There was a low hiss and an alarm rang for a few seconds as Ally and South stepped into the bright whiteness of the store. They walked past the anti-theft devices, the shopping baskets and headed for another PC standing in the grocery aisle. South showed his ID and nodded, his hands absently touching the shelves of vegetables. He turned his head and saw the crowd of suits and uniformed officers tucked back in a small office, holding cups of steaming drinks.

'There she is.' Ally pointed to the back wall of the store, where milk and other dairy products were stacked neatly in a refrigerated department. The girl sat huddled with her back against the shelves.

South could see her eyes were red with tears streaming down her cheeks as she shakily held the large knife to her throat. It looked cumbersome in her small hands. The doctor was crouching a few yards away; she had long straight, dark hair. He could see her smiling, her mouth opening. He wondered what sort of thing you say to a young girl with a knife to her throat, then stormed into the office. 'How did this all start?'

A ginger-haired police constable stepped forward, holding a mug that read: BEST EMPLOYEE. Ginger eyed South. 'You this DI she asked for?'

'That's right.' South walked to a nearby desk and leaned his backside on it. 'Now, would you mind telling me what exactly happened here, before a young girl slashes her own throat? Anyone?'

An Indian gentleman walked forward and nervously rubbed the side of his face. 'I'm the manager of the store.'

South looked at him. 'And what happened?'

'She just came in and seemed like she was just

shopping like everyone else who comes in here.' He looked down. 'Then the next thing I know, the security guard told me she's standing at the back of the store holding a knife to her throat. Somebody called the police.'

The ginger constable stepped forward. 'She asked for you after we got here. Do you know her?'

South looked ginger in the eyes and shook his head. 'No. Does anyone know why she wants to kill herself?'

'Perhaps you broke her heart.' The ginger constable turned to his colleagues and laughed.

'Stop bloody laughing,' South said.

'Alright, alright,' Ginger said and put down his mug of tea. 'Perhaps it's to do with her face.'

South turned to the ginger constable. 'What? What about her face?'

Ginger pointed to his own face. 'She's got some weird red birthmark down one side of her face. Right ugly thing. No wonder she's upset.'

Ally said, 'Even with her birthmark, Sergeant, she'll always be a damn sight better looking than you. Now, get your people out of here. Wake your ideas up and get out!'

South stood back and watched the uniforms place their mugs down and quietly remove themselves from the office. The manager looked lost for a moment, his eyes jumping from Ally to South.

'You can stay, Mr….' South began.

'Bhogal.'

'Let's go and find out what this girl's up to.' South stormed from the office with Walker behind him. He stopped by the crouching doctor and lowered himself to her level. The doctor turned to him and he notes she's all dressed up as if she was about to eat dinner in a fancy restaurant. 'You must've been in the middle of something when you got called out.'

The doctor turned to him, then looked up at Ally. She smiled slightly, and turned her eyes back to the girl. 'A friend's engagement party. I'll be forgiven… eventually. I take it you're Detective Inspector South? I'm Tia Moreno.'

'Mark.' South put out his hand, but she didn't take her hands away from the floor. South looked over to the girl, who was watching them. He now saw the red birthmark and imagined the thoughtless comments she had had to suffer. 'Do you know why she wants to kill herself?'

'She'll hardly talk to me. It's you she wants to see. Do you know her?' Moreno turned to South.

'No, never seen her before. I better introduce myself.' South moved forward and watched the girl flinch a little, the knife making a deeper dent in her neck. 'Hello. Amy, isn't it? I'm Detective Inspector Mark South.'

The girl blinked away her tears. Her eyes sharpen. 'You…you could be anyone.'

South took out his ID and threw it near her feet. He watched her free hand scrabble on the floor and grab his identification. Her eyes reached out to him as more tears moved down her cheeks. 'I'm going to do it.'

'I understand that, but I don't understand why. Please, tell me.' South moved forward a little.

Amy looked up. 'Just you. Tell them to go, please.'

South turned to face Ally and Tia Moreno. 'You better get yourselves back to the manager's office. I'll call you if I need you.'

Ally helped the doctor from the floor and they walked slowly back to the office, leaving the girl and South facing each other. South crouched down. 'So,

186

what's this all about, Amy? What is your surname by the way?'

'It's Glade, but it doesn't matter anyway,' she said and relaxed the knife a little, moving it away from her neck. He thought about what he'd been taught about hostage situations and attempted suicides, people about to throw themselves from roofs. 'What about your family?'

'What about them?' Her blue eyes widened.

'Won't they be upset if something happens to you?'

'They don't care. They don't understand what it's like for us.'

'Us?'

She nodded, looking at the blade. 'People like me.'

'Like you? What do you mean?'

She shook her head. 'Don't be like that. Don't pretend you don't see it, all over my face. It's ugly.'

'I can see you have a bit of a birthmark, but that's about it.' South leaned to his side, adjusting himself and getting a little bit closer. 'I really don't think it's worth killing yourself over. You're a pretty girl.'

She pointed the knife at South, jabbing it wildly towards him. 'You don't know what it's like! You don't hear what people say to me!'

'People can be cruel.'

'They have to be shown.' Her teeth bit together, more tears rolling down her cheeks.

'Shown how?'

The girl lifted the knife to her throat. 'Like this.'

'No, Stop!' South reached out his hand, his trembling fingers a couple of feet from her.

The girl relaxed the knife a little. She looked at South and the hand he was holding out to her and his scared expression. She lowered the knife and a wave of tears began to build.

South kept his eyes on the knife as it dropped into her lap. He looked up to the girl's face as her mouth opened and closed, the tears running onto her dry lips.

'He told me to ask for you,' the girl said, quietly.

South pulled himself across the floor until he could reach out and grab the knife. He threw it behind him and listened to it clatter against the wall as he wrapped his arms around the girl. She gripped him and shook with the sobs, her words mumbled into his shoulder.

Andrew Nelson was dreaming of Heather. In the dream he could smell her perfume, the one in the blue bottle she always put on before they would go out. She was standing by her dresser, already to go out on the town, smiling and doing a twirl. He could see her and she looked happy. In the dream, he wanted to hold her, to reach out to her, but as he touched her skin, it became cold. His hands burned from the ice that covered her. Her skin became fragile and fell away from her body and landed around his feet. He looked at the pieces, large lumps of white skin that formed parts of her body. He knelt down and picked up her wrist and hand. He looked up and blood was running from her mouth. He turned and ran. He couldn't run any more and he was being sucked back towards her, her hands reaching out to strangle him…

Nelson's head shot up as the garage door opened. He could barely make out anything, then heard the feet scraping along the floor. A bag thumped to the ground. The footsteps got nearer until he could see the familiar figure standing over him, the dead eyes staring at him through the mask.

A gloved hand patted Andrew like he was a dog. The figure moved back and grabbed something from his bag, then came back empty handed. He reached down and picked up a bottle of water and removed Nelson's gag.

He knew the routine and took the water down his throat. After he drank, he looked into the eyes of his captor. 'So what's going to happen to me?'

The man looked down at him. 'That's up to you.'

'Up to me?' Nelson said. 'What do you mean?'

'It's time you told the truth.'

'I have been! You kept asking me and I kept telling you, I didn't kill Heather!'

The figure got closer and held a finger up to his mouth. 'Keep your voice down, Andrew. Or this could be over very quickly.'

Nelson nodded and swallowed. 'Are you going to kill me?'

'I am the jury. This is your trial.'

'No, please, just listen…I didn't…'

The figure looked deep into Nelson's eyes. 'You raped and strangled her.'

'I didn't. I swear I didn't.'

'Then who did? Who raped and murdered your girlfriend? Sorry…your ex-girlfriend.'

'I don't know.' Nelson hung his head.

'If you admit you did it, I'll let you go.'

'No, you won't.'

'I swear. Just admit you did it and I won't kill you.' The figure rose and put a hand into his jacket. Nelson watched the hand come out holding something. He couldn't see what it was. He heard a metallic clicking sound and saw the blade flick out towards his face.

'Just tell me and I'll use this to cut you free. I won't slice you open and let you watch your guts fall out of your stomach. Tell me, Andrew.'

'You'll kill me.'

'No, I'll set you free.'

189

Nelson looked at the knife, then up at the eyes. They seem less threatening. What choice does he have? 'Alright… I…I killed her.'

'And you raped her?'

Nelson coughed, and gulped down a sob as he nodded. He looked at the knife, saw the figure back away a little, the gloved hand gripping the handle of the knife tighter. He looked up into the eyes and saw them burning.

'No, please, don't. Let me go, please. You promised… you said you'd let me go!' He tried to move himself away from the blade, struggled to use his weight to push the chair backwards. It didn't move. The knife was pulled back. Nelson shook his head, feeling the tears crawling down his face. 'You said you'd let me go!'

'I know I did.'

The knife jabbed out towards Nelson. He didn't feel anything. The second movement of the blade brought an ice cold burning. Nelson looked down at his side, where pain was starting to burn across him. He saw bubbles of black blood spilling out of him and he tried to scream. The knife entered his chest. Andrew felt the blood gurgling in his throat and tasted the blackness as it swallowed him.

TWELVE

Sunday, 25th April 2004

It's so quiet in the corridor that South had to sigh to make sure he hadn't gone deaf. In his hand he held a mug of milky tea, the way Amy said she liked it. One sugar. He turned to see Ally coming down the corridor towards him, her face showing nothing. She stopped and shrugged her shoulders. 'Can't get hold of Fred. He's not answering his mobile.'

South nodded and looked towards the interview room. 'Well, let's talk to Amy then.'

Ally walked in and smiled at the girl. Amy's eyes were still swollen from her tears, but it didn't detract from the sharp blueness of them.

South took a seat after Ally sat down. He smiled at Amy as he pushed the cup of tea towards her. 'Get that down you. Nice and milky like you said.'

Amy looked down at the tea, then up at South. 'Thank you.'

'I hear a bit of brummy in your accent.' Ally sat back.

'Yeah, I'm from Birmingham. Sparkhill.'

South took out a handkerchief and slipped it across the table. 'How old are you, Amy?'

Amy picked up the handkerchief. In those small movements, the way in which she moved her body self-consciously, South could almost hear all the ignorant comments made about her face.

'I'm eighteen,' she said and brushed her hair so it hung over her birthmark.

'Why did you ask for me, Amy?' South sat forward. She blinked. 'Does it matter?'

'Yes it does,' Ally said. 'We have to know why you picked that supermarket. Why walk into such a public place? Why not stay home in Birmingham?'

She sipped the tea. 'Because people should know the hurt they cause.'

'The hurt they cause when they call you names?' South asked.

Amy nodded.

'So you were going to publicly kill yourself so people would realise the hurt they've caused?' Ally asked.

'We were going to show them all. It was the only way and now I've let them all down.' A tear bubbled from Amy's eye.

'Let who down, Amy? Who are they?' South said.

'Michelle Hawks. Steve Murphy. And the rest.' She blew her nose.

South reached his hand out across the table. 'You know them? You've met them?'

Amy shook her head. 'No, I never met them, but they suffered like me. They did what I couldn't. They gave their lives so people would know.'

'So, how did you hear of them?' Ally asked.

'Through the website.'

'The Solution? The suicide website?' South looked into the girl's eyes.

'Yes. We'd chat to each other about our experiences. It was the same for all of us. We'd all been treated so badly in our lives and our families didn't care. Poor Michelle, and her hand. She told me that her husband wanted kids, but she couldn't stand the thought. What

192

if the kid had the deformity, she'd ask? What if her own child grew up to hate her because of her hand?'

'What do you know about John Kerry?' South wished Fred were there. He would like him to hear all this, the pieces fitting together.

'He had a problem I could never understand, but I felt for him. I'd heard of people who had eaten people out of survival, and afterwards they couldn't give it up. John wanted so badly to eat part of another person, but he was ashamed of himself too. He knew he'd have to do it, but he knew he couldn't live with himself afterwards.'

Ally said, 'What about Mrs Earl?'

The girl seemed to smile a little. 'I'd heard of her. Richard said she had cancer and didn't want to die slowly and to be a burden to her sister.'

'Who's Richard?' South asked.

Amy breathed deeply and looked at her hands. 'He's the one who found us all. Without him we'd all be living our lives without people understanding what we're going through.'

'He organised it all?'

Amy nodded. 'He told us what to do. He helped us to plan it.'

'He told you to walk into that supermarket and put a knife to your throat?' South asked and leaned towards Amy.

'He said it was the best way to show everyone the pain and suffering I was going through. He said the whole world would listen.'

'What do you know about Richard? Where does he come from? What's his full name?' South tried to smile.

'He only ever called himself Richard. 'I don't know where he came from, but he said he'd travelled around helping people with problems like ours. He told me in a recent email that he'd decided long ago what his path would be. He was chosen to help people like us.'

'Do you still have any emails from him?' Ally asked.

'At home somewhere.' Amy looked up questioningly. 'You want to stop it, don't you? You think it's a bad thing that he's done?'

Ally sat forward. 'Helping people kill themselves is a criminal offence. We can't let him go on doing this. He poisoned John Kerry.'

'John knew what would happen.' Amy put down the tea, her eyes burning. 'He wanted to die. How is that wrong?'

'It just is.' Ally folded her arms. 'John Kerry needed help. If Richard wanted to really help, then he would have told all of you to get professional help. You feel suicidal, you call the Samaritans, you don't walk into a supermarket with a knife to your throat.'

South put a calming hand on Ally's arm. 'Look, we're going to need your home address. We need those emails. Help us, Amy, and perhaps we can help others like you.'

Amy made sure her hair was covering her birthmark. 'And what's going to happen to me?'

South smiled. 'We'll make sure you get the help you need.'

'You mean you'll send me to a loony bin?'

'You just stay here and we'll contact your family.' South got up and nodded for Ally to follow him. They were about to walk out of the room, when something occurred to South. He turned around. 'What about the spiders? Where do they come into this?'

She looked blank. 'What?'

'The spiders.'

'I don't know. I hate spiders.'

He nodded and joined Ally in the corridor.

'She's a lovely girl that one,' Ally said and rubbed her tired eyes.

'She didn't know anything about the spiders.' South looked at the door of the interview room as if he was trying to see through the wood and back in at Amy. 'Why wouldn't this Richard tell her about the spiders?'

'I don't know. I really don't understand.'

'Maybe she didn't know the full story,' South said. 'All the other people were older. They would be more determined to go through with it. Amy, she didn't seem like the real suicidal type to me. I just don't think she would've gone through with it.'

'And your point is?' Ally asked.

'Wouldn't our mysterious friend have guessed the same thing?'

Ally nodded. 'He probably would have.'

'He was relying on it. He knew she wouldn't. Why?'

'He wanted her to talk to us. He's teasing us.'

South smiled. 'He's playing a game. He's trying to kept us interested.'

The slow buzzing of the stairlift got louder until Martin Fairservice appeared sitting in the machine at the bottom of the stairs. Fred looked at him from his armchair, looked at the thin, pale form of his only living relative.

Fred looked down into his lap. Neither him nor his brother functioned properly, he felt. He got up and walked to his brother, who looked at him helplessly. Fred picked him up and carried him to the leather recliner and put him down. It was like caring a chair, a small lightweight chair, he thought. Fred sat back down.

'You came in late again,' Martin said, 'must have been early in the morning. That should be a promising sign, but somehow I don't think it is.'

'I don't want to talk about it.' Fred bent forward and put his head in his hands.

'You went out to the pub, so what happened?'

'Nothing.'

'I don't believe that,' Martin said. 'Something must have happened.'

'We had a few drinks and talked and that was that.' Fred walked to the kitchen, filled the kettle and switched it on.

'You didn't make a move?'

'I didn't feel like I had any moves to make.'

'Did her husband turn up?'

'You want a cup of tea, Martin?'

'No. Did her husband turn up?'

Fred took his tea and stood with his back against the window, looking down at his brother. 'No, he didn't. Just forget it.'

'I want to help you.'

'You don't need to.' Fred sipped his tea.

Martin gripped the chair with his bony hands and pulled himself up a little. 'I want you to have a normal life. When I'm gone, you'll be all alone. You need someone.'

Fred laughed at this. 'And having an affair with the neighbour's wife is going to make me feel better?'

'Maybe. You need something exciting in your life to kept your mind busy. If your mind isn't busy, then it dies too. I should know.'

Fred looked at the books on the coffee table. 'Perhaps I should read more.'

'You don't need to read. You don't need to sit and watch television. Life is out there.' Martin pointed a finger at the window. 'Your work should keep you busy.'

'My work? They're going to take that away from me soon.'

'Don't let them. Fight them. Prove them wrong about you.'

'They're right.' Fred rubbed his nose.

'No, they're not right.' Martin looked into his brother's eyes. 'I know you. You can do your job better than any of them. You can catch this guy you're after and then you'll be back on top again.'

'I think it might be too late for that.' Fred looked down.

'It's never too late,' Martin said.

Tony Harris' wife cooked a great Sunday lunch, especially when it was pork on the menu. He smelt it as he stepped out the front door carrying a bucket of warm water and a leather shammy. He was wearing an old blue short sleeve shirt and a pair of jeans, ready to wash his car. The rain of Kent had marked the bodywork and mud was splattered up the wings.

Harris spied his son's car parked across the street as he poured the bucket of water over his car. Then he heard the rumble of an engine behind him.

'Tony Harris?' a voice asked. Whoever it was, they sounded like they smoked sixty-a-day.

Harris stopped mid wipe. He stood still, hoping it wasn't the same voice he hadn't heard for two years and hoped he'd never hear again. He turned slowly and looked at the Silver Mercedes. In the passenger seat sat the owner of the voice, a slick haired, muscular Italian. His mouth was surrounded by a jet-black goatee beard. 'Hello, Tony. Thought we'd pop around and see you. You busy?'

Harris chewed the inside of his mouth as he threw the rag down on the bonnet of his car, then headed down the drive. He stood looking into the car, at the man staring at him. He couldn't see Italian's eyes because of his sunglasses, but he recalled perfectly what they looked like; small, brown and beady.

'What do you want Franco?' Harris asked, feeling tired all over.

Franco took off his sunglasses and laughed. 'I haven't seen you in two years and this is the way you say hello?'

'You want me to pretend to be your friend Franco? Fine. How you doing, old mate? Long time no see.'

Franco laughed and then turned to the man driving. The driver was black and muscular. He looked like a bouncer.

'See, that's what I was saying,' Franco said. 'Tony's always good for a few laughs.'

Harris dipped his head to have a good look at the driver. 'So, you're being driven about now, Franco? You that important?'

Franco laughed. 'No, no. The bastards took away my licence. I got stopped when I was driving home from a club. Three year ban.'

Tony shook his head. 'So, what do you want?'

Franco jumped out the car. He threw his sunglasses on the passenger seat and leaned his back on the door. 'Mr Skouvakis wants to see you.'

'Why?'

'You know why.'

Harris looked away from Franco and up the suburban street. He'd moved not long after his last dealings with Skouvakis and Franco. He knew then it would not be difficult for them to find him. Everybody left a trail behind. It all came down to computers.

Those little microchips will get you in the end. He'd wondered if they might turn up after they found Byrne's body, but he put it out of his mind. He told himself not to even think his name, let alone say it. 'I don't know who killed Michael Byrne.'

'You can tell that to Mr Skouvakis.' Franco smiled.

'You tell him. I'm a policeman.'

Franco laughed again. 'So? What the fuck does that mean? Who cares? You were a policeman three years ago. It didn't stop you talking then. It didn't stop you doing a lot of things.'

Harris turned his back on Franco and walked up the drive. 'Tell him I might come and see him if I get time.'

'Tuesday night, he'll be in his pub in Bow,' Franco shouted and climbed into the car.

Harris watched the car roar out of the street, then swore to himself. He felt sick as he thought about the past.

The doorbell rang and Fred looked from the kitchen towards the door. He took a glass and filled it full of water and swallowed down a couple of painkillers. It was 12 p.m. and Fred still had his slippers and pyjamas on as he shuffled towards the door and opened it. He looked into the face of Mark South.

'What's wrong?' Fred asked. He opened the door wider and blinked.

'Nothing urgent,' South said. 'I just wanted to talk to you.'

Fred stood back, waved his colleague in and followed him into the lounge. 'Sit down.'

South sat and faced Fred. 'Is your brother here?'

Fred pointed a thumb towards the back of the house. 'He's in the garden. He likes to sit out there

199

when the suns out. He's reading another one of his books.'

'Did you hear about what happened last night?'

'No, what?'

'A young girl walked into a supermarket in Church Street and held a knife to her throat. She was going to kill herself.'

Fred sat up a little. 'Was? You stopped her?'

'Yes. She wasn't going to go through with it. She's just mixed up. They've got her in Chase Farm's psychiatric ward for observation.'

A sigh came from deep within Fred as his eyes rolled. 'That's great. She'll be pumped full of drugs and she'll be no better off than when she went in.'

'Well, that's all we could do. Where were you? You didn't answer your mobile.'

'I was busy.' Fred pulled himself up and started for the kitchen. 'Tea?'

South shook his head. 'She asked for me.'

'Why? Does she know you?'

'No. She was told to by our friend, the suicide assister.'

'What did she say? It might be a wind up. She might've found out about the case...'

'No. She knew too much.' South folded his arms. 'The person behind all this put her up to it. And the others, because they wanted to die. Even the cannibal, Kerry.'

Fred nodded and pushed his hands into the pockets of his robe. 'So, if we catch him, the best we can hope for is doing him for assisting a few suicides? What's the point?'

'He calls himself Richard.'

'Of course. The Shakespeare book.' Fred entered the kitchen and filled the kettle. 'How old is she?'

'Eighteen. Her name's Amy.'

'Eighteen? He knew she wouldn't kill herself.'

'That's what I said. He wanted her to talk to us.'

Fred looked towards the back door and saw the shape of his brother through the glass. 'And what about the whole spider motif?'

South laughed a little. 'That's the strange thing, she didn't know anything about it. I don't think it has anything to do with what he's doing. I think the suicides and the spiders are somehow separate. The spiders are just a little teaser.'

'Doesn't make sense.'

'I don't think it's meant to. We've been trying to build some connection between the spiders and the suicides, that's where we've been going wrong.'

Fred came back into the room and sat down. He was feeling his pain subside a little. 'What do you mean?'

'I mean the suicides are his thing. The spiders in the mouths were meant to attract attention.' South sat back. 'I don't know why. I don't really know what I mean. I just can't fit the deaths of the old people with the suicides. I kept lying awake trying to figure where the spiders come into it. I thought perhaps the spiders were supposed to represent the people who died. Spiders are also misunderstood by the way they look, but it's too much of a stretch. So, I just think the spiders are some kind of message to us.'

Allowing his mind to rewind, Fred found himself holding his mother's hand and it was comforting. If he could he'd grip tighter and not let her go. He was walking along with her, smelling her perfume and the leather of her knee length boots. She was wearing a worn suede skirt that was very short. He turned and looked into the open door of the flat and stood there watching the policeman. The dead old man was in his seat. The policeman's fingers opened the lips and he watched the spider crawl out of the mouth again. Then he was being pulled back along by his mother, her hand tightly gripping his wrist. After that, the rest of the afternoon was just his mother and Aunt Sylvia smoking. He sat and drew what he'd seen, carefully drawing the old man's head and the spider leaping from his chin.

'Fred?' South said.

Fred pulled himself back from his dream, letting go of his mother's hand. 'When I was nine years old my mother took me to my aunt's…'

'Are you alright?'

Fred waved away South's question. 'Listen. When we were almost there, I saw an open door and looked in. In the room there was a dead old man sitting in an armchair. There were policeman there. They were examining him, probably making sure it was natural causes. They opened his mouth and a spider crawled out.'

South nodded. 'This happened when you were nine? How old are you now?'

'Forty-five.'

South nodded. 'So, what has this got to do with this case? Thirty odd years ago you saw a spider crawl out of a dead man's mouth and then last week it happens again. It's a coincidence.'

'Is it?'

South sat forward. 'What else would it be? It's just the fact that it seems so familiar that it's got you a bit freaked out. I'd be the same.'

'What if someone found out about it and decided to mess with my head?'

South shrugged. 'How likely is that?'

Fred laughed a little and relaxed in his chair. There are no monsters in the wardrobe or under the bed. He expected South to pat him on the knee, get him a drink of water and tuck him in.

'Also,' South said, pulling out a piece of paper from his pocket. 'Ally found two similar cases, one in Wales and one in Scotland. One was a guy who was born without arms who somehow managed to shoot himself in the head, and the other was a paralysed guy with shrivelled up legs who managed to climb on a chair and hang himself.'

'And you're convinced this is the same guy? Our suicide assister?'

South nodded. 'We looked into their histories and both had expressed a desire to end their lives. I think this fucker has travelled to London and carried on with his little game. He probably thinks he's helping people. We need to profile this bastard, find out what sort of person does this. We can't let him get into the heads of any more eighteen year olds. It's just wrong.'

'I could talk to my therapist. She's also a criminal psychologist.'

South got up and looked down at Fred. 'Don't worry about the spider thing. We'll figure it out.'

Fred got up as South walked to the door, opened it, and said, 'And don't worry, we'll find who murdered Byrne.'

THIRTEEN

Monday, 26th April 2004

The magazines were stacked up on a small table in waiting room one, a long and wide room with walls painted magnolia and covered in posters about illnesses and vaccines. Fred sat himself on one of the plastic chairs that lined the right hand wall and watched a small blonde girl play with wooden blocks on the floor. He watched as the mother dragged the child away crying. He picked up a car magazine, flicked through it and then threw it back down on the pile. He sat as more people came in, taking up the seats, all mostly silent apart from the women with children. He looked at his watch and counted down the minutes, looking up at the electronic sign that called for various patients to different rooms.

The electronic sign chimed and Fred looked up and saw his name flashing, directing him to room 5.

'Morning,' Doctor Silverman said and fiddled with his skullcap while he tapped away at his computer with the other hand. He wrote something down, his tongue tapping away on his bottom lip. 'Haven't seen you for a while. What's the problem?'

Fred coughed as he sat up and looked past Silverman's head at the small sink and the green paper towels. 'I've been in pain lately.'

Silverman turned in his chair and faced Fred. He nodded, his sharp nose shining. 'And where is this pain?'

'In my back.'

'And have you pulled something or does this pain come and go?'

'Well, it's not really my back. It's lower down. It's more my…rear.' Fred smiled and tapped his leg.

Silverman leaned forward. 'How long have you had it?'

Fred lifted his eyes to the ceiling. 'Maybe a month. Month and a half. It's been gradually growing. I've been taking painkillers, but they're not really working so well now.'

All the time Fred talked, Silverman was nodding, his brown eyes staring into Fred's. 'Sharp pain? Dull ache?'

'Bit of both really.'

The nodding continued, until Silverman stood up and washed his hands. Fred saw him scrubbing his nails and then drying his hands with a paper towel. He looked at Fred, his eyes flickering. 'Any blood in your stools?'

Fred breathed deeply. 'I have noticed some. I think.'

Silverman took some latex gloves from a box near the sink and slipped them on. 'Right, can you remove your trousers and lie face down on the bed?'

Fred stood up and did as he was told, making sure he folded his trousers and placed them on the chair. He lay down on the bed and waited. He felt his pants being pulled down and then Silverman's fingers prodding him about. Fred gritted his teeth as the fingers became a little more thorough in their search. He counted at least a minute before Dr Silverman spoke. 'Right, that's that. You can put your trousers back on.'

As he pulled up his trousers, Fred heard the snap

of Dr Silverman's gloves coming off, then being discarded. He seated himself and looked at the doctor as he scribbled something down.

'OK, now I don't want to worry you.' Dr Silverman sat back a little in his chair as his face lost its natural smile. 'I'm sending you to have a prostate examination at a clinic in Chase Farm Hospital. It will be this week or next week. You're now in the age group when we have to keep an eye on things like this. So, it's better to be safe than sorry. The hospital will phone you very soon. OK?'

Fred nodded.

'Now, try not to worry.' Silverman smiled.

'I won't. Thank you, Doctor.' Fred got up and left the room, then stood outside the door for a moment. He looked down to see his hands shaking.

Fred's hands were still shaking when he picked up the medical book in Edmonton Green Library. He thumbed the pages and let his eyes sweep over the described symptoms. He looked for erectile dysfunction, while staring round the library occasionally to make sure no one was spying on him.

When he looked back at the book, he began to read again, trying to absorb knowledge like his brother. A young black boy stopped by his legs and showed him a book his mother was allowing him to get out. Fred turned back to the book, swiping the pages, hunting for the right chapter.

A hand slipped a book into a space in the shelf right next to Fred. He followed the hand along to an arm and then up to the head. Scott Brown smiled at him. The librarian was wearing a woolly hat.

'Diagnosing an illness by yourself can be a dangerous thing,' Brown said and slid another book onto the shelf.

Fred sighed. There was something strange about Brown's eyes, and his whole person, but he couldn't put his finger on it.

'I bet you see people diagnosing themselves with all sorts of illnesses.' Fred closed the book and placed it back where he found it.

'You do remember me?'

'Of course. Scott Brown, the librarian.'

Brown pulled his hat down tighter around his ears. 'Hope you're not ill. Surely policemen haven't got time to be sick?'

'No, we haven't really. I was just looking something up for work.'

Brown reached for another book among a trolley of returned books. He slipped the book into the shelf, then turned to Fred and pointed a finger at him. Fred noticed some of his fingernails were painted black.

'I bet I could help,' Brown said.

Fred didn't know what to say. He thought of the only book the case had involved and looked at Brown, wondering how educated he was. 'Know anything about Shakespeare?'

Brown stopped with a small paperback in his hand and scratched his nose. 'Didn't he write some plays?'

Fred laughed.

'Which play?' Brown said.

'Richard the Third.'

'Fancy a herbal tea?'

'What?'

'I'll get a copy and we can look over it while we drink a cup of tea.' Brown pushed the trolley further along.

Fred looked at his watch. He imagined a morning briefing already in full swing, his absence being duly noted. Then again, he told himself, he was on his way out and this could be seen as part of his investigation. 'That would be helpful.'

Brown pulled his hat down further over his head, adjusted the front, then smiled at Fred. 'Right. I'll just find us a copy.'

'Dear Amy,

Yes, death can be a scary thing, but life can be too. Do not fear it. For us, the marginalised people of society, death can only be a warm bosom to rest our heads. Martyrdom will be a sanctuary from this world of abuse. Do not think of your family, because that will only make you weak. They cannot understand what you've been through, what we've all been through. Think of Michelle and Stephen and John. Think of Christ on the cross, suffering for our sins. You will not be alone. God will take you with open arms, holding another of his children to his heart. Be strong.

Yours Richard.'

South looked at the email that had been faxed to him along with several others that morning. Ally read over his shoulder as they were sitting down in the incident room, the chattering voices of their colleagues snapping at their ears. South shook his head and looked at Ally. 'They all read like this.'

'Martyrdom?' Ally said. 'I can't wait to meet this Richard.'

'RIGHT!' DCS Jameson slapped his hands together, then stared into the faces of the front row, where Ally and South were seated. 'I'm not a happy man. In fact, I'm very pissed off. We are getting nowhere fast, people.'

South watched Jameson breathe deeply, his face

all red. Jameson slapped the whiteboard where a photograph of Heather Beckley was stuck. South felt a couple of the PCs jump a little in their seats.

'This young girl's being buried this week. Her family will be beside themselves with grief and we should've at least given them some comfort. We should've had the bastard locked up by now.' Jameson nodded, then scanned the room.

South looked at Harris, who was rolling his eyes as he sat by the whiteboard.

'This is not good enough.' Jameson took a moment to look at Heather's photograph. 'I want to go back over everything. Our prime suspect, Andrew Nelson, is still missing and we need to locate him. I want Heather's family talked to. If we've got a vigilante, then I want to know about it. He's a slippery little fucker, so perhaps he got a friend to hit him while he was in his car to leave his blood behind. It's not that far fetched. He must have known we were on to him. Talk to everyone again. Go over everything.'

Jameson walked along to the other side of the board and looked at the photographs of the suicide victims. 'The same goes for this lot. I know a lot of you haven't been taking this all very seriously, but we still need to get to the bottom of this. People are dead. South now tells me that these people all chatted to each other over the internet. So, what we are basically dealing with now is some kind of cult. An eighteen year old girl walked into a supermarket just down the road and threatened to slash her own throat just on the say so of the bastard who started this website. I repeat, this happened just down the road. He's laughing at us.'

Jameson looked over the room, then at South. 'Where's Fred?'

'He went to the doctors,' Ally said. 'That's fucking

great.' Jameson sighed and patted the board again. 'Just go over everything. Read the statements. Read the emails South has got. Make copies. Each team know what their actions are for the day. If you don't, read the action list. Just get on with it.'

Ally and South remained in their seats as their colleagues rushed off and began to tap on keyboards and make phone calls. South looked at another email, then passed it to Ally. She held it in her hands as she said, 'He would have to know when the old men were likely to pass away.'

'He would've been keeping a pretty close eye on them.' South leaned back and stretched.

Ally put the email back on his lap. 'Perhaps Watkins died and then he moved Murphy in over the road. Murphy took his overdose like a good boy, then he goes over to check on Mr Lovegrove.'

'He probably got lucky. Watkins had only been dead a couple of days. Lovegrove, over a week. All he had to do when he knew Lovegrove was dead, was to get the book over to Hawks' house or send it to her. That would've been her cue.'

Ally puffed out her cheeks. 'It's crazy. How do you get these people to take their own lives on cue?'

South turned in his seat and faced her. 'What about that cult in Switzerland that thought an alien ship was going to pick them up once they were dead? Hundreds of them stood around and drank poison, right on the button. This? This is just a plain old suicide pact.'

'So how would he kept an eye on the old men?'

South thought for a moment. 'Meals on wheels? Someone might've noticed a strange visitor. Anyway, he would have been around a lot.'

Ally nodded. 'Better go and ask the neighbours a few questions.'

Having been led through the back of the library, Fred found himself in a small square room with four armchairs and a large circular coffee table at the centre. A table with tea and coffee making facilities sat inside the door, where Scott Brown made their drinks. Fred looked about him, taking in the large film posters on the walls and noticing the lack of books in the room. He picked up the large edition of The Complete Works of William Shakespeare.

Brown placed a cup of milky tea before Fred, then seated himself and sipped his drink. 'Is this to do with Steven Murphy?'

Fred looked up. 'Well, I can't really discuss that.'

'No, of course not. It's just that I'm quite sure he had that book out at one time.'

'Would make sense.'

'I can smile and murder whilst I smile,' Brown said. 'Shakespeare?'

Brown nodded. 'Something Richard The Third said in the play. He's tired of being looked upon like a freak, so he decides to become king, then he knows everyone will have to sit up and take notice of him.'

'Is that what it's all about? He becomes a villain because he looks like one in people's eyes?'

'Ugly on the outside. Why not be ugly on the inside?'

'What if someone felt like King Richard does, and wanted to strike out at the world?'

'Then they'd be a very angry person. Full of rage.'

'But they'd be deformed as well, wouldn't they?'

Scott Brown looked at his cup. 'I suppose. To be teased and marginalised, they'd have to stand out. I know what it's like to be different. People always look at me weirdly because of my eyes.'

211

'Your eyes?' Fred asked, sitting forward.

'Yeah, I was born without eyelashes. It's weird I know. But I can only imagine what someone with a real deformity must feel like. You either accept it and get on with life or...'

'Or you get mad at the world. And you find others who feel the same way and get them to sacrifice themselves for a greater good.'

Brown nodded. 'Is that what's happening? Is this to do with that woman stabbing herself?'

'Sorry, I've said too much already. But thanks for listening to an old man ramble on.'

Brown laughed. 'Old man? You're not old.'

'I feel like it. Won't be long before this old man is out of a job.'

'I sometimes think humans weren't meant to work. Not in offices or for companies or anything like that.'

'How long have you worked here?'

'Only a year or so, I think.'

Fred nodded and pulled himself out of the chair. 'Well, thank you. I better get back to work.'

Scott Brown said, 'If I can help some more, just come by.'

Fred shook the librarian's hand, then headed back out of the building. He'd been trying not to think about his hospital appointment and the hands that would prod him, delving into his most private regions. It would be like his own post-mortem. The vision of Tracey Boswell leaving the hotel room flooded into his brain. He blocked it out, took out his mobile and saw that he'd been called several times. He swore and walked down the library steps.

Damp air greeted South when he stepped out of Ally's car and found his vision clouded with mist. He looked at the row of ex-council houses in Gough

Road, examined the exteriors of the houses, the way some had been given extensions and others still had the original brickwork.

Lovegrove's house had a jungle out the front of it. After digging around a bit, it became clear he and his wife had lived there since leaving the East End during World War Two, when the bombings started. She'd died ten years ago and the old boy had lived on with only his pension to keep him.

Suddenly Fred came into his mind. When his brother was gone, Fred would be alone, suffering a similar fate to the many old people like Lovegrove. He told himself not to be so sentimental.

'You've got to feel sorry for the old boy,' Ally said and got out of the car.

'What about the kids?' South asked.

'Live in Hertfordshire. Got their lives all sorted, so why should they worry? Probably got a nice four hundred grand house and a dog.'

South laughed at her bitterness. 'And you don't want all that?'

'I don't really know. I like my life the way it is. Can't imagine me married, with kids and stuff. I like my career too much.'

'Fair enough.' South stepped up to the hilariously large porch that had been slapped onto the narrow house.

Ally pressed the doorbell and looked over the front of the house. 'Some people don't deserve houses like this. Not if they haven't got taste.'

'Perhaps you should join the Metropolitan taste police.' South smiled.

A dark skinned young woman, with lavish long black hair, opened the door holding a mug of tea. She looked at South, then Ally, while pulling a clip from her hair. South's eyes automatically jumped to her frilly blouse that was unbuttoned a little, revealing her ample cleavage.

'You're not selling something are you?' She flickered her brown eyes between them.

'Not today.' South showed his ID. 'DI Mark South and this is DS Ally Walker. I take it you know your neighbour died last week?'

The woman put her tea down on a small table near the door and leaned against the doorframe. 'I only found out the other day. It's terrible. I used to say hello to him and chat sometimes. He was a nice enough fella. I thought he died of old age though. Did someone do him in?'

'No, there weren't any suspicious circumstances,' Ally said. 'We have to follow these things up though. Do you remember him having any visitors?'

The woman frowned and fiddled with a silver chain around her neck that had a name hanging from it. Maria, it said. Maria looked upwards, as if she was reading something on the ceiling. 'I don't really remember anyone. I'm usually busy with my kids.'

'You here about Mr Lovegrove?' a croaky voice asked from behind them.

Ally and South turned to see a tiny old lady with blue tinged hair. South smiled and stepped closer to her. 'You were friends with Mr Lovegrove?'

'Yes dear,' the old lady croaked again. 'I live opposite, you see. I've known Bill for years, but I've been going to the hospital with my husband all the time, so I hardly saw him. I feel terrible about it all.'

'I wouldn't be too hard on yourself, love,' South said.

The old girl smiled and looked over at the house William Lovegrove spent his last moments in. 'Him and his wife were very close. He didn't really go out much after she passed away.'

Ally nodded and said, 'And do you know if he had any visitors? Anyone who might have popped around now and again?'

She thought for a moment, a bony and veined hand stroking her chin. 'Well, I can tell you that his kids didn't come round much. It's a real shame when they ignore their parents like that.'

South smiled. 'But can you remember a man coming around and seeing him at all? Would probably be quite often.'

'I tell you what, come to think of it…' She looked to the heavens for a moment, then nodded. 'There was a man who used to turn up sometimes. I did see him knock on the door and I wondered if he was a relation or something.'

'And can you describe him at all?' Ally asked.

'Oh dear. I don't think so. I remember he wore a hat. One of those hats all the kids wear these days, the sporty ones. Those rappy people, or whatever they are called…they wear them. Anyway, that's the only person I can think of.'

South smiled. 'Well, thanks anyway. You've been a great help. Look after yourself.'

Ally smiled and followed South to the car. She climbed in and looked over at her colleague. 'That's why we need more CCTV cameras around, so we don't have to rely on eyewitnesses. They're so unreliable.'

'You are joking?' South asked, his eyes bulging. 'More cameras watching everyone? I agree with cameras in major cities, in the trouble spots, but not everywhere. I believe in good old fashioned privacy.'

She started the engine. 'I like my privacy, but I also like the idea of a lower crime rate.'

He laughed. 'You want to be watched twenty-four hours a day? I don't.'

'No, you don't even like your curtains left open. Talk about anal.'

South spluttered for a moment as he struggled to put his seat belt on. 'Excuse me, but I don't like to be on display. What do you say to that?'

'Fancy a drink after work sometime?'

FOURTEEN

The piles of paperwork and statements were strewn across Fred's desk, but he could no longer look at it all. His hand drifted through the pile of papers and pulled out Amy Glade's statement. South had attached an envelope filled with the emails she received from the mysterious Richard. He'd read them all and found little that spoke to him, nothing which gave him any particular clue to his identity. Amy Glade mentioned in her statement that she believed he was deformed in some way, but she didn't know how. Was one or both of his hands deformed or perhaps a leg? Could they be on the look out for a limping and self-conscious crazy person?

Fred looked back to the case of Mr Saha and his taxi ride into the Deformity Society charity shop. Most eye-witnesses made no mention of anything that stood out, that would mark out the assailant as anything but run of the mill. Normal height, wearing a balaclava and gloves. Dark top and black trousers or jeans. Average. No limp. No arm missing. No legs amputated at the knee. Fred looked round, noticing someone standing in the doorway.

Rich Vincent smiled, then walked into the room holding a few pieces of paper in his fist. 'I see you're very busy, Detective Inspector.'

Fred nodded. 'Those for me?'

The IT expert looked at the paper. 'You're not going

217

to be happy.'

'I didn't think I would be.'

Vincent rested his backside on the corner of the desk and laid the crumpled pages before Fred. He could see figures and numbers filling the pages, but it meant nothing to him, so he raised his eyebrows at Vincent. 'What does all this mean?'

'We'd be here all day if I tried to explain. Basically, I've been working on this day and night. I looked through the lists the ISP gave me, after a lot of time wasting. I ran the programme and found the phone number and address that our man was at when he up loaded the pages of his website.'

'And?'

Vincent's fingers played with his nose piercing for a moment. 'He's smart. He must've parked up outside the house and used a laptop. He just tapped into their computer and uploaded the pages. The house belongs to a family, and no password protection. He knew what he was doing.'

The phone on Fred's desk rang and he looked at it for a moment, then gave an apologetic face to Vincent. He picked up the receiver as Rich Vincent left. 'DI Fred Fairservice.'

'Good Afternoon. This is Peter Cowes from The Highland Bank. I'm just phoning to enquire about several withdrawals made from your account over the last two weeks.'

After Fred gave the necessary security information, he said, 'Withdrawals. How many?'

'Ten so far. Each have been for the maximum of two hundred and fifty pounds. That's two thousand, five hundred pounds so far. The withdrawals were made with the card issued to Martin Fairservice. You understand that we have to check unusual withdrawals like this for security purposes.'

'Yes, that's OK. I just remembered that my brother, Martin, was using the money to take a trip, so it's OK. Sorry about that.'

'I'm sorry to trouble you, Mr Fairservice. Thank you for your time.'

Nearly three thousand pounds, Fred said to himself. What could he say? He couldn't say his brother was shut up in doors, being eaten away by a disease and was unlikely to be using the cash machine. Then again, he thought, Martin might have got someone else to do it for him. Why? He wasn't worried about the money, not at all. It belonged to Martin too. He had told his brother that when he got the card issued to him, way back when he could still get about with his canes. He thought he might need money one day, just in case something happened to him on duty. Why now? He shook away his thoughts.

He reached for Amy Glade's statement. She was the closest they had got to the suicide cult leader and Fred couldn't believe she didn't know anything about the spiders and what they might represent. She was hiding something, he thought, and picked up the phone to call Chase Farm Hospital. He'd been to the psychiatric department along time ago to talk to a young junkie who might know the name of a dealer they were after. He was useless, just a pale, staring, shell of a man. He looked twenty years older than his twenty-five years and so skinny and brittle. It wasn't him who had affected Fred, who made his heart dive into his stomach and caused him to swear never to go back again. No, it was the young girl he met when leaving. The exit had been in front of him, he was about to escape when a desperate, harrowing cry came from behind him.

'Don't leave me here,' the young woman pleaded, her eyes glassy and dark from the drugs they were pumping into the patients. 'Please, don't leave me here. Please.'

Fred had turned and walked into the air outside the ward, then drove away with tears in his eyes.

Now he was about to go back again.

Walker and South reached the reception desk in the old people's home. A black nurse, with a slight Jamaican accent, greeted them. She talked to them without looking up, her eyes staring down at something she was reading. 'Yes?'

South showed his ID and looked over the desk to see what had gripped her attention. 'Sorry to disturb you when you're so busy, but we need some information about one of your residents. George Hammond. He died the other day.'

The nurse looked up at their faces. 'Why? You think we murdered him or something?'

South laughed. 'No, not at all. It's just part of another inquiry. We need to know if he had any regular visitors. Maybe a man who came and looked in on him?'

'Wait a moment.' The nurse looked under the desk and pulled out a book. 'The visitors have to sign this. Mr Hammond's Niece came to see him quite a bit, I think I remember.'

South leaned on the counter while Ally walked away from the desk, looking at some watercolours on the corridor wall that led into the main lounge area. The nurse shook her head. 'No, all we have is her niece signed in.'

'Thanks anyway,' South said and walked over to Ally. 'Just his niece.'

'What are we going to do? There must be loads of

visitors to this place. It could be any one of them.'

'Let's go and talk to Watkins' neighbours, maybe they saw something.'

Ally leaned her back against the corridor wall, her eyes almost closing. 'We should be working on the Heather Beckley case. We need to find Andrew Nelson.'

South leaned on the wall. 'Everyone's working on that case, but no one knows where he is. Until we find him, we haven't got a case.'

'I just keep seeing those pictures of her body every day and I feel sick to my stomach. Her poor parents.'

South gripped Ally's shoulder as they headed to the exit. 'If something's happened to Nelson and the blood in his car is from a violent struggle, then we might have to talk to her poor parents.'

'And who would blame them?'

South stepped onto the pavement and checked his mobile phone. 'We'd still have to bring them in.'

'And where the hell is Fred?'

The psychiatric ward at Chase Farm Hospital was exactly as Fred remembered it. He parked his car in the small car park opposite the glass and metal walls that kept the patients inside. Not all of them though, Fred realised as he saw a nurse directing a stubby-looking man with a thick black beard, back in through the doors. With 'Care in the Community', Fred knew most of the patients would be back on the streets within a matter of months. The drugs they filled them up with were there to combat the after effects of the drugs that had cracked open their junkie brains in the first place. The other patients, the ones who one day stopped making sense to their families and friends, sat in their rooms dosed up to the eyeballs, or were stuck in front of a television.

He smelt the kitchen when he stepped inside. It was the stench of the same easily digested slop they always served. He felt the vomit try to clamber up his throat as he turned towards the young male nurse behind the reception desk.

Fred took out his ID. 'DI Fred Fairservice. I need to see Amy Glade. She was admitted yesterday.'

The nurse looked at the ID, blinked several times before looking up at Fred, then at a larger female nurse with long red hair. 'Anita, there's a policeman here who wants to see Amy Glade.'

Anita turned around in her swivel chair, then slowly got up and faced Fred. 'You called earlier? I hope you're not going to upset her. She's been in a right state. Bless her heart.'

'I just want to ask her a few questions,' Fred said and watched the nurse tap the counter, then turn to the young man. 'Put Amy in the tearoom and clear out anyone in there. You can talk to her in there, officer.'

To Fred's relief, it was only a few minutes before he was shown into the tea room, a surprisingly large triangular room surrounded by glass so the patients could look out on the gardens. A few large leather armchairs were positioned about the room. It was only when Fred stepped further into the room he saw Amy was already seated in a chair with its back to the window. She looked fragile against the enormous armchair.

Fred walked slowly over, careful not to startle her. She turned slowly and looked him in the face as he seated himself, but her eyes seemed blank. 'Amy?' he said. 'Amy Glade?'

There was a slight nod of her head, and the fingers of her left hand fluttered like newspaper in a breeze.

'Do you mind if I sit and talk to you?' Fred asked

and sat forward, trying to smile as brightly as he could.

'How long will I have to stay here?' She blinked.

'I don't know. Perhaps when your parents come…'

'They're happy for me to stay here.'

'I'm sure that can't be true.' Fred smiled again. 'Listen, if you talk to me, I might be able to help you.'

She came to life in small movements. 'You have to promise to get me out of here.'

'I'll do my best.'

'Promise?'

'OK, Amy, I promise.' Fred sat back in his chair. 'Who is Richard, Amy?'

'I don't know.'

'You emailed each other, so you must have some idea.'

'I let them all down.' She looked down at her hands.

'No, you didn't. You did the right thing. I need to know who Richard is, so he won't do it again.'

She looked up, a flicker of light appearing behind her eyes. 'Are you Fred?'

'That's right.'

She nodded a little. 'He mentioned you.'

'He mentioned me? When?'

'In his emails to me.' A little wistful smile crossed her face.

'There was no mention of me in the emails we have.'

'I burnt those ones like he told me to.'

'Listen, Amy, you have to tell me everything. How does he know me? What is this all about?'

She looked up and smirked. 'He's not doing anything wrong. They wanted to die. And anyway, he's only answering a calling.'

'From God?'

'Maybe. Who knows? He said that he was reached

out to.'

'Who reached out to him?' Fred slipped down from his seat and crouched at her feet.

'I don't know.'

'How does he know me?' he pleaded.

'He's done his research, I suppose.'

'Please. You have to tell me where he is. This is very important.'

'I don't know. I really don't know!'

He got up and looked at her, examining her young face for any signs of lying, but she was too out of it for any of that. 'OK, Amy. You think of anything and you let me know. Because I really need to find him.'

'Don't they have CCTV cameras positioned some-where around here?' Ally asked and looked up at the surrounding walls of Fisher Court. Opposite her, a few yards away, was the flat in which the body of Steven Murphy had been discovered a week earlier. South looked at the flat and recalled the animal blood all over the walls. He tried to see through the front wall and pictured Murphy's body in several pieces, arranged for the best effect. Fred was right about that much. It wasn't a brutal murder; it had just been made to look that way so they wouldn't just let it go.

South laid out the facts in his mind, forming them like a series of snapshots. Perhaps it was Steven Murphy's idea to take an overdose, to slip into a peaceful sleep. That would leave his helper to cut up his body and create the macabre scene.

'Did you hear me?' Ally asked and joined South as he stared at number 5.

He turned to her slowly. 'Sorry? What?'

'What about CCTV cameras?'

'None of them work. Some money was poured

224

into this place a few years ago, to help fight the drug dealers around here, but now the cameras are broken or vandalised.'

She nodded. 'Typical. What're you thinking?'

'Just that Fred was right. He cut up Murphy's body to get our attention. He sliced off the lump of flesh for Kerry before sticking the head in the oven as a last little joke. Because Kerry was going to cook and eat him.'

Ally turned to face Watkins' flat. 'And then he daubs some of the blood on Mr Watkins' door, so we'd find him with the spider in his mouth. But why?'

South stared at Watkins' building, then turned to face his neighbour's door. South took out his notebook and flipped open the pages. He read his notes and looked up at the door again. 'Karen Mills.'

'The neighbour,' Ally said and started towards her door. She rang the bell and listened to a child screaming something.

Karen Mills opened the door with a look of absolute exhaustion on her face. 'What is it?'

Ally and South showed their IDs. Ally smiled. 'Hope we haven't come at an inconvenient time.'

'There's never a good time in this house,' Karen Mills said.

'Well, we really need to ask you some questions,' South said, ignoring her pained expression.

She sighed, then opened the door and let them through. South watched her go to the kitchen where she seemed to be preparing a bottle of milk for her baby.

'So?' she said. 'I've answered lots of questions already. I should be getting paid for it.'

South laughed and stood under the archway that led to the kitchen. 'Did Mr Watkins have any regular visitors?'

'I wouldn't know really. Why're you so interested in him? I thought he just died of old age.'

'Let's just say we take an interest in the elderly.' South smiled.

'You're the only ones who does then,' Mills said and picked up her baby from a carrycot on the kitchen table.

Ally came to look at the baby. 'Look at you. He's gorgeous.'

Karen Mills smiled at her boy and rocked him a little. 'Right little handful, like his sister. Look, I think I saw a man at Watkins' door a couple of times. I'd go out shopping and I'd look back at my door to make sure I'd shut it properly and there'd be this man standing there at his door.'

'How often would you say this happened?' South asked.

Mills placed the bottle into her baby's mouth. 'Maybe three times. He could've been here more times. I just figured it was a relative or some friend. I don't know. I don't nose into other people's business.'

'And what was he wearing?' Ally asked, her eyes still on the baby.

'Dark hooded top. The last time I saw him it was one of those freakishly hot days a couple of months ago, so it was strange that he had his hood up. But then again, you see loads of kids with those hoodies on.'

'But this was a man?'

'Yeah, I think so. Was normal height. Looked like a man. I'm used to seeing the back of men.' Karen Mills laughed and smiled at her baby. 'Aren't I, sweetheart?'

'I know how you feel,' Ally said. 'Right, we'll leave you to it. If you remember anything else, let us know.'

South watched Ally move past him, heading for the door. He turned back to Karen Mills as he thought of something. 'Did he have a bag with him, this hooded man?'

Karen's head sprung up. 'Yeah, I think he did. A rucksack.'

'Thank you.' South followed Ally out of the door, where she started writing a few notes down, resting her back on the wall.

'He brings something with him when he visits,' South said to himself. 'He wears a hat or hooded top, obviously to obscure his face. If he does have a deformity, then no one has pointed it out.'

'Perhaps that's why he wears the hat or hood.' She nodded, a slight smile appearing on her face. 'To obscure the two little horns on his head.'

'Very funny. Now, we've got to figure out why these old people let him in. We need officers to go round and find out if anyone saw him and try to get a description. We've been focusing on the suicides, but we haven't been looking closely enough at the deaths of the old men. If we look into them a bit more, then we'll get closer to the truth.'

Fred stood just inside the front door, hesitating before he entered the lounge. He could already picture the wiry frame of his brother sitting reading, his brain pulsating behind his withered face.

It was early afternoon and Fred couldn't face going back to Edmonton Police station, not after seeing Amy Glade held in captivity at Chase Farm. He still couldn't get the smell of the place out of his nostrils. Everything else, the whole investigation, had clambered out of his brain. He'd even forgotten about the money taken out of his account until he reached home.

'You're early,' Martin said and turned down the

volume on the television as Fred came in. 'There was a message on the answer phone for you. Something about a hospital appointment. Hope everything's OK.'

'Nothing's wrong. Dr Silverman wants me to go for a check up. High blood pressure, that's all.' Fred saw the curtains were nearly closed apart from a thin gap that allowed the sun to spray a stream of light into the room. He watched the dust spin around in the light as he took off his jacket. 'And how have you been, Martin?'

Martin picked up a book near him and opened it up, his eyes scanning over the words. 'Not bad. Solved the case yet? That's what's giving you high blood pressure, the case.'

'Perhaps. I spent the afternoon in Chase Farm psychiatric ward.'

Martin lowered the book. 'Any particular reason? Or just popped in for a chat?'

'A young girl walked into a supermarket the other night with a knife to her throat and said she was going to kill herself.'

'But she didn't and now she's locked up with the lunatics? That'll do her good.' Martin raised the book again.

Fred looked at him for a moment, trying to remember the sort of person Martin had been before he was a victim of disease. He half wanted to let the money disappear from his mind, but he had to be sure it was Martin who took it. 'The bank called me today.'

Martin kept looking at the book. 'Trying to sell you some insurance or something, I expect?'

'No, they informed me that quite a large amount of money had been withdrawn from my account.'

'Really?'

'Yes. Have you seen the card I gave you lately?'

Fred got up and stretched.

'You said it was my money too or was that just something nice to say to your dying brother?'

Fred looked away, nodding his head. 'I'm more surprised that you actually got to the bank.'

'Home helps are good for other things.'

Fred smiled, then sat down again. 'So, two thousand, five hundred is a lot of money. What do you want it for?'

'Perhaps I need it.'

'OK then. What do you need it for?'

'Does it matter?'

'I'd like to know.'

'Can't a dying man have any secrets?'

Fred jumped up as his stomach flipped over. 'Don't. Don't start talking like that.'

Martin picked up a book. Fred stepped closer, looking down at the slight figure lying under the huge blanket. He realised he couldn't even make out where Martin's legs began and ended. 'If you wanted money, you should have just said.'

'And you would have just handed over that much money? I have to disagree, dear brother.'

'Just tell me what you want it for.'

Martin looked up cautiously. 'OK, I was going to do something nice for you. I wanted to help you.'

Fred was speechless for a moment. 'For me? Help me? How?'

'It doesn't really matter now, actually,' Martin said and looked at his watch as the doorbell rang.

Fred answered he door and faced Tracey Boswell. She looked surprised. 'I didn't expect you to be in. I rang the bell in case.'

'You came to see Martin?' Fred asked, feeling the burn of embarrassment covering his chest and face.

'Yes. Are you OK? How have you been?'

'Fine. Why don't you come in?'

Tracey hesitated for a moment, before Martin called her in. She stood awkwardly in the lounge, looking between Fred and Martin.

'Well, I'm going to go out,' Fred said and put his jacket and shoes back on. 'I've got more details of the case to sort out. I'll be back soon.'

Fred stepped out of the house and stood on the doorstep for a moment. He imagined them both sitting in the living room discussing him, chatting away about the fact he has failed as a man. He pictured his colleagues at work complaining about him as an officer, and now he had his personal life in shreds too. He jumped into his car and drove out of the square.

FIFTEEN

Tuesday, 27th April 2004

Dave Farrow woke up, not at his usual 5 a.m., but two hours earlier. He tried to adjust his vision as he sat up a little, looking around the large double bedroom, trying to discover why he'd woken up so early. He could see the amber glow of the street lamp outside the window. He looked down at his wife, Jean, who had somehow managed to wrap herself up in the duvet. Maybe that's why he'd woken up, he guessed, then swung himself out of bed. Jean stirred and mumbled something as he grabbed the bedside table to steady himself.

He wasn't certain he could hear it at first, but then he stopped dead, sure someone was opening the boot of a car outside. He'd become suspicious of late, watching the skip outside his home in case any of the neighbours, or anyone else for that matter, started dumping rubbish in there. Skips were not cheap to hire these days, he'd told his neighbour, Derek, in the hope that he got the picture. They always waited until you had hired one and then start getting rid of their unwanted junk. Last time it was a stained mattress he'd found dumped in the skip.

Dave ran a hand through his hair, then stood frozen, listening to the sound of someone dragging something from their car. Shit, those cheeky bastards. He hurried over to the window, pulling the curtains apart so he could get a sneaky look. He looked down into the street where he could see a figure dragging something along the pavement. Whoever they were, they had something large wrapped up, ready to throw it in the skip. Fuck them, he muttered and grabbed his jeans and shirt. He put them on as his wife turned over and wiped her sleepy eyes. 'What you doing, Dave? What time is it?'

'Go back to sleep. Someone's dumping something in the skip.' Dave hurried down the stairs and up to the front door, where he slipped on his shoes and prepared to catch them in the act. As he opened the door, he heard a car engine roar down the street. Its brake lights flashed on as it turned sharply right. He faced the skip and saw the blue plastic sheet the offending object was wrapped in. He looked again up the street as he stepped out into the blue-black haze. He walked around to the side of the skip where the object lay, then stopped dead, his eyes focusing through the bad light. He reached for one of the lamps attached to the side of the skip and held it up, letting the orange light fall upon the end of the plastic. He stepped forward, laughing at the ridiculousness of what he thought he might have seen. He bent his head and lifted the plastic. He jumped back. Then he pulled back the sheet further and stared at the two bare feet.

The sun was barely up when South arrived outside the semi-detached house where the forensic team had set up their working tent, fixing it over the skip and front garden. The SOCOs came and went, their bodies covered in protective clothing. South parked outside someone's drive, realising the neighbour would probably be out and complaining in a matter of minutes. He didn't care. He got out and watched for a moment as the SOCOs carried bags of dirt from the skip and sifted through them for evidence. It was painstaking work and he didn't envy them. He was happy enough to receive the information they gave him and build on it from there.

South slipped under the blue and white cordon and stood watching the SOCOs entering and exiting the tent. He could hear movement, could see the uniformed officers opening the gates of the neighbours' houses. He grew up in a street like this. The same houses and just the same sort of neighbours, except everybody was friendlier then, he decided. These days no one took much notice of anything. If your burglar alarm was ringing all night, they just complained about noise.

'Morning South,' Jameson said and patted him on the back. 'Bit early for finding bodies.'

South pointed to the tent. 'Do we know who's in there?'

Jameson nodded. 'We've managed to identify the body and you'll never guess. Our friend Andrew Nelson has at last turned up. Hasn't been dead for long.'

South raised his eyebrows. 'So someone did grab him? They must've had him somewhere for a while before killing him. Do we know how he died?'

'They found a flick knife tucked inside the plastic he was wrapped in and a few holes in him.'

Jameson searched in his jacket pocket and brought out his notebook. 'Forensic are giving it the once over, and let's hope whoever killed him left us a trail. They usually do.'

South stepped closer to the tent and tried to peer in, but all he saw was the dented bottom of the yellow skip. 'He was wrapped in plastic?'

'The bloke who found him said it's a kind of sheeting they use in the building industry, so that could be a possible lead. Also Nelson's shoes were covered in dust. They reckon it could be cement dust.'

'So we're possibly looking for someone involved in the building trade?' South asked and watched another SOCO step out of the tent holding a tub filled with rubble. South turned back to Jameson. But why dump Nelson's body here? He must've known we'd find him right away.'

Jameson stopped looking through his notebook. 'Of course. He wanted the body to be found. And the murder weapon for that matter. This, son, is one very careless murderer. They've given us everything. The body, the weapon and we know the motive.'

'Do we?' South asked.

Jameson looked at him as if he'd told him a racist joke. 'Yes. This has to be revenge. Whoever killed Nelson wanted to get him for killing Heather. Simple as that. Why, what were you thinking, South?'

'I don't know. Just think it all seems a bit too straight forward.'

'Murder usually is. Ninety-nine percent of the time you'll find A hated B and that's what led them to kill them. Jealously. Anger. It all comes down to human responses. But you know all this, you've seen it all before.'

South nodded as he saw a SOCO coming towards them carrying the flick knife in an evidence bag. As the SOCO held the bag up, South's eyes were fixed on the dried blood on the blade. 'So he used a flick knife. Interesting.'

The SOCO nodded. 'That's right, boss. They've taken most of the plastic sheet away from him. It's not pretty. Also, I should tell you they've found a print on the handle. Looks like a partial thumb print.'

Jameson took the bag and held it up and stared at it, a smile spreading across his face. 'Good. Let's get Heather's brother and father in. Get them printed and see if we can get a match. This could be over very quickly.'

The SOCO nodded and walked back to the tent. South wondered about Nelson and his guilt. He wondered where his justice was and whether it really lay in a skip, thrown away like a piece of junk. 'So, that's it, Nelson's her killer and we forget all about it, just file it away?'

Jameson laughed. 'Don't start thinking too much, South, you'll strain something. Nelson did her in. End of story. But we'll make sure of it, just like we'll make sure his killer gets what's coming to him.'

Fred had only just got to work when he received the order to meet DCI Harris and go and fetch Allen Beckley. They found him at work, under a sink, at a building site in Brimsdown. More apartment buildings were being constructed, developing the old industrial Enfield back into a village like it was a hundred years ago. Harris and Fred stood by Beckley until he looked at them out of the corner of his eye.

Fred produced his ID for the plumber to see.

Beckley dusted himself off and looked at his identification. 'Does this mean you've found something out about my daughter's murder? Have you caught that fucking bastard Nelson?'

Harris said, 'There was been a development in the case, Mr Beckley.'

Fred watched Harris put a hand on Beckley's shoulder, walking him towards the street. Harris, lowering his voice, said, 'Andrew Nelson was found dead this morning.'

Beckley froze. 'He killed himself, didn't he? The fucking bastard. He's got off lightly, the little…'

'He was murdered, Mr Beckley. We need you to come down to the station with us and answer a few questions.'

Beckley blinked for a moment, before the anger reached his eyes and face. 'You think I had something to do with his death? My daughter's murdered and now you want to lock me up? Fuck off.'

Harris grabbed Beckley's arm as he turned away. 'Mr Beckley, you really need to cooperate with us. It'll make everything easier.'

'You want everything easy, don't you?' Beckley stared up at Harris. 'No, fuck off.'

Harris took a deep breath before saying, 'OK, fine. Allen Beckley, I'm arresting you on suspicion of murder. You do not need to say anything, but I must warn you that it may harm your defence if you do not mention when questioned something which you later rely on in court. Anything you do say may be given in evidence. Do you understand?'

'This is a joke.' Beckley spat on the ground.

'This is no joke,' Harris said and pushed Allen from the building site with Fred following behind.

'Seems you don't really have anyone to confirm where you were this morning, Mr Beckley,' Harris said, sitting in the interview room. He pushed a mug of tea towards him. Fred sat with his arms folded, looking across at the plumber. He looked over his worn denim shirt that had hardened stains on the front. Then he looked up at his thinning fair hair that had been cut very short. Fred couldn't imagine the friendly face of Beckley murdering anyone, but he knew it didn't count for much. The plumber's face, with his tiny dark eyes and laughter lines, could easily change with anger. A daughter's murder could change everything.

'You'll have to take my word for it then,' Beckley said and grabbed the mug of tea.

Fred listened to the tape machine winding, recording every word. 'Your wife didn't see you this morning at all?'

Beckley shook his head. 'We don't sleep in the same bed, so when I got up for work she didn't see me. I always leave really early. I've always been an early riser. I shower, have a cup of tea and sit in the kitchen and then head off to work. My mind's been all over the place at the moment, thinking about Heather. My dead daughter, remember her?'

Harris nodded. 'I know that. But we need to know where you were at half three this morning.'

Beckley looked up. 'I was still sleeping. Where was I supposed to be?'

'Someone dumped Nelson's body in a skip at about that time. They wrapped it up in a plastic sheet and threw it away. They knew we'd find it, so it goes to show they couldn't have cared less. That's the sort of thing an angry father might do.'

'Fuck off.' Beckley hunched forward. 'I was in bed.'

'Well, that's great news, Beckley. Prove it.' Harris smiled and leaned back.

'I can't. I was there and that's that.'

Harris nodded a little. 'You work on a building site, so there must be quite a bit of cement dust around.'

Beckley's eyes narrowed. 'Yeah. What's that got to do with anything?'

Harris tapped the table. 'Was it just you or did you and some of your work colleagues keep him tied up on your site until you decided what to do with him?'

The plumber's mouth opened and for a moment he

looked as if he was going to laugh. 'Shut up. You're not going to put this on me, mate. You lot are not going to stitch me up, not after you couldn't even get Heather's killer. You fucking…I'm not having this.'

Fred looked over at the plumber, watching his whole body stiffen as he sat back and folded his arms neatly across his chest, his mouth tight shut. 'We have the murder weapon,' Fred said.

Harris nodded. 'Yeah. It was dumped right along with the body, but you know that, don't you?'

Beckley unfolded his arms. 'No, I don't know that. You're just making all this up. I suggest you let me go. Andrew Nelson can rot for all I care.'

Harris slowly turned to Fred. 'Well, how do you like that?'

The door to the interview room opened and Ally leaned in. 'Fred, Tony. I need you out here.'

They followed her out into the corridor and watched her looking uncomfortable. She fidgeted for a moment, then shrugged her shoulders. 'The fingerprint didn't match Allen Beckley's. We've just had the son, Jason Beckley in too and he's no match either. Didn't think it was him anyway. But that's the least of our problems.'

Harris sighed. 'Get to the point, Ally, I'm about to have a baby here.'

She nodded and played with a strand of her hair. 'We got a match on the print. It belonged to Michael Byrne.'

Harris laughed for a moment. 'Oh, that's fucking great. Wonderful. Did you hear that Fred, mate? Fantastic.'

'I got in contact with Kate Morcom and she confirmed that Byrne kept a flick knife in his car. The print must've been left on there from the last time he

238

handled it.'

Harris leaned his back on the wall, looking ready to laugh. 'He must have got out of the car with the knife, then the killer bashed his brains in and grabbed the knife. He made sure he didn't clean Byrne's prints off.'

Fred stood watching, his hands deep in his pockets, taking in all the information they were spilling out. 'The killer wanted us to know he killed Byrne too. He wanted us to have the weapon and the body.'

Harris looked at Fred. 'But why? Why those two? What connects them? Did they play golf together?'

Ally shook her head. 'I doubt Nelson and Byrne kept the same social circles. Sounds like we've got a vigilante going round.'

'Neither of them would be hard to find,' Harris said. 'Byrne in his club and Nelson's work place wouldn't be hard to locate. But why? Is it just revenge or what? Someone just decided to go after them because we weren't doing our job?'

'Maybe the post-mortem will tell us something,' Fred said.

Harris seemed to be thinking. 'Someone else might.'

'What do you mean?' Ally asked.

Harris looked at her, seeming to try and size her up. 'I'm going to see an old contact in the underworld tonight. He might be able to tell me about Byrne's murder.'

'Not if he was killed for no reason except someone's idea of justice,' Ally said. 'I wouldn't if I was you, not without talking to Jameson.'

Harris said, 'Forget him. I'm going to chat to my friend and see what he has to say. That's all.'

Ally shrugged. 'What do you think, Fred?'

Fred looked Harris over and saw the DCI was giving him a strange look, his eyes burning out to him.

'Harris will do what he's going to do. Let him get on with it. It might help.'

'Thank you,' Harris said. 'Thanks for your concern, Walker, but I'll be fine. These people trust me. Now, you better tell Beckley he's free to go.'

SIXTEEN

Later that day the entire team stood watching Dr Farmer, and a younger assistant, slicing up Andrew Nelson. South looked at the body and the several stab wounds that seemed to be collected around the right side of his body. Farmer, dressed in his green gown, his hands covered by latex and blood, lifted his vital organs from the corpse and gave them to the young assistant to weigh.

South looked at his colleagues and didn't see any real emotion, except maybe curiosity, their eyes carefully watching the procedure. He watched a lung being taken out, Farmer holding it up and taking it away.

Dr Farmer walked over to them, and stood next to the Perspex shield that kept them separated from the post-mortem room, and took the mask from his face. 'Nelson's attacker stabbed him fifteen times around the chest and stomach. He penetrated his lung too. Nelson would have seen his own blood gurgling out. Not nice. He would have survived at least five minutes after that. He was sitting down. And there were no defensive wounds, but he had rope marks on his wrists.'

'He was tied up,' Jameson said.

Farmer nodded. 'Yes. The assailant was right handed. Nelson died at least a couple of days before you found him.'

241

South looked upwards, his mind thinking back. 'That could be Saturday.'

Harris laughed. 'So, he didn't take the weekend off.'

'There were large amounts of cement dust in his lungs,' Farmer said. 'I'd estimate he was held captive somewhere with very little ventilation. In fact, his whole body and clothes were covered in the stuff, so he would have been held in a confined place.'

Jameson ran a hand through his hair. 'So the killer kept him tied up for all this time and then stabbed him, then dumps him in a skip for us to find. What was he doing? He killed Byrne outright, just beat his brains in. Why hesitate with Nelson?'

Ally stepped forward. 'Because Byrne was a known gangster. Most people knew he was up to no good. Maybe the killer decided he warranted his execution. But he couldn't be sure that Nelson killed Heather.'

South listened to her words, then heard rain starting to tap away at the glass ceiling above the autopsy room. 'So he waited for a confession.'

'Maybe he tortured him,' Harris said.

'No,' Farmer said and looked over at the body his assistant was cleaning up. 'There were no signs of any other violence apart from the stab wounds. He was well nourished too. The killer kept him fed and watered until he decided what to do with him.'

South was thinking of the knife the killer had taken from Byrne. It wasn't the only weapon the killer had taken. 'But what's Nelson's killer going to do with Byrne's gun?'

'If he has it at all,' Harris said and leaned on the partition, looking over the blue-skinned corpse. 'Look at Nelson here, he wasn't shot, although he got what was coming to him.'

Jameson grabbed Harris by the elbow and pulled him upright. 'I don't want to hear any of you saying anything like that when the press is around. Nelson is dead. He was murdered, just like Heather, so we have to deal with that. We have to find her killer and Nelson's and Byrne's.'

'Haven't we already found Heather's killer?' South pointed to Nelson's body.

Jameson looked at the cadaver as the pathologist covered it with a sheet. 'We still have to prove that. His kidnap made that difficult, but now, my friends, we can continue. Anyone have any idea about how Byrne and Nelson are connected?'

'Maybe they aren't,' Ally said. 'Maybe we've got some nutcase who decides he's going to do the world a favour. I don't think there is any connection between Byrne and Nelson. I've already looked into whether Nelson even went to any of Byrne's clubs and it's a negative. They just didn't move in the same circles. Nelson wasn't into drugs either, although he'd been in trouble for GBH. The usual drunken behaviour on a Saturday night, but that's about it. If he murdered Heather, then that's his first real serious crime.'

Harris puffed out his cheeks. 'If he murdered her? What's that supposed to mean?'

Ally turned towards him. 'I know you men reckon you've got this weird instinct for spotting the guilty party, but I think that's just wind.'

'So, Ally, you don't have women's intuition?' Harris laughed.

'No, actually I don't. I have to rely on my brain and the evidence. Yes, I know Nelson was a smart arse git, but I think that's just the way he was.'

Fred opened his mouth for a moment, his hands deep in his pockets.

Jameson stepped towards him. 'What were you going to say, Fred?'

'Just that it had to be Nelson who killed her. He's the only one who had a motive. Even his killer seemed sure of it.'

Jameson nodded. 'Well, like I said, we need to go over everything. We have to examine the forensic evidence from Heather and make a case against Nelson if we can, so we can close this. And we need to find where Nelson was being held. Forensic are sweeping through Beckley's place of work, so we should have some results from there. We'll also look into the possibility his friends or co-workers were involved and find where they store their equipment. We'll concentrate on the Enfield area for now. Anyone else got any ideas?'

Harris nodded. 'I was thinking about going and seeing Skouvakis tonight.'

Jameson turned to him sharply. 'When were you going to mention this? You thinking of going on your own?'

'I think that'll be best,' Harris said. 'He won't like it if we turn up in a gang. He'll talk to me on my own.'

Jameson looked from Harris to Fred. 'What about Fred? You both investigated him and Byrne together.'

'With all due respect to Fred, I don't think Skouvakis ever liked him.' Harris smiled at Fred.

'You're welcome to him,' Fred muttered.

Jameson sighed. 'OK. OK, Harris, just don't get in any trouble. See him and then call me to tell me what went on. See if he knows anything about the gun too. You lot better get on with the rest of the case.'

South watched his colleagues walk out of the room, but he stayed for a moment looking at sheet on the table, the shape of a stretched out human lying underneath it. He imagined Nelson tied up, sitting in a chair, then a knife going into his body several times. He tried to imagine the pain at first, then thought about whether Nelson deserved it. Did he kill Heather? Why was the killer so convinced he had, or was he just trying to cover his own tracks? There were so many unanswered questions; he was beginning to wonder if it would have an ending at all. The usual pattern of one person hating another and being so jealous it leads them to kill wasn't forming. South was beginning to believe the motive for both Byrne's and Nelson's murders were someone's sick sense of justice. He had another strange feeling. The killer had to know a lot about both men and both cases. The only thing he could see linking Byrne and Nelson was the fact that their team happened to be investigating both cases.

'I know what you're thinking,' Ally whispered as she appeared at his side.

'What?'

'Exactly what I am.' She raised an eyebrow.

'And that is?'

'That the only people who are interested in seeing justice in both the Nelson and Byrne murders are us. We could point the finger at Heather's family, but what've they got to do with Byrne, unless there was something they aren't telling us?'

'So?'

'So, is the killer among us or is he getting his information from us?'

'It can't be someone from Edmonton nick. I can't believe that. One of our own decided to start killing criminals? Why start with Byrne, a small-time gangster? I can understand Nelson. Seeing those pictures of Heather is enough to send any of us into a revenge-crazed rage. No, I don't believe it.'

'Well, whoever did it beat Michael Byrne to death and decided to take his knife and gun. Then a while later they kidnapped Nelson and kept him tied up for three days, then stabbed him to death with Byrne's knife. And they knew we'd find the print on the handle.'

South looked deep into her eyes. 'You think they want to be caught?'

'I think they just don't care. It didn't matter to them whether we find the body or the weapon. They're just in it to get revenge. I think they're keeping us dangling just long enough to finish what they started.'

Fred pointed his key fob towards his car and listened to it bleep, then turned towards his front door. He stopped as he heard a long screech of words coming from Tracey Boswell's home. He moved closer, crossing his own front window and standing against the wall of the house. He heard the mumbled shout of a man, growing louder with every rant. Fred moved away, but spun around again as something smashed. He hovered for a moment and looked about the empty street, seeing the sun going down and the red clouds wrapped around it. He listened to the shouting, then a sudden desperate scream. He imagined Tracey Boswell fending off her large and very angry husband, his builder's fists bashing her face. Whatever her husband had found out, Fred realised he had to put a stop to it.

He rang the doorbell, stood looking into the light of the hallway, waiting for a figure to come towards the glass. At last he saw the figure of a man coming to answer the door.

'Yes?' Mr Boswell growled. 'You're from next door,

aren't you?'

'That's right. I heard some shouting and screaming.'

Boswell looked back into the house. 'So? What's it got to do with you?'

Fred took out his ID. 'I'm also a policeman.'

'Good for you. What do you want me to do about it?' Boswell's body took up most of the doorframe.

'I'd like to see if Tracey is alright.'

Boswell eyed Fred for a moment, then moved backwards, leaving the hallway clear. 'Fine. Come on in. I wouldn't want to be accused of anything.'

Fred walked into the lounge and found Tracey standing in the middle of the room, her eyes wet with tears. 'Fred?' she said.

'I came to see if you're OK. I heard all the noise.' Fred watched Mr Boswell walk into the room and smelt the alcohol emanating from his pores.

Tracey tried to laugh it off, but it seemed to stick in her throat. 'I'm fine. It's nice of you to come round, but I'm fine. Just a bit of a row.'

'Now you can sod off, Fred.' Boswell smirked.

'Look, I'm here in my professional capacity, so if there is anything wrong, perhaps I can help.'

Mr Boswell huffed. 'Alright, Fred, I'll tell you what's wrong…'

'Terry, just shut up, please.' Tracey reached out an arm to her husband, but he jerked it off as he picked up a thick envelope from the coffee table.

'Look at this.' Terry shook the envelope in Fred's face. 'Seems my lovely wife had been up to her old tricks.'

'Shut up, Terry.' Tracey grabbed his elbow.

'You shut up.' Terry turned to Fred, the envelope clenched in his hand. 'There was over two grand in this envelope. Where did that come from?'

247

Fred looked at the brown envelope, then at Tracey. She looked away quickly. He recalled her entering his house, asking to see Martin. 'I'm sure that's none of my business, Mr Boswell.'

'It might be if you knew what this cow used to be.' Boswell turned to face his wife, his mouth fixed in an evil grin. 'Looks like she's back selling herself again. You stupid fucking cow.'

Fred stepped over to Tracey. 'Why don't you get some stuff together and I'll take you somewhere?'

Tracey looked at Terry, but he turned away. 'Alright, I'll be back in a minute.'

Fred nodded and walked back down the hall and out the front door. He waited out in the night air, then strolled to his car and reversed it until he sat outside Tracey's house. She hurried out of the front door carrying a small holdall, then jumped in beside him. She smiled, wiping tears from her eyes. 'Thanks. I'm sorry about all that. He gets weird when he's been drinking.'

Fred nodded, his hands running over the steering wheel as the engine hummed. 'Is it true, what he said?'

She looked out through the windscreen. 'He talks rubbish.'

'I'm not going to judge you, Tracey. Just tell me the truth.' He looked at her profile, seeing another tear roll down her face.

'Yes, it's true. That was a long time ago. It's the same old story. I was after money. Things were tight.'

'Martin gave you that money, didn't he?'

She looked down at her nails. 'It's just some money I've been saving up.'

'Don't lie to me. I know Martin gave it to you. He told me.'

She looked sharply at Fred. 'He told you?'

'No. But now I know. So what exactly was he paying you for?'

She was silent, looking down.

He faced her, moving round in his seat. 'Did you do something for my brother?'

She nodded slowly. 'So...are you going to arrest me for prostitution?'

'So that's what my brother was paying you for?'

She looked at him strangely for a moment. 'I don't know what to say.'

Fred placed a calming hand on hers. 'Did you have sex with Martin?'

'He paid me for sex, but...well, it didn't happen. I told him he didn't have to pay me, but he did anyway.'

'That's Martin.'

'He said...he said I'd be making you feel better.'

Fred turned to her. He didn't understand. Then he saw her eyes and recalled the way she looked when she left the hotel room that night.

SEVENTEEN

Harris parked a couple of streets away from the Ship Public House in Bow, then walked back towards it, looking over the decrepit exterior and the way it looked so lonely. The buildings that used to stand next to it had long since disappeared and now it stood as a solitary reminder of the old East London, the time when the local people used to horde into the pub and sing around the piano. Harris shook his head as he saw the mustard colour paint of the exterior that had been discoloured by all the passing traffic. The warm lighting glowing from inside looked inviting.

Only a few old men sat by the dark wood bar that stretched along the centre of the room. A man in his thirties with short spiky hair stood behind the bar, serving. Harris walked to the bar, ordered a lager and stood around looking for a familiar face. The pub didn't fit with the memory of the hard-faced club owner he'd dealt with three years ago. He pictured his face in all its strangely pale glory, and the way his grey hair was always oiled and slicked back. And the moustache, the neat brush of grey hair on his top lip.

'You're early, Tony.'

Harris turned around and faced Franco, who was smiling, holding a Guinness in his hand.

'Where's Mr Skouvakis?' Harris asked.

Franco turned and pointed to the far corner, right near the back of the pub. Harris could see the familiar shape of the man he'd met on several occasions, had shared several drinks with, but never really liked. He followed Franco to the booth where Skouvakis sat, then stood looking at the club owner and the muscle men who were sitting either side of him.

Skouvakis nursed a glass of red wine as he looked up, his pale skin very tight around his bony face. He smiled brightly. 'Good evening, Tony. You moved and you never let me know. That's rude. Sit down.'

Harris pulled out a seat and felt a draught coming from a door on his left. 'You look well.'

Skouvakis pointed to the door. 'I'm sorry about the breeze, but that door there leads to the toilets. This place is a real shithole I'm afraid, but soon it'll be refurbished and given a new name. Young people will come and dance and drink themselves stupid.'

Harris sipped his drink. 'Sounds great. What did you want to see me about?'

Skouvakis looked towards his two bodyguards. 'This man used to be so funny. What happened to you, Tony? Make me laugh.'

'I'll tell you a joke later. Is this about Michael?'

'That came as a shock. I really took it hard. We were very close as you know.'

'Hmm…look, you wanted to talk to me, so just get on with it.'

Skouvakis leaned forward, his grey-blue eyes staring into Harris. 'Have you forgotten about all the good times we've had? Is that it?'

Harris looked over at the two bodyguards.

Skouvakis followed his eyes. 'Franco, take these two to the bar. Get yourselves some drinks, boys.'

Harris watched them all amble away, then sat closer to Skouvakis. 'As I remember it, things didn't exactly end very rosey.'

'Business is like that sometimes. OK, let's forget about all that. Who killed Michael?'

'I don't know.' Harris picked up his lager.

'You don't have any clues?'

'See, that's the difficult part, Mr Skouvakis.'

'What happened to calling me Dennis?'

'Listen, we haven't turned up anything. We've had people interviewing his staff in his clubs and everyone else we can think of, but no one has given any plausible reason why he should have been killed. Of course, we both know he made a few enemies, but nothing serious. He ran your clubs. He was your front man, so I came to see if you know anything.'

Harris saw Skouvakis' moustache twitch for a moment, a drip of red wine hanging from it. 'Like you say, he was my front man. He ran my clubs and I paid him well. Anyone who might have gone after him, would have me on his back and he'd know it. If someone killed him, then they were angry and stupid.'

Harris nodded. 'Does the name Andrew Nelson mean anything to you?'

'Sounds familiar. Should I know the name?'

'He was the young lad who was suspected of murdering his ex-girlfriend. He vanished a little while back, but he's just turned up dead, dumped in a skip.'

'And what's this got to do with Michael?' Skouvakis sipped his wine.

'We found the murder weapon with his body. It was a knife and it had Michael's prints on it.'

Skouvakis nodded. 'He kept a knife in his car, I remember.'

'And did he keep a gun in his house? Because it's gone missing. We believe his killer has it.'

'Well, someone's been having some fun and games. I don't know Andrew Nelson, but maybe Michael did.

Maybe this Nelson killed Michael and then someone killed him. I don't know. This is your job.'

Harris drank his lager and looked around the pub for a moment. 'If someone's going round killing out of the pure joy of it, then they may have his gun. I just hope this didn't have anything to do with his business dealings.'

Skouvakis looked suspicious. 'You think they might come after me?'

'I don't know. We don't know what this is about. I'd watch your back if I was you.'

'Whatever happened to your friend? The other policeman.'

Harris looked up, a little surprised. 'You mean Fred?'

Skouvakis nodded enthusiastically. 'Yes, Fred. He was a strange man.'

'He's on his way out. He'll be out of the force by the end of the year, maybe sooner. He'll get his pension and that'll be that.'

'He nearly caused us a lot of trouble back then.'

'Nearly.' Harris sipped his lager, then felt an icy draught clench his back as a man entered the pub through the toilet door. 'This is an awful place.'

'Not for long. Soon there'll be music and dancing. Perhaps pole dancers.'

'So, do you still have massage parlours filled with young girls?'

Skouvakis grinned. 'I'm not sure if I should discuss that sort of thing with you any more. You're a DCI now, so that means you've got ambition.'

'True. It's probably a good job we don't mix socially any more.'

Skouvakis laughed. 'Circumstances have made it this way. I enjoyed our business arrangements the way they were. It's a shame. I still remember you and your people marching into my establishment, tearing the place apart. It hurt.'

'That's the way things had to be.' Harris finished his lager.

'Yes, that's right.' Skouvakis smiled as one of his friends brought him another glass of wine. 'You'll find out who murdered Michael, won't you? I want to make sure that this person isn't going to make more trouble for my business.'

'You have to tell me if you find out about anyone who might've had anything against Michael. That's the deal.'

Skouvakis lifted his drink as if to toast. 'Here's to that. To revenge.'

'To old times and better times.'

Skouvakis leaned closer. 'The old times were the better times.'

'Perhaps, but they ended badly.'

'But we survived. And we keep on surviving.'

Harris smiled politely. 'But I wonder for how long?'

Alone and tired, Mark South stepped into the White Hart in Southgate, a pub situated about two hundred yards from the tube station. The station itself looked like a large flying saucer had crashed landed in the middle of the town.

He walked into the compact pub and looked at the young barmaids and the customers huddled around the bar that ran down the centre of the place. He ordered a pint and grabbed a table by the window.

'Oi, Ally,' someone shouted as South looked up and saw Walker stepping in the door.

She waved at a young man with a shaved head who was sitting on the corner of the bar. 'I know you're pleased to see me, but keep it down.'

'You gonna nick me? Go on, nick me.' The young man stood up, smiling.

Walker was wearing a very dark red dress and heels, and looked very good. He jumped up to buy her a drink. 'What do you want?'

'Vodka and Diet Coke.' She placed her coat on the back of a chair then sat down.

South brought back their drinks. 'What is it with you women and your diet drinks?'

'Fat Coke means you'd be looking at a fat cow.'

'I can't imagine you being fat.'

'Hello tart.' A young woman, with shoulder length blonde, came over and gave their table a wipe. 'Haven't seen you in a while. You were supposed to call me. We all went out last night in Town. I was absolutely pissed.'

Ally laughed. 'Sorry been busy at work. Anyway, it only takes you two drinks and you're pissed.'

'True,' the woman said and shook her cloth at Ally. 'Give us a call next week or I'll slap you next time.'

'OK babe,' Ally said, as the young woman walked behind the bar.

'They certainly know you in here,' South said and leaned forward.

'This is my local. That was Sarah, a very good friend of mine. So, here we are.' Ally picked up her drink.

South nodded. 'You look good.'

She smiled, her cheeks reddening. 'I wonder how Tony is getting on. Someone should've gone with him.'

'Sounds like he's better off on his own. He knows what he's doing. Perhaps they'll tell him if Nelson had something to do with Byrne.'

'It doesn't seem likely does it? Nelson's just a little arse wipe bloke who did the dirty on his girlfriend. If anyone should've been mad it would've been Heather, not Nelson.'

South shrugged. He didn't want to keep talking about the job, but he knew Ally would only be satisfied when she'd talked it all through. 'Maybe she attacked him, and he grabbed her neck and squeezed and then suddenly she's dead.'

Ally shook her head. 'No, she was tied up before she died. She was held somewhere, then strangled. We need to talk to all of Nelson's friends. And the people he worked with. Someone must know what's going on.'

'Well, that's for tomorrow morning.' South took a gulp of his lager and listened as music started to play from the juke box. Robbie William's Rock DJ kicked in.

'I'm really starting to worry about Fred,' Ally said. She leaned over and pulled a paper bag out of her coat. She placed the bag in front of South, slightly pushing it towards him. 'I found all these packets of painkillers in his desk drawer.'

'What were you doing going through his desk?'

'I was looking for a statement. But look at them. That's a lot of painkillers.'

South looked into the bag and saw three boxes of painkillers. 'Well, he does seem to be in a lot of pain. He probably bought them in bulk in case he ever ran out.'

'You can't buy that many painkillers in one go anywhere. You'd have to go to different shops.'

'Because they're worried you might try and top yourself.' South's head sprung up. 'Is that what you're thinking? You think Fred's going to do himself in?'

Ally sighed deeply. 'I don't know. But look at them all. It's not right, is it? The receipts say he bought them all on the same day. That's not a good sign in my book.'

'Maybe they're for his brother. He's not well.' South reached in and pulled out the receipts, then stuffed them back in again.

'His brother has a rare form of MS, so any pain he's in isn't going to be helped by those pills. He has to get prescribed medication from his doctor.'

South put down the bag, then looked up into Ally's eyes. 'So, what do you want to do about it?'

Ally reached out and patted the bag. 'For starters, I think you should make these disappear, just in case. But try and talk to him. Find out how he's feeling.'

'I'm not a counsellor. Anyway, I thought he was seeing a therapist. She's the one he should be talking to.'

'I know, but he probably resents the fact that the force has made him see her. I bet he didn't really tell her how he felt. Detectives have to keep their feelings tucked away, so we become very good at it. The therapist probably only scratched the surface. I know he's not happy and he's obviously not well. His brother's dying and he's never really ever got over his mum's death. Inside, he's just a big ball of hurt.'

South sighed. He'd been hoping to get Ally a little drunk, but he hadn't been planning on anything sexual, just to get to know each other better. He was aware of the proverb that recommends not shitting on your own doorstep, but he also realised you have to grasp romance wherever you find it. When you're a copper, he thought, you only ever try and pull the people you're working with or the ones you're trying to nick. And when you're spending most of your time working the streets of King's Cross, that's not really a good philosophy. 'I'll talk to him.'

'Good. Now, I'll get us some more drinks and you can tell me about your life before you came back to

257

London.' She smiled and walked to the bar. She leaned over the bar ordering her drinks, then turned her head and smiled again at South.

Skouvakis was on his second bottle of wine. It was not the cheap stuff from the supermarkets, but the good and expensive bottles he'd shipped in from Europe. He took a mouthful of wine and swirled it in his mouth, taking in the fruity and oak flavour. He swallowed, then looked up and saw Franco standing by his table. A cigarette hung from his mouth, his Zippo lighter inches away from the end of it.

'You want me to take you home?' Franco asked as he lit his cigarette.

Skouvakis picked up his glass of wine. 'Not yet. I have to piss.'

Franco pulled out a stool. 'Can I sit down?'

Skouvakis nodded.

Franco sucked on his cigarette, something obviously on his mind. 'Tony doesn't want anything to do with us any more.'

Skouvakis placed his glass on the table. 'Of course not. Why would he? He's got a good thing going now. He thinks of himself as straight. He's moved to a better neighbourhood too. Before he used to live among the people he was arresting. He wants to be clean now. He wants to be better than us.'

'He's not…'

'No, he's not better than us. He used to be one of us and he's never forgotten that. He took my money and thanked me for it. Not even all the soap in the world could get him clean. He's kidding himself. It didn't matter to him that those girls working for me had no choice in it. He learnt to look the other way because it suited him.'

Franco tapped his cigarette into an ashtray. 'Will he tell you who killed Michael?'

'They don't know. But someone else was killed with Michael's knife. And someone has Michael's gun. I'm concerned this has to do with all of us. We need to find out who killed Michael and end it. Now I really have to piss.'

Skouvakis raised himself, feeling a dull ache in his back. He saw Franco reach out for him, but waved him away and carried on towards the toilet. The cold from the street grasped his body as he pushed through the door, then the smell of bleach and stale piss invaded his nostrils as he walked into the small lavatory. He stood facing the wall, his trousers undone, hovering himself over the long metal trough. He smiled a little and relaxed, feeling the relief spread across his body as he emptied out his bladder. He knew he'd feel the same sort of relief when he found the person who'd murdered his friend and, in consequence, upset his business dealings. Michael was a good club manager, a man clean enough to make everything seem above board. Now he was gone and there were few men he could trust.

Again, the cold from the street outside rushed towards the toilet. He heard the door behind him open slowly as he shook himself over the trough. He zipped himself up and prepared to turn and pass another customer.

He faced the figure and saw burning eyes looking out through the balaclava. 'What do you thing you're doing?'

A gun came out from the man's jacket and he pointed it at Skouvakis. The club owner looked at it, then up at the masked man. 'Is that supposed to scare me? Fuck off out of my pub.'

Two shots echoed around the space. Skouvakis stumbled back to the urinal, his eyes watching the man stepping sideways out of the room. He grasped at his wounds, looking down at the blood on his hands, slipping down to the floor, feeling the cold wet floor bite at his backside. He heard the street door shut as loud voices started shouting inside the pub. He saw Franco entering the toilet, his face twisting with horror. He came nearer, but Skouvakis felt everything growing darker.

EIGHTEEN

Wednesday, 28th April 2004

North Middlesex Hospital sits along Silver Street in several large and bulky connected buildings. A small tower block is central to everything around it, including the outpatients' department that slivers out from under its belly. This was where Fred was born and where he will probably die. It was inevitable.

After a nurse told him to urinate into a bottle and weighed him, he was taken to some chairs in a corridor where he waited. He smiled politely to the mostly black nurses who passed by. He could see they were busy and didn't even have time for pleasantries. He would have been the same if he'd been at work, but now he was just another sick person being churned into the system. He watched them hurry along the corridor holding a file or pushing a trolley.

An Asian doctor appeared, walking delicately as he adjusted his pink tie a little. The dark suit was strained around at his large stomach. Fred looked up into the dark eyes that returned his stare. No smile, just a professional examination and nod. 'Come in please.'

Fred stepped into the large room. It was part of the old hospital, where the rooms were covered in cracks and the paint and furniture were from a long time ago. He looked down at the dark green tiled floor and the lime green walls. A screen sat in the middle of the room enclosed around an examination table. Fred turned and watched the doctor collapse into a chair by a large metal desk that had been painted to look like dark wood. The doctor pointed to a chair beside him. 'Sit down.'

Fred sat and listened to a shovel being scrapped along pavement outside the window as the doctor tried to stretch out his shirt collars a little, his dark skin hanging over them. He opened the file on his desk and looked through it for a few minutes, nodding to himself, looking at Fred. 'How old are you?'

'Forty Five.' Fred looked back over to the window.

'Still quite young,' the doctor said and looked at the file. 'And you are having a lot of pain?'

'Yes. Quite a lot of pain. In my backside.'

'Have you felt the need to pass water a lot more lately?' The doctor pointed his dark eyes at Fred.

'Quite a lot.'

'And do you have any blood in your faeces?'

'A little.'

The doctor nodded, opened another page in the file, then shut it and turned to Fred. 'Although you are below the age where we would consider you a risk of any prostate problems, I feel we should look into it. You understand?'

Fred nodded.

The doctor smiled. 'I will send you for a few tests. A blood test and a prostate examination. This will tell us a little more about the situation. You understand?'

'OK.'

The doctor started to fill out a couple of forms while Fred sat and looked about the room, listening to the pen as it scraped along the sheet of paper. He turned back to face the doctor and saw that he was holding the sheets of paper out to him. 'Give these to the nurse and she'll tell you where to go.'

'Thank you.' Fred took the papers and left the room.

South was the first to enter the interview room at Bow Police Station. Jameson followed him, shutting the door hard and facing Tony Harris who was nursing a cup of tea. Harris watched them and said nothing, just looked down again, his shoulders hunched over.

Jameson leaned over the desk as South seated himself opposite Harris. 'What the fuck happened, Tony?'

Harris sipped his tea. 'Skouvakis was shot and killed. What do you want me to say?'

'And where the fuck was you?' Jameson grabbed a chair and slumped into it. 'I mean, you were having a drink with him not a few minutes before he was killed.'

Harris nodded, then looked at both South and Jameson. 'I know. I left and got half a mile away from the pub when I saw the squad cars screaming back from where I had come. I called in to find out what had happened and then raced back to the pub. I've been here all night. They've been asking me some real stupid questions.'

Jameson laughed without humour. 'I'm not bleeding surprised, you pratt. They must be laughing themselves stupid. Edmonton has an officer on the scene just before Skouvakis is done in. It's bleeding comical.'

Harris nodded. 'I went back to the pub and the barman's being interviewed outside, telling the local coppers everything. I walk up and he got a look at my boat race and said, "He was there!". Then I'm in the nick answering all these bloody question. I feel a right idiot.'

Jameson laughed again. 'Someone's taking the piss.'

South pulled his chair closer. 'So, someone waited 'til you left, then shot him? Did they walk right into the pub? Did anyone see anything?'

Harris shook his head. 'No, apparently Skouvakis was taking a piss. There was a door that leads from the street right into the pub toilet, that's why it's so bleeding cold in the place. The shooter must have walked straight in there and pulled the trigger.'

South nodded. 'And you left the pub and was driving home?'

Harris looked at him suspiciously. 'That's what I said, wasn't it? Why, what are you getting at?'

South sat back a little. 'Nothing. Just trying to get a picture of the scene. It just seems like whoever killed him was pretty well prepared for it. They knew where he was going to be that night and was just waiting for him to drop his pants.'

Jameson looked at South. 'So, you're saying he knew Harris was meeting him? Then it could've been one of his own people. Someone trying to get up the ladder?'

South shrugged. 'What about the gun he used? What's the chances that it's the gun taken from Byrne's house?'

'Well, we haven't any way of knowing. We don't know anything about Byrne's gun, so we can't do a ballistics test or anything.' Jameson rubbed his eyes.

'Convenient for the killer,' South said. 'This is too much of a coincidence to not be anything to do with Byrne's murder. We don't know exactly why the killer went after Byrne and Nelson, but it won't stop us finding him.'

Harris put down his tea and shook his head, his eyes staring out to South. 'Excuse me, Mark, but you might not have noticed, but we've just about messed up the investigation so fucking far. We've managed to find exactly fuck all people who can tell us anyone who might have it in for Byrne, and absolutely sod all link between him and Nelson. If you ask me, this fucking bastard has it in for us. He's in it to make us look stupid, so we should start looking for people who we've put away.'

Jameson looked across at Harris for a few moments as his fat hand tapped the surface of the desk. 'He could be right. Byrne died a few days back and the killer took his knife, then kills our only suspect in the Heather case. Why? Maybe just to fuck it all up. He even left Byrne's knife with the body, just to have a good laugh at us. Then this. He waits until now to kill Skouvakis, probably with Byrne's gun. He's laughing at us, that's the only reason.'

South leaned over the desk and put his face in his hands. He soaked in the darkness of his hands, then allowed his palms to come into focus. He wished he could offer another suggestion, but what Jameson had said so far made sense to him. The killer of all three of the victims was somewhere having a laugh, not worrying if he got caught or not, because it was all part of some game. 'If he's just trying to fuck up everything for us, then that's the motive. For some reason he must hate us. If we've got motive, then we can get him. He would've left a trail. There'll be a link from us to him.'

Jameson groaned as he pulled himself out of his chair. 'Well, we've got uniforms questioning the passing traffic and the locals. We might get a description of a car or something. He might have dropped something. The bins around that area are being searched in case he dropped the gun in there. I wouldn't want to hold on to it, would you?'

South looked up and saw the raised eyebrows of Jameson. 'Depends. He might not've finished with it yet.'

Fred was looking through a battered copy of People's Friend magazine when a nurse called his name. He looked over the faces of the men waiting beside him in the small room lined with padded seats before he got up and followed the Indian nurse along the corridor. She told him to enter a cubicle and undress. He saw the green gown he was supposed to put on and sighed. He slowly undressed and slipped on the gown, listening to two nurses talking. The nurse returned and directed him to the next room where a bed was positioned next to a window. He was told to sit on the bed, so he climbed up and looked down at his puffy white legs and the faint yellow hair scattered over them. He tried to pull the gown down over his knees and felt like a girl on a night out wearing a short skirt.

'Hello.' A middle-aged doctor, with a thin line of silver hair across his scalp, stood in the doorway. 'We'll need the machine for this.'

A nurse appeared and passed him a file. 'I'll get the scope.'

The doctor looked at Fred for a moment as he flipped open the file. He nodded and tapped his lips with his forefinger. 'Mmmm…right. OK, Fred, we're going to examine your prostate using a probe, which will allow me to view my progress on a screen. I'll probably ask my colleague in to take a look, just for a second opinion. You might find it slightly uncomfortable. Please lie down on the bed, facing the window.'

Fred moved his body across the bed, hearing the gown grind against the long paper sheet that he was supposed to lie on. He tried to get comfortable, pulling himself onto his arm and felt a slight breeze around his backside. Oily wheels crossed the floor behind him and he guessed the machine had arrived. He heard latex gloves being stretched and put on, then a hand pushing up his gown, baring his backside to whoever might enter the room. This was no position for a policeman to find himself in, he thought, and wanted to laugh before wanting to cry. He stopped and gritted his teeth as he felt a finger exploring his rear, putting pressure on his anus.

The machine hummed to life as the finger went away for a second.

'OK, I'm going to start inserting the probe now. Try and relax the best you can.'

Fred gripped the bed and felt his stomach move up to his chest, desperately trying to manoeuvre itself away from the object that might invade its world any second. It was worse than the finger, and slower, the pressure pushing him apart, making the invasion increasingly lacking in dignity. He nearly bit down on the plastic bed as the probe pushed through his anus and entered the unknown. He listened to the sound of the machine, trying to keep still and ignore the pain.

'Could you keep still please?' the Doctor asked.

After a few minutes of probing, Fred heard the steps of another person entering the room. A cough echoed around the room, then there were lowered voices. Fred wanted to turn and see who had joined in the examination, but didn't move. He closed his eyes again.

'This is it, Mr Fairservice,' the original doctor said, pulling the probe out a little.

'How are you feeling, Mr Fairservice?' a foreign voice asked.

'Not too bad, given the circumstances,' Fred said,

lowering his head to his chest.

'No, of course,' the other doctor said. 'Let me have a look.'

'Have a look here and see what you think,' the first doctor said.

Fred gritted his teeth again.

'It's a bit tight, so I think you better inflate it,' the foreign doctor said. 'This may be a little uncomfortable.'

Fred felt his backside stretching, a burning sensation exploding from his anus as he gripped the bed. Whatever they are doing, he thought, they should do it quicker.

'OK, Fred,' the original doctor said, pulling out the probe. 'You can get dressed now.'

South sat in the car after turning off the engine. Ally sat beside him reading a piece of paper. He looked out through the windscreen at the large yellow sign that had been placed on the corner where Michael Byrne was beaten to death. The sign read:

METROPOLITAN POLICE
WE ARE APPEALING FOR WITNESSES
CAN YOU HELP US?
MURDER ON Saturday 24th April 2004 AT ABOUT 3:30am.
In strictest confidence please phone 020 8883 0120

'Why are we sitting here then?' Ally asked and put the sheet of paper down on her lap.

'Just needed to think for a minute.' South turned to her. 'He kills Byrne and dumps him in the river for us to find at a later date. He also took his knife and uses it to stab Andrew Nelson to death. At some point he entered Byrne's house and ransacks his office and takes his gun.'

'Which he kills Skouvakis with.'

South nodded. 'Probably.'

'Not probably. It has to be.'

'It could've been a professional hit. A rival could be after getting Skouvakis out of the way.'

Ally folded the piece of paper. 'You make Skouvakis out to be this big criminal mastermind, but he's not. Yes, he's got some rackets going and deals drugs, but he's not the mafia.'

South tapped his fingers on the steering wheel. 'Could be Russian mafia. I looked into the case they were trying to build against him a few years back. There were rumours about girls being smuggled in and used as prostitutes. When they were asking around his name kept coming up.'

'But nothing was proved.'

'Some Eastern European girls were found working at his place, but they weren't illegal. They were masseurs, supposedly. Harris and Fred were investigating him.'

'That's right. And they couldn't get anything on him.'

South thought back to his private conversation with Fred after his therapy session. It seemed like weeks ago now and he felt as if he'd been back in London years. 'Fred told me that a girl contacted them. She told them she'd been kidnapped and brought over from the Ukraine. She said she was being forced to sleep with men.'

Ally eyed South as she turned around in her seat. 'What girl? They never said anything about a girl.'

'They couldn't. The girl insisted on going back to work so she could help her friends get out too. Harris persuaded Fred to let her, but they never saw her again.'

'She just disappeared?'

'No. Do you remember a young girl being found in

269

the Thames, near Hounslow?' South stared into Ally's eyes, willing her to remember.

She nodded. 'That was her? She was chopped up, wasn't she?'

'Yeah, they cut off her arms and legs to keep her from being identified. But Harris and Fred knew who she was.'

Ally let out a gasp. 'I can't believe those two let her go back to that. The fucking bastards.'

'They had a chance to get something on Skouvakis. They could've saved a few more girls who were even younger. I would've done the same.'

'So, why're you telling me this now? You think this had something to do with Skouvakis being killed?'

South shrugged. 'I don't know. It just keeps coming back to me. Fred told me it all after Byrne turned up in the river. But now Skouvakis is dead... I can't stop thinking it has something to do with this.'

'That was a few years ago. You think someone just decided to kill Byrne and Skouvakis now, after all this time? Why?'

'Maybe the opportunity came up.'

'And who?'

'Maybe she's got family. Maybe a father who thought we didn't do a good enough job finding his daughter's murderer. After all, they never did find her killer. But Skouvakis must've been involved. Perhaps someone who knew he was involved is after revenge.'

'But it doesn't fit with Andrew Nelson.' Ally raised her eyebrows.

He nodded. 'I know. That's the problem.'

'Unless this person thought there was a connection. Anyway, we're supposed to be going over to Nelson's work, remember? Like Jameson said, we have to go over this again and again. Also, a colleague of Nelson

270

has been away on holiday for the last two weeks. Chris Ray. Let's go and find out if he can shed some light on Heather's murder.'

South started the engine. 'Yeah, the least we can do is resolve her murder. That's something we might actually do right.'

NINETEEN

Fred walked into the office and saw the doctor properly for the first time. He had balding silver hair and a long face. Fred sat down as he was directed. The room was larger, with cream coloured walls and windows looking onto some trees and a small patch of grass surrounded by parked cars. It was also closer to the main road and the rumble of traffic vibrated through the floor.

The doctor played with an expensive looking pen for a moment, his dark eyes glancing over a sheet of paper lying on top of Fred's medical notes. The doctor sat up and folded his arms. 'The prostate examination has given me a little cause for concern. You had a blood test this morning, is that right?'

Fred nodded. 'Yes.'

'And a urine sample?'

'Yes.'

He nodded, his eyes looking over at his computer for a moment. 'The results of those tests won't come back yet, but we should press on. You understand what the prostate does?'

Fred raised his shoulders for a moment, unsure where to began. 'I think so.'

'It helps to produce semen and it lies under the bladder. With age the prostate enlarges and this causes problems with passing water. This usually becomes a problem in later years, usually after the age of fifty.

You see?'

Fred sat up a little. He felt his backside start to twinge with pain as if it had heard the doctor's words. 'Yes.'

'The examination of your prostate showed an enlargement of the prostate and possibly a tumour.' The doctor sat up, not taking his eyes off Fred. 'This could be benign or malignant. Of course, at this stage, we can't be completely sure of anything. I'll send you for some X-rays, which you can have today. But I will need you to come in after I get those back to have part of the tumour removed for a biopsy. OK?'

Fred nodded. He took the words in, hearing the doctor's well-spoken voice and then sat there wondering if they were missing him at the station. He looked at the doctor and noticed he was looking at him blankly, perhaps waiting for him to react.

'I wouldn't worry at this point,' the doctor said, and started scribbling something on a slip of paper.

'I'll try not to.' Fred took the piece of paper, read the word X-ray, nodded and left the room.

South barged through the large glass door, narrowly missing a man carrying a large cardboard box out of the BG Furniture store. He stopped as Ally walked past him, his eyes scanning over the huge shop floor, watching the customers trawling the long aisles that seem to stretch miles back.

'I bought my furniture from BG,' Ally said.

'From here?' South began walking again, passing by the tills, all manned by middle-aged women or teenage girls.

'No, I don't come to Loughton to do my shopping, there's one along the North Circular,' Ally said, then pointed to a man in a dark blue suit. 'He looks like he could help us.'

South took out his ID. The man screwed up his face. 'Do you want to ask me some questions or do you need some furniture for your nick?'

'Very funny…' South looked at the man's name badge. 'Eddie? We want to talk to Christopher Ray. Where is he?'

Eddie rolled his eyes and beckoned them to follow him as he stepped towards a phone on the nearby wall. He picked up the receiver and pressed a button. South and Ally stood by, listening to Eddie's request for Chris Ray to come to the tills echoing around the whole building. 'He'll be here in a minute.'

'Anywhere we can talk to him in private, Eddie?' South asked.

'See that office?' Eddie pointed to small office to the side of the tills. 'In there.'

Chris Ray stood outside the glass door of the office for a moment, looking back to where he'd come from, seemingly unsure of where to go. South watched him, smiling to himself, looking over Ray's stocky frame, dark spiky hair and pointy nose. He jumped up after a second and opened the glass door. 'Chris?'

Chris Ray creased up his nose and nodded. 'Yeah? Why?'

South guided him into the office. Ray's feet scraped along the carpet in his worn grey trainers that must have been white once. 'What's happened, man? Who're yous guys?'

Ally sat behind the desk and showed Ray her ID. 'Sit down, Chris.'

'I ain't done nothing, innit?' Chris sat down, not taking his eyes off Walker.

'I hope not Chris,' Ally said. 'You've just come off holiday I hear.'

'Yeah. Tenerife. What of it?'

'Nice tan,' South said. 'Tell us about Andrew Nelson.'

'What you want me to say, man? He's fuckin' dead. You know that, don't yous?' Chris Ray reached into his pocket and took out a pack of cigarettes.

'I don't think you're allowed to smoke in here, Chris.' South pointed to the no smoking sign.

'Who gives a toss?' He lit up and seemed to relax. 'He was me mate, like.'

'What about Heather?' Ally asked and folded her arms.

Chris laughed. 'Heather? Yeah, I suppose. I didn't spend that much time with the lady, but yeah, she was OK. I had my own business to see to.'

'Really?' Ally said and looked at South.

'Fuck yeah. Me and Andy did some gigs. We DJ and shit. We had some well good times.'

'What did you think when Heather went missing?' South asked.

Ray shrugged. 'I didn't think nothin'. She was crazy sometimes. She was always on his back, man. I couldn't have handled that, know what I mean?'

'What about when she was murdered?' Ally asked.

He shrugged again. 'I didn't think Andy did it. No way was he going to do her in. No way. He had another girl. Why would he kill her? You tell me that.'

South rubbed his hands together. 'Well, she's dead and he was the only suspect, Chris.'

'Yeah? Well, who the fuck killed Andy, innit? They probably did Heather too. Why aren't you sorting that out?'

'Why do you think we're here?' South raised his eyebrows. 'Now, Chris, is there anything you can tell us about your friends, Andy or Heather? Like the last time you saw Heather?'

275

Chris Ray took a deep lungful of smoke. 'I can't remember when I last saw her, man. She worked over Enfield Town and I sometimes would see her talking to his old man.'

'Andrew's father?' South asked.

Chris nodded. 'Yeah, he has a flower stall near the shopping centre. I've driven through and she's there talking to him. I think I saw her there just before I went away.'

South raised his eyebrows at Ally. 'That's interesting. Were they close? Did they get on especially well?'

'How the fuck should I know, innit? Talk to his old man.'

Ally got up. 'We did, but he never mentioned seeing her at his stall. You sure about that?'

Chris laughed for a moment, smoke bellowing from his mouth. 'Oh come on, why would I lie? I saw her. Talk to him. Talk to Jon, man.'

Ally stepped closer to him, bending towards him a little. 'We intend to, Christopher.'

Fred stepped through a door marked Emergency Exit and stood breathing in the air. Across from him sat the car park, packed as usual. He took out his phone and turned it on. Immediately it told him that he had three missed calls: one from Jameson, one from South and another from a number he didn't recognise. He phoned the last number back, ducked under the bus shelter, and stood next to a young couple in an embrace.

'The Williams Residential Care Home, can I help you?' a woman's posh voice said.

'This is Detective Inspector Fred Fairservice. You called me a little while back.'

The woman seemed to hesitate for a moment before

letting out a sigh of recognition. 'Yes, that's right. Some of your people were here a little while ago. One of our residents sadly died and someone requested a list of visitors.'

'That sounds about right.' Fred started heading across the road towards his car. 'We need to go through the list and ask them a few questions.'

There was an unimpressed sigh on the other end. 'Well, I'd really rather you came to see me before I give out a list of my clients. It's a matter of privacy.'

'I understand that.' Fred hated it when well-spoken managers started getting all above themselves, forgetting about anyone who might have been hurt or killed. He felt like telling her to send the list anyway or he'll come down there and feed the phone to her. And not through her mouth. He took a deep breath as he reached his car. 'But you have to understand that this is a criminal investigation.'

'If you want the list, come by here this afternoon. I have some time free.' The phone clicked and Fred stood with his mobile to his ear and no one to talk to. He put his phone away as he saw an elderly gentleman coming down his garden path. He recognised the look in the old man's eyes as he stood at the end of his garden, huffing and puffing. 'You're blocking my drive. I can't get out.'

Fred looked and saw the back of his car was slightly blocking his drive. He took out his ID. 'Sorry. Official police business.'

'I don't bloody care. What if I had to get out in an emergency?'

Fred slid into his car and started the engine. He rolled down his window and watched the man getting closer.

'What if my wife was ill?'

'There's a hospital around the corner.' Fred smiled.

'Very bloody funny. What's your name? I want to make a complaint.'

'Detective Inspector Fred Fairservice. Call Edmonton Police station. Now bugger off.'

Fred drove off, feeling the pain in his backside stabbing at him. He gripped the wheel and nearly hit the brake as a raging pain seemed to spear into his spine. He pulled the car over after darting a glance in his rearview mirror. He swallowed a couple of pills, but knew the pain would be intense before they kicked in. If they kicked in. He bent his head down and tapped his forehead on the steering wheel, trying to use pure will power to drive the pain way, and felt a tear travelling down his face.

They parked by the market and walked towards the shopping centre. Ally was ahead of South and he spent the short stroll looking her over and generally desiring her. After the night in the pub, they had gone their separate ways, him drifting off back to his sister's and her...well, doing whatever it was she did. He'd gone home and imagined her slipping off her clothes and settling into bed.

'I can see his stall.' Ally pointed to the entrance to the shopping centre. South could just about make out the corner of his barrow and a bush of brightly coloured flowers. In a few seconds, they turned the corner and saw a tall man in a thick sheepskin coat with a money bag around his waist. South noticed that he had the same sort of hair as Nelson, fair and a little wavy. His face was red in the cheeks and his eyes startlingly blue. Nelson served an old woman and then turned to face South and Ally. 'Fresh roses for the lady?' Nelson asked, smiling.

'You're a smooth one.' Ally showed her ID.

Jon Nelson put some change away in his bum bag and turned to rearrange his flower stall. 'Ain't you supposed to be busy finding my son's killer?'

South stepped forward, making sure Jon Nelson got a good look at him. 'Believe it or not, Mr Nelson, but we are in the process of finding his killer. But let's not forget your son's girlfriend, Heather.'

He nodded and folded his arms, his eyes seeming to look across the street. 'Heather. Yeah, she was nice.'

'When was the last time you saw her?' Ally asked.

Nelson frowned and rubbed his cheek. 'Can't really say. Things weren't good between Andy and her, so I left them well alone.'

Ally ran her hand over a bunch of pink carnations. 'So you can't remember a particular time before she went missing?'

He shrugged. 'Not really. Sorry.'

South huffed. 'She didn't ever visit you here? Didn't come by for a chat, say?'

Nelson looked down. 'Might have come by here sometimes. She was a friendly girl.'

'She worked in the solicitors down the street,' Ally said.

He nodded. 'That's right. Yeah, she did pop by. But I can't remember when I last saw her.'

Ally walked over to the cart and peered beyond the flowers at something. South watched her, then turned back to Jon Nelson and said, 'We have a witness who said she came by here the day before she went missing.'

'She might've. I don't really remember.' Nelson dipped a hand into his money bag.

Walker came back around to face Nelson and held up some thick string for him to see. 'Do you mind if we take some of this?'

'Why? What do you want it for?' Nelson's eyes were fixed on the string.

'Heather was tied up with some string like this. Whoever killed her might have got it the same place as you. It may help.' Ally smiled.

South placed a hand on Jon Nelson's shoulder. 'Come with us back to the station and we can talk about this string.'

A black nurse directed Fred along the highly polished floor and into Mrs Nadine Wainwright's office. Mrs Wainwright looked up, her sagging and tanned skin hanging loose from her jowls. He recognised her hairstyle from any eighties photograph of Margaret Thatcher. She smiled politely as she put down her pen and sat up straight. 'Detective Inspector Fairservice?'

'That's correct.' He stepped in further and looked about the large square room with its mahogany furniture and John Constable style paintings on the walls. He figured she must have visited every antique shop in Enfield to get the right official look for her office. She sat proud like her furniture and looked Fred over. She didn't seem impressed. 'I'd like to see some identification, please.'

Fred smiled politely as he showed her his ID.

She nodded. 'Thank you. This list you wanted... please, take a seat.'

He pulled up a chair and watched her as she examined a sheet of paper. She put on a pair of ornate glasses and said, 'I'm sure the sons and daughters of my residents don't want their names bandied about.'

'Well, with all respect, I'm sure they want us to succeed in finding the person who broke in here that night.'

She looked up sharply. 'Broke in? Who broke in?'

'The person who broke into the old gentleman's room. You know, the one who put spiders in with his dentures.' He sighed.

Wainwright looked at him as if he'd just passed wind. 'It was a prank, surely? I don't think any of this warrants a police investigation.'

'Well, we do. Think about the safety of your elderly residents.'

'They are perfectly safe.' She removed her glasses.

'All we need is the list and all this will be over. And there'll be no need for us to phone your clients and tell them that their parents are in danger here.' Fred sat back a little.

Wainright looked at him carefully, then folded the piece of paper and slid it across the desk. 'You win. I want that list back though.'

Fred nodded as he took the piece of paper. He slipped it inside his jacket and got up. 'Thank you for seeing me.'

Fred stepped out the door and stood there for a moment, breathing deeply, imagining her still inside writing away. She was just another stuck up manager who couldn't give a toss about him or the job he had to do. Perhaps she did care about the people she looked after, but to him it sounded like she cared more about her reputation and the sons and daughters who palm their sick parents off onto her care home.

He thought about his mother and the day he took her to the home. He didn't like doing it and there hadn't been a day since he hadn't thought about the way she looked each time he visited her. She got skinnier and her eyes more dull, until he couldn't stand to see her like that. It was lucky she didn't know what was going on around her much of the time. Her mind had long since crumbled, melted away as she sat in the home, peering at the television with a slight dismal look on her face.

Fred started moving again, then stopped by a window that allowed him to spy into the day room. The residents were sat in there, their blankets covering their legs as they stared up at the television. Two women sat talking to each other, one of them constantly knitting, her eyes never peering down at what her hands were doing. That's why so many grandchildren end up with oversized jumpers, he thought.

He was about to move on when he saw a shelve of books sitting on the right of the room. Most of them were battered and worn. He opened the door and walked in, the old people in the room barely noticing, the roar of the television drowning anything else out. He could barely hear the knitting, the soothing sound of the needles tapping together in a constant rhythm.

He reached the books and ran a hand over them, noting most were yellowed-paperbacks with a few hardbacks thrown in. He took a book out, flipped through the pages and then shoved it back. Then he stopped as he saw a thick hardback book with a plain brown leather cover. He pulled it out a little and saw the words 'The Complete works of William Shakespeare'. He pulled it out.

'After something to read, dear?'

Fred looked over to a chair a few feet away and saw a tiny woman smiling at him. Her hair looked suspiciously dark brown and her small face was pink and wrinkled. 'Yes, I was looking at this book.'

'Aren't you a bit young to be in here or are you just visiting?' Her eyes opened wider and so did her smile.

'I'm a policeman. My name's Fred.'

'Nice to meet you, Fred. I'd just take it with you if I was you. Most of them are too blind to read anyway, love.'

'Well, don't tell anyone then.' He closed the book and smiled as he walked from the room.

South was buzzing as he walked into the incident room and heard the chatting voices of the awaiting uniforms. He spotted Harris in the far corner, standing solemnly with a mug of something hot in his hand. He could see that Harris' usual bright and chirpy manner had deserted him. He wondered how many digs he'd got that morning as he travelled around the station, trying to avoid the amused eyes of his fellow cops. Jameson stepped out of his office and nodded when he saw South enter. South was surprised by the fat man's next move. He saw the large thumb appear from his fist, giving him a big thumbs up.

Ally sat by the big whiteboard with a spare seat beside her for South. He sat down and Ally gripped his shoulder as she said, 'This is going to be a good day.'

Jameson slapped his hands together, gaining the silence of the room. 'Right people, we haven't got much time, so let's get down to business. Things are looking up for once. This morning we were looking like a right laughing stock, but this afternoon, thanks to DS Ally Walker and DI Mark South, we've had a breakthrough.'

Jameson bent down and picked up the four evidence bags and held two in each hand at shoulder level. In each bag sat a thick piece of string. 'Take a good look. We've got a warrant to search the home of Jon Nelson, Andrew Nelson's father. Looks like he might have had a lot more to do with Heather Beckley than any of us realised. Now, search his house from top to bottom. Some of you will be looking over his lock-up, so don't

283

leave any area unexamined. We're looking for string like this. This string was used to tie Heather up. We need the rest of this string. Now bugger off. Harris has got the address. Go on, go!'

Jameson placed the evidence bags back on a nearby seat and beckoned Ally and South over. He smiled slightly, bending towards South. 'Where's Jon Nelson?'

'In room 2, and his solicitor has just arrived,' South said.

Jameson nodded. 'Right. Have you read him his rights, because we don't want any fuck ups at this stage?'

'Yes, It's all done,' Ally said. 'He's down there sweating.'

Jameson nodded. 'Right then. Go and get the truth out of the bastard.'

'Are you going to charge my client?' the slim solicitor said as South sat down. A beam of sunlight made a slanted yellow square on the desk. South looked at it for a moment, savouring the situation. He smelt Ally's perfume as she sat down next to him, then heard her opening a cassette tape. She placed it in the machine. She talked calmly then, saying the time and date, telling the tape who was present.

'Are you going to charge my client?' the solicitor repeated.

'Maybe,' South said and looked at Nelson. 'We need him to talk first. We need to straighten out a few facts.'

'I suggest you don't answer any more questions, Mr Nelson.' The solicitor ran a hand through his silver hair.

Nelson nodded. 'I haven't got anything to say.'

Ally leaned forward. 'We have officers searching

your house and lock-up right now, Jon. Isn't there anything you want to tell us?'

He shook his head.

'For the record, Jon Nelson has indicated that he doesn't wish to add anything,' Ally said calmly. 'When was the last time you saw Heather Beckley?'

'My client has already told you that he saw her alive and well two days before she went missing,' the solicitor said.

South turned to Jon. 'Were you very close, Jon? Did she come and see you often when you were working?'

Jon looked up for a second at South, then looked down at the desk.

'She was very pretty, wasn't she?' Ally asked softly. 'Your wife left you two years ago, didn't she?'

'What the fuck has that got to do with anything?' Jon's eyes burned.

'Just trying to paint a picture of events,' Ally said. 'It'd help us if you could tell us something useful. That's if you didn't have anything to do with her…'

'You think I killed Heather?' He looked back and forth between Ally and South.

South pulled out an evidence bag containing a piece of string found tied around one of Heather's wrists. 'See this, Jon? For the tape, I'm showing Jon Nelson the string that was used to tie up Heather Beckley. You use string like this don't you, Jon, in your job I mean?'

'That string could be used by anyone. This is ridiculous. This is offensive,' the solicitor said, sat back and folded his arms.

'That could belong to anyone.' Nelson went back to staring at the table.

'To your son, perhaps? Is that who you think killed Heather? Who tied her up and then strangled her? Did your son squeeze her throat until her face turned blue?' South stared at Nelson.

Nelson shrugged. 'Me and my son didn't get on that well since me and his mother split up. I wouldn't know what he got up to.'

'So, you think he could be capable of murder?' Ally asked.

Nelson looked up into her eyes, his mouth twisted with a frown. 'Well, he's not capable of anything now, is he? So that's that, isn't it? So you can let me go.'

Ally put her hands together, resting her chin on them. 'If we find some string on your property that matches the working end of the string used to tie up Heather, then that means you'll be going to trial for her abduction and murder. Simple as that.'

'Look, my client has given you his DNA. He's cooperated in every way. Now, are you going to charge him?'

South tapped the desk lightly. 'How tidy is your house, Jon?'

'What?' Nelson stared at South.

'Do you clean regularly? Do you have a woman that comes in? I mean, you work every hour that God sends, I imagine. Up at the crack of dawn getting the flowers, then shutting up late in the evening. Do you ever get the chance to tidy up?'

Nelson's mouth opened slightly.

South smiled. 'Was she there? Is that where it happened? Did she come over? Did you get her there to talk about Andrew? Perhaps you got her a bit drunk, is that it? Then things got out of hand. She started screaming and…'

'No. Nothing like that happened, ever.' Nelson's head dropped.

'So tell us what happened,' Ally pleaded. 'We'll find that string and her DNA.'

Jon Nelson looked at his solicitor for a moment, then back at Ally. 'I've got nothing more to say.'

South tapped the desk. 'Her DNA was all over that string we took off her. Pieces of her skin imbedded in the string. Perhaps her DNA will be on the rest of the string, maybe in your van. We know you killed her, Jon. Just get it off your chest now. Tell us what really happened so we can tell her parents. Think of Mr and Mrs Beckley. You know how they feel. Your son's dead too. Put their minds at rest.'

Nelson turned his head and seemed to be looking towards the door of the interview room. He didn't say anything, just shrugged.

The solicitor coughed and sat up. 'OK, so are you going to charge him now?'

South turned and took in the solicitor's look of superiority. 'No.'

'No?' the solicitor repeated.

South smiled and gave humourless laugh. 'Not until we've finished looking around Mr Nelson's van, his lock-up and home. Then we'll talk. You're going back downstairs, Mr Nelson. But don't worry, we'll give you a nice cup of tea and some food. Sausage and beans alright?'

South got up and signalled for Ally to follow him out of the room. In the corridor, South told a uniformed officer to take Jon Nelson back to the cells. Ally watched the uniform head into the room, then turned to South. 'We might not find that bit of string. Then we'll have nothing to hold him with.'

South ran a hand through his hair as he let out a deep breath. 'There's still the chance we might find her DNA.'

'But that'll only tell us she was at his place. He could admit she was there and that wouldn't prove anything. We'll have nothing to hand over to the CPS.'

'Well, let's hope they find something then.' South stormed off down the corridor.

TWENTY

Fred had never seen the incident room so empty. He walked in and saw only a couple of officers on the phones or doing paperwork. He kept walking and headed into his office, holding a carrier bag under his arm with his stolen book inside. He put the bag on his desk, sat down, then looked in his drawer for the rest of his painkillers. He didn't find them. He could have sworn he'd left them in his top drawer. He shut it and looked up, seeing a large figure in the doorway.

'Nice of you to show up, Fred.' Jameson entered. 'Where the bloody hell've you been?'

Fred looked through a file on his desk. 'At the hospital. Then I went to talk to Mrs Wainwright.'

'Who?' Jameson sat down.

'The woman who ran the old people's home. We needed a list of regular visitors so we could go through them and clear them from the inquiry.'

'What inquiry?'

'The suicides and the dead old men we found.' Fred looked up.

'That's gone out the window, Fred.'

'But we haven't found out who killed Kerry.'

'That's because no one cares who killed Kerry. No one but you, mate. Look, all those people killed themselves. End of story. And the old people just died. Kerry wanted to die. Alright, so someone helped him, but that's just a loose end. We haven't got the resources to chase around some stupid arsehole who's helping sad twats kill themselves. A young girl has been murdered. Byrne's killer is still running loose. The same person who probably killed Andrew Nelson. On top of that, Skouvakis was shot and killed last night. Did you know that?'

'I heard.'

'Scotland Yard has taken over. They seem to think it was a professional hit. They didn't find any usable prints and the bullets dug out of Skouvakis haven't told them much either.'

Fred sat back a little, looking towards the window opposite. 'So the spider thing is being dropped?'

Jameson nodded, then leaned forward. He smiled. 'Look, Fred. People have been worried about you for a while. It's obvious you're not well, mate. You spend most of your time in hospital or in the therapist's office. We know you're popping pills like they're Smarties. What the fuck is wrong with you anyway?'

Fred rubbed his eyes, trying to give himself time to think. 'They don't seem to know. Keep giving me tests.'

'Bloody doctors.' Jameson sat back. 'Them upstairs have been having words. They think it might be best if you take the rest of your leave starting now.'

'You mean I'm out? They want me off the job?'

'I'm sorry. I'll look into the pension business, see what we can sort out. It'll give you the chance to get well again.' Jameson patted the desk, then eased himself up. 'By the way, looks like we might have Heather Beckley's killer.'

Fred looked up, a little shocked. 'Andrew Nelson's dead, isn't he?'

'Yes, but looks like his father, Jon Nelson, might be our man after all. Found a special kind of string on his stall that matches the stuff Heather was bound with. How about that?'

Fred nodded. 'That's…that's good news.'

'Yeah, now all we have to do is find out who killed Andrew Nelson and Michael Byrne and why.'

Fred watched Jameson shuffle out of the office, then looked for more painkillers. He found his last packet in his coat and swallowed two. He couldn't help thinking about what Jameson had told him. He'd wanted to finish the job, to tie up the loose ends before he went, but he'd suspect ed they might jump in and cut him off before he got the chance.

It was all over. They'd won. He'd messed it all up.

Fred felt the tears pour down his face. His body shuddered as he sat there feeling his tear ducts burn. The pain gripped his body, so he grabbed the desk, trying to blot out any thought, trying to picture a nice peaceful scene.

He saw the dead bodies. The old men. The suicides. Mrs Hawk with a knife sticking out of her gut. Byrne with his brains beaten in. Nelson lying on the slab in the post-mortem room. There'll be justice for Heather Beckley now, he thought, and wiped away a tear.

He'd really messed up.

South was coming towards the incident room when he saw Jon Nelson's solicitor waiting for him. He smiled politely as South reached him.

'So?' South asked, folding his arms across his chest.

'My client would like to talk with you,' the solicitor said. 'He has some more information.'

'Mr…what's your name?' South asked.

'Benjamin Estall.'

'Mr Estall, is there any chance he's about to confess?' South leaned back.

'My client said he's innocent of the murder of

Heather Beckley. But he wishes to add something he thinks is relevant to the case and might assist you.'

'OK.'

Ally and South seated themselves opposite Mr Estall and Jon Nelson. Nelson looked at them both in turn.

'So?' South asked. 'What is this information?'

Nelson coughed a little. 'I thought I better tell you now because if it came out later it might make me look guilty.'

Ally sighed. 'Just tell us, Mr Nelson.'

Nelson nodded. 'Me and Heather were seeing each other.'

Ally turned to South and raised her eyebrows. 'Really? Tell us more.'

Nelson cleared his throat. 'Well, it started when she used to come and visit me on the stall when I was working. She'd turn up at lunchtimes and tell me how pissed off she was with Andrew. I'd listen of course. Then we started going for lunch together. It was nice.'

Ally nodded. 'Go on.'

'Well, one day she suddenly tells me she loves me.' Nelson looked from South to Ally, searching their faces for some kind of reaction.

Ally leaned forward. 'Heather told you that she loved you?'

'Yeah. It was a real shock. I didn't know what to say.'

'She was a very attractive girl,' South added.

'That's right. Well, I guess I did the wrong thing, but I kept meeting up with her. Then she started turning up at my place. One thing led to another.'

South let out a laugh. 'Let me get this right, you and your son's girlfriend started having an affair?'

Nelson nodded. 'Yeah. I know I shouldn't have, but

I'm a man. My wife had buggered off. I felt guilty, but I knew Andrew didn't give a stuff about her. I really liked her.'

'So,' South folded her arms. 'What you're telling me now is that if we find any of her DNA at your home, there's a perfectly innocent explanation? You were seeing each other? You loved each other?'

Nelson stared at South. 'Yeah, basically. I thought I better explain now. There's more though.'

'And what else have you got to admit?' Ally asked.

'Well, she was a bit kinky.'

South slapped the desk. 'Don't tell me, she liked to be tied up and you just so happen to have some string?'

'Yes, I know it sounds stupid, but I tied her up with the string I kept for work. It was a while back. I reckon she kept it. Maybe someone else used it to tie her up.'

South turned to Ally with a slight smile on his face. 'Right then. OK, well, we will take that information into account and get back to you.'

The inside of his house was too quiet. Fred stepped in and shut the door, all the time listening out for the sound of the pages of a book being turned. Inside the living room, he saw the empty leather chair where he'd got used to his brother sitting. A terrible thought sucked at his stomach for moment as he stopped dead. He looked up towards the ceiling, wishing he could see through the rafters and into Martin's room. What if something had happened to him? His brother could now be lying in his bed, cold. The doctors gave no hint that he might drop dead, only how his brother would melt away each day; it was not exactly how they worded it, but basically they said there would be, after a couple of years, a living skeleton inhabiting the same house as him.

Fred took a step on the carpeted stairs, lifting himself up, feeling the pain in his backside had softened. He took another quiet step, lifting his head to see towards Martin's room.

'Fred?' Martin called out.

Fred stopped. For a moment he stood still, holding onto the bannister, gripping it and feeling the tears rise from the corner of his eyes. He wiped his eyes and coughed. Now he collated the feelings he was having as he travelled up the stairs, adding it all up and realising that what he felt was not relief. He wanted his brother to be dead. He tried to justify this, adding together the pain his brother suffered with the lack of life he endured. Yes, that was the source of his disappointment.

Fred felt the carrier bag tap against his leg as he stepped into his brother's room. He couldn't remember the last time he was in there. He'd had no reason to go in, it was his brother's private world where he reached out through the internet and then slept. Sleep was his only escape from the pain. Fred watched his brother sitting up in bed, holding a large book out in front of him.

'How come you're home?' Martin asked, lowering the book.

'It's over.'

'What do you mean it's over? What's over?' Martin's bony fingers slowly moved the heavy book to the bed.

'My job. They've finally pushed me out.'

'Can they do that?'

'Of course. It was only a matter of time. Probably for the best.'

'What are you going to do?' Martin said.

'What do you mean?'

'Maybe you can fight it.'

'It's over. I've done my bit.' Fred looked at the carrier bag with the Shakespeare book inside.

'What about the case you were working on? The spider thing?'

'Out the window. Not enough resources.' Fred took out the book and flipped through the pages, then opened it to the centre. He took out the list Mrs Wainwright gave him from his pocket and stuck it between the pages and shut the book.

'So, that's it?'

Fred looked up at Martin and saw the sad eyes peering across at him. 'That's it. The end. All over.' Fred got up, carrying the large book under his arm.

'Tracey came by to say goodbye.'

'Where's she going?'

'Don't know. I didn't ask. She's left that idiot though.'

Fred nodded. 'Good.'

'She told me that she told you about the money and what it was for.'

Fred kept looking down at the book under his arm. 'Did she?'

'Yes. Aren't you going to say anything?'

'Like what?'

'Aren't you feeling angry?'

Fred searched himself inside and out, looking for some kind of emotional response that he could pass off to his brother. He opened a door inside himself and felt the emptiness of a vacated room. 'No.'

'I paid her to sleep with you. Didn't that piss you off?'

'Why did you do it?'

'So she'd sleep with you. I thought it might make

you feel better. Put a spring in your step.'

Fred nodded. 'Then you did it with good intentions.'

Fred started heading out of the room, until he heard Martin call him back. He looked around at the dishevelled figure under the enormous duvet. 'Yes?'

'Don't give up on the spider thing. At least try and solve it. There's nothing saying you can't still investigate it.'

'I'll think about it.'

Jameson was sitting in his office with the phone pressed against his ear, while South and Walker stood outside leaning on either side of the door. They knew he was talking to the forensic team, waiting to hear the results of a test performed on the string found in Nelson's home and on his stall. South was breathing deeply, listening to the muffled phone conversation. He heard Jameson saying 'yes' a lot, and watched his fingers tapping on his desk.

'It's going to be alright,' Ally said.

He looked at her and saw her nod, a slight smile appearing on her lips. He smiled or at least tried to. 'I'll take you out and get you pissed if it's OK.'

'OK. I look forward to it.' She raised one eyebrow as Jameson put down the phone and walked out of the office.

'So?' Ally asked.

Jameson's face gave little away. He sighed. 'Forensic took all the pieces of string they found and put them against the ones used to bind Heather. One of the ones on the cart matched the string used to tie her up. It matched one hundred percent. The string used to tie her was cut from the string he used at work.'

South stepped forward. 'But that only supports what he admitted.'

Jameson smiled. 'Well, the forensic people informed me that the string around her wrists was only tied once. Something to do with the fibres or something. So, if he did tie her up it was done before she died. He's lying.'

South smiled and tilted his head back. 'The fucking bastard.'

'Is it enough to get a conviction?' Ally asked.

'We've got him on tape admitting tying her up and having a sexual relationship with her. We've got the string that tied her up, which exactly matches the string he owned, fibre by fibre. He's fucked. Go and tell him.'

Nelson looked anxious as they stepped back into the room. South pulled out a chair and sat down. Ally put another tape in the machine and recorded herself stating the time the interview started and who was present. She looked at the solicitor, then at Jon Nelson, and cleared her throat. 'Got some news back from the search of your house, Jon.'

Nelson looked from Ally to South. 'What?'

Ally leaned forward, putting her hands together. 'We matched the string on your cart to the string used to tie up Heather's wrists.'

Nelson opened his mouth slightly, shaking his head a little. 'But I told you about that…'

'But the forensic tests tell us that the knots on her hands were only tied once. The string from your stall matched the end of the string that was used to tie her up just before she died. That was silly of you, Jon. You made a big mistake keeping that string. It proves you're lying. Yes, you did tell us you tied her up, but your story is too thin. A jury won't buy it. So, anything to add?'

Nelson looked into her eyes, then at the desk. 'The

jury won't buy your story.'

South leaned forward, making sure Nelson saw his eyes. 'Yes, they will, Jon. You murdered Heather. You got her back to your place for whatever reason, tied her up and then strangled her. I don't understand what she was doing there, but her wrists were bruised and cut from when she'd been struggling. That proves that she was fighting back. We will get a conviction.'

Nelson looked away, seeming to look across at the wall. 'Well, you better charge me then.'

South looked at Ally. 'Would you like to do the honours?'

After walking out of the house, Fred found himself driving back towards Edmonton Police Station, unsure of what he was doing. He felt slightly dizzy, his heart seeming to rampage against his rib cage. He pulled over, saw the concrete building of the library, then parked. He sat for a moment, trying to control his breathing, looking up at the shabby grey-stone walls and the water stains from the North London rain. He got out and walked across to the library, passing a frumpy-looking woman and a child with bright ginger hair. He walked up the steps, his vision blurring as he felt the dusty concrete under his feet. Cool air greeted him inside and the smell of the books. The quietness was what he needed and trudged to a desk. He grabbed a paperback and opened it, not wanting to seem out of place. The words seem ed to run into each other. He felt hot, the sweat pouring down his forehead. He took out a tissue and wiped his eyes and nose.

'You back again?'

Fred looked up from the book and saw Scott Brown looking down at him, a smile stretched across his pale face. Brown peered at the book he was reading. 'Jackie

Collins? Didn't think I would ever see a policeman who's into Jackie Collins.'

Fred turned the book over and looked at the front cover. He allowed himself to laugh, then the book fell from his fingers.

Brown looked at him suspiciously. 'Are you OK? You look white as a sheet.'

Fred nodded. 'I'm fine. Just needed to sit down for a bit.'

'It's the workload you coppers take on. It's not good for you.' Brown picked up the book.

'Well, I won't have to worry about that any more.'

'What do you mean?'

'I'm being put out to pasture. I've had my time it seems.'

Brown nodded. 'I see. I'm sorry about that. Well, I hope you managed to solve the case you were working on.'

Fred sat back and looked up at Brown and noticed his hat. This time it's a purple woolly hat. 'I wished. You should've seen me earlier. I stole a book from an old people's home.'

Brown smiled. 'Well, they say that if policemen weren't policemen, they'd be criminals.'

Fred nodded. 'That's me set up then. Old peoples homes today, bank robberies tomorrow.'

'Got to start somewhere.'

Spots danced in front of Fred's eyes for a moment. He shook his head, blinked and then lifted himself up and saw Brown staring at him strangely. He stepped around the table as his body became heavy. He swayed a little and gripped the desk. Brown's arm appeared around his back, supporting him.

'You going to be alright?' Brown asked.

'Yeah, just get me to my car and I'll be fine.'

'I don't think you can drive in this state. I'll drive you home.' Brown pulled Fred along to the exit and helped him down the steps. The policeman felt his legs melting away, somehow not recognising his feet as his own any more. He didn't feel pain either, not a twinge, and that was what was worrying him as the librarian helped him towards a battered black VW Polo. Fred felt his legs being lifted into the vehicle, then the car gently rocking as the door slammed beside him. His head swirled again, and his eyes beginning to close.

After quickly slipping the file in his drawer, South saw Harris coming towards him. 'Good result, eh?'

Harris carried a cardboard box full of papers and dropped it on South's desk. South looked at the files and saw it was the Heather Beckley caseload. 'This for me?'

Harris smiled and clapped his hands together. 'Yes, South, old boy. You and Ally got your man, so you can get all that statements over to the CPS.'

'Thanks a lot.' South lifted out the top file, then dropped it back in.

'My pleasure. Gives me more time to play golf.'

South leaned back in his chair. 'Still got to find out who killed Nelson and Byrne yet. Don't forget that.'

Harris looked behind him, then pulled up a chair and sat down. 'I thought you and Walker were going to sort that out for us too. That not right?'

'What's your problem?' South folded his arms.

'I was working on finding Heather before you even came along, mate. And I wasn't even asked to sit in on the interview. That's what's fucking wrong, South.'

'If you're pissed off because you looked a right pratt with the Skouvakis thing, don't take it out on me, right?'

Harris sprung up, his lips curling back. 'Fuck off.

You fucking…look, fuck Skouvakis. Someone paid someone to kill him, so fucking what? No one cares. Yeah, I was there to get info. I left and he got shot. His fucking bad luck.'

South put his hands behind his head. 'You and him go back a fair bit, don't you? You and Fred was after him for those young birds he was supposed to be smuggling into London, that right?'

Harris folded his arms across his chest. 'Actually, smart arse, Skouvakis was just the glorified delivery guy. We figured out he was helping them get in, probably through some Albanian or Russian gang. But nothing came of it.'

South sat up. 'So, you never met any of the birds who were smuggled in? No one came forward as a witness?'

Harris' expression changed. He no longer looked angry, only a slight show of curiosity appearing across his face. 'What's this all about? Why're you asking all these questions?'

'Just wondering.'

'Scotland Yard has taken over the Skouvakis case. End of story. You keep your nose out.' Harris pointed a finger across at South.

'Just seems funny that the killer waited until a copper was on the scene.'

'Oh fuck off. What's that supposed to mean?'

'Perhaps someone had an old score to settle with Skouvakis.'

'Meaning me? I go and see Skouvakis, then walk out the pub and then double back and shoot him? Fuck off, South.'

'Yeah, it's ridiculous, isn't it?' South smiled. 'Someone would have to be stupid to do that, or very sly.'

'They checked me for gun residue, South. They found nothing. So you can fuck off.' Harris got up again.

South laughed a little. 'Alright, mate, sorry, didn't mean to wind you up.'

'Yeah, right. Anyway, why're you so worried about Skouvakis getting offed anyway? Let Scotland Yard deal with it. They think they've got it sorted.'

'But you don't?'

Harris shrugged. 'Don't really know. Skouvakis must have had a lot of enemies by now. The bastard's had his fingers in a few pies for a long while now. He'd been inside for a couple of things when he first arrived in England.'

'Like what?'

'An armed robbery of some Post Office somewhere and possession of drugs. But he must've learnt a few things inside, because he's managed to kept clean ever since.'

'On the surface.'

Harris nodded and stuffed his hands in his pockets. 'Yeah, on the surface. He's got plenty of dirty washing somewhere. We shut down a few businesses that were doing some money laundering a few years back. Word was he was heavily involved, giving his pay packet a wash and then sending it out of the country. But nothing came up. We nicked some other lowlifes though.'

South got up and walked around the desk. 'What about his massage parlours?'

'He had a couple up the road, but they've gone now.'

'He was running a prostitution ring from them, wasn't he?'

'That's what we thought. Anyway, the fucker's

dead, so it's all over.'

South let out a deep breath. 'If only. Did you know that the global sex market is worth nearly four billion a year?'

Harris whistled. 'I'm in the wrong business.'

'These poor girls think they're coming over to study or work a normal job, but the smugglers take them to some dingy flat and tell them that they owe them the travelling money and they have to work it off. So, they end up having sex with strange men.'

Harris shook his head. 'It's bloody awful.'

'And some of the girls are just kids.'

'So, I ask again, why all this interest?'

South took out a handkerchief from his inside pocket and blew his nose. 'I had a similar case up in Manchester. Slave labour and that sort of thing. Found out a couple of my colleagues were a little involved.'

'Bastards.' Harris lifted up a file from South's desk and opened it.

'Fred told me that a girl came to see you and him. She wanted out or something.'

Harris dropped the file to his lap. His eyes burn out to South. 'He fucking said what?'

'Melanie or something, wasn't it?' South returned Harris' stare.

'Can't say I remember. Was a while back now.' Harris got up. 'Right, I better get some work done.'

'You must've felt like shit when she turned up like that, all cut up.'

Harris turned around and looked deep into South's eyes. 'Don't start trying to pull my chain, South. I'm a straight bloke. Ask anyone. I like a joke, yeah. It's what gets me through the day. But I hate people like you, who have to keep digging away at stuff that should be left alone. Yes, a girl came to us, then she disappeared.

303

Her own fault. Not ours. Now just keep it to yourself.'

South watched Harris walk out the office, then sat behind his desk again. By his feet was a box. He reached in and brought out a file. Inside were Fred and Harris' old paperwork. He looked through the statements and nodded to himself. Someone must have been working with Skouvakis, someone on the force tipping them off. He put down the file and stared across to Fred's empty desk.

TWENTY-ONE

When Fred was just a kid, not long after he saw the spider crawl out of the old man's mouth, he became friends with a new kid who came to his school. Fred thought for a moment as he tried to sit up on a maroon sofa that was covered in cigarette burns. Shane. Shane Valance. He was a small kid, but he was tough, always in fights. He didn't stay at the school long and didn't come back after one particular summer. His home, which was a grubby little flat on the estate near Carterhatch Lane, was just like the one Fred was sitting in. It could be the same worn sofa.

Fred could smell stale cigarette smoke in the material, but not in the room. The walls had been recently painted magnolia, the uninventive colour of a man living alone.

Fred sat up feeling groggy and rubbed his eyes. Opposite him was a closed door and he tried to hear beyond it, listening out for signs of life.

He could have been asleep for hours, but he looked at his watch and saw it had only been about an hour. He thought back and recalled being practically carried to Scott Brown's car. This must be his flat, he thought and got up. He opened the door and found himself on a small landing, the toilet and bathroom opposite him, while a very neat and tidy bedroom lay to his right. He felt his bladder swelling and stepped into the sparse bathroom, unbuttoning his flies. He didn't feel any pain as he started to feel a slight trickle of urine splash against the toilet bowl.

For a man living alone, there wasn't much mess. He saw no hairs around the bowl or in the shower. Everything looked so clean. He finished urinating, but as soon as he stepped away from the toilet, he felt the pressure to go again. He tried not to think about his prostate and moved back across the landing.

There was definitely no one else in the flat, so he stepped into Brown's bedroom, and stood there for a moment, looking around at the magnolia walls and the single bed. He looked at the shelves of books that lined one of the walls, recognising some of the titles, his eyes scanning through them.

The sound of the front door opening made Fred hurry out of the room. He got to the landing and stood there smiling as Brown hopped up the stairs carrying a bag of shopping. 'Was out of tea bags and milk. You feeling OK?'

Fred looked down at his hands which both felt light. His whole body felt lighter too. 'Yeah, fine. Thanks. Sorry about that.'

Brown shook his head as he entered the tiny kitchen. 'No problem.'

Fred followed him into the kitchen, where Brown filled the kettle. 'Weird though, isn't it?'

'What do you mean?'

'Well, you come to where I work to investigate some crime, and now you're in my home.'

Fred laughed a little. 'Yes, I suppose it's a bit weird.'

'Do you believe in fate?'

Fred laughed, then saw Brown had a perfectly serious look on his face. 'Never really thought about it.'

'I don't really. But I believe in synchronicity. You

know, when it seems that events are fitting into place, directing you to one specific event?'

Fred listened to the kettle starting to bubble. 'I don't think we are directed anywhere. We do what we do because we want to. I don't believe in God either.'

'Me neither. That's something we've got in common.'

'I suppose so,' Fred said and watched the librarian make two teas. After being handed his tea, Fred wondered about Brown's life. One thing he'd noted about the living room was the lack of a television set. People who are able to go without television always amazed Fred. With his brother's illness there also came an incredible amount of crap programming. 'You live here alone?'

Brown nodded and took his tea through to the lounge.

Brown sat down and folded his arms. 'I've lived alone most of my life. I don't think I could live with another human being.'

'I know what you mean. I live with my brother. He's ill and has to be looked after. I don't mind it, but being in such a confined space with another person does get to you.' Fred sat in a brown leather armchair.

'People are untidy, generally,' Brown said. 'I hate mess. I've never been messy. Never. It was the way I was born and now if I see mess or waste, I lose it.'

'I spend most of my time at work. That keeps me and Martin separate. We have a woman who comes in and looks after him.'

'And now you haven't got a job any more.' Brown picked up his tea and looked at it for a moment.

'No, and that's probably for the best.'

'Why do you say that?'

'Because…well, it was only a matter of time before

I messed up. There was things I wanted to sort out…
but now that doesn't matter either.' Fred didn't feel
strange at all telling Brown all this. They say a stranger
is easier to talk to and Fred had to agree as he sipped
his tea. Brown, although he looked a little weird, with
his eyelashes missing and his red woolly hat pulled
down over his head, was somehow calming. He was
like Dr Sheila Evans in a way.

Fred got up.

'Time to go?' Brown got up too and walked him to
the door. 'Well, pop in the library if you're around. I'll
recommend some good books.'

Fred nodded. 'I will. Thanks again.'

Fred watched the door close behind him and stood
looking out across Enfield Highway, realising he was
outside the flats just off of Carterhatch Lane. He smiled
a little as he travelled down the grey stairs, the smell
of urine gripping his nostrils. He passed a couple of
kids riding bikes, then started walking home.

He tried not to think of anything as a cold wind
gripped his body and tried to brush him sideways
into an old woman. He wanted to forget his job, to
keep on walking, but then he saw Green Street Library
on his right, where everything pretty much started.
He stopped for a moment, looking up at the stone
building, when a thought tried to clamber into his
head. It was the list in the book. Maybe he should've
given it to South, he thought, then recalled they
had filed away the spider case. It was over. He kept
moving, feeling a light rain jabbing at his head.

South was going through the file on Skouvakis when
Jameson came into the office and stood by his desk.
He had a sandwich in his hand. He stood chewing for
a moment, looking down at what South was reading.

He bent a little and saw the photograph of Skouvakis. 'Ugly little runt, wasn't he?'

South looked at the picture, seeing the pale and stony-faced man with a small dark moustache. 'He didn't look very threatening.'

'They never do. He was a right ruthless bastard though. I'm surprised someone had the balls to walk in there and shoot him.'

'They must have hated him.'

'Looks like someone was paid to kill him.' Jameson took another bite of his sandwich. 'If you go along with what Scotland Yard think.'

South looked up. 'And do you?'

'Well, that's their theory. We told them about Byrne and Nelson and the gun, but they don't seem interested. What can we do?'

'It says here that an undercover police officer was the source of information about the girls being smuggled in. What happened to him?'

Jameson pulled up a chair. 'You want to start digging around that again? It came to nothing last time.'

'Maybe because the investigation was sent down a dead end.' South flipper through the file and shook his head. 'There's nothing here after they raided Skouvakis' massage parlours. Nothing. There must've been other leads, surely.'

'Harris and Fred didn't find anything. The undercover officer said the same. It went quiet. The fuckers who smuggled these girls in aren't stupid, South. They're watching us as much as we're watching them. They know when we're on to them.'

'That's what's scary. Maybe Skouvakis had one of our lot on his side.' South raised his eyebrows.

Jameson sighed. 'That goes without saying. The

money they make from bringing in these Eastern European girls adds up to millions. They find a copper who isn't too happy with his job and his life style and they've got him. All they have to do is wave a wad of cash under his nose.'

South saw regret in Jameson's eyes, but ignored it and said, 'You think that's what happened with the Skouvakis thing?'

Jameson looked at the remainder of his sandwich, then chucked it in the waste paper bin. 'Put it this way, we had a bloody good tip-off about a flat he was using to put the girls up in and that he used his massage parlour as a cover for prostitution. We raided the flat and the parlours and they were clean. In fact, each place looked like Mrs Mop had been around to give them a nice spring clean. One of the uniforms found a bin bag in the alley next door and there were needles inside. They usually get the girls hooked on junk so they become dependent on them. The money they make from selling themselves out weighs the cost of the smack.'

'We raided a place once, back up north.' South leaned back in his chair, raising his eyes to the ceiling. 'They had all these girls sleeping on the floor. Just blankets thrown over them, the poor cows.'

Jameson nodded and tucked his shirt into his trousers. 'So, what are you thinking then? You want to look into Skouvakis' business dealing?'

'Well, I'm curious to see if any of our people are involved in this.'

Jameson got up and stuck his hands in his pockets. 'Well, that's why they sent you back down here, wasn't it? To weed out the corrupt officers? If any of us are corrupt, then you've got to get on with it. Good luck.'

TWENTY-TWO

Thursday, 21 October 1999

After fetching a cup of poor quality tea from a vending machine, Fred walked down the hospital corridor to where his brother was sitting, leaning on his cane. It made him look like a country gentleman. Martin still wore his smart suit from his banking job, his hair slicked back and his skin clean-shaven. Fred handed him the tea and watched his brother sip and pull a disgusted face. 'I don't know why I bother.'

'Are you going back in?' Fred asked, nodding towards the door to the ward where their mother was lying.

Martin looked to the door, holding his tea a couple of inches from his mouth. 'I think she's done with me. It's your turn. You're her favourite.'

Fred looked at Martin. 'You're not going to come back are you?'

'What would be the point?'

'The point is she's dying. This is our mother. You only get one.'

'And thank fuck for that,' Martin said, then quickly winked.

'Look, it won't be long. The doctor told me that her heart's giving out.'

Martin nodded. 'She won't be here tomorrow.'

Fred looked up, confused by his brother's statement and the certainty in his voice. 'What makes you say

311

that?'

'She told me. In there.' Martin pointed towards the ward.

'She told you? She's decided to give up? Just like that?'

Martin nodded. 'Just like that.'

'It doesn't work like that.'

'Of course it does. If she wants to die, she'll die.' Martin looked at Fred as if he was stupid.

Fred shook his head and jumped up. He looked across the ward and saw the orange curtain drawn around her bed. With the light from a lamp shining through the curtain, he could see the shape of Mrs Wright, the neighbour from across the street, sitting at their mother's bedside.

'Are you going to buy the house off the council?' Martin asked.

Fred shrugged. 'I suppose. We grew up in that house, so I suppose I should.'

'Good.' Martin pointed his cane towards the curtain. 'Here's Mrs Wright. It's your turn.'

Mrs Wright ambled out of the ward and stood looking through her handbag for a moment, her plump body blocking the door. Fred watched her search through the bag, occasionally looking in wonder at her jet-black hair and warty face. For a moment, he thought she was going to give them a pound each like she used to do when they were kids. She pulled out a handkerchief and blew her nose. 'Hello, lads. She wants to see you, Freddy.'

Fred smiled and walked through the ward, hearing the coughing of the other patients, all elderly, all near death's door. He heard the television in the corner, some news programme being broadcast loudly, but kept his eyes fixed on the curtain around his mum's bed. An Indian nurse appeared from out of the curtain and walked past him carrying a sample of urine. He could see a light rain spitting at the window through the black night as he turned and looked at the skinny figure under the green blanket.

The old woman smiled, tried to pull herself up but had no luck at all. Fred quickly stepped over to gently support her back while he fixed her pillow. Her white hair was longish and sat in untidy curls around her ears and neck. He could smell peppermints, her favourite sweets, as he sat down. A bottle of Lucozade sat on the bedside cabinet and reminded him of his own sick days from school.

'Look at you,' his mother said, with a quick sweep of her blood shot eyes.

'Look at you.' He laughed.

'Martin's not looking too bad, is he, Freddy?' She pointed a bony finger towards the corridor.

'Not too bad. He'll be alright. Don't worry about him.'

'It's you I worry about. That bleeding awful job you do. Why did you want to become a policeman, for gawd's sake?'

'Not this again.' Fred sat back a little, the smell of hot meat pies drifting past his face. 'It's just a job.'

'And a dangerous one, my boy.' Her voice croaked a little as she pointed to the bottle of Lucozade. 'Pour me a bit of that will you, love?'

Fred took a plastic cup and poured the orange liquid into it, feeling the gases burst into his face. He passed it to her and watched her sip the drink. Her eyes, all glassy and pink, remained on the television for moment, until they travelled along the beds, looking at the other old bodies around her. 'Look at these lot. Mrs Thorne over there has just had a new hip put in.

313

She's in agony most of the time. And, to make matters worse, she keeps wetting the bed. They have to kept changing her sheets and gawd does she moan?'

Fred smiled. 'You'll be out of here soon enough.'

For the first time, her pink eyes properly looked at him. She blinked for a moment. 'You know that isn't true, Freddy. I bloody well do, if you don't. I told Martin and I'm telling you, I won't be around much longer, so you'll have to look after each other.'

'You're not going anywhere, Mum.' Fred put the cup on the table and then his hands on hers. He felt the wrinkled skin under his palm and it was so cold. 'But of course, we're going to look after each other.'

'Martin isn't well, Freddy.' She put a hand on top of his. 'You have to look after him. Promise me.'

'Of course I will.'

'You can both live in the house together. Promise me you'll both live there.' Her hand pressed down on his.

'All three of us will live there.'

She paused for a moment, before lifting her hand off his and sitting back. 'You've got to do what you can to help him. If he wants something, you've got to get it for him. I don't want him suffering the way I have all my life.'

Fred smiled. 'I'll do my best.'

'Promise me. Swear that'll you'll help him.'

'I swear.'

'Now, I don't mean to be rude, love, but I need to get some sleep.' She smiled.

He laughed a little and bent down and kissed her cheek. He could smell peppermints again and suddenly he was filled with a small amount of panic that he couldn't explain. He wanted to tell her something, anything that would communicate his love for her, but he couldn't find the words. He stood for a moment, and squeezed her hand. 'I'll see you tomorrow.'

She nodded slowly and drifted off.

TWENTY-THREE

Thursday, 29th April 2004

South had tried several different numbers for Nick Hatch by the time Ally appeared out of her front door rubbing her tired eyes. She opened the gate, pulling a face at him as he sat in his car, his mobile phone pressed to his ear. He beckoned her towards the car and saw her hair was still wet. She climbed in and brought the chill of the early morning air with her. She went to pull her seatbelt on, then stopped and looked at him angrily. 'It's seven in the morning. It's bloody early.'

South nodded at her, then took the phone from his ear and stared at it for a moment before shoving it into his inside pocket. 'I can't get a hold of this Nick Hatch person.'

'Who? Who's Nick Hatch?'

'He's the undercover police officer who worked with Harris and Fred when they went after Skouvakis. He was the one who had all the leads.'

'What's this got to do with us? I thought Scotland Yard CID were taking care of Skouvakis' murder.'

'They are. I'm interested in what happened when they raided his massage parlours. He'd obviously been tipped off. Maybe one of our lot was involved.'

Ally turned around to face him. 'Why are you looking into that? Why now? That was a few years ago. And what did you mean on the phone when you said don't dress like a copper?'

He looked down at her tight black T-shirt and faded Levi Jeans. 'Very Good. We can't go turning up looking like the filth. We don't want to fuck up any case he might be working on, do we?'

She sighed. 'You didn't answer my question. Why are we digging into this now?'

'Because the illegal trafficking of people for cheap labour and prostitution needs to be stopped. That's what we are going to do.' He started the engine.

'And Jameson is alright with this?'

South slowly drove the car along the street. 'Of course. It's a crime that needs solving. We found Heather's killer, didn't we? Now we're on this.'

She put her seatbelt on and sat back. 'But there are other crimes on our books. Like Fred's spider thing. We still don't know who put that young girl up to walking into that supermarket with a knife to her throat.'

South shook his head. 'She put a knife to her own throat, Ally. Those other people committed suicide. Yes, OK, some weirdo is out there putting ideas into their heads, but we haven't got anything to go on. We haven't got the resources to chase him around the country forever. If he was a serial killer maybe, but he's not.'

'And we've got Byrne and Nelson lying in the morgue.'

South gave her a quick look as he steered the car along an empty street. 'I know. And uniforms and other teams are looking into that. We can't do everything. I know you want to find out what happened and so do I, but for now we have to look into this.'

'Yes sir.' Ally grimaced. 'I didn't even have time to dry my hair properly.'

South laughed a little while watching the road.

A little while later, South stopped the car along the high street outside a parade of shops. South studied the newsagent, the pet shop and the women's clothes shop. They were the sort of shops that always seemed as if they should be closed. The fashions in the window of the boutique looked as if they were from the sixties, while the pet shop seemed to belong in the post Second World War era. Up a little way was an Indian restaurant called Ghandi's. He turned and looked at Ally, pointing his thumb in the direction of the restaurant. 'There's a good Indian back there.'

She raised her eyebrows. 'I think it's a bit early for curry. Yes, it's only half past eight. Maybe a fry-up.'

'There's a café over there. I'll treat you after we pay a visit to that block of flats over there.'

Ally looked over at the greasy spoon across the road. The big red and yellow sign over the café read: Alan's Place.

Inside she could see the figures of builder types huddled over cups of steaming tea, while a tall and skinny lad removed empty plates from tables. 'Lovely. I can already feel my arteries hardening up.'

South got out and felt a light rain flickering across his face he looked up at the massively tall and grey tower block. He could already smell the acrid stairs and stale urine.

He watched Ally making her way across the street towards the glass and steel entrance, pulling her coat tighter around her. He quickly followed, finding her holding open the large door for him, his nostrils already picking out the smell of piss in the dark foyer. They avoided the lift and began climbing the concrete stairs until they reached the 5th floor.

'I see they've got CCTV.' Ally pointed to a small

camera adjusted to sweep the balcony.

'I bet it doesn't work.' South stopped her before flat 51. He looked over the dark red door, noting the damage around the lock area. A couple of pieces of graffiti were scrawled near the letterbox.

'This is where Hatch lives?' Ally whispered.

South rang the doorbell, then flapped the letterbox a couple of times. 'This is the address I managed to get.'

They stood there for a while, staring at the door, looking through the small window into the kitchen, but there was only darkness. South pointed back along where they had come, so they travelled back down to the street. South pointed to the café when they get back down. 'I'll buy you breakfast.'

Ally nodded. 'Yes you will. A nice bacon sandwich.'

Only a few customers sat hunched over their fry-ups as South and Ally came through the door, smelling the tea brewing and bacon sizzling in a frying pan. An elderly Chinese woman smiled at them as they approached the counter. South ordered a big breakfast and Ally's bacon sandwich, looking forward to eating something substantial. He hadn't been to East London for a good few years, he recalled, remembering his mate who used to police the Isle of Dogs. It was the days when the far right were at their peak and the presence of the police was a daily occurrence for the Island's population. Whole groups of police vans would be patrolling the area, watching for trouble from both the far right groups and the left wing extremists. Clashes always seemed moments away.

'Not a bad cup of tea,' Ally said as she sat down at a table near the kitchen. South seated himself and stared out the window at the front of the café, his eyes scanning the street. Outside he saw a flower shop van pull up and a middle-aged woman start pulling batches of flowers from the back.

'I wonder if he still even lives there,' South said.

'God knows. Someone in his nick must know where he is.'

'Better not mention stuff like that.'

Ally shrugged and turned towards the door when it opened and the increasingly hard rain came in as a bulky-looking man entered. South turned to see him walking across to the counter, his hands in the pockets of his baggy combat trousers. South looked up at the man's head and saw his short fair hair and a scar over his right eye. The man leaned on the counter and ordered his food, his eyes occasionally focusing on South and Ally.

The man kept looking at them and smiling slightly, knowingly. A bigger smile stretched across his face as he took his tea from the Chinese woman, his back resting on the counter. He caught Ally's eye and winked. He came over, stood by their table, and pointed to a vacant chair next to Ally. 'Mind if I sit down, darling?'

Ally didn't say anything as the man pulled out the chair and sat down. He drank his tea and smiled at them both. After putting down his tea down hard on the table, he rubbed his hands together and laughed. 'Look at you two straight-faced idiots. Who sent you over here for fuck's sake?'

'Who are you?' South asked.

'I live at the flat you knocked on a little while ago.' He smiled again, taking in their puzzled expressions. 'Oh come on, you two can't be that thick. I'm Hatch.'

South nodded. 'You're Hatch? How did you know we were in here?'

'It didn't take a lot to know you'd be sitting in here

waiting for me to make an appearance.' Hatch took a plate of toast from a tall waiter. 'So, what do you want?'

South said, 'Information.'

Hatch laughed. 'Fuck me, I knew that. Look, I've got a whole situation going on here, mate. I can't be talking to filth, can I? What would that look like?'

'You are…' Ally began.

Hatch placed a finger to his lips. 'OK, darling, we all know the score, right, so let's kept it short and sweet. What do you want?'

'You remember Skouvakis?' South asked.

Hatch, about to take another bite of his toast, hesitated for a moment, his blue eyes peering carefully at South. 'Yeah. He got knocked off the other night. I read about it in the paper, so fucking what?'

'You worked on the investigation into him being part of a prostitution ring, didn't you?' Ally asked.

Hatch went to open his mouth, but stopped as he watched the young lad place Ally's bacon sandwich before her. He nodded politely to the lad and then brought his chair closer to the table, leaning nearer to South. 'You think that his death had something to do with prostitution?'

'Maybe,' South said. 'You were the officer that informed Edmonton nick he was part of a trafficking ring. You found out that he was bringing in girls from Eastern Europe and forcing them to sell themselves for money.'

Hatch picked up a piece of toast and studied it for a moment. 'It wasn't Skouvakis bringing in the girls. He wasn't that powerful. He was just a delivery boy. Look, mate, I did my fucking part, I told them what I had found out and then I got out.'

'What did you find out?' Ally asked, lifting her

bacon sandwich to her mouth.

Hatch looked at her slyly. 'Like I said, darling, Skouvakis was taking delivery of the girls after they were smuggled into London. I heard that he was putting them up in houses he bought, letting them sleep rough on the floor or whatever. They'd think they were being helped to build a new life or something, but then they'd find some sweaty bloke handing over cash so he could have his way with a nice young foreign girl.'

A plate of greasy fried food arrived on the table and South pulled it towards himself. 'But when the raid happened, they didn't find anything? That right?'

Hatch nodded. 'That's right. None of the properties had anyone in them and none of the girls were in the massage parlours. He must've been tipped off.'

South picked up a fork. 'Who tipped him off do you reckon?'

Hatch shrugged. 'How the fuck do I know? Could've been anyone.'

'Anyone working the case?' Ally said, chewing her sandwich.

Hatch nodded. 'Must've been. Not surprising either.'

'What's not surprising?' South asked.

'Well, a lot of money is at stake, isn't it? We're talking millions of pounds. Skouvakis took delivery of the girls, but he has to give money to the smugglers. It's a big multi-million pound operation.'

'Billions worldwide,' Ally added.

Hatch nodded. 'That's right. So, if you find a copper who's willing to take an envelope of cash every now and again, you'll have the law on your side too. And with that amount of money in the balance they aren't going to let one person risk it all going down the toilet either, are they?'

South nodded again. 'So, they wouldn't hesitate at bribery or murder, that's what you're saying?'

Hatch folded his arms. 'Multi-billion pound industries do not let lives get in their way. Look at the fucking arms industry. They make money from killing. Princess Diana was going up against them, wasn't she? She was a high profile member of the Royal family trying to get land mines banned. Land mines make a lot of money for the arms industry.'

Ally stopped eating and stared at Hatch. 'You reckon Diana was knocked off by the arms industry?'

Hatch sat back and smiled.

South shook his head. 'Look, we are getting off the subject. Who was got at?'

Hatch gave a little humourless laugh. 'Anyone could've been got at, mate. How the fuck do I know? Look, I'm risking my cover talking to you today. I'm right in amongst it with some right wing fuckers and now you've got me trying to remember something that happened a few years back. I can't fucking remember.'

South wiped his mouth. 'It's just funny how the operation went dead after that. You and the other officers couldn't find anything more. That was lucky for Skouvakis.'

Hatch's eyes burned into South. He raised his hand slowly, his index finger stretching out to South. 'Don't start making those sort of accusations, mate. I'm clean, you fucking…look, someone got scared or got rich, I don't know, but the operation went tits up.'

South looked at Ally and raised his eyebrows. 'OK, Hatch, OK.'

'What about the girl who ended up in the Thames, minus her limbs?' Ally placed her crusts on the plate and stared at Hatch.

Hatch shrugged. 'There was no way of knowing if she was one of his girls. She was identified, eventually, by a family member who came over from somewhere near Russia, I think. He said she'd come over to study English, but that was the last time he'd seen her. She must've been causing someone some trouble.'

South pushed his plate across the table. 'Is there anyone you can put us in touch with? An old informant, perhaps?'

Hatch sighed. 'Look, I'll do what I can. Give me your number. Don't contact me again, right?'

South took out his card and gave it to Hatch. 'Right.'

Hatch got up and looked them both over. 'And it should only be one of you. No offence, sweetheart, but you should stay out of it. I'll be in contact.'

Ally watched Hatch step out into the rain. 'Well, that was interesting.'

'Yeah.' South picked up a piece of bacon and shoved it in his mouth. 'Sounds like they might've had more than one copper on the books.'

'Did you hear what he said? They won't take kindly to another copper sniffing around.'

South smiled at her. 'I'll be discrete.'

TWENTY-FOUR

For a moment, Fred thought he'd woken himself by screaming in his sleep. Then he heard a pain-swollen moan. He pushed back his bed sheets and put his feet into his slippers. Another cry took him quickly towards Martin's room. He knocked, then pushed open the door and saw the bony shape of his brother curled up like a baby. Only a thin sheet covered Martin's body, his spine visible through it. Fred walked around the bed and looked down at his brother's face, seeing his eyes were tightly shut. His lips were pulled back, his teeth gritted. When Martin opened his eyes, tears trickled out of them. The snarl lessened and Martin struggled to smile. Fred knew his brother, understood that he wasn't emotional, not in the way other people are. He never liked to be held as a child, his mother once said.

Fred didn't know what to do. He crouched down and listened, but his brother showed his gritted teeth and clamped his eyes shut. No sound arrived this time.

'Have you taken your tablets?' Fred asked.

Martin's eyes flashed open. 'Yes! Of course I have.'

'You better go back and see the specialist.'

'And what will that do? I'm dying, Fred. There's nothing they can do. Jesus Christ!'

'I've got some strong painkillers. If you want some?'

Martin struggled to nod.

Fred moved to get up, placing his hand on the bed for a moment, then stopped as he felt a bony hand grasp his. He looked down and saw his brother's hand. He crouched down again and looked at Martin's closed eyes. He recalled the promise he'd made to his mother. The grip loosened and Fred took this moment to fetch the tablets and some water.

'I don't know how they'll react with your medication,' Fred said as he gave a couple of the pills to Martin.

'Does it really matter?'

'I suppose not.'

Martin passed him back the glass and tilted his head back into the pillow. He let out a deep breath and a grinding laugh. 'Oh God, what a life.'

Fred got up and stepped quietly towards the door.

'I can't go on like this for long,' Martin whispered.

Fred's stomach churned as he reached the door. He knew it was only a matter of time before his brother started talking like this. He walked out of the room, stood on the landing for a few minutes before sitting down on the stairs. He raised his knees up to his stomach, wrapping his arms around them, and buried his head into his knees. His own pain had faded for the moment. He hadn't told Martin about his own hospital visit and what they have found. Fred rocked a little, knowing he was going to have to deal with Martin's situation pretty soon.

South didn't enjoy dealing with the press, so when Jameson grabbed him and told him about the press conference that was going to have to be given, he couldn't hide his nausea.

Jameson looked surprised. 'Come on, I'd thought you love getting the glory.'

Jameson guided him into the large hall filled with rows of journalists, all eagerly waiting for a bite. He looked over their hungry faces and saw a few middle-aged men, a couple of women and some younger looking lads with cameras. Most were from the local rags, perhaps a couple from the nationals. Heather Beckley's murder had, unsurprisingly, touched a large number of people and built up the usual call for vengeance and tougher sentencing. He imagined the scene when Jon Nelson would get sent down, huddled out of the Old Bailey under a jacket as angry members of the public hurled abuse. The police van would take him to prison, surrounded by photographers, reaching up their cameras, manically flashing away.

South saw Ally sitting behind the two tables shoved together in front of the stage. She looked surprisingly relaxed. She sat up as Jameson arrived in his uniform, his highly polished buttons bulging as he seated himself. South blinked as the cameras started flashing before him. Jameson called for quiet, then gazed around the room gradually and cleared his throat. 'OK, now I'm sorry we had to crowd you all in here, but we called this at the last minute so we could inform you and the public of what's happening in the Heather Beckley murder case.'

'Have you got someone for it?' someone called from the back.

Jameson peered at one of the younger members of the press. 'We have charged a forty-eight year old white male with her murder. We believe we have substantial evidence of his guilt and will be handing over all of it to the Crown Prosecution Service. Seated either side of me are the arresting officers, Detective Inspector Mark South and Detective Sergeant Allison Walker. Their work, along with the rest of the team's, has led to this arrest. Now, I welcome any questions you might have, although we only have a limited amount of time.'

Jameson pointed to a wiry looking man in the front row. The man sat forward. 'Can you name the suspect?'

Jameson shook his head. 'No, not at this time. The lady in the white blouse.'

An attractive woman with long dark hair stood up. 'Have you any leads on the murder of Andrew Nelson and is it true that the murder of Michael Byrne and Andrew Nelson are connected?'

South sat forward. 'The murder of Andrew Nelson is still being thoroughly investigated by a strong and resourceful team of officers. We have several leads. We are looking into the possibility that Michael Byrne and Andrew Nelson were killed by the same man.'

A large man with a short grey beard stood up. 'So, are we to believe their murders had nothing to do with Heather Beckley's death? Is the man you've charged with her murder under suspicion of their murders too?'

Jameson sighed. 'There is no evidence to suggest that the man we have in custody had anything to do with either death. They are being investigated as separate cases.'

The long dark haired woman stood up again. 'Byrne was involved in organised crime, wasn't he? And Andrew Nelson was the main suspect in Heather's killing, so is revenge the reason they were targeted? Could there be a vigilante doing your work for you?'

'We're looking at all angles, but that is doubtful,' South said.

'Right, that's it people. Thank you very much for coming today, but we have lots of work to do.' Jameson stood up and watched the press begin to leave.

A few uniforms escorted the press from the room and left South, Ally and Jameson sitting behind the long desk. Ally tied back her hair and looked over at the other two. 'I think we handled that OK.'

South laughed. 'But we didn't have very many answers for them. We still don't have any idea who knocked off Byrne and Nelson. And I'm not convinced that Skouvakis' murder isn't connected.'

Jameson got up and unbuttoned his uniform. 'Me neither, but let's wait until we find out what Scotland Yard turned up. Their people might find that a contract was put out on him. It has the hallmarks of a hit, but Byrne's murder was violent. Personal. Whoever did that to him was full of rage. The same with Nelson.'

'Maybe that's the way it was supposed to look,' Ally said. 'Maybe they killed Byrne and Nelson in a fit of rage, but when it came to Skouvakis they didn't have time for anything more than two bullets. The killer's probably got Byrne's gun, so why not use it? He made it look like a hit to put us off. Wouldn't a hitman dump the gun afterwards? The area was searched and no gun turned up.'

South shook his head. 'No, he might have dumped it somewhere else. Fuck, I don't know.'

Jameson shut the door and faced South. 'What about Hatch? What happened with him?'

South said, 'He didn't give us much to go on. He hinted at a lot.'

'Like what?' Jameson asked.

'Like everyone on the case could have been taking bribes or scared or both,' South said.

Jameson's face changed. His teeth were bared as he shook his head. 'That's bollocks. There was no way. I'd know if a whole group was taking back handers.

Fuck him. Maybe he was taking bribes, how do we know he wasn't? He's not one of us.'

'He knows a lot more than he's letting on,' Ally said and stood up. 'The way he paints it, you'd think Skouvakis was a ganglord. If anyone is scared of anyone, it's the people bringing in the girls. They're ruthless, dangerous people.'

Jameson said, 'And who are these people?'

South shrugged. 'Russian Mafia? Albanians? They work with British people to organise the whole operation. Ally's right, they're a ruthless bunch. They wouldn't bat an eyelid at slicing up some Ukrainian girl.'

Jameson loosened his tie, his eyes staring out at the back wall. 'So, maybe one of our boys tipped him off about the raids. Maybe he also told them about the girl and they had to get rid of her. The other girls would be too shit scared to say anything to anyone. Plus, they probably kept them too well guarded to let them tell anyone.'

'So, how did she get out and talk to Fred and Harris?' Ally asked.

Jameson thought for a moment. 'You two better have a word with them. Separately though. Get them to go over the statements they made at the time. I don't believe for a moment either of those two would be taking bribes, but we need to go over old ground.'

South adjusted his tie. 'Hatch said he's going to give me a contact, someone who might know about the whole trafficking operation.'

'He said that? You better have some people backing you up. Take Ally and Harris.' Jameson patted South's shoulder.

South nodded. 'OK. I'll make Hatch come along too.'

Jameson nodded and left the hall.

When Jameson was out of earshot, Walker turned to South. 'You're thinking of going alone, aren't you?'

'I have to. Hatch's an undercover policeman, he'll know if I've got back up.'

Ally sighed. 'I don't like the sound of this.'

Tony Harris was briefing a room full of uniforms, most of which looked like they had just had their backsides wiped and pushed out the door of Hendon. He was in the incident room, just about to tell the constables to get on with making more inquiries, when his mobile rang. He pulled the phone from his jacket and saw a private number. He answered, held up his palm for the young wooden tops to see, then walked to the window. 'DCI Tony Harris, can I help you?'

'Yes, Tony, you can,' Franco said, laughing, 'call me on this number right now. 020 8245 2376. It's fucking important. And use the landline.'

Tony looked over at the group of young coppers who were now talking to each other, laughing about something, then pulled a nearby phone towards him and got an outside line. He dialed the number. It was picked up immediately and he heard cutlery and plates being thrown in a sink on the other end. He could almost feel Franco's warm and stale breath as his breathing filled the line.

'That was quick,' Franco said. 'Hope I didn't disturb you, mate.'

'Get on with it.' Harris checked that the uniforms were still chatting away to each other. 'What do you want?'

'Don't you want me to talk dirty to you for a while?'

'Fuck off,' Harris whispered, his stomach turning over.

'We need to talk. In fact, we have to talk. We have a problem.'

'What sort of problem?'

'Girl trouble. The serious kind, Tony. Meet me outside the Dixeyland Fried Chicken across the street in five minutes and I'll fill you in.'

Harris looked over to the other side of the street where the takeaway sat on the corner, a big yellow sign above it with a picture of an enormous chicken's head on it. It sat next to a small patch of wasteland, and beyond it was the train station, a perfect place to hold a private meeting. It was also the most perfect place to stab a copper and leave him there to bleed. 'OK, but just you on your own.'

The line went dead and Harris stood looking down at the street for a short while, turning over the phone call in his mind.

He looked over at the small patch of worn grass underneath the railway bridge. He'd be out in the open. He turned to see the young constables sitting quietly, staring across at him. He smiled for a moment, then spotted Ally and called to her.

She strolled over. 'Yes, Tony? What can I do for you?'

'Could you brief these lot on the circumstances surrounding the murder of Michael Byrne? I've got to pop out for five minutes.' He gripped her shoulders and winked at her.

She looked annoyed for a second. 'Did you get the message about talking to us about Skouvakis and the case you and Fred worked on?'

'Yes, but I don't see why I should have to answer to anyone about that.'

'Look, I'm your friend, Tony, remember that. We're just following up a few leads and we need to go over the investigation with you and Fred. That's all. We've talked to Nick Hatch, the undercover officer.'

Harris patted her back and hurried off as he shouted, 'That's great, Ally. I'll be back in five minutes, maybe ten.'

Harris hurried across the heavy traffic coming down the High Street, holding his hand up as a Turkish teenager shouted something from his suped-up car, dance music blaring out the windows. He got a similar shout from a man in a blue van, then reached the pavement, looking up at the big chicken's head. He might have felt hungry if the thought of talking to Franco again wasn't spinning around in his gut. He looked into the small takeaway and saw two young girls and a man in oily overalls waiting to be served, but no Franco.

'Oi,' Franco called from around the corner.

Tony looked around for a moment as he approached Franco, who was smiling, his hands firmly in his pockets. 'Didn't think you came out in broad daylight, Franco. Do you fancy me? I mean, you do keep finding excuses to see me.'

Franco's was wearing a three quarter length leather jacket, with his collars pulled up around his neck. His usual olive skin looked a little paler today. Franco nodded towards the patch of green grass and the little dirt track as a train rumbled overhead. 'This is important.'

'I'm sure it is. Couldn't we have met over a nice game of golf?'

Franco smirked. 'Football's more my game. Golf? That's just for wankers in stupid trousers.'

Harris laughed. 'True. So, what's so important? I'm a policeman, remember? I'm a busy man.'

'My boss is dead. He was my friend too. Pretty

much family.'

'Don't start me balling, Franco.'

'You were there before they shot him.'

Harris said, 'I didn't have anything to do with it, if that's what you mean?'

Franco waved his hand. 'I know that. You wouldn't be that stupid. Mr Skouvakis knew that one day something like that might happen. He talked about it sometimes, mostly when I was around his gaff, playing poker. He knew that someone he'd upset might sneak up on him. That's why he kept us around.'

'They nearly caught him with his pants down.' Harris smiled, but stopped as he saw Franco's anger. 'So, you're after the person who paid for the hit?'

Franco shook his head slowly. 'They'll figure it out in time. In the meantime, we still have business to do. Skouvakis kept things together, but now people are going to take advantage of his absence. Thing is, we got another problem.'

Harris heard a car come down the dirt track and turned to see a silver car pull up. The door opened. He turned to look at Franco and saw him nod to the man climbing out. After slamming the car door, the man, dressed in a dark blue sweatshirt and jeans, headed over.

Harris focused in on the man's face and instantly knew he'd seen his particular mug before.

'Do you remember Hatch?' Franco asked.

'How you doing?' Hatch said and took out a pack of fags. He slipped one between his lips and lit it. With one eye closed, he looked at Franco. 'So, what have you two discussed so far?'

'Nothing much,' Franco said and leaned against the wall of the takeaway. 'Look, Tony, one of your lot is asking a lot of questions.'

Harris felt his heart vibrate and nausea fill his stomach. 'Yeah, I know.'

'DI Mark South and some bird,' Hatch said and blew smoke up into the air.

Harris sighed. 'So?'

Franco stood up straight. 'So, I don't want this fucking wanker turning over our operation. We've got to sort it out. Or sort him out.'

'Fuck off. I remember the last time you sorted someone out from my nick.'

Franco winked at Hatch. 'It did the trick though, didn't it?'

'You don't have to work with him every day, do you?' Harris said.

Hatch huffed. 'Look, South's waiting for me to make contact. I give him a name and place. He comes alone and, when he does, we make sure he didn't mess around with us. You don't even have to show up or anything, Harris, just make sure you've got our backs. This is your shit too.'

Harris nodded grimly. 'Don't I know it.'

'I don't think you do,' Hatch said. 'You may have turned your back on our little business deal all that time ago, but it still fucking stands that you helped us get away with it. If it wasn't for you, we'd have lost all those girls and a lot of fucking money. Remember the people over the water, the rich fucking gangsters in Russia won't be very pleased if it all goes tits up. So, you better keep your trap shut.'

'You think I'm going start bragging about…oh, fuck it.' Harris shook his head. 'Just do what you're going to do. South is a smart arse tosser anyway. But don't you dare lay a hand on Ally. I mean it.'

Hatch flicked his cigarette at the grass. 'Don't worry, we'll leave your girlfriend out of it. I'll get

South alone. I'll tell him I've got a contact for him to meet, then I'll get separated from him and leave our friends to deal with him.'

'What are you going to do?' Harris asked.

Hatch looked at Franco for a minute. 'That depends on what our friends feel like.'

TWENTY-FIVE

Fred felt strange as he gripped the handle of the door, about to enter the office and sit in his usual comfy chair. He was no longer a policeman and it seemed to him, in consequence, he no longer should have to see the police psychologist. The visits were a guilty pleasure, he realised, as he opened the door to Dr Sheila Evans' office. She sat in her chair, this time wearing black slacks and a dark purple jumper. Her eyes flicked up for a moment from her notebook, while she put a Dictaphone back on her small coffee table. She uncrossed her legs and stood up. 'Hello, Fred, sit down.'

He felt like telling her that he no longer worked for the police, but stopped himself and relaxed into the chair, feeling a longing to talk to someone, to confess everything in his mind. Every bad thought about his life, and the feeling that his brother was a heavy crushing burden on him, wanted to burst out of his mouth, but he remained silent.

'How have you been feeling lately?' she asked and her eyes held his.

Fred looked down. 'Weird, I suppose.'

'Weird? In what way?'

He shrugged. 'I don't know really. Just sort of weird.'

'What about work?' She wrote something in her notebook.

'It's over.'

'What do you mean?'

'They're making me leave. They think it might be for the best.' He looked up.

'And how do you feel about that?'

He shrugged. 'I don't know. I think I've done all I can. Maybe they're right. I'm probably not thinking straight anyway. I did my best to tie up the loose ends and get everything sorted, but it'll just keep going on.'

'What about your life away from work? How do you feel about that? What will you do?'

He thought for a moment, tried to picture himself at home, watching television or reading a book like his brother. Then he recalled the letter he saw that morning from the hospital and the appointment for him to have an operation. They want him to have a piece of the tumour removed. It would tell them whether it was malignant or benign. He already knew. He'd never thought about God much, but then, sitting facing the older beauty of Dr Evans and knowing he'd never touch or kiss her, and that his brother would soon be dead, he felt only hate. He hated someone who might not even exist. Somehow he hoped he did, so he could blame someone for his situation other than his own bad luck. 'Maybe I'll travel. I don't suppose I'll be coming here any more.'

The doctor looked thoughtful for a short moment. 'Well, it's your job that brought you here, but if you still feel like you need help, then maybe you should kept seeing someone.'

'But not you?'

She smiled. 'Well, the Metropolitan Police arrange these sessions, but…'

'It's OK, I think I'm going to be OK. I've faced my demons.'

'Have you? Is that what you feel like you've been

338

doing lately?'

'I think so.' He looked over at the wall. 'I'm not sure what my demons are, except the stuff that got me here. But I think I had to face everything and try and defeat them. Now I think they've gone. I've done the right thing. I hope. I keep thinking about my mother and the last time I talked to her.'

Doctor Evans stopped writing. 'You haven't talked about your mother much.'

He shook his head. 'She died a while back now, before Martin got really ill. I think she knew that he was going to get worse. She made me promise to look after him and do the best for him. And I have tried to.'

'But you don't feel like you have?'

'I don't know. He's in so much pain a lot of the time. The other day I came home and he wasn't downstairs in his chair as he usually is. I knew he must be in bed and for a moment I thought he might be…that he might not have woken up.'

Doctor Evans nodded. 'And how did that make you feel?'

Fred looked at his hands and felt the self-disgust rise through his body until it was sitting in his mouth. 'Relief. I don't know if it was for him or me, but I wanted it to be over.'

Doctor Evans' face changed slightly, becoming less professional and more sympathetic. 'That's nothing to feel bad about. Of course you don't want him to be in pain. And you can't be expected to live your life around him. It's a perfectly normal human response.'

'That's what I keep telling myself. Everything I've done lately has been a normal reaction to everything happening to me. I've done what I thought was right. Surely, that's all I can do?'

'That's all anyone can do.'

'Thank you,' Fred said and stood up.

Doctor Evans seems a little surprised as she looked up. 'You don't have to go yet. The session hasn't ended yet.'

'Well, I should really get home and see Martin. Thank you for everything though.' He held out his hand and watched her smile.

She stood up and took his hand. 'You're welcome, Fred.'

He turned and walked out of the office. For some reason, the dead old man sitting in the chair all those years ago came back to him, his face grey and his mouth open slightly as the spider escaped. He wondered if the old man felt relief.

South checked his watch as he opened the front door and stepped inside. He heard the sound of his sister and Shane eating. He was late again and felt especially guilty, because he really couldn't say work was wholly the reason for his dinner being cold. He walked into the front room and saw them look up at him, both of them finishing off their meals. He was still thinking about Ally Walker. He'd finished the evening by chatting to her about the Hatch situation. She didn't like the fact he was going to meet the undercover officer alone. She told him they couldn't trust anybody at this point. Not even Harris or Fred, although Ally had said it was unlikely Fred would ever sell out. South sort of agreed, even though he kept remembering what Hatch had said about the power and money behind the smuggling operation.

His final thought was of the young girls shipped in and forced to have sex with various men, a thought that made him want to throw up.

He watched his son eat and ignored his sister's

look of disappointment.

Somewhere out there in London were young, scared girls bedding down for the night or being made to stand on street corners, probably drugged up to their eyeballs. He took off his jacket and put it on the back of a chair. He smiled and walked over to his son.

'Hello, Dad,' Shane said.

'Looked like I missed dinner.' He ruffled Shane's hair and nicked his last chip.

Emma frowned as she picked up her empty plate. 'I can warm yours up.'

'Thank you.' South took a seat opposite his son. 'And how're you doing?'

Shane put his knife and fork down. 'OK. I'm going to be playing football after school now.'

'That's great.'

'Did you arrest anyone? A kid at school said the police don't have any powers any more. Or that they put people in prison who aren't guilty.'

'We do the best we can. We don't go around putting innocent people in prison because we feel like it. You know I wouldn't do that. Your mate is talking rubbish.'

'He's not my mate. He's a shit.' Shane played with his fork.

'Oi. Language.' South tried not to laugh. 'Anyway, I caught someone the other day.'

'It was in the local papers today,' Emma said and pointed to the newspaper on the coffee table.

South heard his phone ringing in his coat, then grabbed it. 'Detective Inspector Mark South, what can I do for you?'

'Hello. Call me on this number from your landline.'

South ran up the stairs and dialed the number registered on his mobile.

'Hello, South,' Hatch said. 'Sorry, did I interrupt

your dinner?'

'No, not at all. What's happening with you?' South was sitting on his bed, the phone cradled in his neck, holding a pen and paper ready.

'You live with your sister now, don't you? You and your son?'

South took the phone from his neck and held it to his ear. 'What's that supposed to mean?'

'Just been checking up on you, mate. Just want to make sure you're straight, know what I mean? Anyway, I'm in a shithole pub right now surrounded by local wankers, so let's get on with this. If you want to know more about what you've been looking into, then you should get yourself over to the Rising Sun in Walthamstow. There's a club next door where they have lap dancers sometimes. In fact, they're here tonight. It's ten quid to get in, but I'm sure you can afford that.'

'You want me to come over tonight? Who am I going to meet?' South scribbled down the name of the pub.

'A contact. He's OK. You can trust him. He'll be in the club pushing tenners into the girls' knickers. See you about ten. Alright?'

South thought quickly, sizing up the risk. 'OK. I'll see you then.'

When South came down the stairs, Emma had his dinner sitting on the table. She and Shane were eating ice cream in silence. Emma looked up and pointed her spoon at him. 'Was that an important phone call?'

'Yes, I think it was.' He sat at the table and looked at his microwaved dinner. South had a distinct hatred of microwaves. He wasn't at all surprised to read the latest cancer fears related to them. He played with a piece of beef for a while, then looked up to see Emma watching him.

'So, are you going out again?' Emma asked.

South watched his son finish his bowl, take it to the sink and disappear up to his room. 'Is he OK?'

'He's lonely at the moment. He got in a fight with that boy he was talking about. Did alright I think though, but you're not around enough. I'm not going to moan at you, because I know what you do.'

'Thanks.' South pushed his dinner away from him. 'I have to go out to meet someone tonight.'

'Tonight? Who?'

'Just a contact I got off another officer.' He smiled.

'You came down here to investigate internally, right?'

'That's right. Look, I'm going to be OK. I'm meeting up with another officer and he's going to introduce me to someone who might have some info for me.' He rubbed his eyes and looked at his watch.

'I hope you know what you're doing, Mark. Meeting strange people in the middle of the night doesn't sound good.' She looked at him like he was crazy.

'You'll be able to read about me in the papers again.'

'That's what I'm afraid of, you git. Don't want to see your name in the obituaries. Be bloody careful. I hope you'll have people backing you up or something.'

He'd thought about getting Ally to come with him, at least to keep an eye on the club, but he didn't want to get her in any trouble either. Hatch had said it was best to come alone. 'Don't worry, I'll have someone there with me.'

TWENTY-SIX

The pages of the book were thick and Fred turned them slowly, listening to his brother's breathing, allowing each hum of life to fill his ears. He didn't know why he was sitting in Martin's room, his aching backside on his brother's black office chair. Fred took two more painkillers and thought about tomorrow's operation. He hadn't told Martin much, just that he had some final police business to handle, knowing he'd be back home in a few hours after the operation. It was a simple procedure. A biopsy. Then they'd know what he already knew, that it was malignant. But he wanted to know if there was anything they could do, any treatment they might be able to give him. Every time he felt the ache of pain from his rear, it reminded him he was still alive.

He turned another page and listened to the sweep of the thick pages, then another shallow breath from his brother.

Martin's eyes opened and he looked about him, at his small world and then at Fred. His skin seemed so pale and thin, as if flesh-coloured muslin has been stretched over his bones.

'You still reading that book?' Martin smiled slightly, his hand reaching for the controls to the bed.

Fred looked down at the pages. 'Keep thinking it'll tell me something.'

'Like what?' The bed slowly rose with an electronic

moan.

'I don't know really. They forced me to retire before I could find out who told that girl to walk into the supermarket with a knife to her throat. Not that I was getting anywhere, anyway.'

Martin sat up. 'Perhaps it's all there.'

'I doubt it.' Fred turned another page and saw he'd reached the beginning of Richard The Third. 'He calls himself Richard in the emails to the girl. Thought of himself as some sort of cripple.'

'Maybe he is. Maybe you should arrest every cripple in London.' Martin lay back. 'Where did you get that book anyway?'

'The old peoples home. It was sitting on the book shelves.'

Martin smiled. 'So, they've booted you out and already you've turned to crime. Excellent.'

'How're you feeling?'

Martin opened his eyes slowly and looked across at Fred. 'Like I'm dying slowly. I can't die slowly, Fred.'

His brother's words punched him in the stomach. 'Well, I don't know what I can say.'

'It'll take months, maybe a year like this.'

'Maybe we can go back to the specialist.'

'Don't talk rubbish. Look, I'm not going to wither away like this. I can't.'

Fred could hear the unusual emotion in his brother's words, a trembling coming from his throat. He dipped his head and brought it back up when he heard the doorbell ring. 'I better get that. I'll be back in a while.'

Fred opened the door to find Ally stood before him. She smiled a little, her eyes glancing behind Fred. 'Hello, Fred, how are you? I thought I'd come round and have a chat.'

Fred smiled. 'Come in.'

She walked into the front room and looked at the empty leather recliner. 'No Martin?'

'No, he's staying in his room a lot these days.'

Ally sat down. 'He's getting worse?'

Fred nodded. 'So, what did you want to talk about?'

'Not going to offer me a drink?'

'Alcohol or coffee?' Fred looked towards the kitchen.

'A coffee would be great.' Ally got up and followed Fred to the kitchen. 'We need you to come in and go over the Skouvakis case.'

Fred looked up sharply. 'You're talking about his murder? I don't…'

'No, the prostitution ring. When you and Tony were after him, and the people who were smuggling those girls in, remember?'

Fred put the kettle down and turned it on. The relief he felt upstairs faded as he looked into Ally's police face. Her emotions had all but vanished. 'Why now? You think that has something to do with his murder?'

'Maybe. South and I are looking into it.'

Fred nodded and took two cups from the cupboard. 'South's on a bit of a roll. What with finding Heather's killer.'

'We got lucky.'

'It's a good job they let me go. I would've had the wrong man banged up.' Fred sipped his coffee.

'Don't say that. You've been through a lot. Anyway, stop changing the subject. What about this smuggling ring?'

Fred walked through to the lounge and sat down. Ally followed him and relaxed into an armchair.

Fred put his coffee cup down on the table. 'There was not much to say. We figured out that there were probably cells operating around London, maybe the whole country. They'd bring in a supply of girls and a cell would put them up in a flat or somewhere and get them working to pay off their travel expenses.'

'The fucking bastards.'

'You're dealing with ruthless people who only care about money. Human lives don't mean anything to them.'

'But you got a tip off?' Ally said and blew steam off her coffee.

'Yeah, some informant told us about Skouvakis' massage parlours. We got the go ahead to steam in there, but we didn't find anything. Then we got the word on two flats he owned. We didn't find anything there either.'

'Convenient,' Ally said. 'What about the girl who came to you?'

Fred looked up, a little surprised. 'South told you about her, did he?'

Ally nodded. 'You must've felt terrible.'

Fred looked into his coffee. 'I've never forgotten the look on her face. She said she was going back to work for them, so she could help us and the other girls and we let her. What the bloody hell were we thinking?'

Ally patted Fred's knee. 'It was just a mistake. You were doing what you thought best at the time.'

Fred looked at Ally's hand, then up to her sympathetic face. He couldn't think of any other colleague who he liked working with more than her, and he couldn't think of one person he trusted more. He imagined himself trying to get back from his operation the next day. He wouldn't be able to drive. 'Ally, I was wondering if you'd do me a favour.'

'What is it?'

'I'm going to need picking up from somewhere

tomorrow.'

Ally frowned. 'Shit, I think we're going to be jammed pack, what with this whole reinvestigation. Is it really important?'

'Not really. I think I'll be able to get a taxi or something.' He smiled for a moment and thought about the investigation that South was on, picturing him searching around London for young lost girls. The girl, Melanie, came to mind and he could see her milky skin and green eyes, a cigarette in her hand as they sat drinking in a pub. He recalled the smell of the smoke from her cigarette; it was some European or Turkish brand. It was a meeting that Harris didn't know about. Fred tried to convince her to leave the country. He thought he could get her away and she had agreed. She'd promised to meet him the next day and he'd believed her. Fred winced.

'Are you OK, Fred?' Ally asked. 'Maybe I can get someone to pick you up tomorrow? Why can't you drive?'

'Car's out of action. Bloody thing. Mechanic mate of mine is coming around to look at it tomorrow.' Fred drank the remainder of his coffee. 'Tell South to watch his back. They're shits those people.'

Ally nodded. 'I will. Well, I better be going. Say hello to Martin for me.' Ally got up. 'And don't forget to come in and go through your earlier statements.'

Fred saw Ally to the door, then sat down. Skouvakis was dead and that was for the best.

Fred heard his mobile ring. It was a private number and he answered, half expecting a salesman's voice.

'Hello, is that Detective Inspector Fairservice?' the voice asked.

'Yes?'

'It's Scott Brown from the library. How are you?'

Fred sat down, glad that it was the librarian and not one of his colleagues. 'I'm OK, not bad, thanks.'

'I was phoning because we've got a book club tomorrow evening. I thought you might be interested. Something to do.'

Fred thought for a moment, remembering his operation. 'Well, I don't think I'll be able to come. I have to go to the hospital tomorrow.'

'Oh dear, nothing serious I hope.' Brown sounded genuinely concerned.

For some reason, Fred felt compelled to tell the truth. 'Well, it's a small operation, but I might be out of it, so I'm going to have trouble getting back.'

'Really?' There was a pause on the other end. 'Well, I can pick you up. What hospital?'

Fred didn't know what to say for a moment, his mind tired of thinking too much. 'Really? Well, that would be great.'

'What hospital?'

'North Middlesex.'

'Well, get them to give me a ring and I'll come and get you.'

'OK, thanks, if you're sure,' Fred mumbled into the mouthpiece.

'Of course. It's OK, I'm used to hospitals, picking people up and stuff.'

'Right, well, thanks. I'll ring you tomorrow.'

'OK, Fred.'

'Well, OK then. I'll see you then.' Fred finished the call and put his phone down, amazed by how things sometimes work out.

South parked as close as he could to the venue. As he passed the pub, which looked like any other London pub, except for the blacked out windows on one side, he glanced at the public bar and took in the colour of the place and the number of bodies. He felt a light rain flickering across his face and looked at the damp pavement that glowed red and blue, reflecting the neon sign that hung over the blacked out windows of the club.

South stepped into the public side and saw the long bar with a straggle of young customers lined up along it. South tried to get to the bar, while trying to spot Hatch. He searched every little table and saw only people drinking and chatting, while a thick cloud of cigarette smoke engulfed his senses.

South ordered a pint, then turned his back to the bar and looked through the door that led to the pole dancing part. It was guarded by a large man in a black suit and silver shirt. A group of girls poured through the door and brought with them a mixture of perfumes. He moved along, gripping his cold pint, thinking it might have all been a wind up, just one copper trying to piss off another nosy copper.

Then Hatch walked in through the door. It had started to rain harder and the undercover policeman's leather jacket was covered in raindrops. He ran a hand through his damp scalp and stuck out his other hand for South to shake. 'Fucking weather.'

'Yeah, typical London,' South said and watched as Hatch pushed through the crowd and smiled at the barmaid.

'Want a drink?' Hatch asked.

'No, just got this one.'

'Oi, Debs, get us a pint.'

South sipped his drink. 'This your local then?'

Hatch looked around him as he took out a pack of cigarettes, then lit one. 'Not really. I come here sometimes. It's a convenient meeting point.'

'Who are we meeting?'

'An old contact. Don't wet yourself, South. In a minute we'll go through…'

Hatch's jacket started ringing and he took out his phone. He walked away from South and started shouting into his mobile. South moved closer to hear the conversation, but Hatch moved into the crowd of girls, losing himself in a sea of perfume and cleavage.

When Hatch appeared again, South heard him say, 'No, come here, you fucker.'

South sipped his lager as Hatch stared at his phone for a moment. He swore again, then put it away. 'The bastard won't come down here. Do you fucking believe it?'

South felt his stomach tighten. 'Do you know where we could find him?'

'I know where he might be.'

Harris picked up the phone and listened to Ally talking about the investigation into Skouvakis' murder. He was listening, but also felt himself shrink, sinking down into his chair as his wife watched. Her face gradually became more and more concerned.

He got off the phone and walked around the house, touching objects as if he was about to pick them up, but then drifting off to another part of the house. At one point, he took out his golf clubs and stared at them. His wife, Ann, came up behind him and looked at the clubs.

'What's wrong? she asked. 'Why are you staring at them?'

'Don't know.' Tony put them away and smiled at his wife.

'Have you got problems at work, is that it?' Ann, with her bobbed black hair and tanned face, stood with her arms folded. 'What's happened?'

'Nothing's happened.' Harris sat down and put on the television. He looked over at the drawn curtains. It was dark beyond them and he wondered how long it would it take him to get to where South was. He wasn't sure what they would do to his colleague. He didn't want to think about it. He knew they were capable of anything. Ally wanted him to come in and give his side of events, but he could hardly face seeing her across the desk. She'd talk things through, looking into his eyes. It wasn't because of the details and having to lie to her; it was because after tonight, he'd have to face her knowing he betrayed them all.

He looked at the TV screen and tried to see the late night football game without seeing the young girl's face. He saw Melanie on one particular day, before she disappeared into the flat, her face bruised. Harris rubbed his face. A burst of fear burned up through his stomach and into his chest. He got up and looked around for his car keys.

'Where are you going now?' Ann asked.

'Out.'

South drove his car to the address Hatch gave him. He pulled up outside the terrace house in a side street off of Wood Green, tucked behind the Shopping City. The streetlights illuminated the front of the house, allowing South to see the curtains were drawn. There was no sign of life inside.

Hatch walked up to South's window. 'He'll be in there, hiding.'

'Who is he?' South looked up at the house and something told him this was all a waste of time. 'No offence, Hatch, but this feels like a wind up. Call me when you've got a real lead.'

Hatch gripped South's shoulder. 'I'm telling you, this fucker used to work for Skouvakis. He knew it all, so go in. He'll be hiding behind the sofa. I'll knock on the front door pretty loud and you go around the back. If he hears me coming, the fucker will do a runner. I swear on my mother's life.'

South looked into the copper's face, weighing up the situation. He wished Fred was there to back him up. He got out of the car. Even though it was nearly May, a cold breeze drifted up the street as South stepped closer to the house. He saw the alleyway leading around the back of the house, then looked at Hatch who was already making his way to the front door. He saw the copper about to wrap his knuckles on the door, so started walking down the alley. South stopped for a moment, his eyes finding the dark and nothing to focus on. He stood for a moment, seeing shapes in the darkness. He started walking towards the archway, realising he'd look like a coward if he didn't at least get to the back door.

He felt paving under his feet, and the strong smell of creosote as he reached out his hand and saw a child's swing along the small stretch of garden. He could barely make it out for a few seconds, but there it was. This was a family home, he thought and looked at the back windows. It didn't feel right.

He felt something move behind him, then heard material scraping against brick. A hand wrapped itself around his neck, while another pair of hands swept away his legs. At least three bodies pinned him to the ground, their breathing pounding away at his face, his own hands scratching at the gritty pathway. He was dragged backwards, the grit of the driveway ripping through his palms.

He'd known something was wrong. He knew it. Shit. Shit. Shit!

TWENTY-SEVEN

Fred looked around his bedroom for a moment as if he expected to see something or someone. Satisfied he was alone, he sat up and reached for his painkillers. He swallowed two, flushing them down with a glass of stagnant water. He grimaced and swung his feet out of the bed. He recalled the dream he'd been having. It was close to being a nightmare, sort of dark and…he shook it away and stood up, feeling his angry, spiteful companion biting at his spine.

An electronic hum came from Martin's room, so Fred stepped towards his bedroom door and knocked. He heard Martin's shallow command for entry and walked in to find his brother sitting at the desk, facing the computer screen. Fred looked at the empty bed and the duvet that was half hanging off it. 'You managed to get out of bed then?'

Martin looked around to him slowly, a splattering of sweat on his pale head. He nodded slowly and turned his head back to the monitor. 'It wasn't easy.'

Fred sat on the bed. 'You should have called me.'

'Why?'

'Because it can't be easy getting from your bed to there.'

'And what would you have done? Carried me? You're always carrying me.' Martin stopped typing and let his head droop.

'I'm your brother.'

'You made Mum a promise. That day in the hospital, the last time we saw her.'

Fred shrugged. 'Yeah, to look after you.'

'No, to do what I wanted. Anything to make things easier. She told me.'

Fred looked up, feeling an iciness down his back. 'When? You didn't go back in, did you?'

'I did go back.' Martin looked away. 'I brought her the pills.'

Fred gripped the duvet. 'You gave her the pills that she used to kill herself?'

Martin nodded. 'She asked me to. I snuck them in. It was up to her. She made me promise.'

'I'm not going to listen to this…I'm going to bed.' Fred got up, a swirl of spots before his eyes. He gripped the doorframe as he heard his brother say, 'I don't want to go on months and months like this. Please.'

Fred walked out of the room and into his bedroom. He looked at the Shakespeare book on his shelf and picked it up, feeling the weight of it in his hands. Something from his dream tried to come back to him, but then retreated back into a pool of darkness. He sunk back down onto the duvet, feeling the warmth of it touching his back as he curled up into a ball.

The journey was soaked in petrol fumes. South had his arms tied behind his back and his shoulder felt as if it had been torn from his socket. The red of the brake lights burned through the hood he was wearing, coating his world in scarlet. He felt every bump in the road and the vibration of the engine. The blackness consumed him until the car stopped and the boot opened.

South sat in a small room, his head covered by the

hood. His hands were tied behind his back, his shoulder wrenched backwards, burning with pain. They had dragged him up a flight of stairs, his feet thudding against each step. He felt a brush of worn carpet at the top of the stairs, then heard voices. Muffled female voices.

The hands that gripped him were large and carried him with ease up the stairs. They pushed him into an armchair. When his hands were secured, he felt the cold barrel of a gun against his temple.

He tried to control his breathing, feeling a draft of cold air brushing his neck.

There was safety in the hood placed on his head, no light or faces to see. He sat back a little. He moved his arms, but the pain burned into his shoulder. An image of Hatch came to his mind. It was a black and white image, his face smug, turning away and walking into the darkness of the street.

There was a slow creak of a door opening across the room and South sat up, his eyes trying to make out anything through the blackness shrouding his face. He mumbled a 'hello', and waited for a reply. A female breath, then perfume, drifted to his nose. He bent closer to the scent.

There was heavy footsteps across the landing as the woman let out a startled cry. 'I'm sorry!'

'Get the fuck out of there!' a man shouted. He had a South London accent, South noted. The footsteps came into the room and stopped, then another set, softer this time, came across the carpet and stopped closer to South. A shadow fell across him as a hand yanked the hood off his head.

South blinked for a moment and looked up at the two men. The one who removed the mask looked down at him, not smiling or showing any emotion, just looking carefully at South's face. This man had a thin, but hard looking face, with dark skin and green eyes. He had receding hair, just a thin strip of black hair sitting on top of his head. South looked away from him and stared at the much larger man who stood by the door. His large blockhead and meaty face was coated in amusement. They both wore shirts and trousers and stank of aftershave.

The one closest to South said something in a foreign language, but the larger man just stared at him blankly. The foreigner started pacing slowly around the room, while South watched him. He noticed the room was small, like a child's bedroom. He could feel the draft from the window behind him, but no light. The patterned carpet looked as if it was from the seventies, as did the peach wallpaper that was coming off the walls. South's heart started to bounce around his chest as an icy sweat ran down his sides, under his armpits. He fiddled with his hands, but they were tied too tight.

'We know what you are,' the larger man said, then stepped closer and stood by the wall.

The foreign man mumbled something again. The larger man nodded and looked at South. 'It doesn't matter that you're a pig. Don't think that we care. We don't.'

The larger man laughed and winked at the foreigner.

'Look, just let me go,' South said, hearing his voice break up.

More indecipherable words were thrown across the room from the foreign man, then the large man laughed again.

'You shouldn't have gone sniffing around,' the larger man said and stared at South. 'Bet you wish you hadn't now. Get us something to sit on.'

357

The foreigner left, then came back with a battered straight back chair. The large man sat opposite South and leaned forward. 'Do you like girls?'

South looked over at the foreigner who started to laugh crazily. The large man smiled a little and said, 'We've got plenty of girls. Nice young girls. Do you like them young?'

The foreigner moved about the room as he laughed, shaking his head. 'No, he don't like girls, he likes wanky, wanky.'

The larger man laughed, then leaned forward. 'You a queer?'

South shook his head. 'No.'

'Yeah. I've got you nailed. You're a queer.' The large man leaned back a little. 'Where's my little friend?'

The foreigner strode out of the room, then came back carrying a small handgun by his side. He shut the door behind him.

The large man leaned forward, closer than before, so South was engulfed in his breath. He grinned, then whispered, 'We're going to kill you and there's nothing you can do. Don't bother crying for help.'

South looked beyond the large man. He stared at the foreigner, then down at the gun he was holding. The foreign man smirked and nodded.

'You're going to cry, aren't you?' the large man said.

South saw Shane, sitting at home watching television, his sister ironing. His heart rattled inside his rib cage as electricity shot through his legs and arms. But he managed to keep his mask of calmness, to stop himself throwing up.

DCI Tony Harris pulled up outside Fred's house and sat for a moment, the engine still sighing. He looked away from the curtains and placed his hands on the steering wheel, lowering his head to it. Slowly, he began to raise and lower his head, tapping it on the wheel. He gritted his teeth and closed his eyes. He sat up sharply and looked to his right. The curtains were drawn, but he knew Fred would be up, probably tucking in his fucked up brother.

Harris pulled the handbrake on and jumped out of the car. He knocked on the door and waited for the hall light to come on, which it did. Fred's shape appeared and opened the door, his eyes opening wide as he saw Harris.

Harris pushed past Fred, but didn't look at him. 'You look a right mess.'

After he walked into the living room, Harris stood staring around the place. He'd been there a long time before and the place still looked just as untidy. Harris saw the fucked up brother's chair and sat in it, looking up at Fred as he entered.

'Make yourself at home, Harris,' Fred said and picked up a remote to turn down the television.

'Why don't you call me Tony like everybody else, Fred? It gets on my fucking nerves.' Harris picked up a book, read the long-winded title and threw it down on the coffee table.

'It's late,' Fred said. 'My brother'll be trying to sleep.'

'Will he? Look, Fred, you're an annoying shit.'

'Am I? Why's that?'

Harris decided to cut to the chase. 'What's South up to? I mean, what the fuck does he think he's doing?'

Fred moved over to his armchair and sat facing Harris. 'His job. Why?'

'He'll get himself killed.'

Fred laughed.

'What the fuck are you laughing at? You know

what I mean.' Harris burned with anger.

'Skouvakis is dead. It's over.'

'What about the ones who look after the girls?'

'What about them?'

'They'll do anything to keep things together. You know that. Whoever killed Skouvakis, has just cut the head off the snake.'

Fred stared at Harris. 'What are you worried about?'

'We walked away, remember? You and me. We could've done something about that dead girl, but we didn't. She'd come to us, but we kept our mouths shut.'

'They didn't find anything to connect her to Skouvakis. If the Yard didn't find anything, then what good were we going to do?'

Harris sat up, his eyes filled with rage. 'We could've told them what we knew.'

'You didn't care at the time. In fact, you were the one who convinced me we couldn't do anything. I keep thinking that you seemed determined to prevent me from telling the Yard anything. Now all this. Why? What happened all that time ago? Was it you who tipped them off? Yeah, we both got warned off, but you seemed to be protecting them.'

Harris shook his head. 'Fuck off.'

'Why're you so worried about South? What's he getting close to? Is it you? You worried that he might find something out? What do you know about Skouvakis being knocked off?' Harris shrugged. 'I don't know anything about that. Maybe it was the others. Skouvakis and Byrne were giving them cover, getting the girls places to operate from, but maybe the others got greedy and decided to get rid of them, take control of the whole thing.'

'No, it doesn't make sense.' Fred sat down again. 'Whoever killed Byrne killed Nelson. Nelson had nothing to do with all the other Skouvakis business.'

Harris said, 'How do we know that? There might be a connection. Maybe he saw something. Who the fuck knows?'

Fred looked up slowly, his eyes widening. 'You're worried they're coming for you too. Or have they been to see you? What've they had over you all this time?'

Harris looked down. 'They threatened my wife and son. What could I do?'

'You had quite a few options.'

'And what about you?' Harris jabbed a finger at Fred. 'They beat the shit out of you. Tortured you! They left you for dead, for fuck's sake.'

'Did they? Why do you think it was them?'

Harris moved closer to Fred. 'Who else would want to torture you for three days? I know about the scars all over your body. What else did they do? What did they say to you?'

Fred looked up, his face emotionless. 'Get out.'

'What about South? He's meeting Hatch tonight.'

Fred looked away. 'Just get out, Tony.'

Harris stood for a moment, looking down at the familiar lump in the chair, then stormed out.

TWENTY-EIGHT

Friday, 30th April 2004

Fred was sitting in a small waiting room, his nostrils being stung by the smell of Deep Heat emanating from an elderly lady sitting near him. He moved his legs and heard the rustle of the green gown he was wearing. He watched the nurses move heavily across the corridor, while a long-haired domestic assistant mopped the floor. He turned and read the sign written on the drinks machine near him, something about it being broken. He looked up at the desk before him, where a receptionist tapped away on her keyboard.

A large nurse ambled his way, her shoes slapping the floor as she looked at him blankly. 'Come with me. It's Mr Fairservice, isn't it?'

Fred nodded, smiled and followed her to the large room filled with little trolleys and screens pulled across half the room. White swing doors led to more corridors at each end of the room. In the middle of the room sat a bed with stirrups at one end.

'Lie down on the table, please,' the nurse said and started looking through a file.

Fred looked over at the trolley beside him and saw an array of instruments that looked as if they could easily be used for torture. He lay back with his arse in the air. The nurse turned and looked at him, her face showing nothing but boredom.

At the far end of the room, the doors sprung open

and a doctor, dressed in scrubs, walked in. His hair was thick and silver even though he looked reasonably young in the face. The doctor smiled at Fred and rubbed his hands together. Fred sniffed the air and smelt detergent hand soap.

'Right, OK, Mr Fairservice, try and relax,' the doctor said as he was handed a chart.

Another nurse came in carrying a tray. Fred saw a syringe and a long tube. He watched as they put the needle in his arm and attached it to the tube. The liquid sped down the tube into his arm and he melted backwards into the table, sinking into a thick, grey mud. For a moment he felt like fighting to stay awake, but then fell helplessly downwards.

Fred moved and his backside screamed at him to stay still. He flexed his arm instead and saw the cotton swab taped to it. He fought with the starched sheets across his body and sat up. His head seemed to be moving even though he was perfectly still, which made him want to puke. He watched an older nurse come towards his bed. Her face looked kind.

She placed a urine bottle by the bed. 'You're awake then? That's good to see. How do you feel?'

'A bit sick.' Fred tried to smile.

'That's to be expected. That's the anaesthetic, but you'll feel fine in a little while.'

Fred could hear a faint hint of an Irish accent.

'Shall I send in the young man waiting for you?' she asked.

'Please.' Fred sat up a little and his stomach turned over.

Scott Brown looked about the recovery room, his face blank until he saw Fred. He moved across the room carrying a bottle of orange juice. 'How did it go?'

Fred looked down towards his backside. 'Have no

idea, but feel a bit sore down there.'

'Well, you'll just have to wait and see what they say.' Brown grabbed a chair and sat by Fred. 'They said you'll be ready to go home in half an hour.'

Fred nodded and pushed his head back into the pillow. 'I suppose I'll get the results in a few days.'

'I should think so.' Brown smiled. 'It'll be OK.'

Fred looked at him for a moment, noticing his latest hat. This time was the kind worn by young skaters. He'd seen them carrying their boards tucked under their arms, with their hats pulled down over their ears. Fred looked at Brown's eyes. He saw the weird baron ridge where his eyelashes should have been. 'Thanks for coming.'

'Don't worry about it. What else would I be doing? Putting books on shelves? Handing out fines?'

Fred allowed himself a laugh. His head seemed to swim towards the ceiling for a moment until he pulled it back. 'Thanks anyway. I couldn't have gone home on my own. I didn't really want to either.'

'Anytime. I mean that.'

'Who's running the library?'

'Doreen. She's old and crazy, but she's really nice.' Brown scratched his ear. 'The place runs itself really. All we seem to do is take the books they bring back and put them on the shelves. You don't need to be a brain surgeon. Now, your job...'

Fred looked at Brown and raised his eyebrows. 'It's not so different. We look through the facts and file them away. Sometimes we manage to put someone away, sometimes it's just another statistic. I haven't done much to help...but I do try. Or at least I did.'

Brown reached out a hand and squeezed Fred's shoulder. 'You seem like someone who's had a lot of troubles, but you keep them wrapped up inside you.

Deep inside you. That's not healthy.'

Fred wiped a tear from his eye and looked at it. 'It's not, but that's the way it is. That's what being a copper is about. You're not supposed to get emotional. But… well, I've done a few things I'm not proud of…but at the time they seemed like the right thing to do, if you know what I mean?'

Brown nodded. 'I'm not a priest, but if you want to pour out your soul…sort of confess, I can make the same vowel of secrecy.'

Fred shrugged. 'It's not the sort of thing I feel I can talk about. It could be incriminating.'

Brown's eyes widened a little. 'I see. Well, I'm not about to go running to the law. To tell you the truth, I haven't exactly led a straight existence. There have been some particularly dodgy moments.'

Fred let out a dry chuckle. 'I see. Then there's my brother.'

'What about your brother?'

'He's dying and there's nothing I can do. He keeps saying things…' Fred swallowed, his head down.

'What things?'

'Asking me to…well, help him along.'

Brown frowned. 'And what do you feel about that?'

'Sick. I promised our mum that I'd do whatever I could for him. Whatever he wanted…but…'

'If it's his decision…'

'Well, if he wants to…well… end his suffering, then he could…easily… I mean, he doesn't need my help. He has strong painkillers.'

'Maybe he's after your blessing.' Brown raised his shoulders as Fred quickly looked at him.

'Maybe.'

'Perhaps he's waiting for you to give him a sign, a gesture.'

Fred watched the Irish nurse come in and smile at him. 'Right, you can take him home now. You feeling ready to go, Fred?'

Fred nodded. 'Yes, thank you.'

DS Allison Walker sat staring at her computer screen, occasionally looking up towards the doors of the incident room. It was still early and South could walk in at any moment. Jameson was in his office, talking on the phone, eating his breakfast from a white paper bag, something purchased from the sandwich shop down the street. Ally smelt the coffee he was drinking as he came in and nodded to her. It smelt thick and black, full of sugar, just the way he liked it. It made her stomach ache for a moment. She never ate or drank anything more than water in the morning, not before ten anyway. She looked up again as the doors of the incident room opened. A PC walked in and handed a sheet of paper to one of the officers manning the phones. She sighed and looked at her computer screen, where she'd been trying to type up a statement.

She took out her mobile and saw there were no missed calls and only one text message. The message was from Sarah, her friend from the pub.

Ally smiled and put the phone away. She quickly took it out again and dialed South's phone. His voice came on, the answer phone message. He was unavailable and it made her worry more, but she smiled a little bit, just because she could hear his voice. She looked towards Jameson's office and saw him still talking on the phone, his mouth bulging with the sandwich he was consuming.

She'd phoned South's mobile late last night, just because he'd asked her to. He'd wanted her to contact him, worried about his own safety. He'd said he thought Hatch would be OK and would probably keep his word about getting the contact to meet him, but still he suggested she call him that night to make sure he was safe. Also, he'd told her not to go to Jameson if a problem occurred. She'd stared at him. Why? He looked at her and shrugged. Embarrassment was the answer. He wanted to do this without Jameson's help, without too much scrutiny from the top brass. He wanted to delve into a murky, dirty world and come up smiling.

South had seen her concern and smiled. 'Alright, if I go and see Hatch and I disappear or something, tell Fred.'

Again, she looked at him like he was crazy. 'Why Fred? What can Fred do?'

'He's on the outside now. He can do more than the rest. He hasn't got anyone to answer to.'

'What if he's one of them? What if he's the one who tipped them off on the original investigation?'

'Then I'll be fucked.'

She took out her phone and saw there were still no missed calls and no messages. She looked around at the bodies of her colleagues as they went about their usual routine, typing and phoning and filling in forms. She went through her address book, looking for Fred's number, and brought it up. Her finger hovered over the call button, but then she cleared it and rung South's phone again. There was no answer, except his comforting and friendly recorded voice asking her to leave a message. She did, asking him to contact her. She put her phone away, cleared her mind and began tapping at her keyboard again.

South felt the gag pulling at his mouth as he lifted his head. He heard a key entering the lock of the door, then watched as the door slowly opened and a slender figure stood in the doorway. The young girl stood before him had remarkably bony arms. He could see the bone in her elbows threatening to split through her pale skin. Her midriff was perfectly flat, the pelvic bones pressing through her flesh. Her baggy trousers hung on her hips, revealing bruising around her pelvis. He looked up and saw shoulder length black hair that framed her head, which was small and white, like a sickly doll's. Two large eyes looked at him, eyeing him, flickering nervously to her left. South noticed the redness on her arms, the group of tiny needle marks.

She raised her bony shoulders over her neck as she looked around the room. She tried to smile, then quickly moved away from the door as heavy footsteps come closer. South saw the foreign man grab her arm and start pushing her down the hall, screaming at her in his native language. After he pushed her along the hall, he came back, wiping lipstick from his mouth, smearing it across his jaw. He smiled as he bent down in front of South, a spout of foreign words and spit coming from his mouth.

'He said he's going to kill you today,' large man said, appearing in the doorway holding a can of lager. 'He's wrong though. Pay him no attention.'

The larger man pulled the foreign man away, then stood in front of South. He grinned. 'I'm going to kill you.'

From the back of his trousers, the large man pulled out a small sharp knife and held it before South's eyes, allowing him to see the silver of the blade up close. 'I'm going to stick this in your stomach. Then I'm going to stab you in the leg or arm. I'll make sure I don't get anywhere that'll make you bleed too much, like your neck or wrist. I'll stab you in your groin next. Probably cut off your little dick. Maybe I'll make you eat it. How would you like that? Ever eaten cock before?'

South stared into the man's eyes, not looking away, making sure he didn't blink.

The man laughed and looked at his foreign friend. 'This here pig's a bit of a hard bastard. I thought he would've cried by now. Perhaps he'll wait until we're gone and then cry himself to sleep.'

'What the bleeding hell's going on?' A middle-aged woman in a short black leather skirt and red blouse came into the room, pulling her dark brown hair from her face. Her eyes bulged when she looked at South. 'Who the fuck is this?'

'Calm down,' the large man said. 'We had to keep him here, he was going to fuck everything up for us.' The large man turned to the woman and hugged her.

She pushed him away and stared down at South. 'Who the fuck is he?'

'A copper.'

Her eyes ignited. 'What the fucking hell? Why haven't you got rid of him yet?'

'What do you suggest we do?'

The woman stared at South, looking him in the eyes. 'Kill him and dump the body.'

South listened as they discussed the logistics of murdering someone and getting rid of their body. But not just any body. His. He looked away, his eyes drifting across the rubbish in the room, an old carton that had one time carried fried chicken. He looked at an old milkshake cup. Perhaps it had contained vanilla milkshake, which Shane liked so much. He wondered what Ally liked to eat when she goes out and promised himself that he'd tell her how he felt when he eventually saw her. If he saw her. No, when he saw her. It was only a matter of time before she led them to Hatch and then here.

The larger man got up and nodded at the woman. 'Alright, sweetheart, we'll shoot him in the back of the head tonight. I've got a silencer somewhere. Then we'll take the body and burn it after cutting off his hands and head. It'll take them longer to identify him that way.'

The woman grabbed the man and kissed his cheek as she smiled. 'You do that. We'll have to move the girls somewhere else though and pretty soon. Just in case.'

The woman, along with her cheap perfume, drifted out of the room. South looked up at the large man, saw his eyes opening a little wider and his eyebrows rising. He bent down and faced South. 'So, later on I'll come in here and give you your last meal. You'll eat, if you can without throwing up, and then I'll shoot you in the back of the head. It'll be quick, so don't worry.'

South mumbled through the gag for him to fuck off.

The large man laughed and patted him on the head. 'That's right. Now you sit here and wait for that moment. You'll probably piss yourself before then. Don't worry, it's an old chair.'

The foreign man appeared for a moment at the door and said something that South didn't understand.

'He said goodbye,' the large man said and left the room, leaving South alone in the dark.

TWENTY-NINE

Fred's skull felt rough against the sofa's arm as his eyes opened. He blinked for a moment and felt a heavy blanket covering his clothed body. He looked at the slightly open door opposite him. He was in Scott Brown's flat and there was the smell of cooking coming from somewhere. Fred pulled back the blanket and sat up, sniffing the air. He still felt a little sick, stumbling a little once he stood up. He went out the room and into the kitchen where Brown stood stirring a pan of soup. He smiled at Fred. 'Fancy some soup?'

'I don't really feel hungry.' Fred smiled awkwardly. 'You brought me here?'

'Yeah. You were pretty out of it in the car and you said you didn't want to go home. You didn't want your brother to know anything's wrong.'

Fred leaned on the sideboard and steadied himself. 'Yes, that's right. I don't want to worry him.'

'You should eat.'

Fred nodded and sat at the small kitchen table. Brown ladled some soup into a bowl and placed it before Fred. He picked up a spoon and began to eat. 'This is very good of you.'

'I just like to help out people in trouble.' Brown sat down and watched Fred eat.

'You think I'm in trouble?'

'You seem to be suffering. You and your brother. It's not right.'

Fred nodded. 'You're right there. If there's anyone up there, they have a sick sense of humour.'

'There's no one up there.'

'You're not religious then?'

Brown shook his head. 'My family were.'

'Were?'

He nodded, his eyes and thoughts seeming to travelling back to his childhood. 'Yes, then things got shitty. They thought of themselves as perfect, I think. My father was a perfectionist and when things started to go wrong for them, he couldn't handle it.'

Fred stopped spooning the soup into his mouth and looked up into the troubled face of Scott Brown. 'What happened?'

'Lots of stuff. Doesn't matter. All in the past.'

Fred dipped some bread into his soup. 'I know what you mean.'

'That's why I want to help you I guess. I understand what you're going through. We're friends, aren't we?' Brown's eyes looked a little wet.

Fred nodded. 'Yes, I think so. Yeah, of course. You've done a lot for me.'

'Good. Whatever else I can do, don't hesitate to ask.'

'I don't think there's anything else anybody can do. I just have to wait now.' Fred sat looking into his bowl of soup, at his own reflection.

'You seem certain that the results will come back and it will be bad.'

Fred took another mouthful of soup. 'I am.'

'Why?'

'I just am. This is bloody good soup.'

Ally had grabbed Harris when she saw him enter the incident room. He'd been out following up some leads most of the morning and then walked slowly

372

into the room, unwrapping a chocolate bar. Walker took him along to the interview room, asking him for a chat.

Harris continued to eat his chocolate bar after seating himself, looking at Ally as she sat down after putting two teas on the table. Harris smiled and grabbed his, dunking his chocolate bar in it. 'You OK, Allison?'

Ally watched him for a moment, then shook herself out of her trance. 'South has disappeared.'

Harris looked up slowly. 'I expect he's still following up this girl smuggling racket thing.'

She shook her head. 'No, he was supposed to be in contact by now.'

'Have you said anything to Jameson?'

'No, Mark told me not to. He didn't want to look like he couldn't do the job.'

Harris dunked the chocolate bar again. 'Well, what're you going to do?'

Ally shrugged. 'I don't know. He told me to tell Fred, for some reason.'

'Fred? Fred isn't one of us any more. What? He trusts Fred more than me?'

She sighed. 'I don't know, Tony. I just…'

Harris looked her in the eyes. 'You trust me, don't you?'

She looked up, her stomach churning. 'This isn't about who I trust. This is about South and the fact that he's gone AWOL. Jameson's given him a few days to investigate this, but soon he'll want to know what's happened to him. What do I say?'

Harris placed his hand near hers. 'You do trust me though? You don't think I've got anything to do with this whole business, do you?'

She smiled. 'No, of course not. But what do I

do? South could be making some contacts out there somewhere or he could be…well, he could be in trouble.'

'Look, give it a couple of days. I know Hatch from back then. I'll try and get in contact with him. I'll see what's happened.'

'That would be great, Tony. Please, if you could do that, it would be a weight off.' She looked brighter and sipped her tea.

Harris smiled back and then winked. He screwed up the chocolate bar wrapper, put it in the plastic cup and launched it at the bin. 'Yes! How about that? He scores!'

After stepping into his house, Fred leaned his back against the door and swallowed two pills. He gulped down some water from a bottle he bought on the way home. In the lounge, he was confronted with his brother, back in his leather chair, with a book spread out before him. He didn't look up, his eyes scanning the pages, a thin splattering of sweat on his brow. As Fred took off his jacket, he saw a folded sheet of paper in Martin's lap. 'Are you OK, Martin?'

Martin looked up, blinking. 'Yes, why?'

'You're sweating a lot.'

'Must be hot in here.' Martin stared at the book.

Fred examined the book. It was the one he stole from the library. 'You found my book then?'

Martin nodded. 'A piece paper fell out of it.'

'Right. Yeah, that's a list someone gave me. Shit. Should have given it to South or Ally really.'

'And let them solve the case?'

'Well, there isn't a lot I can do now. I can't go around arresting people, can I?' Fred sat down and removed his shoes, massaging his toes.

'Where were you today?'

'Sorry?'

'Where do you go now that you're out of work?' Martin's eyes flickered over to him for a moment.

'I go out. I do stuff.'

'That's good. You really should be trying to find out who got those people to kill themselves. Perhaps, firstly, you should find out why they killed themselves.'

Fred turned and looked at Martin. 'What? What do you mean? They killed themselves because they thought that would be the easy way out. They had problems.'

'What problems?'

'Steve was a junkie and he obviously didn't like himself very much. I wouldn't either if I was hooked on that shit.'

'And the woman who stabbed herself?'

'She had a deformed arm and she was afraid her child would be deformed too, I suppose.' Fred rubbed his face and let out an exhausted laugh. 'Look, Martin, can we just forget all this? I'm not a policeman any more, OK?'

'What about the cannibal?'

Fred shook his head. 'I think he was religious. Wanted desperately to eat another human, but couldn't live with himself if he did. They were all fucked up.'

'And the girl with a knife to her own throat?' Martin lowered the book and stared at Fred.

'She had a birthmark over her face. People would point at her and make fun. She considered herself ugly and obviously that can have a terrible effect on a young girl.'

'Do you agree with what they did?'

Fred glared at his brother. 'No, Martin, I don't. But if people are going to kill themselves, then they're going to do it! There's nothing I can do. All I can do is

375

try and clean up the fucking mess.'

'What about people who are in pain? Like Mum was?'

Fred buried his head in his hands. 'Don't. Just… stop talking.'

'I want you to say you understand.'

'How can I?' Fred looked up, his eyes sizzling.

'She made me promise.'

Fred sat up sharply. 'OK, yes, she made you promise to take in the tablets and you did. She's dead and gone. Yes she was in pain. I understand.'

'Then help me. You made a promise to Mum.' Martin had tears in his eyes.

Fred turned to him and saw the tears travelling down his face, heading into his mouth. He could see Martin's eyes were sore, that he'd been crying all day. He tried to imagine the pain his brother was suffering, then looked at Martin and sighed. 'I've been thinking about it. Just give me time.'

'OK.'

'I need time to…to think about it.'

Ally Walker sat parked in Harris' street. She was in Sarah's car, borrowed while she was working in the White Hart. She had binoculars and a camera and sat eating a sandwich, watching the warm and welcoming lights of the houses around her. It was getting dark and most of the houses still had their curtains open.

She pulled herself out of her dream and looked towards Harris' car, which was still parked on the lengthy drive of his nice and luxurious home.

In a strange way, she felt awkward about spying on Harris, watching him and his family. Harris' son had returned home, his arm around his girlfriend, a pretty, but short girl with blonde hair.

She poured herself a cup of coffee from her flask, then spooned some sugar in, tasting it and frowning. Why she was camped outside Harris' house? She couldn't really begin to understand, but something in her gut had been eating away at her, twisting, trying to tell her something. She set down her coffee on the dashboard and picked up the binoculars. A figure came out of Harris' house. She concentrated the binoculars on the front door and saw Harris putting on his jacket and turning off the alarm on his car. He slid in and started the engine, then reversed off the drive and headed in Ally's direction. She ducked down in her seat, hid herself until he passed by, then started her engine and turned her car around in time to see his brake lights at the end of the road. She stayed back a little, allowing him to get a little way in front.

Underneath the amber of the streetlight, Harris was sitting in his car, his eyes travelling along the shops and restaurants. He stopped on the bright windows of the twenty-four hour bakery and café. This being Wood Green High Street, he knew the local druggies would be getting the munchies pretty soon. He hated sitting among them, smelling the sweet, acrid scent of wasted lives all around him. He got out of the car, locked the doors, then stood for a moment, watching the café and hesitating. He swore under his breath and stormed towards the cafe.

He got to the window and looked past a group of young black girls, who were sitting giggling and breaking into song, then focused towards the back corner. He saw Franco nursing a small cup of something. As he entered, Franco nodded to him. The bright ceiling lights reflected off the white walls, making Harris blink as he approached the gangster.

'You're early, Tony.' Franco let the smoke drift out of his mouth and finished his coffee. 'Want a coffee or something?'

'No.' Harris folded his arms, keeping his face blank. 'I want to talk about our problem.'

Franco held up his hand, then got up and fetched another coffee. After he sat down, he smiled again. 'Alright, say what you're going say. I'm listening.'

'You have to let him go,' Harris said.

'Let him go? I don't think the lads are going to think that's a good move.'

'Tell them.'

'They're trying to protect their investment. There's a lot at stake. If they get caught they'll go to prison for a long time, and they aren't going to risk that. Plus, he's seen their faces.'

Harris lowered his head and sighed.

'You alright? You look ill.' Franco stared at Harris' face.

'No, I'm not. This is the end. Oh shit...what the fuck...' Harris sat back and looked up at the ceiling.

'Calm down. They'll get rid of him and that'll be that. Nothing's going to come back to you.'

'What about Hatch?'

Franco let out a laugh. 'Hatch? Do you think Hatch is going to jump right into the shit? Fuck off. He's up to his neck in this. He's not stupid. Anyway, he's worried about you.'

'Me? What does he think I'm going to do?'

'You're a policeman, Tony.'

'So's he!'

'Not like you, Tony. Not like you.'

Harris looked around the café, smelling the coffee and the bread being baked. 'Yeah, and that means I've got to keep this from getting out. I can't risk South blowing the whistle either.'

Franco sipped his coffee, keeping his eyes on Harris. 'What about your loyalty to your fellow pigs?'

'Well, I think that's gone out the window now, don't you?'

'They'll kill you if you do anything to fuck this up.' Franco stared at Harris. 'You, your boy and your wife. They told me to tell you that. It doesn't matter to them that you're filth. It's never mattered to them. They didn't let a young girl get in their way, so they ain't going to let you either, or your mate.'

Harris looked into Franco's dark eyes and nodded. 'I know. Tell them to leave my family out of this. They've got nothing to worry about. What will they do to South?'

'Get shot of him. I don't know how, but they won't find the body. They're too good for that. It'll be done tonight.'

Harris thought for a moment, picturing Ally waiting for her hero's return. 'Not tonight. Tell them not tonight.'

Franco looked confused for a moment. 'Why? What're you thinking?'

'They'll be expecting to hear from South. They know he went to see Hatch before he disappeared, so they'll go after him. We need time to lead them away from us. We could force South to phone someone, leave a false trail.'

Franco rubbed the stubble on his chin. 'I don't think they'll wait.'

'Phone them. At least phone them.'

'I can't.'

Harris leaned forward. A sickness filled his stomach. 'Why not?'

'They told me to cut contact.' Franco took out his

mobile. 'And I can't phone them on my mobile.'

'There's a payphone over there.' Harris pointed to the phone next to the men's toilet. 'Call them. Tell them they have to wait. Do it. Trust me, if we're going to survive this, they have to wait.'

South struggled as they held him down. Mr Large gripped his shoulders, easily pushing him back as the woman held the syringe above him, flicking the end. He was thankful she knew what she was doing for a split second, then a terrible thought entered his head. Are they going to give me an overdose? He shouted through the gag, but the woman looked blankly at him, then turned away.

'You'll fuck this up if you keep moving,' she said and pointed the needle at his arm. She tapped his vein and then he felt the prick of the needle.

Then he forgot to struggle, and sunk down through the floor.

'That's better, isn't it, luv?' The woman bent down towards his face. He could smell her cheap perfume, stale cigarette smoke, but soon he was drifting further down, his eyes heavy, sinking with the rest of him.

'We'll get him to the car in a few minutes.'

'I'm not coming,' the woman said.

'I didn't expect you to fucking come.'

'Oh fuck off.'

South could smell rotten timber when he drifted out of his dream. For a moment he felt like he was choking, until he was breathing. He wasn't dead. When he looked into the dark, he saw a torchlight travelling across the floor, a single source of light spreading out to him. He called out to the light and watched the black figure growing behind it, creeping slowly from the floor to the wall and up to the ceiling, spreading out and engulfing the entire building. The torch danced for a moment until it stopped and became rigid.

The figure came closer, a face appearing out of the darkness, a face that made South want to cry. The same large man looked down at him, his eyes emotionless. From behind him stepped the foreign man, this time wearing grease-stained overalls. South noticed the large man was wearing something similar. He started to crawl backwards, using his legs to push himself along the concrete floor.

'Where are you going?' the large man asked, then grabbed South and hoisted him over his shoulder while the foreigner laughed.

'Shut up,' the large man said as he dropped South. 'You going to do this or am I?'

The foreign man turned to a bag on the floor and searched through it, eventually bringing out a small gun. South saw the shape of it for a moment and started shaking. He heard himself pleading through the gag, feeling both disgusted and desperate.

'It'll be over in a minute,' the large man said. 'Should've kept your nose out. It's not our fault.'

South watched the gun travel behind him in the foreigner's hand, then closed his eyes. He saw Shane's face, then the boy's mother. A hand touched his shoulder and he wanted to bite it. The gun was dug into his head, pressing into the back of his skull, while fear bubbled in his stomach. He felt the vomit coming up to his throat, but swallowed it down. As he coughed, he heard the foreign man laugh and talk in his own language.

'Just shut up and do it,' the large man said.

South heard something though the pounding of blood in his head, some kind of muffled tune somewhere. The large man fished his phone out of his pocket as South watched, his eyes blinking, feeling the remainder of his tears stinging his cheeks. Then he felt the barrel of the gun being pushed against the back of his head.

'What?' the large man shouted into the phone, walking into the shadows. 'I said not to fucking call me! Yes, I did. Yeah, why? Oh fucking hell. You're fucking joking?'

The large man walked back into the smouldering light of the torch, his face concentrating on South. 'Right. Fuck. Alright. I'll call you back.'

South blinked again, looking into the large man's thoughtful face. Eventually, the big man bent down and stared at South. 'Those should be tears of joy, mate. You're fucking lucky you are. Well, for now you are.'

The foreign man asked something from behind South. The large man pulled himself up with a moan and looked at his friend. 'Not tonight. Let's get him in the boot. We're taking him back.'

With more anger in his voice, the foreigner asked something again. The large man froze for a moment and nodded. 'OK, but don't kill him.'

The foreign man came around South, walking slowly, stalking him. He put away the gun and walked off towards the bag he'd brought. When he came back, he was carrying something small and black, a cruel smile carved into his face. He lifted the cosh up, his teeth gritted, stretching his hand far above his head. South flinched and shut his eyes.

THIRTY

Saturday, 1st May 2004

It was still quite early as Ally Walker sat in her car parked outside Fred's place. She looked at the clock on the dashboard and saw it was only 9 a.m. When she looked at herself in the rearview mirror, she saw bags under her eyes. It wouldn't have bothered her if she'd spent the night boozing, but all she'd been doing was lying in bed. She'd been picturing Harris sitting in the café opposite Franco Orlando. At first, she hadn't recognised Franco, but then she had followed him and took his car's registration number. Turned out he had an arrest record for armed robbery, and stealing cars and selling them abroad. She wondered why Harris might be talking to him, hoping he was some kind of informant, but it didn't fit his history. Then she looked through his file and found he'd been working for Skouvakis. In fact, she found out he was a loyal friend and practically family.

Ally took out some make-up and tried to make herself look less tired. She stopped as she realised there was no one she wanted to look less tired for. She got out the car, slammed her door and headed across the road, then walked up to Fred's door and pressed the bell. After a few moments, a stocky shadow moved inside, unlocking the door. Fred stood rubbing his eyes and pulled his robe tightly around himself as he smiled slightly. 'Allison? You OK?'

She nodded, leaned on the doorframe, and let out a sigh. 'No. I'm not alright. Actually, it's Mark South who might not be alright. Can I come in?'

Fred let her through and she sat down in an armchair. He stood looking down at her, his confusion showing. 'Want a cup of tea?'

'No, no thanks.' She looked up at him, her cheeks red and her mouth pinched. 'Look, I think he's in trouble. He went to see Hatch and hasn't contacted me since.'

Fred sat down. 'Well, there's not much I can do. Tell Jameson.'

'I can't. South told me not to. He wanted me to contact you if anything went wrong. Why would he do that?'

Fred shook his head. 'I don't know. What does he think I can do?'

'I don't know. What can we do?'

'I don't know much about Hatch.'

'Is he OK, I mean is he on the straight and narrow?'

'I don't know. He always seemed OK.'

Ally thought for a moment, weighing things up in her mind. She sat forward. 'Fred, do you think Tony could've been mixed up with Skouvakis?'

Fred looked away. 'Why do you ask that?'

'I followed him last night. I don't know why. Something in my stomach told me to. Well, he met with Franco Orlando in a café in Wood Green High Street. Don't you think that's odd?'

Fred sat back in his armchair. 'Perhaps he's after information.'

'Franco isn't the informant type. Maybe Harris was the one who tipped off Skouvakis that time.'

Fred shook his head. 'Harris? No, he wouldn't be that stupid.'

'He's got a family. Maybe they threatened him.' Ally raised her eyebrows.

'Then he would've told us or somebody.' Fred got up. 'Let's have a cup of tea.'

'I don't want anything. I don't trust him, Fred. I've worked with him for a few years now and I've never had any reason to think he was bent, but now... I just don't know. When I sat across from him the other day, when I asked him about your investigation, he had a weird look on his face and something told me he was tied up in it all. I know it sounds stupid…'

Fred smiled as he stood in the kitchen doorway. 'Women's intuition?'

'That's a load of bollocks. I'm talking about the feeling you get when you're a copper and you know something's not right. Now he's meeting up with Franco Orlando for God's sake. That's not right.'

Fred grimaced, clenched his teeth and leaned his back against the wall.

Ally jumped up. 'You OK? You don't look well.'

'I'm alright. Just a bit of pain in my back.'

'What is wrong with you, Fred? I know there's something wrong with you. I found strong painkillers in your drawer. Lots of them.'

'So, it was you who nicked them?' Fred straightened himself. 'It's just some pain.'

Ally grabbed him by the shoulders. 'What pain? Have you been to the doctors?'

'Yes, and the hospital. They don't know what's wrong.' Fred sat on the sofa.

Ally followed him, then stopped as she heard her phone ringing. She pulled out her mobile and saw a strange number calling her. 'Hello.'

'Ally? It's me, Mark.'

'Where are you? Where've you been?'

'I've been trying to track down an informant Hatch put me on to.'

'But you didn't call me.'

South's voice came back, echoing in her ear. 'I know. I'm sorry. Let Emma and Shane know I'm OK.'

'Where are you?'

'I can't say. Hatch helped me with some info and now I'm staying at a hotel, sort of undercover.'

'Tell me which hotel and I'll come and meet you,' Ally said.

'No, I'm fine. I'll be back in a couple of days. Just make sure everyone knows I'm OK. Got to go...oh, it's the anniversary of my wife's death tomorrow. Remind Emma to put some flowers on Shelley's grave, will you?'

Ally didn't say anything, just heard the phone go dead and looked at Fred. 'He said he's OK.'

Fred smiled. 'See. He's fine.'

Ally tried to smile and found it impossible. All the muscles in her face seemed to have frozen into a frown. 'I suppose. I don't know. He sounded strange.'

'He was probably in company. Want that tea now?'

She shook her head as she put her phone back into her jacket and stood up. 'I hope you feel better, Fred. Let me know if you want anything, won't you?'

Fred smiled, but as Ally went to leave she thought she saw something dark cross his eyes.

South was finding it hard to sleep. Even though the woman had given him some painkillers, which he'd tried to thank her for through the gag, he still felt the stinging bruises on his ribs, and his face seemed to be growing larger by the second. The large man had just stood there watching in the darkness as the foreigner kicked the shit out of him, swearing in his native tongue. He felt his shoes smash into his ribs and he could only cry out with each blow. For a short while, the foreigner had been sitting on top of him, landing punch after punch into his jaw. South had felt himself oozing away, drifting into unconsciousness, just before the large man made him stop.

South tried to move his jaw and immediately tears came to his eyes. A burning sensation crawled across his face, as if someone was inserting a red-hot poker through his cheek and into his gum. He adjusted himself in the armchair, feeling his ribs tearing into his insides.

The door opened and the large man walked in with a bottle of water and a knife. He removed South's gag and let him drink. 'Want something to eat?'

South looked him in the eye, showing his contempt. 'Why bother? You might as well let me starve.'

'No, that would be slow. Interesting thought though. We might need you to make another phone call to your mates.'

'Fuck off.' South looked down at his feet.

'That was a good job you did. That should put them off our trail for a bit.'

South looked up. 'Not for long. They'll get Hatch, then you'll be fucked.'

The large man leaned towards him. 'And you, mate, will be six foot under.'

'Maybe.'

'No maybe about it, mate.' The large man pulled over a chair and sat down for a moment, looking at South's face. 'My mate really beat the shit out of you.'

'I had my hands tied behind my back.'

'He would've anyway. Trust me. He hates policemen.'

A thought dug its way through South's body, rising

above the pain. 'Let me go and I'll try and make it easy on you.'

'Fuck off, copper. I'm not a fucking moron. I'm up to my eyes in shit. This is my livelihood. I can't let this get fucked up now. I know you're a policeman and if we kill you…well, we're going to go down for some serious time, but what the fuck. It's too late now. Nothing personal, mate, but I don't give a shit about you. I know you've got a kid, a boy and yeah, I'm sure he's going to be fucking upset, but he'll get over it.'

South felt all the pain in his body travelling to his mouth. 'If you mention my son again, I'll rip your face off. I'll kill you, I fucking swear.'

The large man lost his smile. 'You're tied to a chair, mate. You're fucked. Just relax. When we do it, it'll be quick. Bang. Right in the back of your head. If you behave, I might stop my mate going around and strangling your kid and fucking your sister.'

The large man jerked back as South ripped forward, snarling, a tirade of abuse escaping his mouth. His chest rose and fell, his heart swelling as he tried to calm himself down.

'Alright, mate. Enough chit chat.' The large man got up and put the chair over the other side of the room. 'I'll bring you some food later.'

After putting the gag back into his mouth, the large man stared at South, his arms folded. 'Maybe we'll spare your family…if you're lucky.'

Martin lay asleep, his breathing shallow, his chest rising and falling beneath the mauve duvet. Fred stood over him, watching, expecting the movement would stop any second. What would he do? Would he try and resuscitate him?

Fred looked around the room, his eyes scanning

the shelves filled with books. Maybe he'll read some, he decides, if he has time. Then he looked at the chest of drawers and wandered over, standing before the massive pine block. Martin was deeply asleep. Fred looked at the top drawer, saw only socks and pants, then slide it shut. He opened the next drawer and shook his head, trying to take in what lay before him. He looked back at Martin before looking at the worn pieces of paper in the bottom of Martin's drawer.

He took out the sheet of thick paper, the kind kids draw on at school. Sugar paper, they called it. Suddenly he was back at junior school, bent over a desk, a pencil in his hand, sketching the old man with the spider in his mouth. The drawing in his hand looked like a masterpiece thirty-seven years ago; now it was the scribbles of an excited child. He always thought he was good at art, but now he knew he was wrong. His mother loved it and put it up in the kitchen. He had to suffer the taunts and bullying of the kids at school. Only Martin was interested in the story, and wanted Fred to tell it over and over.

Fred took out another drawing and examined it. He shook his head, put the drawings back and slowly shut the drawer. He faced his brother and thought sure his breathing hadn't changed.

Fred began turning over everything in his mind. He thought about the letter that arrived that morning from the hospital. The consultant wanted to see him at 11 a.m. on Monday morning. He read the letter a few times, as if he might get more information from between the words, but nothing came.

Martin moved a little in his sleep, his breathing becoming heavier, more rasping. Fred looked at the pill bottle by his bed. His brother had taken quite a few, but not enough to do the job. He wouldn't let himself. Fred walked across the room and stood in the doorway. Yes, he had decided to help his brother and to hell with everything. If he was right about Monday, then it wouldn't matter what happened afterwards to him. He smiled at his sleeping brother and shut the door.

THIRTY-ONE

Sunday, 2nd May 2004

Ally got up and saw the blackness turn to blue, then the pink clouds stretching across the horizon. She sat down on her bed with her dressing gown wrapped around her, playing the phone conversation with Mark South over and over again. She slipped on the ridiculous slippers her mother had bought her last Christmas, the ones with a puppy's head on them, its tongue hanging out of its mouth. Then she laid her head on the pillow and found the light invading her eyelids. She buried her head in the pillow and heard the voices pecking at her ears. Harris' voice came the loudest, his calm chocolate-coated speech telling her everything would be OK.

Walker turned over onto her side and faced the wall, her eyes still tightly closed. She felt her stomach churn and she shook her head, seeing the image of Harris walking into the café and sitting and talking with a known criminal thug. She pushed out that thought and tried to dissipate the voices in her head. She didn't want any thoughts at all, just peaceful sleep, but an endless blackness opened up all around her and she was floating in it…

She saw Fred coming out of the darkness, his face screwed up, contorted with pain. She heard his voice telling her South would be fine. Before she opened her eyes and sat up in bed, she recalled her own conversation with Mark's sister. She had phoned Emma and told her Mark was working undercover.

When she sat up on the bed, she felt a little light-headed. She hadn't eaten for a while and decided to make some toast. In the kitchen, halfway through buttering some toast, she recalled South telling her to remind Emma about flowers for his dead wife's grave.

She ate a piece of toast as she dressed, grabbing her car keys and heading out the door. When she arrived, she jumped out and hurried to the door, rung the bell and saw a female figure coming through the frosted glass.

'Hello,' Emma said and looked a little surprised.

'Hi, I thought I'd pop by,' Ally said and smiled politely.

Emma stepped back a little. 'Come in.'

Ally went through without saying another word. She looked at the clock on the wall and realised it was nearly 8 a.m. and turned around to apologise to Emma. 'Sorry, it's still quite early.'

Emma patted her arm and walked to the kitchen. 'Don't worry about it. I've got house work to do anyway.'

Ally looked around the room and saw a pile of washing to be put away. 'I couldn't sleep.'

'Why? What're you worried about?'

Ally sat at the dining table. 'I don't know.'

Emma frowned. 'It's Mark, isn't it? Is he in trouble?'

'Where's Shane?'

Emma pointed upwards. 'In his room. Go on, what's wrong?'

'Just worried about him being out there somewhere. I'm sure he's OK.'

'I thought he said he was OK, didn't he?' Emma tried to look into Ally's eyes.

'Yes, but you know…you can't help worrying.'

Emma smiled. 'What's going on between you two? He's mentioned you quite a bit.'

'Nothing. We work well together.'

'Come on. When he talks about you, he always has a twinkle in his eye.'

'It was good to hear from him.'

'I bet. What else did he say? When's he coming home? Shane's missing him.'

Ally shrugged. 'Not sure. Soon, I think. He's following up a lead to do with a whole prostitution thing.'

Emma sighed. 'He was the same up north. I think he's dived into his work since…well, you know.'

Ally nodded. 'He must miss her.'

'Yeah, of course, but I think he's over the worst of it.'

Ally remembered Mark's request. 'Oh, he said to remind you to put flowers on his wife's grave tomorrow. Said it was the anniversary of her death.'

'He's bloody crap!' Emma blurted out. 'It's next week. Men are useless. You'd think he'd remember that Jane died a year ago next week, wouldn't you?'

'Jane? That was her name?' Ally felt her body grow heavy, her heart twisting in her chest.

'Yeah. Jane was lovely. It's so sad, isn't it?' Emma shook her head. 'Do you want some tea?'

'No, I better go.'

'You sure?'

'Yes. Right. I'll see you soon.' Ally let Emma walk her to the door, then smiled and said her goodbyes. She climbed into her car, still seeing Emma at the door, watching her as she started the engine. All the time she watched his sister at the door, she kept hearing Mark say his wife's name. Shelley. He'd said her name was Shelley. Oh shit, Ally said to herself and drove away.

Tony Harris declined his wife's offer of the remainder of her roast potatoes, and placed his cutlery on his plate. He sat back and picked up his glass of red wine and stared at it for a few moments. His wife sat forward. She had been watching him for most of the meal. 'A penny for your thoughts.'

Without looking away from his wine glass, he replied blankly, 'They're worth more than that.'

'Really? And how much do you think they're worth?'

Tony blinked and came out of his dream. 'Sorry, darling?'

'Hmmm,' she said. 'What is wrong with you at the moment?'

Harris sipped his wine. 'Nothing. Just busy at work. Got a lot on my mind.'

Ann Harris stood up, and picked up their plates. 'I know that look you've got, Tony. Tell me what's going on.'

Harris laughed and reached for his wife's glass and filled it up. 'Have some more wine.'

'I remember what happened years ago, Tony. I can see the look in your eyes. You're hardly speaking to me and you're drinking too much.'

'Don't. Just stop talking.'

'You came in drunk every night back then. Do you remember?' Ann reached out and took her tissue and wiped some wine from her husband's chin. 'One night I woke up and you were crying your eyes out, sitting on the end of the bed. I asked you what was wrong…'

Harris held up his hand. 'Please, Ann. I told you to forget all that.'

'I had. But now look at you. You've got the same look in your eyes.'

Harris poured himself some more wine. 'It's fine. I'm OK.'

'Please tell me.' Ann gripped his hand. He looked at her hand grasping his. 'Oh, God.'

She ran a hand through his hair. 'I know when you're in trouble, because you stop cracking jokes.'

He bent his head and nodded a little. 'Shit. Oh shit, God…Ann.'

'What's happened?'

Harris looked up at his wife and saw a tear in one eye. 'What happened last time… it's happening all over again.'

'It'll be all right.'

'It won't, not this time.'

'You sorted it out last time. You told me you did.'

Harris broke away from his wife and stood by the window, looking out into the darkening sky. He watched a car crawl along the road, his mind racing, imagining South somewhere, a gun probably at his head. He turned and looked at Ann. 'Remember I told you that new boy had started, the one who came down from the north? Mark South?'

Ann nodded. 'Yes, what about him?'

'He's started looking into the whole thing, what happened a few years back when I…when I tipped off Skouvakis.'

'And you think he'll find out it was you? Isn't Skouvakis dead now?'

Harris smiled at her. She's so strong usually and so organised and together. He'd always prided himself, in a weird way, that he was the only one who could make her breakdown. No one else could get to her like he could. Harris sat back in his chair. 'I looked into

South's background. It was easy really. I know plenty of people willing to do me a favour. Well, guess what I found out? South was sent down here to root out any corruption. They've been doing the rounds for ages around London, making sure everything is above board. Of course, they know it's not. They know several officers have been taking bribes. You know I'm not like that, don't you?'

Ann tightened her grip on his hand. 'Of course I do. They threatened you and us.'

'I did what I had to do. The thing was...'

'What?'

Harris let the memories flash across his face, filling his eyes with pain and regret. 'There was a girl. One of the girls Skouvakis had locked up, one of the prostitutes...she found me and Fred. She came to us wanting help. I knew then that if she got to anyone else she could take us all down...Skouvakis and me. When she said she'd help us by staying working with Skouvakis, I could have laughed. It was perfect.'

Harris gripped his face. 'Oh shit. What did I do?'

'What did you do?' she asked, her eyes widening.

'I told Skouvakis about her.' Harris looked into his wife's eyes. He felt his wife's grip loosen, then saw her slender fingers retreating across the table. 'I had to. I couldn't risk loosing everything. If they had thought I had helped her...'

Ann's lips quivered for a moment. 'What happened to the girl?'

Harris kept looking at her, watching her shrink away from him. 'They found her...they found her in the Thames. She'd been there a couple of days. They tried to stop us identifying her by...'

'Stop!' Ann turned away and then got up, heading for the kitchen.

Harris followed her. 'What could I do?'

Ann stared at him. 'And what will this other officer do?'

Harris leaned back against the wall. 'Nothing. They won't let him.'

Ann looked at him, her face full of questions. 'What do you mean?'

Harris flinched as his wife grasped his shirt, shaking him a little. 'What are they going to do, Tony?'

'They've got him somewhere. They'll kill him.'

Ann let go of his shirt. 'You can't let them do it. You've got to stop them.'

'I can't.'

Ann jabbed a finger at his face. 'You're going to go and stop them somehow. Or else.'

THIRTY-TWO

Monday, 3rd May 2004

Walker was putting together documentation on that particular Monday morning, trying to push Mark South out of her mind. Every bit of evidence still had to be collected for the Nelson court case. The date hadn't been set, but they had to get the piles of paperwork to the Crown Prosecution Service. There were also witnesses to deal with. So much work. They needed a conviction on this, so there was no room for fuck ups.

Ally stopped typing and let her head fall forward an inch from her keyboard. When she looked up after a minute, she saw Harris standing before her, two cups of steaming coffee in his hands.

'You alright?' she asked, feeling her suspicions crawling up her spine.

He shook his head. 'Want a coffee? I got you one.'

'Sit down.'

Harris put down the coffees and seated himself. He looked over the piles of papers and boxes around her desk and sighed. 'The Nelson case?'

'Yep. What a lot of shit, eh?'

'South's in trouble.'

'I know. Where is he?'

'They've got him somewhere.' Harris looked down.

'Where? Where the fuck is he, Tony?'

'I don't know. Really!'

'Jesus Christ!' Ally jumped out of her chair and

slammed the office door. She stood over Harris, feeling her chest prickling with fire. 'You knew all along, didn't you?'

'It doesn't matter. We just have to sort this mess out.'

She slapped Harris hard across the shoulder. 'It doesn't fucking matter?!…you…wanker! Where is he? Or do I have to get Jameson in here? If it wasn't for the fact that he made me promise not to involve Jameson, I'd have set him on you already.'

'We can fix this.' Harris' eyes pleaded with her.

'How? Tell me how we can find South when he could be anywhere in London? Fuck! He could be anywhere in the country, couldn't he?'

Harris shook his head. 'No, he's in London. I know that much. Franco's people have him.'

'Then we go to Franco and keep kicking him in the balls until he tells us where he is.' Ally leaned on the desk.

'No, he won't know where. These people work by themselves. They're in contact with Franco, but they don't trust anybody but their people. They're like family.'

'That's so lovely.' Ally moved back around to Harris. 'You know you're finished, don't you?'

'Not if we do this right. Don't worry, I know those type of people. They won't kill him. They'll keep hold of him for a while.'

'OK, what do we do?'

'We need someone not on the force to help us. Someone who isn't risking their neck.' Harris looked into her eyes.

'Fred?'

Harris nodded.

This time Fred was sitting in a much larger waiting

room. It was more like a long corridor filled with chairs and tables. Along the lime green walls were white doors where the doctors had their offices. He picked up a lad's magazine and flipped through it, looking at the young women in bikinis smiling seductively at him. He closed the magazine as he saw a small, dark, and olive-skinned child staring at him. The child's deep brown eyes looked at him over the top of a chair. Fred smiled and the child's head disappeared.

Another nurse, Indian this time, walked up to Fred. He sat up, only to hear her call someone else's name. He saw an old man stand up with difficulty and follow the nurse down the corridor.

Fred looked at his watch. He'd been there for nearly half an hour. He looked up and read a poster about giving blood and then another about inoculations. He lowered his head and looked at his shoes as he began to think about his mother, picturing her in her hospital bed. He remembered the hospital informing him that she'd somehow smuggled in lots of painkillers and taken them all. They were apologetic and couldn't understand how it had happened.

He recalled the promise he made to her before her death.

Forty-five minutes passed before the nurse called Fred's name. He stood up and followed her along to an office. Inside, he found the consultant reading through a file. He looked up to Fred blankly and pointed to a chair. Fred sat and folded his arms, seeing the hesitation in the doctor's eyes. He closed the file and looked at Fred. 'We've examined the X-rays and your blood test results. I've also looked at your biopsy and consulted with a surgeon.'

Fred watched the awkward hand movements of the consultant, his eyes seeming to search the room for some answers. 'I'm afraid I have some bad news. Judging by the biopsy and the X-rays…'

Fred lifted himself above the sound of the consultant's voice and drifted over the room. He only took in part of the speech. He listened to the part about the tumour being inoperable and carried on floating off.

He left after shaking the consultant's hand, and headed into the white corridor where patients kept on crawling by.

He didn't listen to the consultant because he'd heard it all before.

A hollow voice was trying to break through South's sleep, but it seemed to be only travelling around inside his head. He opened his eyes and saw a face smiling at him. He smiled and didn't know why. His mouth felt dry as he smiled again at the young, pretty woman standing before him. Her smile disappeared as she pulled the gag from his mouth.

'I'm sorry,' the woman said in perfectly good English, but with an Eastern European accent. She knelt and looked kindly at South's face. She touched his forehead.

'What's your name?' South asked.

'Fran. You've got a bad cut on your eye.' She stood again and folded her arms across her chest.

'Can you help me get out of here?'

The woman looked behind her at the closed door, where there was the sound of another female voice muttering something. Fran turned back to him and slowly shook her head. She brushed some light brown hair from her face, revealing acne scars on her sharp cheekbones.

South smiled at her. 'Please, I have a kid, a son,

who I want to see again. Please help me.'

'They'll kill me.' The girl bit her lip and moved back a little.

'Fran? I'm a policeman. Get me out of here and I'll be able to get help. You could phone the police.'

She shook her head again. 'I can't. The police won't help. They'll just find me and kill me. They did it to another girl.'

'Did you know a girl called Melanie?'

'No, but I know what happened to her. The police didn't do anything.'

'Fran? Fran?' South called her name until she looked into his eyes. 'We will now. The police will take notice. You'll be alright. Can you leave here at any point?'

'No. If we go out they send someone with us. We go to a house or somewhere and they take us there. We are never alone. I couldn't call the police anyway.'

South hung his head. 'OK, let me think. Has a man with a shaved head been here? Stocky? You know, a muscular-looking man? He's called Hatch.'

Fran nodded slowly. 'Yes, he's taken me to some places. I went with him to a club and then a house to meet some people.'

'So, he spends a lot of time here?'

'He'll be here tonight. He stays over sometimes. He usually gets drunk.'

South nodded and looked around the room for a second until his eyes focused on the window to his right. He saw the small body of a spider and its eight dried legs pointing to the ceiling. He looked at Fran. 'Are you scared of spiders?'

'Not really. I don't like them much.'

'What about dead ones?' South let her follow his eyes to the window.

She shrugged. 'What do you want me to do?'

'Have you got a very small plastic bag or something?'

The woman looked back towards the door. She smiled a little. 'I think I can get one of the small bags they put their drugs in. Is that what you want?'

'That would be great. Now get one and put that spider in it.'

She looked at the spider, then walked towards it. She scooped it into her hand and looked up at South. He smiled a little, seeing the obvious confusion in her eyes. 'If you can slip that into Hatch's jacket pocket, it would be really helpful. If he's got a small pocket somewhere on his coat, put it in there.'

'I could write a note,' Fran said brightly.

South shook his head. 'No, if he found that he would know something was up. This way, if he finds it he'll think someone's having a joke. Trust me. Can you do it?'

The woman looked at the dead spider and nodded. 'OK. When he comes he'll leave his jacket downstairs. I'll do it when he goes to see one of the girls. OK?'

South smiled.

She cradled the small dead creature in her hand and looked at it every now and again as she opened the door to the room. South saw the key in the door as she left. He heard her lock the door, then listened as the heels of her boots hit the floorboards along the landing. He leaned back and imagined the dead spider in Hatch's pocket. He began to pray to himself. If they managed to arrest Hatch, then they'd search him. He just hoped Fred would see the spider.

THIRTY-THREE

Fred was standing on the steps of Edmonton Library when his phone started ringing. He looked at the number calling. The sun had risen over the clouds and was shining brightly, burning the backs of his eyes. He looked at his phone again. Allison Walker. He watched her name blinking at him, but let it become a missed call, then walked into the library.

It wasn't so busy now and he walked along the shelves, letting his hands brush the paperbacks. He looked at two grey-haired women hovering around the crime section and kept moving until he approached the desk. There was a young girl behind the counter. She looked up at him as she lifted up a pile of returned books. He saw braces on her teeth as she smiled. 'Need some help?'

'Is Scott Brown here?'

'He's out the back. I can call him.'

Fred rested on the desk. 'That'd be good of you.'

The girl disappeared through the door and quickly reappeared and opened the counter. 'You can come on through. He's through that door.'

Fred walked into the small lounge area and saw Scott Brown at the computer typing something. He acknowledged Fred and finished typing, his hands moving quickly over the keyboard. Fred looked at the familiar sight of a beanie hat on his head, pulled down over his ears. At that moment, Fred felt a shudder of pain grip his back, so he quickly grabbed a chair.

Brown gripped his shoulder. 'Is it bad? What can I do?'

Fred shook his head as he dug out some painkillers from his pocket. Brown grabbed a glass and filled it full of water and handed it to Fred.

After the tablets had drifted down his throat, Fred laughed. 'This is typical. You get the death sentence and it's almost a relief, but the pain it just keeps getting worse.'

Brown pulled two chairs together and made Fred lie down. 'What did they say at the hospital?'

'Nothing they can do now.'

'Want me to do anything?'

'There's nothing you can do. I have to see to Martin and then…'

Brown bent forward. 'Then what?'

'I don't know.'

'You're not going to tell him?'

'No. There wouldn't be any point.'

Brown sat up a little. 'I knew you were ill the first time I saw you. You can see it in people.'

'Really?' Fred said and shut his eyes, a thin sheen of sweat appearing along his hairline.

'I see people walk in and out of this place and I can tell what's wrong with them. There's the women looking for romantic novels and you know their husbands don't show them any kind of affection. Basically, they're all looking for escape. They say you shouldn't judge a book by its cover, but I think you should. You always should.'

'I've never been looking for an escape.'

Brown nodded. 'No, you'd rather have the pain. I suppose it reminds you that you're still alive.'

'You OK?'

Brown looked up from his hands and there were tears in his eyes. 'Yes. It's just sad. Tragic. You have to ask yourself how this can go on. What sort of world are we living in?'

Fred heard his phone ringing and looked at the name on the screen. He sat up with difficulty and answered the phone. 'Hello.'

'Fred?' Ally said, sounding breathless. 'Thank God for that. Where are you?'

Fred stood up with the help of Brown and walked to the back of the room. 'I'm in the library.'

'Which one?'

Fred watched Brown sit at his computer, then spoke softly into the phone. 'Edmonton Library. Why?'

'Can you meet us in the café opposite the station in about five minutes?'

Fred heard the desperation in her voice. 'Us? Who's us?'

'Just meet me in five minutes, OK?'

'OK. I'll be there.' Fred shut off the phone and walked awkwardly over to Brown. 'I have to go. Thanks for looking after me, again.'

Brown looked away from the screen and didn't give any show of emotion. He simply looked at Fred and blinked a little. 'When…if you're ever ready to… help your brother…well, if I can help in anyway?'

Fred touched Brown's shoulder. 'I couldn't. Look, I'll be in touch.'

'You said you wouldn't be able to go through with it yourself.'

Fred shook his head and looked at his feet. 'I just…'

'Well, come and see me if you need to.'

Fred smiled and walked out the door.

Us. That's what Ally Walker had said, and he wondered who exactly she meant. But more than that, he thought of Martin and the terrible thing he might have to do. But how could he possibly help his own brother die?

Ally moved her black coffee around the table. Harris smiled at her, but she couldn't bear to look at him for very long, so she looked out the window of the café. She looked past the three builders sitting by the window and out to the street where the traffic groaned along the high street. She noticed the pedestrians were now wearing lighter clothing, getting ready for another short-lived summer. She looked back to Harris and narrowed her eyes. 'So, have you told me everything now?'

'I've told you all I can.' Harris picked up his mug of tea.

'But is that everything?'

'There's nothing else.'

The door of the café opened and Fred entered, heading towards her. She put down her coffee, smiled at him and gestured for him to take a seat next to her. She saw him staring at the seat with a look of impending doom.

'Your back still giving you trouble?' she asked.

'It's getting better. What's this all about?' Fred looked at Harris and Ally.

Ally frowned. 'Mark South. He's missing.'

Fred looked at Harris and breathed deeply. 'I thought he phoned you?'

Ally shook her head. 'He did, but they must've made him do it. He's been held captive somewhere in London. We know that he's being held by the people who were working with Skouvakis, the ones forcing the girls into prostitution. We haven't got long to find him.'

Fred leaned forward, adjusting his back. 'How do

you know all this?'

Ally looked at Harris. 'Harris here, he told me quite an interesting story about what happened between you lot and Skouvakis.'

Fred looked at Harris for a long time. 'What did you tell her?'

Harris sat back. 'That Skouvakis made us an offer we couldn't refuse. That he threatened our families and our lives. Then he proved that he could get to us anytime, by grabbing you and…well… you know the rest.'

Fred let out a strange, sickly laugh. 'Jesus...you know about the girl, Ally?'

Ally nodded. 'They found her in the Thames. Yes, I know about that.'

'But somebody had to have grassed on her,' Fred said and shot a look at Harris.

'Maybe we'll find out who did it,' Ally said. 'It must've been Hatch who led South into the trap. We need to talk to him.'

Fred said, 'Wait. How do you know Hatch is part of it? We never had any reason to suspect him. He's the one who led us to the whole business in the first place. Who told you about Hatch?'

Ally nodded to Harris. 'Our friend here has been to see Franco Orlando on the quiet. He's been chatting to his old pal, trying to get Mark out of trouble or so he said.'

Fred stared at Harris. 'Was it you who tipped them off about the girl? Did they threaten your family or did they stick a wad of money under your nose?'

'Don't go there, Fred,' Harris said.

Fred nodded for a moment, his eyes turning to Ally. 'So, why don't we go and shake the truth out of Franco?'

'He doesn't know where he is,' Harris said. 'They don't trust Franco, but Hatch will know.'

'He won't tell us,' Ally said. 'He'll be risking his livelihood and his life.'

Fred leaned forward and rubbed his face, while the other two watched him. He stopped and revealed his red, tired face. 'I'll get him to tell us. I can get him to talk. I'm not a copper any more. You two could get in trouble or worse, but what does it matter to me? He won't be scared of fellow officers, but he might be of an ex-policeman with a grudge.'

Ally nodded. 'He might.'

Fred looked at her. 'That's what you wanted me to say, wasn't it?'

She shrugged. 'I thought about it.'

'I have nothing to lose,' Fred said.

'What do you mean by that?' Ally asked.

'Nothing. Let's go and find Hatch.'

Ally got up and took out her notebook. 'I have an address. But we've got little chance of finding him now. Me and Tony will stake out his place and call when we know where he is.'

Fred nodded, got up, looked back at them, then walked out and headed off down the street.

Fran came into the room carrying a plate of food and put in down on the floor a couple of feet from South. He saw she was dressed a little more provocatively, with a low cut purple top that advertised her cleavage, and a very short denim skirt. He looked at her pale legs and the bruising on her thigh. She smiled a little and turned to face the large man walking in behind her.

'You better feed him.' The large man watched Fran lift the plate and carry it to South. After she removed his gag, she got a fork full of takeaway curry and lifted it to South's lips.

'I'm not really hungry,' South said.

Fran looked to the large man, who shrugged and said, 'Well, if you want to starve that's your look out.'

'What's the point of eating when you're planning on shooting me and dumping my body somewhere?' South looked at Fran, seeing the sympathy in her dark eyes.

The large man put his hands in his pockets. 'I thought you were sure that you were going to be rescued. Not so sure now?'

'Fuck off,' South growled.

The large man turned and strolled from the room, but South could hear him just outside the door, chatting to someone.

'What's the time?' South asked and took a mouthful of curry from Fran's fork.

'It's late. That man, the one you called Hatch, has just left. I don't like him.' Fran shovelled some more food onto the fork. She smiled. 'It's good that you eat. Do you think your friends will come for you?'

'Did you do as I asked?'

Fran nodded. 'He fell asleep afterwards, so I had a chance to slip it into his coat.'

South stopped chewing and stared up at her, imagining what she'd been through. He began to chew again and leaned his head against her shoulder. He felt her hand stroke his hair, feeding him in silence. When the plate was empty, she picked it up and looked at him for a few seconds before going out of the door. He heard the door being locked and closed his eyes.

THIRTY-FOUR

Tuesday, 4th May 2004

They were all sitting in Harris' car, facing the tower block where Allison had said Hatch lived. Fred ate a sandwich slowly, his eyes staring out the back window. He adjusted himself as a crackle of pain shot along his spine. He looked up and met Harris' eyes in the rearview mirror. He looked away, stared at the back of Ally's head, then sat forward and put a hand on her right shoulder, causing her to turn around and face him.

'Yes, Fred?' she said.

'You two don't have to be here for this.' Fred looked between her and Harris.

Ally struggled to turn around after taking off her seat belt. 'I'm not going anywhere, not until I know where Mark is.'

Harris laughed. 'What is it with you two? Is it the fact that you've solved a case together, so now you have to screw each other?'

Ally spun round to face Harris. 'Fuck off, Tony. Don't you bloody well dare sit there and say crap like that. It's your fault that he's in this shit. Shut your trap.'

Harris smiled a little as he tapped the steering wheel. 'Fine. If I had known that screwing after a case was the usual procedure…'

'What? You thought I would've screwed you? Sod

411

off.' Ally stared at the entrance to the tower block, her jaw grinding.

'No, I would've been shagging Fred long ago.' Harris laughed.

'He'll come out or come in sometime,' Fred said and put the remainder of his sandwich back in its paper bag. He sat back a little, closing his eyes, taking a deep breath. Martin appeared before his closed eyes. He tightened his eyes and felt the blackness around him as he heard a car roar past. Martin floated through the darkened pink of his fleshy eyelids, his body all screwed up, his face twisted.

'There's a few blokes coming down the street,' Ally said and leaned forward.

'Looks like a mob of thugs,' Harris said.

Fred moved to the middle of the back seat and put on his glasses. He focused on the seven men marching down the street. Harris was wrong. There were only three skinheads, while the others were suited, their hair short, but smart. 'That's Hatch, isn't it? On the left?'

Ally said, 'Yeah, that's him. What's he carrying?'

'Looks like leaflets. He's supposed to be a Nazi, isn't he?' Harris asked Ally.

Fred opened the back door and started to get out. He heard Ally's door opening and touched her shoulder. 'Stay here. I need to talk to him on his own. Please.'

Ally stared at him and then pulled her door shut.

Fred stood up and felt the sun on his face, prickly down his jaw and flashing yellow in his eyes. He held a hand to his forehead, shading his eyes and saw the figures coming slowly past the entrance of the tower block. They must have been going to the café. He started moving and stopped by Ally's window. 'Give me some restraints.'

Harris shrugged, then put some restraints in Fred's hand. Fred walked on, his hand around the cuffs, squeezing them a little, feeling their shape.

Hatch was saying something to one of his friends as Fred walked past. Fred suddenly swung round, grabbed Hatch's elbow and stopped him in his tracks. Hatch pulled his arm back and stared Fred in the face. 'Who the fuck do you think you're touching?'

'I'm Detective Inspector Fred Fairservice. I need to talk to you.' Fred eyed the other men, especially an angry-looking young man behind Hatch.

Hatch looked Fred over. 'Now what have I done? You want to look at these leaflets? Look, nothing offensive on them. Freedom of speech, mate.'

'Well, let's take a look at your flat. Maybe we can find something there.' Fred nodded towards the entrance to the tower block.

One of the suits in the group stepped forward, adjusting his round glasses. 'Look, you can't just start grabbing people in the street. We're part of a political organisation…'

'Shut up, Roy,' Hatch said. 'You lot go in the café. I'll see what this copper wants.'

Fred watched the others crowd into the café, their eyes still looking out through the window as he and Hatch started walking towards his building. Hatch turned to Fred as they got to the entrance, then poked Fred in the chest. 'What the fuck is this about?'

'South. There could be a serious problem. We need to talk.' Fred looked along the street nervously.

'I don't know anyone called South. Now fuck off.'

Hatch turned his back on Fred, so he grasped his right wrist and pulled it behind his back. Fred clamped the restraint on his wrist as he pushed him against the door, slipping a foot towards Hatch's feet, tripping him up. Hatch let out a shout as Fred grabbed his left wrist and clasped the restraints together. Hatch pulled his head from the glass, his cheek red and his eyes glaring. 'You fucking cunt. What do you think you're doing?'

'Let's go inside and talk.' Fred opened the glass door and smelt urine and stale rubbish bags as he pushed Hatch inside the grey lobby. 'Do the lifts work?'

'Fuck off.'

'Do you want me to go to the café and tell your friends who you really are, officer?' Fred pointed to the lifts.

'You could've just come and talked to me.' Hatch started walking to the stairs. 'I remember you.'

Fred stayed silent, watching Hatch go up the stairs. Fred looked out on the estate below as they climbed higher, seeing a graffiti covered playground and some old electrical goods thrown into the centre of the square. An Asian woman and two children rushed across the square and disappeared inside another battered door.

'This is my floor,' Hatch said. 'Now, take these cuffs off me, wanker.'

Fred pushed him along the balcony towards his flat. 'When we're comfortably inside. Keys?'

'In the right pocket of my jeans,' Hatch said. 'Just don't grab my knob.'

Fred smiled sarcastically and opened the door with the keys. He looked in the hallway and smelt fresh paint, then looked in further, and pulled Hatch along with him. He saw the lounge, then pushed Hatch onto the sofa.

Hatch stared up at Fred. 'Now could you take these fucking things off?'

Fred shook his head. 'Tell me where South is.'

Hatch's expression changed slowly, a grin appearing. 'I know you're not a copper any more, so why don't you tell me what this is about?'

'This is about getting Mark South away from your friends.'

Hatch smiled and sat up. 'Let me see, mate, you want me to get my business partners to give up a fellow policeman who's about to blow the whistle on our little set up? So we all end up in prison?'

'That's right.' Fred nodded and looked around the small flat with its black leather sofa and matching armchair. A Saint George's flag was stuck to the window, while old heavy metal posters were pinned to the walls. 'Look, I don't give a shit about your little set up. Just give me Mark South.'

'I don't know where he is anyway. In fact, I don't even know what you're talking about.'

Fred walked away and leaned against the wall. He breathed deeply for a moment, images of South shooting through his mind. He saw South lying on a floor, his blood soaking the carpet until everything around him was black. He looked at Hatch. 'If you don't tell me, I'll beat the crap out of you with anything I can find.'

'Yeah, right.' Hatch laughed.

'I'm not a policeman any more.'

'So? What? Are you going to kill me? Fuck off.' Hatch relaxed and laughed.

'Let me tell you something that happened to me today.' Fred sat down in the armchair. 'I went back to my consultant after a few tests. I've been having these pains in my backside. Real bad pains. I have to keep taking these strong painkillers to get it to stop. So, anyway, I go to my consultant today and he tells me that the tumour they've found on my prostate is inoperable. So I'm going to die in a few months.'

Hatch stared at Fred. 'Lovely story. You have my deepest sympathies.'

'Don't you understand? I don't give a shit any more. So, if I can save Mark South and get your pals banged up, then it'll have been worth killing you. I'll only live with the guilt a few months, if that. I'll take it to my grave.'

Hatch wasn't smiling any more. Thoughts were flashing across his face. 'That's all bollocks.'

Fred took out his painkillers and threw them into Hatch's lap.

Hatch looked at them. He looked up at Fred, his eyes narrowing, scrutinising the ex-copper. 'They could be for anything. Don't mean you're dying.'

Fred shrugged.

'Give us a fag,' Hatch said. 'They're in my coat pocket.'

Fred got up and ran his hands through the pockets until he took out a pack of cigarettes and stuck one in Hatch's mouth. He started looking through the pockets again for a light. His hand grabbed something plastic and pulled out a tiny bag. It was one of the small bags that drug dealers sell Marijuana in. He examined it, expecting to see some green dried leaves. His eyes widened when he saw a small dead spider, then looked at Hatch. He held the bag out to him, making sure the undercover cop saw it.

'What's that?' Hatch asked.

'This is a sign. This means you know where South is.' Fred looked at the bag again.

'What the fuck're you going on about?' Hatch rattled his restraints.

Fred looked around the flat for a moment, his eyes

travelling across the rest of the furniture. He stomped out to the kitchen and then to Hatch's bedroom. He opened a cupboard and saw a claw hammer. He felt the weight of it in his hand. When he came back into the lounge holding it, Hatch's eyes grew wide. 'Are… you going to light this fag or what?'

Fred patted the hammer in his palm and gritted his teeth. 'Or what.'

'Get these restraints off me and fuck off, you old worn out shit bag…fucker. GET THESE OFF ME NOW!'

Fred raised the hammer up to his chest. He looked at Hatch's knee and then brought the hammer down and tapped it heavily. Hatch let out a yelp and struggled to climb back up the sofa, away from Fred. 'YOU FUCKER! I'LL FUCKING RIP YOUR…'

Fred hit the other knee harder.

Hatch pulled himself back and yelled.

Fred found Hatch's elbow and prepared to slam the hammer down.

'Alright. Alright. Shit.'

'Where is Mark South?' Fred grinned and stood holding the hammer over his head.

Hatch's eyes were fixed to the end of the hammer, blinking, his face getting paler. 'Fuck. Don't do this. This will muck everything up.'

Fred lifted up the hammer. 'I'm a dead man already.'

'Shit.' Hatch lowered his head. '24 Town Street, off Tottenham High Street. Thanks a lot, now I'm a dead man.'

'Yes, you are.'

'What the hell're we going to do now?' Harris turned around, taking his eyes off the house where they were holding Mark South. He looked at Fred on the back seat, hearing the rustle of a carrier bag. Fred

417

pulled out an old style truncheon and smoothed his hand over it. He lifted it, giving Harris a better view.

'Oh right, so you're just going to go in there and start smashing people over the head with that?' Harris said.

Walker looked over the black baton, then into Fred's eyes. 'They're probably armed. We have to call for an armed response team.'

'What if they take too long?' Fred asked. 'What if they're about to execute him? I'm sorry, but do we really have the time?'

Harris put his head on the steering wheel for a moment, then looked up. 'I have an idea.'

'Yes? And what is this idea? To be honest, Tony, I don't trust you any more.' Ally rolled down her window a little more and looked out at the street.

'You'll have to trust me, Allison.' He put his head closer to her. 'Please. I swear that I'll do whatever I can to get him out of there. I swear on my family's life. Trust me. I've fucked everything up in my life, and my career, but I'm not going to let you down now. Please trust me.'

Ally turned to Fred. 'What do you think?'

'Let's hear what he has to say.'

After they had parked further along the high street, Ally and Fred sat staring to their right at a café bar called Pacino's. They could see the two girls behind the counter serving customers sandwiches and coffees. Fred smelt the fresh coffee being made. He saw Franco arrive in a Mercedes, which he parked close to the café, putting coins into a parking meter. The ex-copper watched the chunky Italian stride towards the café, wearing a white polo shirt and beige chinos. He stepped inside and Fred imagined Harris sitting at a table, waiting.

'He better not fuck us over.' Ally opened her takeaway tea and blew the steam away.

'I don't think he will,' Fred said. 'If he does, I'll kill him.'

THIRTY-FIVE

Harris was about to lift his espresso to his lips when Franco walked in. The girl behind the counter saw Franco and called out his name and laughed about something. Franco smiled, said something, but kept walking towards Harris' table near the toilets.

Franco's face was calm and collected, but his dark eyes sparkled with suspicion as he pulled out a chair and sat down. 'So, why have I travelled halfway across London? What's this about?'

Harris sipped his coffee and wiped his top lip. 'We've got a serious problem and I don't know what to do.'

Franco frowned. 'What the fuck's happened now?'

'I've found out that they know about us lot. They know everything somehow. They even know where South's being held.'

Franco leaned back and looked at Harris as if he'd called his mother a prostitute. 'Who does? What the hell're you talking about?'

'Some special task force have been working on this without our knowledge. They didn't trust me, so they must've known I was in with you lot. Shit. This means I've got to leave the country.' Harris rubbed his temples.

'Calm down.' Franco looked behind him, scanning the street. 'Where are these people now?'

'Probably camped outside the house where South's

being held. They've probably got an armed response team on the way.'

'Where's South being held?' Franco gripped Harris' shoulder.

'Just off the High Street. Town Road. Number 24. Why, what're you going to do?'

Franco rubbed his nose for a moment and looked around the café. He looked into Tony's eyes. 'You sure they'll be camped outside?'

'Will be soon.'

Franco got up. 'Come on, you're going to show me this house.'

'Me? No way.' Harris lifted up his drink.

'Yes, you. This is your neck too, you dickhead.'

Harris sighed. 'Look, let me phone my wife first. If I'm going to die, I want to have said goodbye to her first.'

Franco shook his head. 'Hurry up. I'm going to pull my car up to the front.'

Harris watched Franco leave, then quickly got on the payphone near the counter. He dialled the phone number Franco had used the night they met in Wood Green. It had been simple to get one of his friends at the station to retrieve the number for him.

A woman's voice answered. 'Hello?'

'You don't know me, but I have to warn you that the police have found where you are. They're closing in. And don't trust Franco Orlando. He's working with the filth.'

'Who...'

Harris put the phone down as he heard Franco's Mercedes roar up to the pavement outside. He walked towards the door and thanked the girls for the coffee before stepping out into the afternoon sun.

Franco waved for him to get in. When Harris

climbed inside, he looked through the windscreen and saw a car up the street with two familiar figures watching him.

South's head jerked up as he heard the crashing feet bounding up the stairs. Then he heard a key in the lock. The door flew open, the large man coming in with his hand still gripping the door handle, his knuckles white. The big man seemed to stare around the room, taking a long time to look at South. Sweat poured down his forehead. South saw the small gun in his jean's pocket and his eyes widened.

The large man stepped into the room and moved quickly to the black cloth that covered the window. He peeled some of the material back, pushing his head to the glass. He swore, then moved away and stared at South. 'You don't make a fucking sound, right?'

South nodded, looking at the gun again.

'If your fucking mates come in here, they'll fucking get it. And the girls and you. Get it? I don't care. I'll shoot you where you sit. I can get a passport and get out of here before they even fucking know what's happened.'

South stared at the man, while he listened for any cars outside, any sign help was on its way.

The foreigner appeared in the room brandishing a larger gun and pointed it at South and said something. The large man pushed the gun down and held it. 'Let's not make it worse until it is worse.'

Everybody in the room froze as there was a knock on the front door. The large man rushed to the window and tried to look out again, swearing under his breath as his hands scrabbled at the black material. 'Fuck. What the fuck's going on?'

'What the bleeding hell's going on, Jason?' The woman rushed into the room, her mouth snarling.

'Don't say my name, you stupid cow,' the large man shouted and stormed off towards the landing.

The woman hurried after him, her hands in tight fists, her chest rising and falling. 'Oi, you fucking idiot, talk to me for fuck's sake. Who's that at the door?'

'I don't fucking know,' Jason shouted. 'Where are the girls?'

'There are three of them in their room and the rest are out on visits.' The woman grabbed his elbow.

'What?' he shouted.

'Who is it? Are you going to answer it? The person on the phone said the police were here.'

The foreign man shouted something loudly at South, but again he didn't understand. South could only watch as the foreigner raised his hands in the air and then stormed off down the landing, ignoring the calls from Jason for him to stop.

South jumped when he heard the first gunshot. The second echoed up the stairs and through his body. He stared at the open doorway, waiting and praying for help.

THIRTY-SIX

Franco parked a little way from the house and stared up at the blacked out windows. He nodded at Harris and pointed at the house. 'They've blacked the windows out. That must be the house.'

Harris looked to where he was pointing and his stomach turned over. 'It is. What're you going to do?'

Franco looked him over and then bent down and searched under his seat. He brought out a large black revolver and wiped it with his hand. 'You and me are walking up to the front door.'

Harris watched the gun being pointed at his stomach, then pictured the bullet ripping through him, making a crater of blood and burnt flesh. 'You don't have to point that at me, Franco. I'm your friend, remember?'

Franco narrowed his eyes. 'You haven't been that friendly lately. Get out.'

'What do you expect me to do? Give you a hug?'

'Very funny, Tony. Get out!' Franco waved the gun.

Franco pointed the gun at Harris as he came around the car, then pushed him towards the garden path. Harris opened the gate and looked at the garden that was bursting with weeds and overgrown grass. Takeaway food cartons littered the whole area, while a crisp packet became attached to his foot. He shook it off and heard the purr of a cat as it rubbed itself on Franco's leg. He kicked the creature away and pushed

Harris on towards the door. 'Knock. Go on, knock.'

Harris took a deep breath and knocked on the door. Franco stepped back a little and looked up at the windows. 'They should see it's me and open up.'

'Why the gun?' Harris knocked again.

'Protection. They can be a bit crazy these people.' Franco smiled and searched in his pocket for a cigarette with one hand. He looked down and managed to start pulling out a fag.

Harris heard footsteps coming fast down the stairs and saw the door opening. Franco looked up as a dark-skinned man pointed a gun at him, then jerked as a shot was fired. Blood exploded from Franco's chest, then he stumbled backwards, raising the gun and firing. The foreigner flinched as the doorframe spat wood at his face. As he fell to his knees, Franco fired again, catching the foreigner in the leg. Harris crouched down, holding his ears as the shots bellowed out. Through his clenched ears, he heard another shot fired and saw Franco's chest burst again. Harris watched him fall slowly, delicately to the path, his head falling across the threshold.

Franco's chest moved very lightly for a few seconds and then stopped.

Harris looked around at the open door and saw no one there. Then he looked at the gun in Franco's hand, prised it from his grip, and looked into the open hallway, through the cloud of smoke. His ears were full of a high pitch whine as he moved into the hall, his eyes jumping around to every available space in the house. He felt a thud in his chest. It was his heart, pumping, rushing blood through his veins.

There was movement upstairs as he put a foot on the stairs. On the wooden steps he saw blood spatters, very far apart, leading upwards.

Fred climbed out of the car, becoming thoughtful. He stepped over to Walker's side as she pressed the button for the electric window to slide down. She made the move to open the door, but he shook his crumpled head.

'Me and Harris...we aren't so lily white any more. You still are. I want you to stay that way.'

Fred turned and looked towards the turning where death was probably waiting. He looked at Ally and saw she was staring at him.

'That girl who died...that was our fault,' Fred said. 'We could've done something. We didn't. I'm finished anyway...so, I'm going around the back. Don't follow. Stay here.'

'What do you mean?' Ally leaned her head out of the window, but Fred ignored her.

The back alleyway smelt of dog mess. Fred sniffed the air and tasted puke rising through his throat. He kept walking, carefully moving away from the stinging nettles. Above him, across the next-door neighbour's garden, he watched large sheets flapping in the breeze as they hung over the washing line. He saw some knickers and T-shirts and watched as the sun burned through them. He squeezed the baton in his hand, then opened the back gate and saw a garden as overgrown as the front. A baby started crying next door. He kept on moving towards the back door.

A familiar pain burrowed into his backside, so he stopped, leaning against the wall for a moment, his breathing hard and fast. He took a few deep breaths and took out his painkillers. He looked at them for a moment, before throwing them into the long grass.

There was a back window, but the dingy-looking brown curtains were drawn. He looked at the back door and saw it looked solid. It was the only new looking thing about the house. They must have had it put there with new dead bolts when they moved the girls in. Fred stood close to it, holding the baton tightly in his hand.

He was thinking about how to get in when he heard the first gunshot. He smashed the baton at the back of the door. He kicked at the door, feeling his foot vibrate. He bounced backwards. As he kicked again, another shot was fired. He saw the door give a little and started bashing at the gap he'd made. He leaned back and smashed his boot against the door.

South watched the foreigner hobble into the room, then put a blood soaked hand on his wound and shout loudly to anyone. Jason pushed past the woman, who was standing in the room, her mouth open, her hands clutching her chest. South watched the tears running down her cheeks.

'Jesus Christ. Is he dead?' Jason knelt down and looked at the wound.

'Put your weapons down,' a voice shouted out.

South leaned forward and could just make out a hand holding a gun coming up the landing. Harris appeared, his face white and his hand shaking a little. Harris' head flickered as he saw the foreigner flip over and point his gun. Harris fired into the foreigner's chest. The foreigner looked down at his stomach, then crumpled down to the floor, his mouth opening and closing, a shallow and grinding breath escaping his lips. There was a gurgling sound, then he lay still.

Harris pointed the gun at Jason, his eyes jumping over to the body of the foreigner. 'You better drop your gun.'

Jason held his gun by his side, gripping it tightly, moving it upwards slightly.

'Now!' Harris barked.

Jason dropped his gun as another wet and crackling breath came from the foreigner.

Harris moved around Jason and kicked the gun across the floor to the skirting board. Then he looked at South, his face still pale and his hands shaking madly. He smiled a little and South could see wetness in his colleague's eyes. Harris stepped closer. Jason lurched up and grasped Harris around the neck, pulling him backwards, his eyes opening wide. South struggled against the ropes, seeing Jason jab something at Harris' back. Harris' eyes opened wide, then he dropped to the floor.

Jason straightened up, a bloody knife still in his hand.

South shook his head and tried to plead through the gag as Jason came towards him. He breathed in and could smell iron in the air. Jason moved closer, his eyes narrowing, his teeth gritted together, not hearing the footsteps behind him.

Fred leaped through the air and flattened Jason to the floor. They pushed and pulled each other, their hands scratching at the floorboards. Fred got on top and gripped Jason's head. He lifted his skull and slammed his forehead into the floor. South stared at Fred's face, seeing the insanity in his eyes. Fred raised Jason's head and smashed it into the floor again and again.

Fred stopped and breathed hard, looking down at the lifeless man under him. He sat up, his chest pounding, then struggled to get to his feet. He stumbled across the room towards South.

South felt a tear drift down his face and enter his mouth as Fred walked towards him. Fred grabbed South's shoulder, trying to hold himself steady, a desperate smile trying to appear on his lips. 'You're alright, mate. You're OK now.'

South turned towards the noise coming from downstairs. A door smashed open. The sound of heavy boots entering the house, storming into every room.

'Clear!' was shouted again and again until an armed response officer moved into the room and stood pointing his Heckler and Koch submachine gun at them. 'Raise your arms! Raise them. Move away from him! Move!'

THIRTY-SEVEN

With his head bandaged and glued together by the paramedics, South sat in a cubicle off the Accident and Emergency Department of North Middlesex Hospital. A DCI had just left him. South had told him everything he knew, like the fact that the foreigner, who turned out to be the son of a Russian human trafficker called Anton Grinkov, was working with the man called Jason, keeping the girls fed and watered so they could keep them working. They would make them work off their travelling money by having sex with men. It wouldn't stop there. They would keep them locked up, forced to sleep altogether in one room with only coats to cover them.

As South had left the building, taken out by the paramedics, he saw the very thin young girls and the needle marks in their arms. Skouvakis was financing the operation, paying the Russians to bring in the girls.

He also told the DCI that a crooked police officer was involved. South noted the shock in the detective's face. South told him Hatch was the only policeman taking money for his services and was probably the one who tipped off Skouvakis all those years ago.

After the debriefing, the detective had informed South that two officers had gone to pick up Hatch and found him on the ground outside the block of flats. His head was spread over the pavement. Mark thought of Fred, but pushed the image out of his mind. The big ugly man had saved him and he would be forever in his debt.

The green curtain was pulled back and Fran came into the room, her eyes red and puffy. When she stepped closer and smiled at him, South saw her bruised face. He touched her hand. 'You alright?'

She nodded slowly, pulling her hair from her face. 'Thank you.'

'I didn't do anything.'

Fran put her hands to his cheeks and held his head. 'I'll be going home soon. I shouldn't have come to this country.'

'It's not all bad.'

'Thank you,' Fran said and removed her hands.

Ally appeared from behind the curtain and smiled brightly. Fran saw her and stepped back through the green curtain with a wave. Ally came over to him, looking at his bandaged head and whistled. 'How're you feeling or is that a stupid question?'

South tried to sit up. 'Like shit. Where's Fred?'

'Disappeared. He didn't stick around to answer any questions. We're in the shit. But at least you're alive.'

South nodded and felt himself beginning to shake again. 'Thank you for coming to save me.'

She laughed a little. 'I had a bit of spare time on my hands.'

South closed his eyes tightly. 'Harris is dead, isn't he?'

Ally put a hand on South's knee. 'They got him into the ambulance, but he didn't last long.'

South sighed. 'What about the one who killed him?'

'He's in coma somewhere in this hospital. Severe head trauma.'

'Fred saved my life.' South reached out and grabbed Ally's hand. Then he felt his body shaking, and tears spilling from his eyes. Ally Walker reached around his back and held him close to her.

He was dreaming of falling and woke up as his back seemed to slam against the sofa. Fred's eyes opened and he felt his hands gripping at his chest. He looked at his fingers and saw traces of blood. He felt nothing, knowing he just killed a man with his bare hands. That was not perfectly true. Satisfaction- it was the only way he could describe it.

He rubbed his head and listened for any noise coming from Martin. There was nothing and he stared at the ceiling for a few moments and then got up. He moved up the stairs slowly, listening out for signs of movement. There were none. He didn't want to be alone right now and needed a brother who could listen to his murderous confession. He had killed. But it was for the best, for all the right reasons.

He walked into Martin's room and found him sleeping soundly. He stood there and looked down at the sleeping figure, the soft breath escaping his mouth. Fred looked down and noticed the splashes of blood on his own shirt.

He put a hand on his brother's thin and wasted leg. Near his hand was the Shakespeare book, face down, opened at the beginning. Fred picked it up and saw there was a library stamp inside the front cover. He stared at it for a moment, his mind buzzing. An Edmonton Library date stamp. That meant something. How did it get into the old people's home? He saw the list poking out and pulled at it. After unfolding it, he scanned the names, his finger tracing the path his eyes followed. He stopped dead at a familiar name, a sudden realisation flowing through him.

He sat there for a moment and looked at his brother.

He recalled his promise and put the book on the floor. He got up, changed his shirt and went out.

Fred arrived at the door and stood there, holding his hand out to the doorbell. He thought for a moment, gathering himself together, trying to push all the scenes of death from his vision. He rung the bell and kept ringing until he heard the door began to open.

'Hello, you OK?' Scott Brown said and smiled.

'Can I come in?' Fred walked in before he got a reply and went through to the small lounge. He sat down heavily and waited for the librarian to come through.

Brown stood in front of Fred. 'Want a cup of tea?'

Fred shook his head. 'What's your real name? Who are you really?'

There was a spasm in Scott Brown's face as he sat back. A breath escaped his lips. It sounded like relief to Fred. 'It took you a long time.'

'Yes, I'm not really the policeman I used to be.'

'Not a policeman at all now.'

'No, that's right. How long have you been killing people?'

Brown let himself smile broadly. 'A few years. I've travelled around Britain, finding people who could no longer live with their problems. I don't murder them. I just help them along.'

Fred put his head into his hands as he said, 'That's not the way the jury would see it.'

'I suppose not. It doesn't matter. I've done my bit.'

Fred looked up. 'And you find them through that website?'

'Mostly. Sometimes I just happen to bump into them. Like Steve. He happened to walk into the library. The rest I met online. They wanted to do it, I just helped them.'

Fred sat forward. 'What about the young girl, Amy?'

'I knew she wouldn't go through with it. It was just a cry for help with her. She was just there to bring you closer.'

'Why me?' Fred stared at Brown.

'Why don't you tell me what you're doing here first? Are you going to perform a citizen's arrest or…'

Fred pushed his face into his hands again as he spoke. He mumbled something.

Scott Brown sat forward, cupping his ear. 'I didn't get that. What did you say?'

Fred jerked his head up. 'I want you to kill my brother.'

THIRTY-EIGHT

South was especially glad he'd discharged himself from the hospital. Even though he felt his head swelling and aching, he could also feel his son leaning against him as they watched television. Emma sat in the armchair staring at him, shaking her head. 'Look at you!'

'I'm alive, aren't I?' South said and patted his son's head.

'Yeah, he's alive.' Shane smiled up at his Dad.

South felt his head beginning to pound. It was as if a shard of ice had been inserted into his eyebrow. 'Have we got any painkillers?'

Emma looked around the house for a moment. 'Er…I think so. Somewhere. Maybe in my purse.'

South waved for her to sit down as he remembered the painkillers Ally stole from Fred's desk. He pulled himself up and felt his son grab his arm for a joke, refusing to let him go as he laughed. South broke free and looked in his overcoat. He found the paper bag and poured the contents out on the table. As he opened the packet and took out the strip of tablets, his eyes fell on the receipt. At first he wondered where they were bought, but then his eyes noticed WHEN and WHERE they were bought. He saw the date and had a strange feeling come over him. The date couldn't be right. He counted the days, checked the dates again. He shook his head and got up.

South grabbed his mobile phone and called someone. There was no answer as he stood there looking across to the curtains. Emma got up and started picking up empty mugs from the coffee table. 'What's wrong, Mark?'

He looked at her, but didn't see her. 'I've got to go out.'

THIRTY-NINE

The warm air sucked at Fred's back as he opened the front door. It was much warmer, but he saw the grey clouds gathering, pushing into each other. In the distance, a darker cloud tried to push them all away. The sun started to dissolve and Fred had a strange feeling when he let Brown into his house. Everything got sucked into the shade.

He remembered a couple of trips abroad when they were kids. He recalled helping Martin dig massive holes in the sand while their parents sunbathed nearby. He'd lie down sometimes, feeling the bright, prickling sun on his young skin and close his eyes. He would swim in the yellow sun above, and feel himself being eaten by it. He was absorbed and nothing mattered. He imagined, with his eyes tightly shut, a blackness swallowing him, and his parents and brother no longer existing. He would open his eyes again and see them sunbathing around him. Martin would be running down to the water's edge.

Martin running.

Fred opened the door to the lounge, let Scott Brown in and said, 'Why did you start all this?'

Brown pulled his hat off his head, leaving a perfectly white, shiny scalp. Fred walked closer and saw there was no signs of any hair growing. He looked at Brown's eyelids. His jaw was perfectly smooth and Fred cursed himself for not noticing before. 'You're hairless.'

Brown nodded. 'I spent my life being teased about my appearance. It's the same old story I suppose, but there you go. I would come home from school and go to my room and cry. My parents weren't very emotional people, so I would hide my feelings. This was the way God sent me into the world, they would say and that's the way I was meant to live my life.'

Fred stepped towards the stairs and rested his hand on the banister. 'Did you try and take your own life?'

Brown took off his coat and laid it carefully on the sofa, then rolled up his sleeves. 'I slit my wrists. Of course, I did it all wrong. I was just a child. Only my father knew and he made me swear on the bible never to try it again. So I never did.'

Fred looked up to the landing, listening. 'But you helped other people?'

'Yes. I happened to meet someone one day who wanted to end their suffering and I realised I could help. Are we going up?'

Fred nodded and started walking up the stairs. He noticed every floorboard that creaked as he climbed to the landing. He entered Martin's room and found him awake and staring at the door. Fred opened his mouth to speak, but didn't know where to begin.'

'Hello Martin,' Brown said and entered the room, then stood watching the brothers scrutinise each other.

Martin turned to Brown. 'Hello…who's this, Fred?'

'This is…' Fred began, but his voice faded away. He looked at Brown, who smiled.

'You know who I am, Martin,' Brown said. 'You sent for me, remember?'

Martin's eyes flickered, as if a switch had been turned on. 'You're him?'

Fred looked between them. 'What? What the hell?

What's going on, Martin?'

'He sent for me,' Brown said, smiling brightly.

'I read about the suicides online,' Martin said. 'So many of them. I knew there must be someone helping them, so I kept on finding websites that might lead me to him. I sent so many emails. I even mentioned the spider, the one you saw coming out of the old man's mouth…just so I would know him when he turned up. When you came home that day and said about the suicides and the spiders, I knew he was near.'

'You wanted me to find him.' Fred looked down to his shoes, nodding, feeling the tears pour out of his eyes.

Martin looked at Fred. 'I knew you would eventually. It's about time. How're we going to do this?'

Brown bent his head sympathetically, then placed a soothing hand on Fred's shoulder. 'He'll be at peace, Fred. That's what you want, isn't it?'

Fred clasped his face in his hands and began sobbing. He sat on the bed, his body shuddering with the force of his tears. Then he got up and sniffed. 'Do what you have to do. I have to…I can't be around for this.'

'Fred,' Martin called weakly.

Fred stopped dead, then faced Martin.

'Tell me you understand,' Martin said.

'I do.' Fred stepped out of room and walked across the landing, where he fell to his knees and cried silently.

Hands slipped under Fred's arms, pulling him to his feet. Fred yanked himself away from the librarian, then swung around to face him. 'What about all those people you killed!'

Brown shrugged. 'They wanted to die. I just helped

the best I could.'

'That doesn't excuse you. It's a sin!'

'You don't strike me as being very religious. I've been watching you, Fred, and I know you're not without sin. You think it's justice you've been giving out, but is it really? Listen, those people were suffering, just like Martin is.'

Fred grabbed Brown by the collar and dragged him close. 'Why all the fuss? Why all the spiders?'

'It was to lure you in. Your brother told me about you in his emails, so I knew I had to let you find me. If you truly wanted my help, then I knew you would search and search until you found me. You never really gave up, did you?'

Fred released his grip. 'I just…'

'Yes, Fred?'

'I just don't want him…to suffer any more.'

'He won't. I promise you.'

South stopped the car outside Fred's house and looked at the receipt in his hand. He didn't like what he was thinking. He opened the car door and slipped out, then rung the doorbell, but nothing happened. He knocked on the door and slammed the letterbox a few times.

A shape arrived at the door and opened it. Fred looked through Mark South, his complexion becoming grey. South faced his ex-colleague, but didn't know what to say. He just passed the receipt to him. Fred opened the door wider and South walked in, looked around the lounge, then sat down in an armchair. He sat back, his hands grasping the arms of the chair, watching Fred trudge to the sofa and fall into it.

'You were in the area, the same road and time when Byrne was murdered. You got those painkillers in a late night chemist in the next street.' South gripped the armrests tighter.

Fred looked at the receipt. 'Yes, that's right.'

'Did you kill him?'

Fred looked up. 'It was the right thing to do.'

'You beat him to death?'

'Yes. I followed him and he pulled over. I took him by surprise and beat him with a baseball bat.' Fred screwed up the receipt and threw it onto the coffee table.

'Why?'

'He was one of the ones who took the most pleasure in torturing me. They kept me for a couple of days. They'd burn me and beat me. And they'd laugh. Every time I close my eyes, I see Byrne's face laughing in mine. Skouvakis would sometimes sit in the corner, just watching. They...they also made me have sex with one of the girls. They put a gun to my head and made me have sex with her. The girl who came to us. Mel... Oh God...that poor...'

South put his head in his hands.

Fred huffed. 'They probably got the info out of her, about me and Harris being on to their operation. They grabbed me and did their worse...the girl...Melanie... was laid on a table and...they made me...do it to her. And they videotaped it...she had a knife to her throat and I had a gun to my head. What was I supposed to do? Tell me what I was supposed to do.'

South looked up from his hands, feeling his stomach turn over. 'What happened to the video?'

'I broke into Byrne's house and got it. I destroyed it.'

'And you shot Skouvakis with the gun you took from Byrne's house?'

Fred swallowed, looked up towards the ceiling and

began to cry. 'I shot him.'

'Why now? Why not back then? Why wait all this time?'

'Because I'm dying.'

'What?'

Fred nodded, his hand wiping away his tears. 'Before I went away I was in agony, but it got worse when I was in Spain, so I went to the hospital over there and they found out what was wrong. I had a tumour. Prostate cancer and there was nothing anyone could do. I even got a second opinion when I got back here, but they said the same thing. It's only a matter of time. I'm a dead man. Why not take something from the whole fucking mess?'

South closed his eyes. 'Why Nelson?'

Fred let out a deep moan. 'Because I thought he murdered that young girl. What was it to me? Just another murderer getting what he deserved. I might as well be the one to set things right.'

'But you were wrong.'

Fred nodded, his eyes clenching shut, his fists opening and closing.

South looked up when he heard the floorboards creak above him. 'Is that your brother?'

Fred shook his head. 'My brother's dead.'

South got up and rushed towards the stairs. 'Who's up there?'

Brown appeared on the landing, holding a pillow in his hands, gripping it tightly. He walked down the stairs and passed South and stood in front of Fred. 'It's done.'

South spun his head between the two men. 'What's done? What's going on?'

Fred looked at South. 'He just killed my brother, but Martin wanted to die, he didn't want to suffer any

442

more.'

South looked at the man holding the pillow.

After a few seconds, Fred took a big breath, stood up, and reached around his back and brought out a gun. In two quick bursts, Fred fired two bullets. The blast of the gun filled the room, pulsating into South's ears.

Brown stumbled backwards, his eyes wide, his mouth gapping. He sucked in a long, harsh breath and collapsed to the floor. Brown blinked for a few seconds, his hands scratching at the carpet, then gasped and became still.

South edged towards Fred. 'Fred, listen to me. Give me the gun.'

Fred seemed to think for a moment, looked at South and then put the gun into his own mouth.

'No! Fred! Listen to me…don't…please!' South threw out his hands.

The gun blast echoed around the room. South felt it bubble and boom in his ears, until a high-pitched ringing filled his skull. He closed his eyes for a few seconds, then opened them and looked at Fred, sitting limply on the floor, the back of his head bulging out. Blood was sprayed across the wall and carpet.

South got on his knees and felt for a pulse, but it was pointless. He got to his feet, and looked at the two dead men. He felt bad, but the voice in his head told him he was lucky. Lucky to be alive. Lucky to see his son again.

He dialled the station's number and waited, listening to the dialling tone.

best it affected you after. I look forward to more novels from this talented man - thanks for sharing your passion with the rest of us!"

AMAZON.CO.UK REVIEW
Murderson is also available from Amazon.com:

London and the South West of England are the hunting ground of a serial killer. The brutal killer, nicknamed The Clock, hunts young men in their thirties, kills them and turns their bodies into macabre clock faces at each crime scene.

Detective Chief Inspector Paul Webb, a tired middle aged policeman with a failed relationship still haunting him, investigates the series of murders with the help of Dr Kirill Fedorov, a man who believes he can spot potential serial killer behaviour in children and cure it. Webb also persuades the now fully-grown Luke Wind, the only British boy that Dr Fedorov cured and treated like a son, to help him find the killer. Fedorov convinces Luke that he should still be able to understand a serial killer's mind, but when Luke looks into himself he begins to doubt that he has been cured after all, especially when the killings begin to look personal.

Printed in Great Britain
by Amazon

17702604R00257